John Billingsley

General View of the Agriculture

of the County of Somerset;

John Billingsley

General View of the Agriculture
of the County of Somerset;

ISBN/EAN: 9783741198489

Manufactured in Europe, USA, Canada, Australia, Japa

Cover: Foto ©Andreas Hilbeck / pixelio.de

Manufactured and distributed by brebook publishing software
(www.brebook.com)

John Billingsley

General View of the Agriculture

GENERAL VIEW

OF THE

AGRICULTURE

OF THE

COUNTY of SOMERSET,

BY

JOHN BILLINGSLEY, Esq.

SOMERSET,
for the
AGRICULTURAL SURVEY
taken by J.C. Billingsley

Sketched by W.m White, 1797

GENERAL VIEW

OF THE

AGRICULTURE

OF THE

COUNTY OF SOMERSET;

WITH

OBSERVATIONS ON THE MEANS OF ITS IMPROVEMENT.

DRAWN UP IN THE YEAR 1795, FOR THE CONSIDERATION OF

THE BOARD OF AGRICULTURE,

AND INTERNAL IMPROVEMENT.

BY JOHN BILLINGSLEY, ESQ.

OF ASHWICK-GROVE, NEAR SHEPTON-MALLET.

AND NOW RE-PRINTED

WITH CONSIDERABLE ADDITIONS & AMENDMENTS,

ACCOMPANIED WITH THE REMARKS OF SOME RESPECTABLE GENTLEMEN AND FARMERS IN THE COUNTY.

THIRD EDITION.

In urbe luxuria creatur; ex luxuria existunt avaritia atque ex avaritia audacia; inde omnia scelera ac flagitia gignuntur. Vos, ô patres conscripti, prospicite patriæ, consulite vobis, cavete plebem; publica privatis, honesta turpibus, utilia inutilibus anteponite.

       Sallust. Catil. apud Euseb. Præpar.

The city derives luxury; from luxury necessarily proceeds avarice; and from avarice breaks forth insolence; thence are engendered all vices and crimes: but this country like, which you call downish, is the beginning of honesty, modesty, and justice.

LONDON:

PRINTED FOR RICHARD PHILLIPS, BRIDGE STREET, BLACKFRIARS;

SOLD BY FAULDER & SON, BOND STREET; REYNOLDS, OXFORD STREET; J. HARDING, ST. JAMES'S STREET; J. ASPERNE, CORNHILL; BLACK, PARRY, & KINGSBURY, LEADENHALL STREET; W. MEYLER, T. GIBBONS, & HAZARD & CO. BATH; COLLINS, WELLS; SHEPPARD & BULGIN, BRISTOL; NORRIS, TAUNTON; CONSTABLE & CO. EDINBURGH; J. ARCHER, DUBLIN; & ALL OTHER BOOKSELLERS;

BY B. M'MILLAN, BOW STREET, COVENT GARDEN.

1798.

[Price Seven Shillings in Boards.]

CONTENTS.

—————

CHAP. VII.

Arable Land.

CHAP. VIII.

CHAP. IX.

Gardens and Orchards

CHAP. X.

Woods and Plantations

CHAP. XI.

Waste Lands

CHAP. XII.

Improvements.

CHAP. XIII.

Live Stock.

CHAP. XIV.

Rural Œconomy.

CHAP. XV.

Political Œconomy as affecting Agriculture.

Middle District.

CHAP. I.

Geographical State and Circumftances.

CHAP. III.

Buildings, farm-houses, yards, stables, &c. 203

CHAP. IV.

Mode of Occupation.

CHAP. VII.

Arable Land.

CHAP. VIII. AND IX.

Grass, Gardens, and Orchards — 220

South-West District.

INDEX.

PLAN

FOR RE-PRINTING THE

AGRICULTURAL SURVEYS.

BY THE

PRESIDENT

OF THE BOARD OF AGRICULTURE.

———————

A BOARD eſtabliſhed for the purpoſe of making every eſſential enquiry, into the Agricultural State, and the means of promoting the internal improvement of a powerful Empire, will neceſſarily have it in view, to examine the ſources of publick proſperity, in regard to various important particulars. Perhaps the following is the moſt natural order for carrying on ſuch important inveſtigations; namely, to aſcertain,

1. The riches to be obtained from the ſurface of the national territory.

2. The mineral or ſubterraneous treaſures of which the country is poſſeſſed.

3. The wealth to be derived from its ſtreams, rivers, canals, inland navigations, coaſts, and fiſheries. And,

4. The means of promoting the improvement of the people in regard to their health, induſtry, and morals, founded on a *ſtatiſtical* ſurvey, or a minute and careful enquiry into the actual ſtate of every parochial diſtrict in the kingdom, and the circumſtances of its inhabitants.

B

Under

Under one or other of thefe heads, every point of real importance, that can tend to promote the general happinefs of a great nation, feems to be included.

Invefligations of fo extenfive and fo complicated a nature muft require, it is evident, a confiderable fpace of time before they can be completed. Differing indeed in many refpects from each other, it is better perhaps that they fhould be undertaken at different periods, and feparately confidered. Under that impreffion, the Board of Agriculture has hitherto directed its attention to the firft point only, namely, the cultivation of the furface, and the refources to be derived from it.

That the facts effential for fuch an inveftigation might be collected with more celerity and advantage, a number of intelligent and refpectable individuals were appointed, to furnifh the Board with accounts of the ftate of hufbandry, and the means of improving the different diftricts of the kingdom. The returns they fent were printed, and circulated by every means the Board of Agriculture could devife, in the diftricts to which they refpectively related; and in confequence of that circulation, a great mafs of additional valuable information has been obtained. For the purpofe of communicating that information to the publick in general, but more efpecially to thofe counties the moft interefted therein, the Board has refolved to reprint the Survey of each County, as foon as it feemed to be fit for publication; and among feveral equally advanced, the counties of Norfolk and Lancafter ' were pitched upon for the commencement of the propofed publication; it being thought moft advifable to begin with one county on the Eaftern, and another on the Weftern coaft of the Ifland. When all thefe Surveys fhall have been thus re-printed, it will be attended with little difficulty to draw up an abftract of the whole (which will not probably
exceed

exceed two or three volumes quarto) to be laid before his Majesty, and both Houses of Parliament; and afterwards a general Report on the present state of the country, and the means of its improvement, may be systematically arranged, according to the various subjects connected with agriculture. Thus every individual in the kingdom may have,

1. An account of the husbandry of his own particular county; or,

2. A general view of the agricultural state of the kingdom at large, according to the counties, or districts, into which it is divided; or,

3. An arranged system of information on agricultural subjects, whether accumulated by the Board since its establishment, or previously known;

And thus information respecting the state of the kingdom, and Agricultural knowledge in general, will be attainable with every possible advantage.

In re-printing these Reports, it was judged necessary, that they should be drawn up according to one uniform model; and after fully considering the subject, the following form was pitched upon, as one that would include in it all the particulars which it was necessary to notice in an Agricultural Survey. As the other Reports will be re-printed in the same manner, the reader will thus be enabled to find out at once, where any point is treated of, to which he may wish to direct his attention.

PLAN

PLAN of the RE-PRINTED REPORTS.

Preliminary Obſervations.

CHAP.

I. Geographical State and Circumſtances.

SECT. 1.—Situation and Extent.
2.—Diviſions.
3.—Climate.
4.—Soil and Surface.
5.—Minerals.
6.—Water.

II. State of Property.

SECT. 1.—Eſtates, and their Management.
2.—Tenures. .

III. Buildings.

SECT. 1.—Houſes of Proprietors.
2.—Farm Houſes and Offices; and Repairs.
3.—Cottages.

IV. Mode of Occupation.

SECT. 1.—Size of Farms.——Character of the Farmers.
2.—Rent—in Money—in Kind—in Perſonal Services.
3.—Tythes.
4.—Poor-Rates.
5.—Leaſes.
6.—Expence and Profit.

V. Implements.

VI. Incloſing—Fences—Gates.

VII. Arable Land.

SECT. 1.—Tillage.
2.—Fallowing.

* Where the quantity is confiderable, the information refpecting the crops commonly cultivated may be arranged under the following heads:

1. Preparation { tillage, manure. }   6. Culture whilft growing { hoe, weeding, feeding. }

2. Sort.   7. Harveft.
3. Steeping.   8. Threfhing.
4. Seed (quantity fown.)   9. Produce.
5. Time of fowing.   10. Manufacture of bread.

In general the fame heads will fuit the following grains:
Barley. Oats. Beans. Rye. Peafe. Buck-wheat.
Vetches · · · Application.
Cole-feed · { Feeding, Seed. }
Turnips · · { Drawn · · · · · · · Fed · · · · · · · · · Kept on grafs · · · ——— in houfes · · · }

PERFECTION in such inquiries is not in the power of any body of men to obtain at once, whatever may be the extent of their views, or the vigour of their exertions. If Lewis XIV. eager to have his kingdom known, and possessed of boundless power to effect it, failed so much in the attempt, that of all the provinces in his kingdom, only one was so described as to secure the approbation of posterity;* it will not be thought strange that a Board, possessed of means so extremely limited, should find it difficult to reach even that degree of perfection which, perhaps, might have

---

* See Voltaire's Age of Lewis XIV. vol. ii. p. 127, 128, edit. 1752. The following extract from that work will explain the circumstance above alluded to.

"Lewis had no Colbert, nor Louvois, when about the year 1698, "for the instruction of the Duke of Burgundy, he ordered each of the "intendants to draw up a particular description of his province. By "this means an exact account of the kingdom might have been ob- "tained, and a just enumeration of the inhabitants. It was an useful "work, though all the intendants had not the capacity and attention "of Monsieur de Lamoignon de Baville. Had what the king directed "been as well executed in regard to every province, as it was by this "magistrate in the account of Languedoc, the collection would have "been one of the most valuable monuments of the age. Some of them "are well done; but the plan was irregular and imperfect, because all "the intendants were not restrained to one and the same. It were to "be wished, that each of them had given, in columns, the number of "inhabitants in each election; the nobles, the citizens, the labourers, "the artisans, the mechanics, the cattle of every kind; the good, the "indifferent, and the bad lands; all the clergy, regular and secular; "their revenues, those of the towns, and those of the communities.

"All these heads, in most of their accounts, are confused and im- "perfect; and it is frequently necessary to search with great care and "pains to find what is wanted. The design was excellent, and would "have been of the greatest use, had it been executed with judgment "and uniformity."

been

been attainable with more extensive powers. The candid Reader cannot expect in these Reports more than a certain portion of useful information, so arranged as to render them a basis for further and more detailed enquiries. The attention of the intelligent Cultivators of the kingdom, however, will doubtless be excited, and the minds of men in general gradually brought to consider favourably of an undertaking, which will enable all to contribute to the national stores of knowledge, upon topicks so truly interesting as those which concern the Agricultural interests of their country; interests, which on just principles never can be improved, until the present state of the kingdom be fully known, and the means of its future improvement ascertained with minuteness and accuracy.

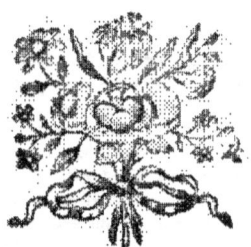

PRELIMINARY OBSERVATIONS

TO THE

SOMERSETSHIRE RE-PRINTED REPORT.

———————

THE following Remarks on the prefent ftate of Agriculture in the county of Somerfet having been made
without an actual furvey, thofe readers who are converfant
with the fubject will be able, no doubt, to point out many
defects, errors, and *omiſſions*.

The Writer, however, prefumes, that though he may not
have fpecifically and exprefsly touched on all the practices
and improvements of the beft farmers, yet that no kind or
clafs of thefe matters has been abfolutely overlooked.

He does not profefs to have given a compleat detail of
the various branches of rural management, but to have dif-
cuffed the moſt *important* articles belonging thereto; and he
has done his utmoſt to treat the fubject in fuch a manner,
and to exprefs his meaning in fuch a language, as might be
beft adapted to the underſtanding and comprehenſion of
common farmers.

Should the fubject of *inclofing, &c. the Waſte Lands*, be
thought by fome to occupy too much room, the writer in-
treats them to weigh in their own minds, whether any thing,
fo nearly related to publick as well as individual good, can
be too diffufely handled, or too ftrongly recommended.

To

To the following Gentlemen the writer is indebted for valuable information, and he begs leave to exprefs his warmest acknowledgements for the fame:

Mr. PERKINS, of Oakhill near Shepton-Mallet.

Mr. ANDERDON, of Henlade near Taunton.

Mr. WHITMARSH, of Batts near ditto.

Mr. ABRAHAM, of White-Lackington.

Mr. MATTHEWS, of Bath, Secretary to the Agricultural Society.

Mr. PAGET, of Cranmoor.

Mr. CROCKER, of Frome.

Mr. LOCK, of Brent.

Mr. WHITE, of Sand near Wells.

Mr. PHIPPEN, of Mere near ditto.

Mr. KINGDON, of Milverton near Taunton.

Mr. DAVIS, of Longleat, Wilts.

Mr. PALFREMAN, of North Devon.

Rev. UNWIN CLARKE, of Monkfilver.

Others who promifed their affiftance, and who, from practical knowledge, were competent to the tafk, withheld their communications, from an *ill-founded* apprehenfion, that the eftablifhment of a Board of Agriculture was preparatory to additional taxation under fome form or other.

This the writer has reafon to mention with regret.

AGRICULTURAL SURVEY

OF

SOMERSETSHIRE.

CHAPTER I.

GEOGRAPHICAL STATE AND
CIRCUMSTANCES.

SECT. 1.—*Situation and Extent.*

SOMERSETSHIRE is a maritime county, in the South-weft part of England, having the Briftol Channel on the Weft—Glouceflerfhire, and the city and county of Briftol, on the North—Wiltfhire on the Eaft—and Devon-fhire on the South and South-Weft.

Its form is oblong, being in length from North-eaft to South-weft 80 miles—in breadth from Eaft to Weft about 36 miles—and in circumference about 200 miles.

The reporter cannot with abfolute precifion ftate the total amount of acres, or the number of inhabitants, in this county; but he conceives the former to be about one million of acres, and the latter about three hundred thoufand. The average value per acre of the inclofed and cultivated land is not lefs now than *twenty-five* fhillings per annum; and at the Revolution the total annual value was eftimated at

375,000*l.*

375,000l. The different appropriations of this furface of land may be arranged in the following way:

			Acres.
Towns and villages	——	——	3000
Publick and private roads	——	—	15,000
Rivers, lakes, ponds, &c.	——	——	2,500
Woods and plantations	——	——	20,000
Meadow and pafture land inclofed		—	584,500
Marfh and fen-land uninclofed		——	30,000
Arable and convertible land inclofed		——	260,000
Common fields	——	—	20,000
Uncultivated waftes [1]	——	——	65,000
		*	1,000,000

The fea-coaft is very irregular, in fome places projecting into lofty and rocky promontories, and in others receding into fine bays, with flat and level fhores. From Start point northward, the coaft is flat, and compofed of vaft fand-banks repelling the inundation of the fea, which, in ancient times, wafhed over thefe fhoals, and flowed up into the country, covering with its waters that extenfive territory now called *Brent-Marfh.* The fea, after its general retirement, paid frequent vifits to thefe parts; and it was found neceffary, to the fecurity of the country, to eftablifh a

---

* Since this account was taken, fundry acts of parliament have been paffed, and are now pending, for the inclofing, draining, and dividing of more than 18,000 acres of marfh and fen land, and 20,000 acres of common fields and uncultivated waftes. Fifteen bills of inclofure have been brought into parliament this feffion (1797) for this county only, whilft, in the adjoining county of Devon, not a fingle application has been made in this century. This is the more extraordinary, as there are immenfe tracts lying wafte in the laft-mentioned county.

Commiffion

Commiffion of Sewers, the members of which fhould examine and infpect the fea banks, ditches, gutters, and fewers, connected with the fea, and order the requifite cleanfings and reparations. The firft commiffion of this kind upon record, was in 1304; and the like offices are extended to this day.

Sect. 2.—*Divifion.*

Somerfetfhire, in refpect to its jurifdiction, is divided into two parts, *eaftern* and *weftern.* The firft containing 19 hundreds, the latter 21 hundreds. It has befides 7 liberties, 2 cities, 7 boroughs, 29 market-towns, 1 bifhoprick, 3 archdeaconries, 13 deaneries, and 482 parifhes.†

Sect. 3.—*Climate.*

In fuch an extent of ground, it may naturally be fuppofed, that the climate is various. Near the fea-coaft winter is fcarcely felt; and from Minehead and Dulverton on the weft, to Milborne-Port and Wincanton on the eaft, the climate (Quantock, Branden, and Dunkry hills excepted) is mild and temperate. As you approach the northern diftrict, and afcend Poulden hill, it changes and becomes more cold and boifterous; and when you proceed farther northward, and gain the fummit of Mendip hills, you feel yourfelf, comparatively, in Lapland. The perpendicular altitude of Mendip hills, compared with the town of Taunton, is fuppofed to be at leaft 1100 feet.

Seed time and harveft greatly vary in different parts of the county: the mountainous parts being nearly a month later than the vales; for which reafon, it is found right, on expofed and elevated fituations, fuch as Mendip, Quantock,

---

† Collinfon and Rack's Hiftory of Somerfetfhire.

and Brandon hills, to sow a fortnight earlier in the autumn, and a fortnight later in the spring, than is generally recommended in books of husbandry or gardening.

Sect. 4.—*Soil and Surface.*

For fertility of soil, and general produce, this county stands eminently high in reputation. The plains are remarkable for their luxuriant herbage, which furnishes not only a sufficiency for its own consumption, but also a considerable surplus for other markets: London, Bristol, Salisbury, and other parts of the kingdom, are annually supplied with fat *oxen, sheep,* and *hogs,* together with *cyder, cheese, butter,* and many other articles, in great abundance. Nor are the hills by any means deficient in their arable productions; yet it must be admitted, that its vicinity to the Bristol Channel, which fills the air with watery vapours unfavourable to the ripening of corn, particularly in the western districts, induces a preference in favour of *grazing* and *dairy* husbandry: and in consequence thereof, vast quantities of grain are annually purchased from the adjacent counties of Wilts and Dorset, to the amount of at least one hundred thousand quarters—by which, the county would be drained of its money, were it not for the coal, cattle, &c. which are sent in return.

MOUNTAINS.

The surface of the inland parts is varied by lofty hills, rich level plains, and bold aspiring woods. The most noted hills are, *Quantock, Brandon* and *Dunkry, Mendip, Poulden, Broadfield* and *Leigh-down, Lansdown, White-down,* and *Black-down.*

The soil of these mountains may be thus stated; *Quantock,* &c. (situated between the town of Taunton and the sea) a thin a thin variable foil, covering a loofe fhelly rock, interfperfed with occafional lime-ftone. *Poulden-hill*, (between Bridgwater and Glaftonbury) a ftrong furface, covering a bed of clay or marl. *Mendip-hills*, (between the city of Wells and Briftol.) *Broadfield* and *Leigh-down*, (near Briftol) a gravelly loam on a lime-ftone rock. *Lanfdown*, (near Bath) a freeftone grit. *White-down*, (near Chard) variable. *Blackdown*, (on the confines of Devon) a thin furface of black earth on a bed of fand or gravel. Almoft every fpecies of foil (chalk excepted, of which there is only a fmall portion in the eaftern divifion) may be found in different parts of the county, and of a quality highly fertile and productive.

FORESTS.

Its antient forefts are, *Selwood*, near Frome; *Mendip*, between Frome and the Briftol Channel; *Exmoor*, between the port of Watchet and the north-weft part of Devon; *Neroche*, near Ilminfter; and *North-Petherton*,* near Bridgwater.

MOORS.

The principal Moors are,
King-Sedgmoor, near Bridgwater.
Eaft-Sedgmoor, between Wells and Glaftonbury.
Weft-Sedgmoor, between Taunton and Langport.
North-moor and Stanmoor, near the ifle of Athelney.
Common-moor, near Langport.
Weft-moor, Curry and Hay-moor, near North-Curry.
Kings-moor, between Ilchefter and Somerton.
Ilemoor, on the river Ivel.

* The parifh of North-Petherton, at the prefent æra, confifts of as good arable and pafture land as any in the county; and may, I believe, be eftimated at the average annual value of 40s. per acre. J. B.

Brent-

Brent-marſh, on the river Brue and Ax.

Weſton-moor, near Uphill.

Banwell and Smeath moors, near Churchill.

Kenn-moor, near Yatton.

Nailſea-moor, north of Kenn.

Clapton-moor, between Clapton and Wirton.

Of theſe many have been incloſed, drained, and improved, in the courſe of the laſt twenty years, as will be noticed hereafter.

SECT. 5.—*Minerals, &c.*

This county produces *lead, copper, iron, lapis calaminaris, manganeſe, coal, lime-ſtone, paving-ſtone, tiling-ſtone, free-ſtone, fullers'-earth, marl,* and *othre.*

SECT. 6.—*Water.*

The principal rivers are, the Avon, Ax, Brue, Parret, Yow, Cale, Chew, Tone, Frome, Ivel, Ex, and Barl.

Of theſe, four only are navigable, viz. the Avon, from Bath to Briſtol, 16 miles; the Brue, from Briſtol Channel to Highbridge, 2 miles; the Parret, from Stert-Point to Langport, about 20 miles; and the Tone, from Taunton to Boroughbridge, 8 miles.

For the ſake of perſpicuity I ſhall divide the county into three diſtricts:—the firſt comprehending the tract of land included between the ports of Uphill and Kingroad on the weſt, and the towns of Bath and Frome on the eaſt. This I ſhall call the *north-eaſt* diſtrict.

The next I ſhall call the *middle* diviſion; and is that portion of land which is bounded by the Mendip hills on the north, Bridgwater-bay on the weſt, and the town of Chard on the ſouth.

The *ſouth-weſt* diviſion will occupy the remainder.

NORTH-EAST DISTRICT.

SECT. 1. *Climate, Soil, and Surface.*

The surface of this diſtrict being very irregular, and inter-mixed with lofty hills and rich fertile plains, the climate is conſequently exceedingly varied. On the weſtern ſide, in-cluding the hundreds of Winter-Stoke and Portbury, the ſoil is, for the moſt part, a deep and rich mixture of clay and ſand; being originally a depoſit by the ſea, which, in antient times, flowed up a conſiderable way into that part of the country. Theſe Moor-lands, as they are called, are at the preſent time ſubject to frequent inundation; and ſometimes, in rainy ſeaſons, are covered with water for four or five ſuccef-five months. The luxuriant herbage produced by theſe lands, when cleared from ſtagnant water, is ſuch as to in-duce, in the mind of a man fond of national improvement, an ardent wiſh to ſee them completely drained.

This, I think, might be effected in the following way: Let a ſluice or dam be built at the outlet of the river Yeo or Yow, the apron of which ſhould be placed near low-water mark. It is not neceſſary to deſcribe theſe ſluices, or outlets, as they are common to moſt counties bordering on the ſea. Suffice it to ſay, that theſe buildings are furniſhed with fold-ing doors, which ſhut at the influx of the tide, and open on its retreat. From a ſluice thus erected, let the bed of the river be lowered to an inclined plane of one foot in a mile. This is ſufficient to produce a current, and it will prevent any great depoſit of ſediment. Let the bottom be contract-ed in its breadth, ſo that the water in time of floods may run with ſufficient rapidity to cleanſe it of mud. In regard to the dimenſions and expence of ſuch a main drain, the reader ſhall be informed when we come to treat of Sedgmoor.

c In

In the parishes of Congresbury, Yatton, Banwell, Winscombe, Churchill, and Puxton, there are not less than three thousand acres subject to frequent inundation. All these lands discharge the greatest part of their waters into the river Yeo, and are under the inspection of the Commissioners of Water-Sewers; but the powers vested in these commissioners by Parliament are not sufficient to enable them to divert the course of the river, or to effect a radical cure.

The tide flows nearly seven miles up the river Yeo; and at six miles from the mouth of the river the spring-tides flow five feet above the level of the adjacent lands.

This would be effectually prevented by the dam before mentioned; and by cutting proper lateral drains, the whole district might be advanced in value 10s. or 15s. per acre: and all this might be done at an expence which two years profit would reimburse. Nothing is necessary but effectual draining to make it as good land as any in the county. It requires no dung, or any extraneous manure, but may be kept in good heart by the contents of the ditches.

To the northward of this district lie the parishes of Kenn, Kingston-Seymour, Cleveden, Nailsea, Chelvey, and Claverham, possessing near four thousand acres, alike subject to inundation.

These parishes are secured from the sea by a wall built with stone and lime, and elevated ten feet above the level of the land within. High tides sometimes overflow this wall, and when a strong westerly wind prevails, at the equinoxes, the wall is frequently broken down by the impetuosity of the waves, and large portions of the land are covered.

Should this happen at the autumnal equinox, little injury is done; but if at the vernal, it kills the best grass, and the crop of the ensuing summer is worth but little. These lands discharge their waters by two rivers, called the Little Yeos.

At

At the mouth of thefe rivers are fluices, fuch as before defcribed, which prevent inundation *from the fea*; but being
not made deep enough at their outlet, and the rivers, by
which the waters are conveyed, not being properly bottomed,
the country is fubject to frequent *land-floods*. This level is
fufceptible of the fame improvement, by a complete drainage, as the former. At the fouth-weft of this divifion lie
the parifhes of Churchill, Hutton, Banwell, Locking, Wef-
ton-fuper-Mare, and Uphill. Thefe lands are for the moft
part occupied by dairy or grazing farmers, and are fubject
to frequent overflowings of the river, which runs through a
dam or fluice at Uphill. It is prefumed, that if the bed of
the river at Uphill, and the fluice through which the water
is difcharged, were deepened three feet, the evil would in a
great degree be removed.

Proceeding northward from hence you afcend Leigh-
down. This is a tract of elevated land, extending from
Clevedon to the Hot-Wells, near Briftol. It is principally
fed with fheep, and confifts of nearly three thoufand acres.
A large portion of this down will not admit of cultivation,
the lime-ftone rock being within two or three inches of the
furface. It is probable that this land will pay more as pafture than any other way. But the chief inconvenience arifes
from the unlimited right of flocking, by which it is burthened with double the number it ought to have; the breed
of neat cattle is greatly injured; and, in refpect to fheep, the
quantity of wool leffened. To illuftrate this obfervation,
refpecting over-flocking, I fhall ftate a cafe in point. A farmer of this diftrict, fome years fince, put twenty-five head
of fteers and heifers into a piece of commonable land: the
fpring being unfavourable to the purchafe of cattle, and a
confiderable fatality having prevailed the preceding winter,
the common was *moderately* flocked; in confequence of

c 2   which

which a profit of two pounds per head was made between the months of April and November. Encouraged by this succefs, and flattering himfelf with the profpect of fimilar profit, he purchafed the next year one hundred head; but others following his example, he, to his great mortification, found that, inflead of profit, he fuffered a lofs of nearly one hundred pounds.

From thefe premifes, may it not be fairly inferred, that the *inclofing* and *dividing* of commons, even in cafes where the plough cannot prudently be introduced, are beneficial both to the individual and the public; as the owner can then apportion his flock to the quantity and quality of his land, and can have them at all times under his eye? But of this fubject more by and by.

Sect. 5.   *Minerals, &c.*

The Mendip hills are famous for their mines, particularly of lead and lapis calaminaris. The former are nearly exhaufled, or at leaft the deep working is fo incumbered with water, that little can be done, and in all probability millions in value may remain concealed in the bowels of this mountain, 'till fpirit enough be found in the country to perforate it by cutting a level, or audit, through its bafe, namely, from Compton-Martin to Wookey-Hole.*

---

* A plan fimilar to this has been talked of in a general way for feveral years paft, but no regular fyftem has been formed. It might eventually prove highly productive to the adventurers; and, whether taken in a provincial or national view, be of great utility. The rifk is certainly fmall, the advantage poffibly great. But there are many concomitant circumftances which call for mature deliberation and able digeftion; fuch as the confent of the proprietors of land, the authority of Parliament, compenfation to the owners of pitches already made agreeable to the laws of the foreft, the incorporation of a company, the appointment of a treafurer, clerk, manager, committee, &c. It will alfo, moft probably, be expected by the proprietors of land, that

more

The diſtance is about five miles, and the depth from the ſurface about one hundred and fifty yards; ſuch a tunnel would not only convey off all water, but the driving it, or the ſinking of the ſhaft or perpendicular pits, might lead to a diſcovery of veins of lead hitherto unexplored, and perhaps as valuable as that now at Weſt-Chewton, which, tradition ſays, yielded 100,000l. within the ſpace of an acre. What the expence of ſuch an adventure might be, I cannot exactly aſcertain; but, for argument ſake, let us ſuppoſe it to be 100,000l.—A thouſand ſubſcribers, at 100l. each, would ſuffice; and as no great number of men can, for want of room, be employed at the ſame time, I would propoſe that the principal money be veſted in government ſecurities, and the *intereſt* only expended; this would keep in conſtant pay more than one hundred workmen, and in all probability, before 10,000l. were expended, diſcoveries would be made highly beneficial to the adventurers, and to the publick; and, even under the worſt ſuppoſition, the only loſs would be that of the intereſt of 100l. to each individual.

In times paſt many thouſands a year have been annually paid to the ſee of Wells for the lord's ſhare (that is, one tenth) of the lead dug on the foreſt within the pariſh of Wells only; and is it not more than probable, that lead, like coal, may be moſt valuable in the deep? On Broadfield-down there are alſo veins of lead; and in the pariſhes of Rowberrow, Shipham, and Winſcomb, there are valuable mines of lapis calaminaris. This mineral is ſometimes found within a

more than one level be driven, that all might have an equal chance of benefit. Such expectation appears reaſonable, and from the ſmall number of workmen that can poſſibly be employed on a level at the ſame time, the intereſt of the capital will be fully ſufficient for carrying on, not only the principal one, but alſo two or more others, from different points, to thoſe parts where, from the antient working, there is good cauſe for expecting to meet with ore. R. PAGET.

yard of the furface, and feldom worked deeper than thirty
fathoms.   Between four and five hundred miners are conftantly employed in this bufinefs, and the average price is
about five pounds per ton.   In the parifhes of Compton-
Martin and Eaft-Harptry are alfo many mines of a fimilar
nature, and a confiderable number of men are conftantly
employed therein.*

The general method of difcovering the fituation and direction of thefe feams of ore (which lie at various depths,
from five to twenty fathoms, in a chafm between two benches
of folid rock) is, by the help of the *divining-rod*, vulgarly
called *jofing*; and a variety of ftrong teftimonies are adduced
in fupport of this doctrine.   Moft rational people, however,
give but little credit to it, and confider the whole as a *trick*.
Should the fact be allowed, it is difficult to account for it;
and the influence of the mines on the hafel-rod feems to
partake fo much of the marvellous, as almoft entirely to exclude the operation of known and natural agents.   So confident, however, are the common miners of its efficacy, that
they fcarce ever fink a fhaft but by its direction; and thofe
who are dexterous in the ufe of it, will mark on the furface
the courfe and breadth of the vein; and after that, with the

---

* There are marks and indications of calamine from thefe parifhes
in the weft, through the whole tract of Mendip to Mells at the eaftern
extremity.   At Merchant's-hill, in the parifh of Binegar, feveral tons
were raifed fome years ago.   It was of very good quality, and more
would have been landed, had not the influx of the water put a ftop to
the works.   At the fame time a large quantity was raifed at Mells, remarkably pure, free from heterogeneous mixture, and of excellent
quality.   It did not there defcend, in regular courfes, between the
lime-ftone rocks, but was found in large maffes or bulks, lying hori-
zontally, at about four or five feet from the furface, on a thin fcale of
free-ftone which covered the rock; and it is highly probable that much
more remains to be difcovered.   R. P.

affiftance

affiftance of the rod, will follow the fame courfe twenty times following *blindfolded*.

At the requeft of many gentlemen I have annexed

The Laws and Orders of the Mendip Miners, commonly called Lord Choke's Laws.

Be it known, that this is a true copy of the inrolled, in the king's exchequer, in the time of king Edward the IVth, of a debate that was in the county of Somerfet, between the Lord Benfield, and the Tenants of Chewton, and the Prior of Green-Oare: the faid prior complaining unto the king of great injuries and wrongs that he had upon Mendip; being the king's foreft, the faid king Edward commanded the lord Chock, the lord chief juftice of England, to go down into the county of Somerfet, to Mendipp, and fit in concord and peace in the faid county concerning Mendipp, upon pain of high difpleafure. The faid lord Chock fate upon Mendipp on a place of my lords of Bath, called the *Forge*; where (as he commanded all the commoners to appear, and efpecially the four lords royals of Mendipp; that is to fay, the bifhop of Bath, my lord of Glafton, my lord Benfield, the earl of Chewton, and my lord of Richmond, with all the appearance, to the number of ten thoufand people) a proclamation was made, to enquire of all the company how they would be ordered; then they, with one confent, made anfwer, that they would be ordered and tryed by the four lords of the royalties; and then the four lords royal were agreed, that the comminers of Mendip fhould turn out their cattle at their out-lets, as much the fummer as they be able to winter; without hounding or pounding, upon whofe grounds foever they went to take their courfe and recourfe. To which the faid four lords royal did put their feals; and were alfo agreed, that whofoever fhould break the faid bonds

fhould

should forfeit to the king a thousand marks, and all the commiuers their bodys and goods to be at the king's pleasure or command that doth either hound or pound.

The old ancient occupation of miners in and upon Mendipp, being the king's forest of Mendipp, within the county of Somerset, being one of the four staples of England, which have been exercised, used, and continued, through the said forest of Mendipp, from the time whereof no man living hath not memory, as hereafter doth particularly ensue the order.

1. *First*, That if any man, whatsoever he be, that doth intend to venture his life to be a workman in the said occupation, he must first of all crave licence of the lord of the soyle where he doth purpose to work, and in his absence, of his officers, as the lead-reave or bailiffe, and the lord, neither his officers can deny him.

2. *Item.* That after the first licence had the workman shall never need to ask leave again, but to be at his free will to pitch within the forest, and to brake the ground where and in what place it shall please him, to his behalf and profit, using himself trustily and truly.

3. *Item.* If any man that doth begin to pitch or groof shall heave his hackes through two ways after the rake. Note, that he that doth throw the hacke must stand to the girdle or waist in the same groof, and then no man shall or may work within his hackes throwe, provided always that no man shall or can keep but his wet and dry groof and his mark.

4. *Item.* That when a workman have landed his oar, he may carry the same to cleansing or blowing to what minery it shall please him, for the speedy making out of the same, so that he doth truly pay the lord of the soyle where it was landed his due, which is the tenth part thereof.

5. *Item.*

5. *Item.* That if any lord or officer hath once given licence to any man to build, or set up any hearth or washing-house, to wash, cleanse, or blow oar, he that once hath leave shall keep it for ever, or give it to whom he will, so that he doth justly pay his lott lead, which is the tenth pound, which shall be blown at the hearth or hearths; and also that he doth keep it tennantable, as the custom doth require.

6. *Item.* That if any man of that occupation doth pick or steal any lead or oare to the value of thirteen-pence half-penny, the lord, or his officer, may arrest all his lead-works, house, and hearth, with all his groofs and works, and keep them as safely to his own use; and shall take the person that hath so offended, and bring him where his house is, or his work, and all his tools or instruments to the occupation belongs as he useth, and put him into the said house, and set fire on all together about him, and banish him from that occupation before the miners for ever.

7. *Item.* If that person doth pick or steal there any more, he shall be tryed by the law, for this law and custom hath no more to do with him.

8. *Item.* That every lord of the soyle ought to keep two miner-courts by the year, and to swear twelve men of the same occupation for the redress of misdemeanors touching the mineries.

9. *Item.* That the lord or lords may make and grant manner of arrests, viz. First, for strife between man and man, for their works under the ground or earth. Secondly, for his own dutys for lead or oare, wheresoever he findeth it upon the same forest.

10. *Item.* That if any man, by means of misfortune, take his death, as by falling of the earth upon him, by drawing or stifeling, or otherwise, as in time past many have been, the

the workmen of the same occupation are bound to fetch him
out of the earth, and to bring him to chriſtian burial at their
own coſts and charges, although he be forty fathome under
the earth, as heretofore hath been done, and the coroner, or
any officer at large, ſhall not have to do with him in any
reſpect.

COAL.

This diſtrict abounds with coal, and with reſpect to this
article is reducible to the ſeparate diviſions of Northern and
Southern.   The former, including the pariſhes of High-
Littleton, Timſbury, Paulton, (with Clutton and Sutton
adjoining to the weſt, and Camerton and Dunkerton to the
eaſt of the diſtrict) Radſtock, and the northern part of
Midſummer-Norton.   The latter, the ſouthern part of
Midſummer-Norton, Stratton on the Foſs, (Halcombe and
Aſhwick adjoining the diſtrict) Kilmerſdon, Babington, and
Mells.

Theſe, meaning the *latter*, are what were heretofore
known by the name of Mendip collieries, and probably they
were once within the verge of that extenſive foreſt, though
now in the midſt of old incloſures.   They being ſtill frequently deſcribed in ordinary books of topography by the
ſame name, (now obſolete in the neighbourhood) this
remark was thought neceſſary for the purpoſe of iden-
tification.   •

In the Northern collieries the ſtrata of coal form an inclination of the *plane* of about nine inches in the yard: theſe
are in number nineteen.   In thickneſs variable, from ten
inches to upwards of three feet.   If leſs than fifteen inches,
they are ſeldom worked.   Coal is now working generally
from ſeventy to eighty fathoms in depth: in a few places
deeper; and by a late introduction of machinery to raiſe it

by the steam-engine, a much greater depth of working will be obtained.*

Profits of working in the aggregate, by no means equal to the extent and risque of the adventure; to a few works considerable; to the majority very moderate.

The coal is of prime quality; pure and durable in burning; firm, large, and of a strong grain; which ensures its conveyance to almost any distance, without injury to its appearance or quality, which cannot be exceeded in any part of the kingdom. Bath is the principal market of consumption; to which may be added, the western parts of Wiltshire, and the next adjacent parts of Somersetshire. The quantity now raised is from fifteen hundred to two thousand tons weekly. A much greater can be supplied, should an increased demand require it. Boys and men, to the number of fifteen hundred, are employed in working it, with wages sufficiently adequate to procure them a comfortable subsistence.

An application is intended to be made to parliament at the ensuing session, for leave to cut two branches of a canal for the accommodation of the collieries of this northern district, to communicate with the rivers Avon and Kennett.† Should the bill pass, a considerable extension of sale may be reasonably inferred. The permanence of the works is

---

* As it may be a matter of consequence to all such coal-works whose situation in regard to water will admit of it, it ought to be noticed, that at Welton, a work in the northern part of Midsummer-Norton, the coal has lately been drawn up by a water-wheel on a new construction; the machinery appendant to which is so contrived as to answer the purpose in the most perfect and cheap manner; the use of horses, as in the old way, being entirely superseded; and the consumption of fuel, as in the new way by the steam-engine, altogether saved. R. P.

† This act has been obtained; and the canal is now (Jan. 1797) nearly half finished.

amply

amply fecured by various contrivances, in preventing the admiffion of the fprings into the deep working.

The number of works twenty-fix. The owners of the freehold from whence the coal is raifed generally receive an eighth of the grofs receipt of fale; but, to encourage the proprietors to greater depths of working, have occafionally complied with a proportionable reduction of this quota, on account of the increafed expences in working; whereby they have derived a profit from coal, which otherwife would have been irrecoverably loft. Some, through ignorance and ftubbornnefs, have withheld this conceffion, and thereby incurred the lofs.

Average price of coal five-pence per bufhel at the pit, (nine gallons meafure.)

The Southern diftrict is on a more limited fcale of working. The ftrata of coal form an inclination of the plane from eighteen to thirty inches in the yard; in fome the plane is annihilated, and they defcend in a perpendicular direction. There are in number twenty-five; in thicknefs from fix inches to feven feet; feldom worked under eighteen inches; in depth from thirty to fixty fathoms at the prefent working. By the fteam-engines, which are now erecting in this diftrict, a much greater depth will be attained. Profits in the aggregate of working very trifling, if any, owing to the confumption of timber, and the expence of drawing water. The coal of various quality; fome nearly equal to that of the northern diftrict; but the greateft part lefs firm, of fhorter grain, and lefs calculated for diftant carriage; but free to burn, wholly divefted of fulphureous ftench, and durable. The fmall coal excellent for the forge, and when reduced to a cinder, called *coke*, by a procefs of very ancient ufage, it furnifhes a fuel for drying malt, which, from its purity and total exemption from fmoke, cannot be excelled,

if

if equalled. The south-weſtern parts of Wiltſhire, the northern of Dorſet, and the eaſt and ſouthern parts of So-merſet, are the markets for conſumption.

The quantity now raiſed is from eight hundred to a thou-ſand tons weekly, which, in the courſe of a few years, might be extended to two thouſand tons, if ſale could be found. Boys and men employed at preſent amount to from five to ſix hundred. An improved method of working has been lately adopted in ſome parts of this diſtrict, by which the ſprings are prevented from inundating the deep working; whereby its extent and duration will be conſiderably promoted.

A canal to the works in this diſtrict, which might be cut at an eaſy expence, has been for ſome time in contempla-tion;* and which not only would benefit the proprietors of the works, by extending the conſumption, but alſo reduce the price to the more diſtant conſumers more than half.

The average price of coal in this diſtrict is three-pence three-farthings per buſhel.

Should the works in the Northern diſtrict be ſtopped, the probable increaſe of the poor-rates would be 2000l. per annum. In the Southern (much more burthened with poor) to ſeven or eight ſhillings in the pound.

At Clapton alſo, a village lying to the north-weſt of Leigh-Down, there is a coal-work which poſſeſſes the ad-vantage of a land-level of forty-four fathoms. At this pit are landed about 240 buſhels daily. The beſt coal is ſold at three-pence halfpenny per buſhel, and the ſmall is ſhipped at Portiſhead-point for Wales, where it is uſed for burn-ing lime.

---

* This is now (Jan. 1797) in execution, and the tonnage, &c. of coal to Frome (nine miles) will not exceed 2s. per ton.

South-east of Leigh-Down is a vale of rich grass land, extending from Bedminster at the north-east, to Brockley and Nailsea at the south-west.

Under this level are supposed to be inexhaustible veins of coal. At present they land 2500 bushels a day. The best coal is sold at three-pence halfpenny, the middle sort at three-pence, and the small at two-pence, per bushel. One of the works is under contract to serve the glass-houses, some time since erected in the parish of Nailsea, at one penny farthing per bushel.

These glass-houses consume about 2000 bushels weekly. The deepest work is forty-two fathoms. The principal vein is five feet thick; sometimes more. The coal takes a south *pitch*, or inclination, never exceeding two feet in a fathom. Little timber is used; but they are much incommoded with water; for the rock which lies above the coal so abounds with fissures, that it is difficult to prevent the *land water* from pervading the bottom of the works.

When the top veins are exhausted, and the proprietors compelled to go deeper, it is a matter of doubt whether any power of a steam-engine may be competent to the task of keeping them dry.

Many people are under alarming apprehensions lest the coal-mines may be exhausted by the extra demand produced by the extension of sale established by the canals;—but such disquieting ideas will vanish, when they are told that more than treble the present quantity could be raised from the pits already in use, did the demand require it; and the increased quantity might be supplied for several hundred years.

CHAPTER II.

STATE OF PROPERTY.

———

Estates and Tenures.

THERE are in this diſtrict many large proprietors from 2000l. to 600cl. per annum; but ſtill the greateſt part is poſſeſſed by the middle claſs, holding from 50l. to 500l. per annum. Part is leaſed out on lives; part is in demeſne, and let out for ſhort terms; and no ſmall quantity is the fee of the occupiers, conſtituting a moſt reſpectable yeomanry.

To thoſe who are ſenſible of the importance of agriculture to ſociety, a contemplation of the cauſes which have principally contributed to its advancement in this county cannot but be highly intereſting. And foremoſt, we may ſafely rank, the *alienation of property*, whereby lands, heretofore neglected and comparatively barren, have been advanced from ſuch their unproductive ſtate to a condition highly fertile and productive. Next, the increaſed population and extenſion of manufactures; together with the enlargement of the city of Bath.

Certain lands now held by their ancient tenures, and conſequently but little improved, preſent a lively portraiture of the former diſgraceful ſtate of the county, when contraſted with its preſent ſtate of comparative perfection.

CHAPTER III.

BUILDINGS.

THERE are many splendid gentlemen's seats, ornamented with extensive plantations, in this district; and the farm-houses and cottages are for the most part commodious and comfortable—but on all the dairy farms, a shameful inattention prevails, in respect to out-houses and sheds for their stock to retire to in the winter months. Cattle are almost univerfally ferved with their provender in the field; and many a dairy farmer, with twenty cows, fcarcely makes, in the whole winter, a quantity of dung fufficient to manure *one acre* of land. Corn being generally ftacked, the barns are fmall, and principally *thatched* with wheat-ftraw unbroken by the flail, which gives to the roof a very neat appearance, and renders the building perfectly fecure from rain. It has been of late too much the practice for parish-officers to proftrate cottages, and to leffen as much as poffible the number of inhabitants in their refpective parifhes; this abfurd and narrow-minded fyftem has received vigour and extenfion from the prevailing cuftom of making the tenant pay the poors levy. It is, however, a practice which cannot be too ftrongly reprobated; and the ill effects of it have been fo mafterly depicted by Mr. *Kent* and other authors, that I fhall not fatigue the reader with a repetition of their arguments. On all the new inclofures (which for the moft part are fituated at a diftance from the inhabited villages) the erection of cottages appears *indifpenfible*, as without them, the wafte of time in going forward and backward to and from work amounts to nearly a quarter part of the day.

It might alfo be added, that many of the cottages now in ufe are on too fmall a fcale. Few of them have more than

one

one room above ſtairs. This is not only uncomfortable, but inconſiſtent with that decency and modeſty, with the importance of which children cannot be too early or too ſtrongly impreſſed.

The rent of theſe cottages varies from thirty ſhillings to fifty ſhillings per year, including a ſmall portion of garden-ground.*

---

* It is but of little permanent utility to the cottagers to give them garden-ground, unleſs you ſupply them annually with a certain portion of manure. J. B.

CHAPTER IV.

MODE OF OCCUPATION.

━━━━━━

Sect. 1.—*Size of Farms. Character of Farmers.*

THE Farms in this diſtrict are not large, ſeldom exceeding 200l. per year, and accompanied with a ſmall proportion of arable. Some of the dairy farms are ſo ſmall, as not
to exceed 60l. or 70l. per year; and many inſtances can be
produced of ſuch little farmers breeding up a large family in a
very reſpectable way. In ſuch inſtances, it is generally found
that the wife undertakes the whole management of the cows,
and the huſband goes to daily labour. There are few trades
in which a ſmall capital can be employed to greater advantage than this. As to the general character of farmers,
truth compels to ſay (and I mention it with regret) that there
is a great want of juſtice, candour, and liberality, in their
conduct towards their landlords, and in their general ſyſtem
of management. If not cloſely watched, they will impo-
veriſh their eſtates by ſelling the little ſtraw they grow to
the adjacent towns; and though dung of the beſt kind may
be bought, both in Briſtol and Bath, for 3s. or 4s. a waggon load, they ſcarcely ever take any back to their farms. `

They are alſo much bigotted to old cuſtoms; and I hope
I am not uncharitably ſevere, if I add, that they are too
juſtly chargeable with a diſregard of truth. This is the
forerunner of all vice, and to the prevailing cuſtom of telling
lies at fairs, may be attributed the looſe morality of farmers
in this moſt eſſential part of human reſponſibility.

` It muſt be acknowledged that there are many exceptions
to this general obſervation.

Sect.

Sect. 2.

Rent is univerfally paid in money; and it is generally cuftomary to receive the Michaelmas rent at Lady-day, and
the Lady-day's rent at Michaelmas. No perfonal fervice
is exacted.

Sect. 3.—*Tithes.*

I muft beg leave to wave a difcuffion of this difficult
though important fubject. Suffice it to fay, that if they
are a grievance, (which I believe few will difpute) it is a
grievance eftablifhed by the laws of the land, and no violent
or harfh methods of relief can be juftified. In refpect to
their influence on the agriculture of *this diftrict*, I fee but
little to complain of: both the clergy and the lay-impro-
priator have been fo moderate in their demands, and in general have agreed to fo reafonable a compofition, that the
progrefs of improvement has received but little check on
this account.

There is one method by which I think tithes might be
fairly and honourably got rid of, and that is by *purchafe*.
The unappropriated tithe-holder could have no juft reafon
for complaint if he were paid a fair value for his property;
and the clergy might *at this time*, from a fund eftablifhed
under the direction and controul of the legiflature, and gua-
ranteed by government, enjoy fuch an increafe of annual
income as would be a fufficient compenfation for any fuppofed advance in the different articles of human fupport,
convenience, or comfort.

Sect. 4.—*Poor-Rates.*

In refpect to the county of Somerfet, the poor's levy is a
more alarming grievance than tithes.

Many

Many parishes, which within twenty years past paid no more than 50l. per annum to the poor, now pay 200l. and unless some plan of prevention be adopted, the evil is not likely to abate. This increase of the poor's rate has been *general*, and may be attributed partly to an increased population, and partly to a growing dissoluteness in the manners of the poor, which ever accompanies national improvement. Active exertions in this way cannot fail to produce a scarcity of labour; and to this, as naturally follows, an advance of wages; but the misfortune is, that such an advance is not accompanied with a growing disposition in the workman to maintain, in a more comfortable way, his wife and family, or to lay by against a time of need. No; if he can earn eight or nine shillings in *four* days of the week, the remaining *two* days are devoted to pleasure, or luxury, and the wife and children are in a worse situation than when more moderate wages compelled him to constant work.

I have known many instances, where the wages of a collier and his family, not exceeding five persons, have been twenty-five shillings per week, and their improvidence has been such, that one week's illness has brought them to the parish for assistance.

I can also look back to the time, when a commendable degree of pride operated on the minds of the lower class, and withheld them from applications to the parish for relief, unless in great distress.

This pride, I am sorry to say, is totally lost, and the boon is now administered by the parish-officer, with *caution* and *reluctance*; and received by the poor, with *dissatisfaction* and *ingratitude*. From what I have said, let it not be inferred, that I wish to depress the poor, or to debar them of that comfort, which their usefulness in society intitles them to enjoy. No sight can be more pleasing to me, than to see

an

an induſtrious cottager, returning from his daily labour, with a chearful countenance, and viewing his wife and children with complacency and delight; and I would contribute to their happineſs as much as in me lies, by humbly recommending to our legiſlators a ſerious peruſal of a pamphlet, publiſhed ſome years ago, entitled, *Twenty minutes Advice on the Poor Laws*. By the plan there ſuggeſted, I verily think the ſituation of the induſtrious poor might be meliorated, and the idle and diſſolute be made to contribute towards their ſupport.* All thoſe who are converſant with the ſtate of the lower claſs of ſociety, muſt know that the period of life in which a workman moſt ſuffers, is when he has five or ſix ſmall children. Then it is that the ſupport of the whole family depends on the father's labour, and his utmoſt exertions is ſcarcely ſufficient to procure them bread; ſhould ſickneſs befall him, he muſt contract debts; and ſhould this repeatedly happen, before he has extricated himſelf, his ſpirits are broken, and the love of freedom and independence no longer exiſts. A degree of torpor and inactivity ſucceeds, from which he ſcarcely ever emerges. To the man in this ſituation, I would, if poſſible, adminiſter relief; and the beſt method I can ſuggeſt is, that of encouraging, by the authority of parliament, *Friendly Societies*, under the regulation of which, the *batchelor* might be made

---

* The practice of farming out the poor ſeems to require correction. It is no leſs diſgraceful to the feelings of humanity than repugnant to the pureſt policy. To preſerve virtue, its native dignity ſhould be countenanced in every order of ſociety, and particularly in that claſs whoſe induſtry ſupplies ſuccour, and whoſe content promotes peace throughout the nation. But how can this be effected by rendering them dependent for ſubſiſtence upon one, who is appointed their provider, only becauſe his terms for their ſupport are leſs burthenſome to the pariſh, than thoſe of his competitors for this office? G. F.

to contribute to the fupport of the *married*; this would in
fome degree check that difpofition to celibacy, which is but
too apparent among the lower orders of mankind; and
would add to the comfort of wedlock, and to the population of the realm.

A progreffive, and too liberal increafe of wages for daily
labour, will leffen the *quantum* furnifhed, and will only tend
to increafe the diffolute manners of the poor; whereas, the
plan fuggefted by the author of the before-mentioned tract
would, *I humbly think*, be attended with the happieft confequences, both in an individual and a national fenfe; and I
hope the time is not far diftant, when this inftitution, or
fomething fimilar thereunto, may commence, and the poor
be extricated from their prefent dependance on the fcanty
bounty of a parifh-officer; and entitled to claim a fupport
from a fund to which they have contributed, and to part of
which they will have a legal and incontrovertible right.

The following are the leading features of Mr. PEW's
plan for the maintenance of the poor, as contained in
Twenty Minutes Advice, before referred to, by which it is
fuppofed that two millions per annum may be faved to the
landed intereft, and the poor better maintained than they
now are:

Claufe 1ft. That a proper officer be appointed for fuch an
extent of diftrict as he may be fuppofed conveniently to fu-
perintend, to take a lift of the names and places of abode of
all males above the age of eighteen, and of all females above
the age of feventeen years, in the fame manner as the lift is
made out for the militia.

2d. That every fuch male pay two-pence per week, and
every fuch female three-farthings or one penny per week,
into the hands of the above officer, for the purpofes hereafter to be fpecified.

3d. The

3*l*. The above officer shall be empowered to furnish employment for all such as are willing to work, and who cannot find it for themselves.

Whether this officer should be chosen annually, in rotation, after the manner of an overseer, or whether he should be a permanent officer, upon an adequate salary, will be a matter of future consideration; but if the latter, he should be paid by the community, and not out of the fund.

4*th*. All the poor being thus sure of employment, the master or mistress for whom they work should be justified in retaining these sums respectively out of their wages; and whether they do so or not, they should (in default of the individual) be answerable to the officer for its payment: all masters and mistresses of families should in like manner be answerable for their servants; and all keepers of lodging-houses, &c. for their inmates.

5*th*. These sums should be carried weekly to the general treasurer of the *division*, who should give sufficient security for the same.

6*th*. Out of this fund, every male, who is really incapable of labour, should (by virtue of a certificate from the above officer) have *a right to demand* from the treasurer five shillings per week for the first six months, should his illness last so long; and four shillings per week after that period, until he again become capable of labour.

Every female should have *a right to demand* two shillings and six-pence per week for the first six months, and afterwards two shillings per week until she was again able to work; she should also be entitled to four weeks full pay at every lying-in.

Every male above the age of sixty-five years, whether capable of labour or not, should be entitled to four shillings per week during life. Every female should, after the same age,

age, be entitled to receive two shillings per week during life.

7*tb*. Any person having three children under nine years of age, should be entitled to one shilling and six-pence per week, until the eldest should have attained the age of nine years; and if he has more than three under that age, he should be entitled to one shilling and six-pence per week for each above that number; and if any one or more of his children should happen to be idiotick, insane, or otherwise so far disabled, either in body or mind, as to be utterly incapable of labour, each of them should still be considered as under the age of nine years, and paid for accordingly.

If a mother should be left a widow, with three children under nine years of age, she should be entitled to receive five shillings; if with two children, three shillings; and if with one child, one shilling and six-pence per week; if with more than three, under that age, one shilling per week for each above that number: it being admitted that all her time is taken up by three, and allowance made for it, but that she is capable of looking after and taking care of a greater number. The wives of men serving in the militia, and in the army or navy, should, during the absence of their husbands, be considered and provided for in all respects as widows.

If a child should be left an orphan, under nine years of age, two shillings per week shall be allowed from the fund for its maintenance; if more than one of the same family, one shilling and six-pence per week for each above that number. As there is probably no less friendship amongst the lower than amongst the higher orders of society, it would generally happen that some friend or relation of the deceased would gladly take charge of the children, provided they could do so without essential loss to themselves: this regulation would effectually prevent that loss; and to compensate, in some degree, for the want of parental affection, six-

pence

pence per week more is allowed for the maintenance of an orphan, or a family of orphans, than for a child, or family of children, who still retain their mother. If, however, any beings should be so *uncommonly unfortunate* as not to be thus *adopted*, the officer above-mentioned should be obliged to provide a receptacle for them, which he will always be able to do for the sum or sums above-mentioned.

8*th*. All children above nine years of age, if in health, should, if they have no parents, or their parents are not able to provide for them, be put out after the manner of parish apprentices.

9*th*. All persons neglecting or refusing to pay their contribution, should be committed to hard labour, in the house of correction, for the space of ——.

10*th*. If the fund should at any time fall short of the necessary demands upon it, the deficiency should be made up by a *parish-rate*, collected in the same manner as at present, but without any sense of obligation on the part of the *multitude*, (for there would be *no poor*) who should in all cases receive their relief *in the nature of a demand*.

11*th*. If the fund (as most probably would happen) should increase beyond the necessary demands upon it, the surplus should on no account be diverted to any other purpose than the benefit of the subscribers. But when the price of grain exceeded that which brings it easily within the reach of the multitude, (suppose 6s. or 6s. 6d. the Winchester bushel) every person who had three children, or more, under nine years of age, should have a right to *demand* such a sum as, in proportion to the number of his family, would reduce the various necessary articles of life (taking wheat as a standard) to a moderate price; and, indeed, I think, in all cases when the price of grain exceeds that proportion at which the *industrious labourer* can afford to come to market, *sound policy*, as well as *common humanity*, requires that all large families should be intitled to receive such a sum as above specified, *although it should be necessary to collect a rate for the purpose.*

SECT. 5.—*Leases.*

Many estates in this district are held by leases for three lives, with quit-rents and herriots, but the greatest part is held for terms of years, viz. fourteen, seven, and three years; and some from year to year.

Some gentlemen, from the best of motives, have been long in the habit of letting their estates at the old rents, though the price of the articles of produce has, in the course of thirty years, advanced one third at least.

How far such acts of kindness may be considered as just to a man's family, or conducive to the publick weal, I much doubt. From the experience which I have had in the agricultural world, I have invariably found lands so occupied in a much worse state than those of neighbouring farmers moderately advanced.

An equitable partition of the advantages resulting from an increase of trade and population cannot by any reasonable tenant be objected to. The one system produces care and exertion, and the other indolence and sloth.

The following are some of the common

CLAUSES IN LEASES.

1*st*. Not to convert into tillage any pasture or meadow land without leave: nor to have more than one half the estate in tillage at one time; and of that half, *one third* at least either to *fallow*, or what is commonly called a fallow-crop, viz. turnips, &c.

2*dly*. To feed and mow the grass alternately.

3*dly*. Not to pare or burn any land without leave.

4*bly*. Not

4*thly*. Not to plant potatoes for *sale* without leave.

5*thly*. To spend all the hay and straw on the premises, and to leave all the dung and straw to the succeeding tenant, without any acknowledgment.

6*thly*. Not to let any parcel of the land to any under-tenant without leave.

7*thly*. To keep the messuage, dwelling-house, barns, stables, &c. in good repair, on being allowed rough timber and the labour of the thatcher.

8*thly*. To pay all taxes and assessments, land-tax excepted.

9*thly*. Not to cut down or lop timber trees, or lop pollards, without leave.

10*thly*. To permit the lord, or his assigns, to search for mines, and to hunt or shoot on the premises.

11*thly*. If pasture land be converted into tillage, the same shall, the first or second year, be manured with not less than one hundred bushels of lime per acre; and after such manuring to have two crops of corn only, and with the second crop to be sown down in a husbandry-like manner with artificial grasses.

12*thly*. At the conclusion of the lease to leave a sufficient quantity of tillage to the succeeding tenant, well fallowed, in a husband-like manner, by proper ploughing, for which the in-coming tenant shall pay a proper acknowledgment.

13*thly*. To keep all the fences, gates, stiles, &c. in good repair, and to leave them so at the end of the term.

14*thly*. To prosecute, if called upon by the landlord, all persons trespassing on the estate, by hunting, shooting, fishing, &c. compensation being made to him by the landlord for all expences incurred by such prosecution; to which are added other common covenants.

SECT. 6.

SECT. 6.—*Expences and Profit of sixty Acres of Grass Land.*

DAIRY-FARM,—TWENTY COWS.

	£.	s.	d.
DEBTOR.			
To rent of sixty acres, at 30s. per acre —	90	0	0
To tithe and taxes — — ——	20	0	0
To the labour of the family serving cattle, utensils,			
salt, and all other articles, 30s. per cow —	30	0	0
To hay-making, &c. twenty acres ——	10	0	0
* To manure — — —	10	0	0
To repair fences — — ——	2	0	0
To accidents with cows — —	10	0	0
To interest of capital — ——	10	0	0
	£182	0	0

CREDITOR,			
By 70 Cwt. of cheese, at 2l. 10s. per Cwt.	175	0	0
By butter — — ——	20	0	0
By calves — — —	20	0	0
† By hogs — — ——	30	0	0
Creditor	245	0	0
Debtor	182	0	0
Profit	£63	0	0

* This charge rarely occurs.

† Though it is not generally practised, a *breeding* flock of hogs must be considered as more profitable on a cow-farm than a *fatting* flock. The whey and skimmed-milk constitute a food well adapted to the rearing of a thriving flock ; and the writer has known many instances of a farmer's selling, at six months old, a litter of pigs for more than thirty pounds; and this was done from the whey, &c. of ten cows, and without the assistance of corn, any farther than the run of the farm-yard, and when pig-meat was only 7s. 6d. per score.

The expences and profits of a *corn* farm, or a farm in *mixed husbandry*, are so variable, that it would be difficult to fix a standard. The old idea of the produce amounting to *three rents* would not do *now*, for the expences of living, of taxes, of wages, &c. are of late years so much increased, that the value of the produce must be augmented in proportion.

One remark, however, may be made, namely, that it is universally admitted by all stewards, that *dairy* farmers pay their rent more punctually than *corn* farmers.

CHAPTER V.

IMPLEMENTS.

THE waggons in general ufe are fmall, compact, and well made: narrow-wheeled weighing from 15 cwt. to 20 cwt.; the fix-inch wheels from 25 cwt. to 30 cwt; the latter drawn with fix horfes, in pairs.

Some years ago waggons of this defcription were made 5 or 6 cwt. heavier than they are now. The reduction of the weight, particularly to thofe who are common carriers, is highly advantageous, being not lefs than fifty pounds per year gained by each team conftantly employed on the road; and if made with good materials, a light waggon will laft as long as a heavy one.

Price of a narrow-wheeled waggon twenty-fix pounds; Six-inch wheel thirty-fix pounds; axle-tree moft commonly of wood. The carts generally ufed for the purpofes of huf-bandry run on broad wheels, and hold about four quarters, or thirty-two bufhels, Winchefter; price about nine guineas: but for road ufe, light carts, drawn by one horfe, are coming into fafhion, and are found the moft advantageous. Price about four guineas.

The ploughs commonly ufed are ftrong fingle ones; fome-times with one fmall wheel, fometimes with a foot only. The great length of the mould-board occafions too much friction, and it cannot be deemed a good implement; but prejudice is ftrongly in its favour, notwithftanding confider-able pains have been taken to fhew the fuperiority of other ploughs.

There are many winnowing machines in ufe, but not a threfhing machine in the whole county. The harrows are

no

no waye fingular in their conftruction, they are, by good
farmers, linked three together, and drawn by three horfes
nearly abreaft, each horfe drawing a fingle harrow.* If any
particular tool be deferving of notice, it is the *fpade*, which is
much narrower and longer than thofe ufed in other counties.
Its length is feldom lefs than eighteen inches, and its breadth
about fix inches, the back part being gently curved to prevent adhefion to the foil.

---

* The method of harrowing practifed by the farmers in South Devon
cannot be too ftrongly recommended.

This operation they perform with two harrows, and two horfes
abreaft, a lad being mounted on the near horfe. The horfes are kept
to a *full trot*, by which one turn of the harrow pulverizes the foil as
much as three or four in the common fauntering method.

CHAPTER VI.

INCLOSING FENCES, &c.

THE fences are quick-hedges, with trees at unequal diftances. And where ftones are eafily got, and lie in a
flat bed, ftone walls, without cement, are built, two feet
wide at the bottom, eighteen inches at the top, and five feet
high; the total coft of which wall is about one fhilling per
yard, running meafure.

I fhall bring forward a comparative view of thefe walls,
with quick-hedges, in treating of the inclofures on Mendip
hills, to which I fhall now proceed.

MENDIP HILLS.

This chain of mountainous land extended, according to
the ancient boundary, from Cottle's-Oak, near the town of
Frome, to a place called the Black-Rock, in the Briftol
channel near Uphill, being a diftance of more than thirty
miles. A great portion of this land having been inclofed,
divided, and cultivated, in the courfe of the laft forty years,
and nearly an equal portion ftill remaining in its open uncultivated ftate, I cannot forward the views of the refpectable Board, under whofe aufpices this report will be brought
forward to the publick, in a better way than by a minute
defcription of the origin, progrefs, and fuccefs of thofe undertakings.

And firft, let us begin with taking a view of the objections which have been ftarted to this fpecies of improvement, and fee if we cannot prove them to be for the moft
part either falfe or frivolous.

1ft. Invafion of the rights and intereft of the cottagers.

2dly. A

2*dly.* A fuppofed injury done to the breeding fyftem.

3*dly.* The expences attending the act of parliament with thofe of commiffioners, and other fubordinate agents employed in its execution.

4*thly.* The expence of buildings, fuch as farm-houfes, barns, ftables, ftalls, and pools, for the purpofe of creating diftinct farms, fuperadded to the expences of cultivation and fencing, altogether conftituting an expenditure which the improved value will not reimburfe.

5*thly.* Injury done to the woollen-manufacture, by leffening the number of fheep, and deteriorating the quality of the wool.

6*thly.* A fuppofed diminution of the rent of the old farms, to which fuch commons were appertenant.

The foremoft of thefe objections carries with it the appearance of a humane attention to the comfort of the poor; but a brief inveftigation will leffen its influence, if not totally refute it.

There are but two modes of inclofing commons. Firft, By unanimous confent of the parties claiming rights, who delegate power to commiffioners, chofen by themfelves, to afcertain their validity, and divide accordingly, under covenants and agreements properly drawn and executed for the purpofe. Or fecondly, by act of parliament obtained by the petition of a certain proportion of the commoners, both in number and value, whereby a minority, fanctioned only by ignorance, prejudice, or felfifhnefs, is precluded from defeating the ends of private advantage and publick utility.

In point of œconomy, the firft of thefe methods is the moft eligible, as it faves the expence of an act of parliament, with equal fecurity to the proprietors. But it is feldom practifed, unlefs in commons on *a fmall fcale,* from the dif-

E ficulty

ficulty of procuring the confent of *every individual claimant*, without which it cannot be accomplished.

In either of thefe methods, it is manifeft that the right of the cottager cannot be invaded; fince, with refpect to legal or equitable conftruction, he ftands precifely on the fame ground with his more opulent neighbours; and as to his intereft, I can truly declare that, in all cafes which have fallen within my obfervation, inclofures have meliorated his condition, by exciting a fpirit of activity and induftry, whereby habits of floth have been by degrees overcome, and fupinenefs and inactivity have been exchanged for vigour and exertion. No ftronger proof can be given of this than the reduction of the poor's-rate, in many of thofe parifhes, wherein fuch inclofing has taken place.*

Upland commons are principally depaftured in the fummer with fheep; and if a cottager were able to flock ever fo largely, the *winter keeping*, and his total inability to furnifh them with food between the fifth of April and the twelfth of May, (before which time thefe commons ought not to be flocked) would be fuch a drawback as effectually to exclude every idea of profit.

On the *moors*, cottagers within a moderate diftance from the common generally turned out a cow or two, perhaps a few geefe, and I believe the latter were the only profitable ftock. Not one in ten rented land to raife winter fubfiftence. In fummer, the moor commons were frequently inundated. The cattle muft be removed, and temporary pafturage hired on extravagant terms. On the other hand,

---

* If in every bill of inclofure it were ftipulated, that a certain number of cottages fhould be built, to which fmall allotments fhould be annexed for the benefit of poor perfons, it would give a falutary fanction to the meafure, and tend to leffen the poor's-rate. W. F.

should the season be favourable, the redundancy of stock from an unlimited right of feeding, by reducing the produce of the cottager's cow so much below what it ought to be, deprives him of every real advantage.

Proprietors or occupiers of large estates, in the vicinity of a common, by turning out great quantities of stock by *day*, and taking them home to feed by *night*, have derived the only benefit which an overfed common could afford.

The cattle of the *cottager*, as well as of the *distant commoner*, under this competition, must unavoidably suffer. The latter may be recruited by occasional removal to better pasturage; the former, having none, must hire, or leave them on the common either in a stunted or starved condition. These are facts of general notoriety, on which it will not be easy to deduce (*communibus annis*) any material benefit to the cottager from stocking; but when the expence of winter support is added, the question is decided, and the presumed *advantage* is converted into a positive *loss*. For ten or twelve shillings per annum, a common right might be rented. Nothing gives with greater accuracy the value of a thing, than fair and unrestrained competition; if so, when the privilege of stocking a common for a year might be obtained for ten or twelve shillings, by a farmer in possession of means to accommodate stocking to every variety of season, what can the value be to a cottager deprived of these? Instead of ten or twelve shillings, the annual nett value of common rights *inclosed* has been from three pounds to twenty pounds per annum, which, as an unquestionable fact, establishes, without scruple or hesitation, the *private* as well as *publick* importance of the inclosing system. Most of the stocking cottagers have rights appendant to the cottages without land, under the denomination of *auster tenements*. To these, allotments are made equal in quantity,

E 2   and

and quality, as to farms of the greatest extent. Here, the cottage claimant, by relinquishing a privilege, injurious rather than lucrative, is placed in a better situation than the proprietor of an extensive farm, who surrenders every advantage of flocking which *capital*, *situation*, and *convenience*, give him, for an equality of allotment with the former, who has no sacrifice to make, but ignorance and prejudice, and who derives from his allotment a clear undiminished profit.

Besides, moral effects of an injurious tendency accrue to the cottager, from a reliance on the imaginary benefits of flocking a common. The possession of a cow or two, with a hog, and a few geese, naturally exalts the peasant, in his own conception, above his brethren in the same rank of society. It inspires some degree of confidence in a property, inadequate to his support. In sauntering after his cattle, he acquires a habit of indolence. Quarter, half, and occasionally whole days are imperceptibly lost. Day-labour becomes disgusting; the aversion increases by indulgence; and at length the sale of a half-fed calf, or hog, furnishes the means of adding intemperance to idleness. The sale of the cow frequently succeeds, and its wretched and disappointed possessor, unwilling to resume the daily and regular course of labour, from whence he drew his former subsistence, by various modes of artifice and imposition, exacts from the poor's-rate that relief to which he is in no degree intitled.

This description is by no means exaggerated. The parish of Wedmore, which abounded with cottage commons, and one of the largest and most opulent in this county, will illustrate its truth and justice. Within twenty years there have been inclosed upwards of three thousand acres of rich moor land, heretofore, when in commons, rendered unproductive by inundations and their consequences, six or seven months in the year, and when passible for the remaining months,

months, of little value from being overflocked; which land is now fet, with liberal allowance of profit to the occupier, from thirty to fixty fhillings per acre. Thefe inclofures are made by ditches, which, by annual cleanfing and fpreading the contents over the furface, afford an excellent manure, with a new and extenfive fource of labour of the moft productive kind, whereby the poor's-rate has been reduced, or at leaft has not exceeded its former amount before any inclofure had taken place.[*]

The fecond objection to inclofing is the fuppofed injury done to the breeding fyftem.

Few obfervations will fuffice on this head. Commons are in general overflocked. Young cattle abridged of their food become ftunted in their growth, and injured in fhape and form. To reftore them in thefe refpects, by better keeping, is fometimes impracticable—always expenfive. It is more than problematical with many intelligent farmers in the neighbourhood, whether, from the circumftances beforementioned, the breeding fyftem on an average of feafons and years has yielded any profit. But this is undeniably certain, that the fame land, when inclofed and improved, will maintain at leaft three times the flock *breeding*, or *any other*, than it did in a flate of nature. Suppofe every acre of wafte land in Great-Britain by inclofure were improved threefold, what would be the confequence? A declenfion of the breeding fyftem? The very contrary; an extention of it very probably in the fame proportion. Without breeding, can you graze or make cheefe and butter? Are not thefe

---

* It may be here noted as a fact, that in moft of thofe parifhes where no inclofure of the wafte lands had taken place, the poor's levy has been *doubled, trebled*, nay *quadrupled*, in the courfe of the laft twenty years.

different

different modes of occupation moſt intimately connected
with, and dependent on each other? Is not the ſame land
convertible to all and every of theſe purpoſes, ſubject to the
controul and regulation of the market for each? Can young
ſtock be kept too well? Should the breeding of cattle exceed the demand, and from a reduction of price no longer
pay the rent of land, will the farmer repine, becauſe his land
is ſuſceptible of other methods of application no leſs beneficial? Surely not. Could he heſitate what to do, when its
high ſtate of culture would direct him either to dairy, or
grazing, as attendant circumſtances might require? And
ſhould the market be glutted with the produce of dairy and
grazing farms, the farmer would naturally recur to breeding
ſtock, or raiſing corn; ſo that all theſe articles would find
their natural level, which the demand for each, whether
inadequate, moderate, or exceſſive, would invariably regulate. But waſte and uncultivated land, being ſolely appropriated to the breeding of ſtock, and not convertible to any
other purpoſe, is without remedy, whenever the market is
overcharged with its produce.

The ſame reaſoning applies to hilly lands in their improved ſtate, by ſubſtituting corn inſtead of dairy or grazing.
From the foregoing premiſes, I think it may be inferred,
that ſince commons of every deſcription, when incloſed and
cultivated, are capable of ſupporting at leaſt three times more
ſtock than they did in a ſtate of nature, no ſerious appre-
henſions ſhould prevail with reſpect to the diminution or
injury of the breeding ſyſtem. I do not mean to deny that
ſome local diſadvantages may occur; but theſe are too trifling and limited to merit attention, and ſtill leſs to impede
the progreſs of an improvement of the greateſt national
importance. The preceding remarks more particularly
apply to the moor, or low lands. In addition thereto I
                                                    have

have to obferve, with heartfelt fatisfaction, its happy effects on the *health* and comfort of the inhabitants of the adjacent villages. Agues, and low fevers, from the humidity of the air, impregnated with exhalations from the ftagnant contents of the marfhes, prevailed very generally during the vernal and autumnal feafons; and thefe for the moft part were obftinate and more frequently fubdued by the drought and heat of fummer, and froft of winter, than by the moft judicious medical treatment. Inclofing and draining have rendered thefe difeafes as fcarce in the *low*, as in the *uplands*, to the prevention whereof advance of wages (from four to fix-pence per day) with conftant employ arifing from the fame caufe, have not a little contributed, by enabling the poor to *live better*, which is generally accompanied with a growing tafte for comfort and cleanlinefs.

The third objection to inclofing, is to the expences attending the act of parliament, with thofe of commiffioners and other fubordinate agents employed in its execution.

I do not mean to contend, that rigid œconomy, and expert management, have been prominent features in this line of publick bufinefs. I am ready to acknowledge, that in fome inftances it has been juftly chargeable with profufion, mifmanagement, and unneceffary delay. In feveral inftances within my own cognizance, the moft enormous expence has been wantonly incurred in obtaining the act, nay, double at leaft beyond the moft liberal eftimate of a fair and equitable charge.

In thefe cafes the excefs arofe from the attendance of fupernumeraries in London, under the pretence of fecuring and expediting the bill, without rendering the leaft fervice in that or any other way. Charges of this fort are not fubject to the controul or regulation of the commiffioners, fince they originate previous to their appointment; and
should

should they refuse payment, a law-suit of hazardous issue might ensue, which, if unsuccessful, would expose them to reproach from the proprietors. The blame therefore must attach to the latter, for not exercising more vigilance at the outset of the business. After passing the bill, *delay in the execution*, so as to withhold the possession of allotments from the proprietors for a year or two more than necessary, has been imputable, and with some colour of justice, to the negligence and inattention of commissioners. It must be acknowledged such conduct is truly reprehensible; since, under many inclosures, especially of low lands, of prime quality, the loss of even a year's occupation, if the inclosure be of considerable extent, might be deemed nearly equivalent to a moiety of the expence. In this neighbourhood, for some years past, this defect has been in a great measure remedied; for unless their proceedings have been interrupted by issues at law, or the inclosure has been of great extent, the commissioners have given the proprietors possession of their allotments within a year from passing the act. This dispatch requires a considerable share of judgment and exertion on the part of the commissioners, as well as sufficient leisure and activity on the part of the surveyor. Another error in management relates to the expence of meetings, which heretofore was very improperly augmented by the attendance of some of the principal commoners for purposes of festivity, without being of the least use; rather retarding than forwarding the business. This practice was general; but for some years past has been for the most part abolished, by a very judicious regulation of allowing the commissioners and their agents a certain sum per day as a compensation for attendance and expences.

The publick will be enabled to judge in what degree the expence of inclosing ought to affect its determinations under
the

the prefent courfe of management, by adducing the following fpecimens of a moor or low land, and a Mendip or
upland inclofure;.

Low Land.

	£.	s.	d.
Act of Parliament, &c. &c. —	510	0	0
Roads ——— —	450	0	0
Subdivifion, Rhynes, or Ditches, 8 feet wide at top, 4 feet at bottom, and 5 feet deep. Price of digging from 1s. 2d. to 2s. per rope (20 feet)	850	0	0
Gates, Bridges ——— —	140	0	0
Commiffioners (3) — ——	200	0	0
Clerk ——— —	60	0	0
Surveyor ——— —	140	0	0
Award and other Law expences —	110	0	0
Intereft of Money borrowed ——	25	0	0
	2485	0	0

Upland Inclosure.

	£.	s.	d.
Act of Parliament, &c. &c. —	300	0	0
Roads ' ——	350	0	0
Fences, part wall, part quick-fets ' —	850	0	0
Gates, &c. ——— ——	56	0	0
Commiffioners (3) ——	200	0	0
Clerk ' ——— ——	80	0	0
Surveyor ——— —	80	0	0
Intereft of Money — ——	35	0	0
	1951	0	0

Under

Under the firſt deſcription, the expence of obtaining the act amounted to upwards of 500l. which, under proper management, would not have exceeded 300l. Near two miles of road; ſtones quarried and broken at ten-pence per load, (eight load to a rope of twenty feet) hallage, at leaſt one ſhilling per rope. Two bridges made; rhynes made for draining the water and fences by ditching, for the ſub-diviſion and allotment of upwards of 800 acres. Com-miſſioners attendance, ſurveyors, ſolicitors, and clerks bills, with every other incidental charge, all of which did not much exceed three pounds per acre. The average value of the land, under a moderate computation, may be reckoned at thirty pounds per acre.

The latter is a Mendip incloſure; quantity of land nearly as the former; a mile of road more; fences partly quick-ſet, partly young living ſtock of hazel, black-thorn, &c. and dry wall. Allotments not numerous but large, which ma-terially curtailed the expence of fencing; road materials cheaply got. Parliamentary charges reaſonable; commiſ-ſioners and agents as in the moor incloſure, all of which did not exceed two pounds ten ſhillings per acre. The average value of the land, as aſcertained by the portions ſold to defray expences, may be reckoned at twenty pounds per acre.*

If facts like theſe be inſufficient to appeaſe the clamours of ignorance and ſelfiſhneſs againſt the incloſing ſyſtem, or to enforce conviction on the unprejudiced mind, the effects of reaſon and argument muſt be altogether fruitleſs.

---

* I never before knew an inſtance of Mendip land in its unculti-vated ſtate ſelling ſo high; the general price is from eight to twelve pounds per acre.

The

That the prefent mode of conducting the bufinefs is fuf-ceptible of further improvement, no one converfant with the fubjeçt can deny. Yet to accomplifh this, many obflacles are to be combated, and perhaps one of the moft formidable is, that of its having been regarded, more or lefs, as a *little fyftem of patronage*. The lord of the foil, the rector, and a few of the principal commoners, monopolize and diftribute the appointments. It is well known, that bills of this fort have found their way through parliament without the inter-vention of a country folicitor. In cafes where no oppofition was meditated, the parliamentary folicitor, and a furveyor, have anfwered every purpofe. By this, a faving was made of from fixty to a hundred pounds; but this might exclude the friend of one or more of the governing party. In fome acts, *five* commiffioners have been appointed; in general there are *three*; but *two* would be fufficient, with power to nomi-nate a third under the circumftance of difference of opinion, which feldom happens; and in fmall inclofures, perhaps one commiffioner would anfwer every purpofe. If a country folicitor be employed, he fhould act as clerk to the commif-fioners, and fave the expence of a fupernumerary in that ca-pacity. Hereby another faving would be made, without any injury to the concern. The office of furveyor is by no means inconfiderable in the aggregate of expence. This might be difpofed of, under a fair competition, to the loweft given fum for executing the whole of the bufinefs, (after the act is obtained) by advertifing for propofals to fuch effect; taking care that the contracting party be competent to the under-taking. This alteration, it is probable, would fave one-third, and in fome cafes nearly half of a bill made out by charges in detail.

In the choice of commiffioners, it is of the utmoft confe-quence to appoint *one*, at leaft, in the neighbourhood of the
inclofure,

inclofure, familiarized with all the varieties of the foil, with the influence of feafons, and with its local peculiarities; whereby its prefent value, and capacity for future improvement would be afcertained with precifion, and the important office of qualifying the land executed with fafety and confidence. The next in the fcale of utility fhould be a perfon converfant with all the forms and routine of the bufinefs; well inftructed from experience in accounts, and in the prices and different modes of fencing, making roads, bridges, gates, &c. of general and comprehenfive knowledge of agriculture, both practical and fpeculative, and of genius to fuggeft fuch modern improvements as are beft adapted to the fituation and foil. Two perfons, thus qualified, are fully competent to execute the office with credit to themfelves, and juftice to the proprietors. But fhould the concern fuffer by the abfence of either, through ficknefs, private bufinefs, or any other caufe, a claufe in the act might be inferted, impowering them, or the proprietors, to choofe a third for the purpofe of avoiding delay. Commiffioners, whofe refidence is at a great diftance, fhould (on account of the extra charges of time and travelling expences) only be reforted to as an alternative, from the impoffibility of getting others properly qualified near home.

The office of commiffioner is, without doubt, the firft in confequence and authority, under an inclofing act, but with refpect to *emolument* the very loweft. Even the clerk's bill of charges, *not* as a folicitor acting in that capacity, but as any other indifferent perfon did in times paft, exceed twice, and fometimes three times the amount of the fees of the former. The publick have been not a little mifled in their conceptions of this fubject. The real fact is, that the whole of the refponfibility attaches to the office of commiffioner, which,

which, in pecuniary recompence, is by far the moſt inſignificant.*

Thus have I impartially ſtated the defects of the preſent ſyſtem, with their correſpondent remedies. In its moſt improved ſtate it will retain ſomewhat of imperfection, which perhaps cannot be entirely obviated.

I ſhall only add, that within a few years paſt, in the neighbourhood of Wells, an incloſure was *farmed* by an attorney of extenſive practice, and well known reſpectability, at a ſum conſiderably leſs than it would have amounted to in the uſual way. The commiſſioners were appointed by the proprietors; the buſineſs executed with ſingular diſpatch, and all parties intereſted perfectly ſatisfied. Fences, roads, &c. were made by the proprietors.

When the incloſing ſyſtem is appreciated by its obvious tendency to increaſe the produce of land, and the demand for labour, to augment the rate of wages to the huſbandman, and to leſſen the amount of the poor's rate, it is a ſubject of regret and aſtoniſhment, that ſo few means have been deviſed by the legiſlature, either to facilitate, or extend its progreſs. How much is to be done this way, a general incloſure act, unfettered by tedious and expenſive formalities, would ſpeedily manifeſt. From the very great number of private acts which have paſſed within the laſt twenty years, ſuch general principles might be ſelected for its baſis, as to implicate almoſt every poſſible variety of claim, intereſt,

---

* Under the allowance of two guineas a day, the nett receipts of a commiſſioner, after deducting daily expences, horſe-hire, &c. does not exceed twenty-four ſhillings; and where a ſervant is kept, eighteen ſhillings per day. This is no extravagant compenſation, particularly when we reflect that the *wear* and *tear* of *conſtitution, clothes,* &c. are left out of the calculation.

and

and property. An act thus conflituted might, without hazard, or injury, be entrufted to a given number of juftices at the quarter-feffions, to difpenfe its powers, and controul its execution; and fuch juftices, I fhould conceive, perfectly competent to determine on the propriety or impropriety of any propofed inclofure.

Thus a total extinction of parliamentary expence would encourage inclofing on the fmalleft fcale, and, with advantages not to be defpifed, would accommodate the moft extenfive.

This meafure, however confonant to the principles of individual benefit, and national policy, would notwithftanding have a hoft of adverfaries to encounter.

Fourth objection.—*The expence of cultivation and buildings, fuch as farm-houfe, barn, ftable, ftalling, pealt, &c. for the purpofe of creating a diftinct farm, &c. &c.*

The low land, or moor inclofures, being principally appropriated to grazing, dairy, or feeding young and poor flock, are not within the limits of this objection. It is therefore confined to the upland or Mendip inclofures.

The nature of Mendip foil, its firft manure, the mode of cropping, the neceffity of fpending thereon the whole of its produce, of hay, ftraw, &c. will be feverally noticed hereafter, and confequently will not be attended to in this place.

By a reference to thefe particulars, the neceffity and advantage of buildings muft be obvious, as not only contributing to the foil its utmoft latitude of improvement, but alfo, when obtained, the means of prefervation therein. Without a barn, ftalling, convenient farm-yard, and pool, neither one nor the other can be accomplifhed.

But it may be afked, are buildings to be provided for every allotment? By no means. I do not think they are admiffible, with the addition of a farm-houfe, on a fmaller fcale of land than 100 acres. The expence to accommo-
dąe

date this quantity with a farm-house, barn, stable, stalling, barton, pool, and pig-stye, should not exceed three hundred pounds.

The next subject of enquiry is the additional value communicated to the land by buildings. Should this be answerable to the expence incurred, the whole of the objection must fall to the ground, notwithstanding its apparent plausibility.

Let us suppose an hundred acres of Mendip land inclosed, and divided into four pieces of *prime* quality, but destitute of buildings; grant a lease of it to a farmer of property and judgment for twenty-one years, (a shorter term would be injurious to the landlord) and I may venture to say, that more than twenty shillings per acre could not be got for it, accompanied with the usual covenants and restrictions to guard against wilful impoverishment. With equal confidence, I may assert, the same land, *with suitable buildings*, would let to the same farmer, for a like term, at twenty-five shillings per acre, with a subdivision of the four pieces into six. The increase of rent in the latter case will be twenty-five pounds per annum. Allow an interest of seven and half per cent. on the capital of three hundred pounds expended on the buildings, which amounts to twenty-two pounds ten shillings, and there will remain two pounds ten shillings as interest on the money laid out to make fences under a subdivision, and if quick-set, to rear them when made. Under this plan, you do justice to the native qualities of the soil, by giving it a separate and independent existence as a farm; and with a lease of proper covenants, you need not fear its being exhausted.

A speculative farmer will be apt to exclaim, Is it possible that the want of buildings can create a difference of five shillings per acre to the occupier? Most assuredly it is;

as will be evident by even a very general statement of the
comparative effects of a twenty-one year's occupation, *with*
and *without* buildings. To begin with the latter; here lime
must be chiefly, if not altogether depended on, as a manure.
This, even with successive cropping with corn, will maintain its ground tolerably well during the first seven years.
Its second application is attended with considerable diminution of its efficacy. From this period, the degeneracy of
the soil is no less rapid than astonishing: it becomes light;
coltsfoot and couch-grass abound; clover and ray-grasses
fail. Intervals of rest of three, or even four years, seldom
recruit its vigour sufficiently to produce even a moderate
crop of oats, which, if followed by a second of the same
grain, would scarcely return the seed. Feed during the two
last years of rest, not worth more than nine shillings per
acre. No turnips for want of dung; no fold, because the
land is too much impoverished to maintain it; straw carried
off, and clover hay only partially consumed on the premises
by reason of the exposed situation. In this unproductive
state, the land must remain during the last nine years of the
term, reduced to the value of ten or twelve shillings per
acre, and with little prospect of melioration.

Painful and disgusting as this representation must be to
every judicious farmer, it is nevertheless strictly conformable
to fact; and many instances might be adduced to establish
its veracity in every point. Such has been, and most probably ever will be, the situation of Mendip inclosures,
without buildings, and more *judicious course of crops. With*
buildings, we have to contemplate effects directly opposite,
under a similar term of twenty-one years. Lime, in the
proportion of twenty quarters per acre, will sustain the land,
with little abatement of its fertility, for the first six or seven
years. During this period, farm-yard manure will be plentifully

tifully fupplied, and may be devoted to turnips, cabbage,
and potatoes, on a confiderable fcale, as it will not be wanted
either for corn or clover for feveral fucceeding years; it may
be appropriated to turnips and clover, affifted by the fold,
which a feed of clover and ray-grafs of the fecond year will
fufficiently maintain. Should thefe refources be thought
inadequate to fupport the whole of the land, from the ninth
or tenth year, piece after piece in fucceffion might be broken
up, and limed afrefh, with an effect very little, if at all, inferior to that of its firft application; as dung and the fold
are found excellent preparatives for the repetition of this
manure. By the alternate ufe of lime, dung, and the fold,
together with the following rotation of crops:

   1ft year, Oats on the Lay
   2d — Winter and Spring Vetches folded off, and Turnips
   3d — Oats and Artificial Grafs Seeds
   4th — Artificial Grafs Seeds mowed
   5th — Ditto fed
   6th — Ditto ditto:

which the improved hufbandry of the laft twenty years has
fuggefted, and which is gradually extending to the mutual
intereft and fatisfaction of landlord and tenant, it muft be
evident, that the land under a term of fourteen or twenty-
one years cannot fuftain the leaft injury, but muft be in a
ftate of melioration and improvement. By the preceding
obfervations, I truft the propriety and advantage of buildings, erected on a fcale of Mendip inclofure of one hundred
acres and upwards, are fully eftablifhed to the conviction of
every unbiaffed mind. Under this ftatement, what plan of
management fhould be adopted for fmaller inclofures? Separate occupation at a diftance from the farm-yard, by the
expence of carting, fo as to preclude the return of produce
in dung, muft neceffarily impoverifh. Muft inclofures of
this defcription then be abandoned to the fate of a wretched

F   and

and ruinous hufbandry? By no means. A remedy is a palliative, if not wholly effectual, may be found. In the greater part of Mendip inclofures, either by allotment or purchafe, or both, a fufficient portion of land has been vefted in an individual, to induce the neceffity of building, with local refidence and occupation of the farmer. The fmaller inclofures fhould be let to the tenant or tenants of thefe farms, for the fame term, and fubject to the fame covenants and reftrictions, under which fuch farms are refpectively held; with, however, a proportionate abatement of rent, by way of an equivalent for the want of buildings. If the lands with the latter be rented at one pound per acre, the former fhould be rented at fifteen fhillings, or at moft at fixteen fhillings; and if either price be obtained, fmaller inclofures would be provided for, on a footing without buildings, equally, if not more advantageous than larger, with them. Perhaps it may be objected to this plan, that by fuch additions Mendip farms would become too extenfive and unwieldy for general occupation. Under an improved fyftem of management, it is now well known that the moft profitable deftination of thefe farms muft be, with little variation, to *corn* and *fheep*; and for thefe purpofes, it is no lefs obvious that farms cannot be well too *large*, provided tenants can be found of fufficient ability and capital to occupy. This, at firft, may create fome difficulty and inconvenience, in letting to farmers in a neighbourhood where the largeft farms feldom exceed two hundred pounds per annum.— This, however, can only be temporary; fince the quality of the foil and the fituation are favourable to corn and fheep, and begin to attract the notice of farmers, who have been accuftomed in other counties to occupy fanns of this defcription on a very large fcale. Thefe, by a fyftem of management adapted to the foregoing purpofes, founded on experience,

experience, and profecuted with vigour, will foon convince thofe of the neighbourhood that *Mendip farms*, thus appropriated, of almoft any extent, may be occupied with as much fafety and advantage as can be reafonably expected or defired.

Having ftated 300l. as the fum requifite for buildings to accommodate one hundred acres of land, I would obferve, that 400l. would accommodate two hundred acres; 500l. four hundred acres; and 600l. five hundred acres; fo that this expence decreafes by an inverfe ratio as the farm is augmented: and in like manner that of fencing, as a large farm requires lefs fubdivifion than a fmall one. Both thefe circumftances further tend to juftify the predilection for *large* farms.

I fhall conclude this head, by adducing an inftance to exemplify the neceffity and importance of raifing Mendip inclofures to feparate and diftinct farms.

About twenty years fince, near fix hundred acres of Mendip land were inclofed, the property of a gentleman of large landed eftate in the neighbourhood. For fituation and quality, it could not be furpaffed by any land of this fort. The contiguity to markets with good roads was another privilege; the quantity was equal to a refpectable farm; and 600l. was judged fufficient to provide the neceffary buildings, in the opinion of thofe who recommended the meafure. A gentleman farmer from Norfolk, of confiderable property, was fo much ftruck with the foil, fituation, and other circumftances, as to declare, that if proper buildings were erected, he would give fifteen fhillings an acre for a term of twenty-one years; this was refufed, nor have any buildings been erected fince. The land was let to the proprietor's tenants of the adjacent farms in different proportions, at not more than twelve fhillings per acre for the firft

nine

nine or ten years, but since, for not more than ten shillings.
Great expectations were formed on the improvement of *the
old farms*, by the produce of the new inclosure being entirely confumed thereon. Thefe, however, are not realized,
for the ftraw was for the moft part fold to the adjacent towns,
and during the firft feven years of tillage, it was no unufual
practice to crop with oats three or four years *fucceffively*;
yet fuch was the fertility of foil, and its aptitude for this
fpecies of grain, that the produce in favourable feafons, with
a fingle ploughing, has been occafionally fix quarters per
acre. The confequences of this wretched hufbandry, with
regard to the foil, are too apparent to particularize, and too
abfurd and ruinous to need any further comment. I fhall
only fubjoin, had a diftinct farm been made in this cafe,
feven per cent. would have been paid for the buildings, ex-
clufively of *an increafe of rent of upwards of one hundred
pounds per annum*, and the land under a proper leafe, inftead
of its prefent reduced rent of ten fhillings or twelve fhillings
per acre, would have attained a permanent value of a guinea
per acre.

The fifth objection involves two diftinct relations :

ift. Deterioration of the quality of wool.

2dly. Diminution of its produce by leffening the number
of fheep.

With refpect to the firft, by way of preliminary, it may
be neceffary to enquire, to what degree has this deterioration
of quality manifefted itfelf by a reduction of price on wool
from fheep of the *fame fpecies*, fed on improved and *cultivated lands*, or on *common* and *wafte lands?* Was this point,
fo effential to the prefent difcuffion, ever afcertained by fair
and accurate experiment? If not, the objection is wholly
hypothetical. If it have, the refult ought not only to be
known but eftablifhed as data to argue from. Nothing of
this

this kind, however, has fallen within my obfervation. I muſt
therefore proceed aſſumptively, and grant, for the ſake of
inveſtigation, a deterioration of quality as far as ſix-pence
in the pound by depaſturing ſheep, which afford the fineſt
Engliſh wool on *cultivated* land, inſtead of waſte or *barren.*
If the conceſſion as to price be ſufficiently liberal, let us enquire how far the publick or individuals are obnoxious to
injury therefrom. The clothier may mix ſomewhat leſs of
this ſort of wool with Spaniſh, the better to diſguiſe the alteration in quality; or if uſed by itſelf, ſome difference in
the texture or feel of the cloth might be the conſequence.
But if the alteration be *univerſal,* in neither point of view
could any particular clothier, nor the trade collectively, be
affected by it; and it is at leaſt probable, the publick at
large would not be endued with ſufficient knowledge of the
manufacture to detect it, or if they did, would regard it as
too frivolous to merit notice. Allow for a moment the
fineſt Engliſh wool to be worth two ſhillings per pound,
from ſheep fed on commons or waſte land, and one ſhilling
and ſix-pence if fed on cultivated land. In the former caſe
the manufacturer of cloth would be a gainer, by having four
pounds of wool for the ſame money as three pounds, and he
could not complain of a proportional reduction of price; a
benefit might therefore, but no poſſible injury could accrue,
to this party in the buſineſs. Let us now advert to the
farmer, who not only repreſents himſelf, but the nation at
large, as being deeply intereſted in the increaſed produce of
land, not only in *this,* but in every poſſible variety of its application. Enquire of the farmer, and he will tell you, that
on an acre of cultivated land, by the aid of turnips and
graſſes, he can keep four ſheep inſtead of one on waſte or
land in common, and this too with an undoubted augmentation both of fleece and carcaſe. He has, therefore, four
fleeces

fleeces and four carcafes inftead of one, with a manifeft improvement in the value of each. Muft he then, from a mere phantom of a grievance which bewilders the imagination of the manufacturer, relinquifh advantages of decided and unfpeakable importance both to himfelf and the publick? Surely not.

The foregoing remarks apply principally to the fmall breed of fheep; but this fort is apparently on the decline in favour of the improved breeds of Dorfetfhire, South-down, and other larger forts, as being more productive in wool, (quality and quantity confidered) in fize of carcafe, and in requiring a lefs given time to graze. Let it be admitted from thefe confiderations, that in courfe of time the former breed fhould become extinct. What then? Should a real degeneracy of the quality of wool, magnified by the fears of the manufacturer, be permitted to militate againft the folid benefit enumerated as above? The quality of cloth as to finenefs is *comparative*. Diftinction would vanifh, pride and vanity would ceafe to murmur, if the wool deftined to the manufacture of cloth were of the *fame* quality, however coarfe. The more *opulent* claffes of fociety might ftill be gratified with cloth made entirely of Spanifh wool; the *middle* with a mixture of Spanifh and Englifh; and the *lower* with that wholly manufactured of Englifh wool. But all this being uniform in its operation and effect, and being evidently calculated to advance national profperity, as well as individual advantage, could create no fymptoms of mortification or difguft. Let us contemplate the fubject under the ftill more interefting claims of humanity. Can the little farmer and the artificer, the labouring manufacturer and the hufbandman, be fed with the fleece? Suppofe this valuable fpecies of animal food were confined to the fmall breed, would there not be a diminution of its quantity fo confider-

able

able as might probably advance the price of mutton from four-pence to fix-pence per pound? Let it be remembered too, that in proportion to the increafed value of the fleece, the farmer will be enabled to reduce the price of the carcafe; for his profit is derived from the *whole animal*, not as fepa-rated into parts. Therefore the more value the fleece, the cheaper he can afford to fell the carcafe.

The next article under this objection, is the diminution of the produce of wool by leffening the number of fheep.

This takes for granted what ftill remains to be proved, namely, that the inclofing of commons, fed principally by fheep, has a tendency to leffen the breed. I fhall confider this objection as applicable to fheep *in general*, and not to any particular defcription or fpecies. Here I have not only my doubts as to the truth of the pofition, but I am inclined to think that the number of fheep will be *increafed* thereby, and this too in a very confiderable degree. For, perhaps, four years after inclofing, an exception may be pleaded, fince this portion of time muft be allowed to a courfe of tillage *neceffarily* previous to the cultivation of fheep feed. This circumftance, as being altogether temporary, fhould not in the leaft operare as a deduction from the validity of the opinion. From this period, when turnips and artificial graffes are brought forward, I would date my calculation.

Recurring to a former obfervation, that Mendip or up-land inclofures were moft profitably applied as corn and fheep farms, I will fuppofe one of this fort to confift of four hundred acres. In its cultivated ftate, one hundred acres may be allowed to fuftain as many fheep as the *whole* did when in common, and a lefs proportion of land than this will fcarcely be allowed for fheep feed. If this be admitted, let me afk what becomes of the futile apprehenfions of *lef-fening the number of fheep.* Let the manufacturer no longer repine,

repine, nor the *timid* fenator be the victim of groundlefs
diftruft: the former will have the fame quantity of wool
provided from a fourth portion of land as was before de-.
voted to the purpofe, and the latter will have the confolation
to reflect that the other three-fourths are raifed, from a ftate
totally unproductive, to a capacity of fupplying its owner
with corn, and pafturage for cattle.

I have fome reafon to believe, that unfavourable impref-
fions have been made on the minds of both houfes of parliament againft a general inclofing fyftem; and thefe may
have arifen from the magical influence of an expreffion long
fanctified by the publick mind, namely, that of the woollen
manufacture being the *ftaple trade* of the nation, to which
even the land, in all its diverfity of produce, muft ever be
fubordinate under every kind of parliamentary regulation.
A little confideration would ferve to detect the fallacy of
this opinion.

. But to recur. In this farm of four hundred acres, fuppofe one hundred and fifty fhould be appropriated to fheep.
On the fame ground of reafoning, this would increafe the
number by the addition of a moiety. Perhaps this proportion of fheep-food is much nearer to the ftandard of practice than the former; if fo, in any ratio, the manufacturer,
inftead of being abridged of his fupply of wool by inclofing,
will have confiderably more, and probably too at a reduced
price.

Such are the facts relative to Wool: the conclufions are
fimple and obvious. The fufpicious manufacturer, actuated
by a fpirit of monopoly which the legiflature has ever been
too much difpofed to countenance, may reft fatisfied that
he can receive no *injury*, but may great *benefit* from the
inclofing fyftem.

The

The fixth objection fuppofes a diminution of the rental value of eflates, to which commons are appertenant.

In *theory*, this may appear in fome degree fpecious, becaufe an increafed produce, without an increafed confumption, would more or lefs countenance fuch an inference.

But admitting the premifes, it induces the neceffity of inveftigating the relative operation of the caufe prefumed. Let us fuppofe a farm with common appertenances to be worth one hundred pounds per year, and that by a deprivation of the common its value be reduced five pounds per year. If the common *inclofed* be worth ten pounds per year, the objection muft give way.

This ftatement, however, beftows a degree of importance on the objection which it fcarce deferves; for in fact, the inclofing both of the low and up-lands has been uniformly accompanied with an increafed produce from both; and it is no lefs true, that fcarce an inftance can be produced of the leaft abatement in rent on the *old eftates*, in confequence of the tenants being deprived of their *commons* by inclofing.

I fhall now proceed to a minute delineation of the general practice of farmers occupying land in this foreft; and endeavour to fhew how far the general end of improvement has been kept in view, how far it has been deviated from, and in what refpect the general fyftem is fufceptible of amendment.

It appears, by the foregoing ftatement, that the expences of the act of parliament, commiffioners fees, roads, dividing and allotting, fencing, drawing and enrolling the award, and all other incidental expences, ought not to exceed two pounds ten fhillings per acre; to this muft be added twenty fhillings per acre for raifing the quick-fet hedges to maturity; and to avoid objections, I will fay fifty fhillings per acre for neceffary buildings, pools, &c.

Let

Let us now endeavour to state the " *cui bono*" of such speculation.

In its open uncultivated state, the value of this waste could not be estimated at more than three shillings per acre; indeed it is a matter of doubt, all circumstances considered, if it were worth *any thing* to the possessors. In its inclosed state, and previous to its cultivation, it might be let for eight shillings per acre; and when cultivated and manured with lime, its value will be advanced to fifteen, twenty, and in some instances to thirty shillings per acre.

Let us state the account both ways.

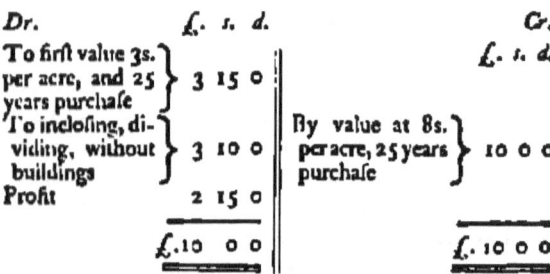

Dr. £. s. d.   Cr.
                                                        £. s. d.
To first value 3s. per acre, and 25 years purchase   3 15 0

To inclosing, dividing, without buildings   3 10 0   By value at 8s. per acre, 25 years purchase   10 0 0

Profit   2 15 0

£. 10 0 0   £. 10 0 0

In this instance the profit is not despicable.

OR, SECONDLY,

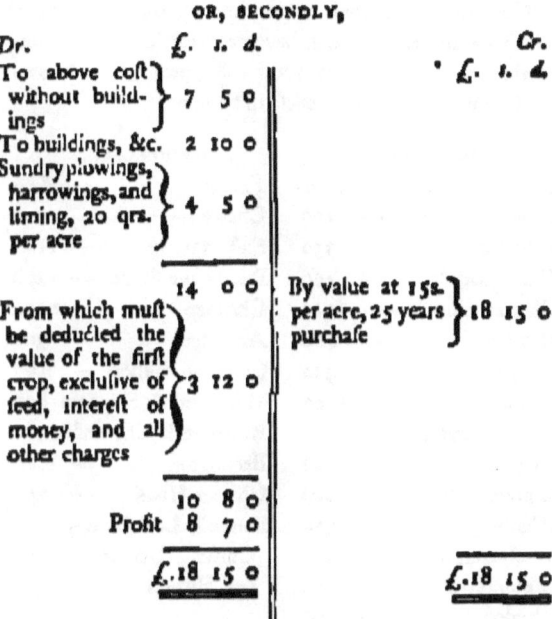

Dr.	£.	s.	d.		Cr.
To above cost without buildings	7	5	0		£. s. d.
To buildings, &c.	2	10	0		
Sundry plowings, harrowings, and liming, 20 qrs. per acre	4	5	0		
	14	0	0	By value at 15s. per acre, 25 years purchase 18 15 0	
From which must be deducted the value of the first crop, exclusive of seed, interest of money, and all other charges	3	12	0		
	10	8	0		
Profit	8	7	0		
£.18	15	0		£.18 15 0	

There are few ways in which money or industry can be employed to greater advantage than this, or in which the publick good can be more promoted; and yet I have frequently heard men, in other respects of sound understanding, ridicule such speculations as altogether visionary, and absurd.

Were it even admitted, that the adventurers in these schemes are for the most part sufferers, yet it cannot be denied that the community is benefited, inasmuch as the land is made to produce ten times as much as it did in its primitive state; and the amount of labour is nothing but an addition to the capital stock of the nation.

Notwith-

Notwithftanding thefe improvements, on the foreft of which we are now treating, have been carried on with unabating ardour and activity, yet it will appear by the following ftatement, that much is left to be done:

INCLOSED.		UNINCLOSED.	
Parifhes	*Acres*	*Parifhes*	*Acres*
Leigh	100	Chewton	2000
Afhwick	350	Eaft-Harptry	1100
Cranmoor, &c.	400	Priddy and Stoke	1200
Charterhoufe	1000	Cheddar	2500
Hayden	400	Axbridge	300
Ubly	950	Compton-Bifhop	500
Bleadon	1000	Winfcomb & Shipham	800
Doulton and Stoke	800	Rowboro' & Churchill	1000
Shepton	800	Berrington	1000
Shuters Bottom	600	Charter-Houfe	350
Weftbury	350	Banwell, Lockftone,	
Weft-Harptry	900	Curfton, Locking, }	800
Compton-Martin	700	and Hutton	
Blagdon	800		
Old-Down	50		
Dinder and Crofcomb	800		
Chilcot and Horrington	800		
Wells	2800		
	13,600		*11,550

* This account was taken in 1794, fince which acts have been obtained for the inclofing of Eaft-Harptry, Cheddar, Banwell, Chewton, and Winfcomb. All the others are likely to follow. J. B.

The

The foil of thefe hills is for the moft part deep, loamy, and of a good confiftence; and were the climate more genial, could not fail of being highly productive *in all feafons.* Occafionally are to be found fpots of land lefs valuable, being of a light fpungy nature, black in colour, and totally unproductive of corn on *firft cultivation.*

Nature, however, has wifely provided a manure within itfelf; for under the furface, at the depth of a foot, is generally found a ftrong clay, which, being fpread after the rate of thirty or forty cart-loads per acre, gives fuch a tenacity to the foil as enables it to produce corn or any crop in great abundance.

And here let me advife a general inveftigation of the fubftrata of all foils about to be improved; for I verily believe, that in moft inftances a manure may there be found near at hand, and congenial thereunto. Do we not frequently find clay under fand, and fand under clay; under flint, *chalk;* under white-lias or ftone-brafh, *marle;* under red earth, *lime-ftone;* under peat-bogs, fea *mud* or *clay?* Are not thefe circumftances fufficient indication to the wary hufbandman, to examine minutely the interior quality of his land previous to applying extraneous and expenfive manures?*

* An incontrovertible proof of the juftnefs of this obfervation was exhibited about twenty-four years ago at Eaft-Cranmore, one of the firft commons on Mendip inclofed by act of parliament. On making the banks round a field of twelve acres, of which almoft the whole was black fpongy earth, a great part of the ditches, confifting of a yellowifh red tenacious earth ftrongly verging to clay, was thrown by their fides to make room for what was thought better mould for the plants to grow in. The field was ploughed and fown on one earth with oats, previous to which the malm, as it is called, by the fide of the ditches was fpread and levelled. The confequence was, that on the black earth there was a very thin crop not equal to the feed fown, whilft round the ditches, where the malm was fpread, there was a fine luxuriant growth. R. P.

The

The climate of thefe hills is cold, moift, and boifterous, during the winter feafon, and frequently immerfed in fogs; but in fummer, the air is clear, falubrious, and invigorating. And it frequently happens that potatoes, French beans, and other fpring crops, are deftroyed in the *vale* by froft in April or May, when thofe on the *hill* are in no degree injured.

The favourite corn crop is *oats*, which are produced in great abundance, and of good quality. The wheat and barley are inferior, being thick in the fkin, and of a dark colour; however, the defect in *quality* is amply made up by the *quantity*; for it is no unufual thing, after the land is manured with lime, to get from twenty to thirty bufhels (Winchefter) of wheat, and forty or fifty bufhels of barley per acre. As to oats, the ufual crop is from forty to fixty bufhels.

But the moft eligible mode of conducting a farm on lands of this defcription, is to grow *comparatively* but little corn, and *that little* in the higheft perfection. To have a great breadth of turnips, cabbages, potatoes, vetches, artificial-graffes, and confequently to maintain a great ftock. To provide all neceffary buildings for fhelter in the winter, and for the purpofes of making mountains of dung, which the large produce of ftraw will enable the occupier to do. If fheep be kept, let the choice be of wedders, (a breeding flock on fuch expofed fituations is hazardous) and let them be folded every night in the year.

By thefe means, lands of this defcription may be carried on in a progreffive ftate of improvement; and if the prefent price of the different articles of produce be not greatly reduced, neither the proprietor nor the tenant will have any reafon to complain.

FENCES, BUILDINGS, &c.

Let us now proceed to a description of the fences, buildings, reservoirs or pools, limekilns, roads, and all other the
needful appendages to such undertakings.

There are various modes of fencing, and each has its advocates, but the two principal are *walls* and *quickset hedges.*

WALL FENCE.

In most instances, the *outside bounds* are a wall fence, five
feet six inches high, two feet and a half wide at bottom, and
fifteen inches at the top, which is covered with a turf of
six inches put on in the form of an arch, making together
an height of six feet. This wall is partly dry and partly
cemented with mortar, or what is commonly called a *lift-
wall.* In some instances, where a flat bed of stone can be
procured, it is made without cement, and if well built such a
wall is very durable. When the ground is level, the foundation of the wall is laid on the turf, and this is to be preferred, as it will not be so apt to sink as when a trench is
dug. The expence of a lift-wall may be thus calculated
per rope of twenty feet running length:

	£.	s.	d.
To quarring or digging eight loads of stone, (25 cwt. each) at 3d.	0	2	0
To halling the same, supposing the distance half a mile, at 6d.	0	4	0
To building per rope, (twenty feet) at 3s. 6d.	0	3	6
To seven bushels of lime, at 3d.	0	1	9
To covering with turf (if done very well)	0	0	3
*£.	0	11	6

* In consequence of the advanced price of wages and of coal, about
fifteen per cent. must be added to these calculations—1797. J. B.

DRY WALL.

			£.	s.	d.
To quarring as before	—	—	0	2	0
To halling ditto	—	—	0	4	0
To building, at 2s.	—	—	0	2	0
To turfing	—	—	0	0	3
			0	8	3

When stones can be got within a wheeling distance, or about sixty or seventy yards, the cost will be reduced about two shillings per rope, and if the wall be *wholly* made with cement, it will be enhanced about two shillings and six-pence per rope.

In making of dry stone walls, two masons should work opposite each other, so that the surface of their work may be always level. Stones also should be occasionally selected of a sufficient length to reach the whole breadth of the wall; this precaution will bind the work together, and render it durable.

QUICKSET HEDGES.

These hedges, if rightly managed and attended to whilst young, are in themselves great advantage and profit; they afford good shelter for the cattle, and they furnish fuel and writh or dead fence for the necessary purposes of the occupier.

The first thing to be done, is to mark out the course of the ditch. The dimensions of the bank on which the quick-sets are planted is generally six feet at the bottom, three and

a half

a half feet at the top, and two feet high.* On each fide is a ditch three feet wide and two feet deep; the fides being made floping, and the bottom not wider than fix inches; this is to prevent the cattle from walking in the ditch and cropping the young fhoots. In making the ditch, the men fhould be particularly careful not to throw any bad earth from the bottom of the ditches into the centre of the bank. If this be done, the growth of the quick will be greatly retarded. The making this bank will coft nine-pence per rope (twenty feet.)

Let the fets be taken from a nurfery formed on a good foil; let them be ftraight in their growth, having been once tranfplanted from the feed-bed, and four or five years old. The fhoots fhould alfo be fmooth on the bark, and well rooted. Thefe fets are worth about one fhilling per hundred.

The bank being thus prepared, and the quick ready, let a trench be cut in the middle of the bank, and let the fets be cut off and laid with the head inclining a little at the diftance of about three inches from plant to plant. Let the roots be then covered with a little of the beft mould, after which fill up the whole trench with rotten dung, or compoft, ftrewing a little more good mould on the top. The digging the trench and planting will coft two-pence per rope.

Nothing more is neceffary than to fecure them from injury. For their defence therefore, and fhelter, two dead hedges muft be made about four inches diftant from the

* In fome inftances there is only one ditch, the earth on the other fide being worked off to a flope; by this plan the bank is kept more moift, and the thorn plants flourifh better.

outfide

outfide edges of the bank.† Thefe hedges are about two feet and half high, and compofed of wreath or bufh wood, with a proper number of ftakes; the expence of materials and labour is about two fhillings and ten-pence per rope. Time of planting the quick either in the months of October, February, or March. It is the practice of fome to plant *two* rows of quick inftead of *one*, but I have not found this plan fucceed well. Some alfo recommend the planting at a greater diftance than three inches, under an idea that *thick* planting retards the growth; but I have invariably found that the hedges planted *thick* thrive the beft.

Some advife the planting of timber trees in the hedge, but I think it a bad practice, as the dripping from them frequently kills the thorn plants, and makes a vacancy in the hedge.

After this, the young quick muft be carefully weeded and hoed twice a year, and particular care muft be taken to prevent their being cropped either by cattle or fheep, both of which are very fond of the tender buds; and if by any accident they have gained accefs to them, and gnawed them, they muft be cut down within an inch and half of the ground. In cold expofed fituations, *two fets* of dead fences are requifite to bring the quick to maturity, and the coft may be thus calculated:—

---

† The expence of fecuring thorn hedges with oak railing is very expenfive, and in fome inftances has exceeded the value of the land fo inclofed—befides, the young quicks are not fo well fheltered as by a wreathed hedge, and confequently do not make fo rapid a progrefs in their growth.

Making

	£.	s.	d.
Making the bank — —	0	0	9
Quick-fets eighty in a rope —	0	0	9
Planting and dunging — —	0	0	2
Two dead hedges — —	0	2	5

(*N. B.* One waggon-load of writh will coft
17s. 6d. and make about fifteen rope of
fingle hedge.)

	£.	s.	d.
Making two dead fences — —	0	0	5
	0	4	6
Weeding plants for three years —	0	0	3
Two additional dead hedges —	0	2	10
	*0	7	7

N. B. The old wood will pay for fundry repairs of the
hedges injured by fportfmen, &c.

In many counties it is the cuftom to plant the quick in
the face of the bank, and where wood for fencing is fcarce,
this method generally prevails.

Having now ftated the different expence of a *mortar* and
lift wall, a *dry wall*, and alfo of raifing a bank, and planting
quick, it may not be amifs to enumerate the comparative
advantages and difadvantages.

A wall is certainly the beft fence for a given number of
years. It covers lefs ground, it does lefs injury to the crops;
if part by accident fall, it is eafily repaired, cattle are kept
more fecure, fportfmen are excluded. Thefe are the prin-

---

* The price of hazel coppice-wood and labour being confiderably
advanced, one fhilling per rope muft be added to this eftimate. J. B.

cipal

cipal advantages, which in a great degree compenfate for the want of fhelter and durability, and in moft inftances where ftone can eafily be got, and I think in all cafes where land is poor and expofed to violent and deftructive winds, it is the preferable fence.

On the other hand, quickfet hedges are beautiful to the eye; and if the climate, quality, and depth of foil, be fuch as to throw out a vigorous fhoot, and minute attention be paid to them in their infancy, they are lefs expenfive, and at the end of fourteen years will yield a fufficient produce when cut down and plafhed to pay all the expences incurred by the firft making; and this cutting may be repeated every twelve or fourteen years without injury to the ftocks. And here let me remind the farmer, that the proper time to cut and plafh his hedges is, when the ground is to be ploughed, or if it be paflure, when the crop is to ftand for hay; for cattle are very fond of the young branches, and by cropping them in the fummer, will greatly injure the fhoots.

But may not thefe two modes be fo combined as to reap the advantage of both, that is, by making both a wall and a hedge? To this there can be no objection but the expence.

A dry ftone-wall, four feet and half high, with fix inches turf on the top, may be built on a fimilar calculation with the foregoing, for fix fhillings per rope; and a low bank may be raifed under it, on which quick may be planted. The growth, encouraged by fhelter and warmth, will be rapid, and in four or five years time the wall may be taken away, and the ftones converted into lime, or ufed on the publick roads, or for any other purpofe. If this fence be made at the time when the land is converted into tillage, one dead fence to fecure the plants on the infide will be fufficient, and that not an expenfive one.

The

The DISBURSEMENT *will be as follows:*

	£.	s.	d.
Building four feet and half of wall, stones and halling included	0	6	0
Turfing	0	0	2
Making bank and planting quick	0	0	4
Sets	0	0	8
One dead fence on the inside	0	1	2
Weeding	0	0	2
	0	8	6
From which deduct the value of the stones at three-pence per cart-load	0	1	6
	*0	7	0

This I think a more eligible mode of fencing than either of the preceding, but still there is another method which I prefer to all others in situations such as that on which we are now treating.

This is making a bank three feet high, and planting on it *full grown floe* or *black-thorn*, setting them very thick, and cutting off the top to the height of three feet. The principal objection that can be started to this plant is, the running of its roots, which are said to obstruct the plough; but I can declare from long experience, that in banks such as I describe, accompanied with ditches two feet and half deep, no such inconvenience has occurred. In most countries great quantities of this black-thorn might be found in coppices, borders of fields, commons, &c. and the owners will

---

* The same addition as before for advance of wages, &c.

be obliged by your digging them up; one good waggon-
load of thefe plants will be fufficient for twelve rope, and
the coft may be thus eftimated:

	£.	s.	d.	
Making the bank	0	1	0	per rope.
Digging up and planting	0	1	6	ditto
Carriage of plants	0	0	9	
	0	3	3	

N. B. The price of carriage muft vary according to the
diftance.

It may be advifeable to mix with the black-thorn fome
hazel or withy ftocks, together with the *large brier*, and to
lay the loppings of the floe along the fummit of the bank,
fecuring them by fmall flakes fo as to prevent fheep from
making a paffage through the flocks. This fence requires
but little repair; the floe will throw out fo many fhoots
from its root, and the briar will fo intwine its branches with
the hedge, as to make it in a few years impervious to cattle
of any kind. And though it cannot be expected to grow
to a great height, yet it will be as clofe and thick as the
farmer can wifh; and, together with the bank, will conftitute excellent fhelter and defence, *and withal* will be made
at the leaft poffible expence.

After inclofing and dividing, the next objects of attention
are fuitable buildings, fuch as a dwelling-houfe, barns, fla-
bles, ftallings, &c. &c. Thefe are placed as near as poffible
to the centre of the farm, and though not elegant, are for the
moft part ufeful and commodious. They are built with
ftone, and generally thatched, the inconvenience of which is
feverely felt; for the moifture of the air, and the powerful
effects

effects of the wind, render frequent repairs neceffary.* A roof will require coating every eight or ten years; it is a harbour for vermin; is more dangerous in refpect to fire, and, every thing confidered, is more expenfive than tile, to encourage the ufe of which, our rulers would do well, were they to repeal the prefent tax upon that article, (or at leaft to allow a drawback on fuch as may be ufed on farm-houfes, barns, &c.) for I think it would not be difficult to prove that the injury done to the kingdom in refpect to its agriculture, is five times greater than the produce of the tax. Exempt from duty, the ufe of tile muft, I think, be general, by which means all the ftraw would be devoted to the purpofe of fubfiftence for cattle, or manure. The expence of a comfortable farm-houfe, with its neceffary appendages, is eftimated at about two hundred and fifty pounds. That of a barn, roomy enough for four threfhers, and capacious enough to hold twenty or thirty loads of corn, one hundred and fifty pounds. Stables, ftalling, pig-ftyes, &c. one hundred and fifty pounds more, making in the whole five hundred and fifty pounds. This expenditure will be fufficient for a farm of five hundred acres. The practice lately introduced of placing the barns on a declivity cannot be too much commended; a warm and commodious ftall for oxen, covered by one roof, is thereby gained. The barn-floor, thus elevated, is rendered more durable, and lefs fubject to vermin; the corn is kept more dry and fweet than on a ground floor; nor can it flip through the barn-floor without difcovery; and I know of no poffible inconvenience that can accompany this plan. Barns, fuch as thefe, are placed

---

* Repair (if poffible) thatched buildings in the fummer feafon. A covering put on then, will laft years longer than one put on in the winter. J. B.

with a fouth-eaft afpect, and the arches of the ftalling front that way. Annexed thereto is a capacious yard, with proper cribs for hay and ftraw, where the animals feed, and retire at their pleafure to their comfortable lodging under the barn.

Nothing is neceffary to complete the farm-yard but a pond or refervoir of water; and as the fituation is on a defcent, fuch pond is foon filled by the common current of rain, or it may be fupplied by fhoots from the roof of the barn.

On one farm, fituate in the parifh of Compton-Martin, the proprietor has made a femicircular farm-yard, and by building a wall on the *outfide*, and round pillars on the *infide*, at the diftance of about fourteen feet from each other, and covering the fame with ftrong lugs or poles, has made an excellent *ftaddle* for corn. To fecure it from vermin, he has placed a row of flat ftones at a foot diftance from the top both of the wall and pillars *infide* and *outfide*. This row of ftones projects about eight inches, and fhuts fo clofe together that no vermin can gain accefs to the corn. On this ftaddle (as it is here called) he places the whole of his wheat crop, except that portion which he intends to threfh for feed; for the moifture of the air in winter renders the wheat on thefe hills fo damp and cold, that the fale at that feafon is very flack, and fhould in moft inftances be avoided. In all my farming excurfions, I never faw a more comfortable covering for cattle, nor a better foundation for a corn mow; and under the fuppofition of its being threfhed in the fummer months, no poffible inconvenience can attend it, for the ftaddle is cleared, and ready before harveft to take another burthen.

POOLS.

The next, and not the leaſt important appendage of theſe farms, are *pools* or *reſervoirs of water*; for on hills ſo elevated few ſprings can be expected. Nothing more ſtrongly verifies the truth of the old adage, " Neceſſity is the mother of invention," than the ſkill exhibited by the maſons of this diſtrict in buildings of this nature. Scarcely ever do theſe pools let through the water, and the coſt, ſuppoſing it to be of the following dimenſions, 40 feet long, 16 wide, and 6 feet deep in the middle, may be thus ſtated:

	£.	s.	d.
Digging out for foundation	2	2	0
N. B. In moſt inſtances this will furniſh a ſuffi-			
cient quantity of ſtone for the building.			
Maſon's labour	10	10	0
Three hundred buſhels of lime	3	0	0
Ten loads of clay and carriage	1	0	0
Eight loads of coal-aſhes and carriage	1	8	0
	*18	0	0

A pool of theſe dimenſions, if properly ſituated, will ſupply eighty or one hundred acres with a ſufficiency of water for the ſtock throughout the year; and if well made, may be kept in repair for ſix-pence a year.

* Some cautious people go to a conſiderable diſtance for lime made from the white-lyas ſtone, which is certainly a ſtronger cement under water than the lime burnt on theſe hills. In this caſe, an additional expence is incurred.

LIMEKILNS.

LIMEKILNS.

As *Lime* is the grand manure of this diftrict, by which
the improvements of cultivation are in a great meafure
brought about, kilns for burning it are numerous, and generally thought well conftructed; their form is that of a
French bottle, the height feventeen feet, the length of the
neck, in which the calcination is wholly effected, feven feet;
its diameter four feet, and the diameter of the belly in the
largeft part twelve feet. They are built on the fide of a
hill, by which means the top is on a level with the adjacent
rock, and the coft is as follows:

	£.	s.	d.
Digging out the concavity	1	1	0
(This will furnifh ftone for the building)			
Building	4	4	0
Lime and afhes	1	15	0
Building a fhelf-houfe for the kiln to depofit the			
lime, and covering the fame	3	0	0
*£.10	10	0	0

In fuch a kiln, may be burnt four hundred and eighty
bufhels of lime per week, and this will confume fifteen
quarters, or one hundred and twenty bufhels of refufe coal,
fuch as is not commonly ufed for any houfhold purpofes.
The coal cofts at the pit two-pence per bufhel, and the dif-

---

* In confequence of the advance of lime, coal, and wages, limekilns now coft about thirteen pounds; and from the fame caufes, the
coft of the lime will be advanced to fixteen-pence per quarter.

J. B. 1797.

tance

tance being fix miles, the carriage is three-pence, the prime coft of the lime therefore is fourteen-pence per quarter, as the following calculation fhews:

Weekly expence.				*Weekly produce.*		
Fifteen quarters of coal, at						
3s. 4d. ————	2	10	0	Sixty quarters,		
Limeburner 4d. per quarter,				at 1s. 2d.		
digging ftones and burning	1	0	0		3 10 0	
	£.3	10	0	£.3 10 0		

The lime produced by one of thefe kilns will amply manure three acres per week; and I leave my readers to determine, whether kilns of this conftruction are or are not to be preferred to thofe in fhape of an inverted cone. The largenefs of the furface in the laft-mentioned muft, I fhould think, require coal of a better quality, and confume a greater quantity.

ROADS.

Laftly, let us take a view of the publick Roads. They are left forty feet wide, and are ftoned twelve feet.

It is ufual to ftone thefe roads one foot thick in the middle, and nine inches at the fides, making thereby a gentle curve.

First

		s.	*d.*	
Firſt forming	—	o	6	per rope of 20 feet.
Digging eight loads of ſtone (25 cwt. each)	———	2	o	
Wheeling or halling ditto	—	3	o	
Breaking ditto	———	3	o	
		8	6*	

Note, The expence of halling muſt vary according to the diſtance of the ſtone.

MODE OF CULTIVATION.

The incloſure being now finiſhed, buildings erected, pools made, and publick roads formed, let us now take a furvey of the expence of cultivating theſe lands, under the following heads: ploughing, manuring, cropping, and harveſting. In this, I ſhall endeavour to draw information from reaſon and experience, and ſhew upon what grounds the practices are founded, ſo that my readers may then take or refuſe them, according to their own judgments.

I have before ſtated, that the foil of Mendip hills is a fine mellow mould, intermixed occaſionally with leſs fertile ingredients, ſuch as ſtone, gravel, clay, and the like; and according as theſe are greater or leſſer in quantity, the foil is worſe or better. In all caſes the huſbandman may diſtin-

---

* I muſt here reprobate the narrow policy of which I have myſelf been too guilty, viz. that of ſtoning the roads only twelve feet wide. In conſequence of its narrowneſs, *one track only* is formed by wheel-carriages, and the repairs are endleſs. On all accounts, experience directs me to recommend ſixteen feet at leaſt. J. B. 1797.

guiſh

guiſh the general nature of the ſoil, by its aſpect on the ſurface, or by the produce thereof. Where the fern grows in great luxuriance, there he is ſure to find deep good land; but weak low furze, ruſhes, or white graſs, are ſymptoms of poverty.

The object to which we now proceed in our diſquiſition may be deemed the moſt important and intereſting, being nothing leſs than the proceſs by which this comparatively barren ſoil is converted into fertile and productive land: and on a nearer inſpection, it will probably be allowed, that few inſtances can be adduced of attempts more ſucceſsful to individuals, or more beneficial to community. This ſoil does not pour forth its vegetable productions ſpontaneouſly, but its qualities and ſtrength are ſuch as to produce great returns, if properly cultivated and manured; and were an ancient inhabitant of theſe regions to return to life, he would be at a loſs to know the name of this apparently new country.

The months of September or October are the beſt to commence the tillage. The inſtrument made uſe of, is a ſtrong foot plough, without wheels, coſt two guineas. The breadth of the plit about ten, and the depth four inches. Four horſes, or ſix oxen, will turn about three-fourths of an acre in eight hours. A man is employed to go after the plough with a ſpade, to repair balks, to dig up ſtones, and to lay the plit flat: this ploughing may be valued from twelve to twenty ſhillings per acre. In this ſtate it remains to be mellowed by the winter froſts till March, when black oats are ſown, after the rate of ſix or ſeven buſhels per acre, and harrowed in by four turns of the harrow on the ſame ground. A few farmers, previous to this ſowing, have lately adopted the plan of *backing* the ſurface, at the expence of five ſhillings per acre: by which means leſs ſeed will do, and the same

fame is more regularly diftributed and better covered; befide, the harking and harrowing is not more expenfive than
the troublefome dragging before-mentioned: the expence of
either of thefe operations may be eftimated at feven fhillings
per acre.

After this, it is rolled at an expence of one fhilling per
acre. Nothing more is done till harveft, and the average
produce may be fet at twenty-five bufhels per acre; the ftraw
of which will pay for harvefting and threfhing (that is, about
eight fhillings per acre.)

Soon after harveft, or indeed at any part of the winter,
the ground is crofs-ploughed with the *double-furrow* plough,
value fix fhillings per acre. Harrowed in March, value two
fhillings; and in April the liming is begun. Four horfes
and two men, with two carts holding thirty-two bufhels of
lime each, (if the kiln be not at a greater diftance than one
mile) will cover one acre and half per day, at the rate of
one hundred and fixty bufhels per acre.

The lime is depofited in heaps of one bufhel, at the diftance of fixteen feet and half every way. Coft per acre
(value of lime included) thirty-five fhillings.

Covering thefe heaps with earth, and afterwards fpreading them, (which fhould be done as foon as the lime is diffolved) are worth one fhilling and fix-pence per acre.

After this the ground is well harrowed, two fhillings per
acre; then ploughed very thin or raftered, five fhillings;
harrowed again two fhillings, and in this ftate remains for
the feed earth. It is found highly advantageous to expedite
the liming, and to finifh all the work previous to the feed
earth by the middle of July; fo that all the ftock, fuch as
cows, fheep, horfes, &c. may have free accefs to the fallow,
or may be frequently driven over it, for the purpofe of making it clofe and compact. The latter end of September,

or

or beginning of the month of October, is the time for fowing; and this is done in two ways, fome fowing under furrow, others harrow in the feed; the latter I think preferable,
as the uncorrupted fward, furze, &c. are by harrowing
brought to the furface, and are a great defence to the infant
plant during winter; whereas, if buried, they keep the
ground hollow, and expofe the roots to injury. Which
ever way it be done, the laft ploughing, fowing, and harrowing, will coft about feven fhillings per acre, to which add
two bufhels and half of feed, value fifteen fhillings, and the
whole expence has been enumerated. No weeding is neceffary, nor is there any other difburfement, fave rolling in
April, which fhould be performed with a very heavy roller,
at the expence of two fhillings per acre.

Let

Let us now recapitulate the expences, and state the average produce per acre.

		£.	s.	d.			£.	s.	d.
First year.					*First year.*				
Dr.					Cr.				
To first ploughing	—	0	16	0					
To hacking and sowing oats		0	7	0					
To six bushels of seed	—	0	15	0	By 25 bushels				
To rolling	—	0	1	0	oats 2s. 6d.	3	2	6	
To one year's rent	—	0	8	0					
Second year.					*Second year.*				
To cross ploughing	—	0	6	0	By 25 bushels				
To harrowing	—	0	2	0	wheat 6s.	7	10	0	
To liming (160 bushels per acre)	—	1	15	0					
To covering and spreading		0	1	6					
To harrowing	—	0	2	0					
To ploughing	—	0	5	0					
To harrowing	—	0	2	0					
To last ploughing, sowing, and harrowing	—	0	7	0					
To two bushels and half of seed	—	0	15	0					
To rolling	—	0	2	0					
To two years rent	—	0	16	0					
		7	0	6					
Profit		3	12	0					
		10	12	6			10	12	6

N. B. The straw in both instances will pay for reaping, harvesting, and threshing.

HARVESTING

HARVESTING AND THRESHING.

The reaping of wheat is generally performed by the acre; and, as the ripening is a fortnight later on these hills than in the vale, there is no want of hands. The price from five to seven shillings and six-pence per acre, including cutting, binding, and mowing. It is always hand-griped as it is called, that is, collected within the palm of the hand before the hook or sickle is applied. All the corn, wheat, barley, and oats, are bound into sheaves and mowed in the field. The price for barley and oats from three to five shillings; besides these prices, the men are allowed for wheat two gallons of beer, and for barley and oats one gallon and half, per acre.

In situations subject to sudden and violent rain, this custom of mowing in the field cannot be condemned, as, in respect to wheat, the day's cutting is secured every evening, and the lent corn can be put together and secured much sooner than in the common method.

The principal objections are, the bringing mice with the sheaves into the barn, or large mow; and the want of sufficient dryness in the corn for winter threshing.

The men of this country are very dextrous in making these mows, so as to prevent rain from injuring the corn; and they frequently remain five or six weeks in the field without suffering any damage.

Wheat is seldom threshed with the straw, but the ears are cut off, and the straw bound in sheaves tied very tight; the circumference of the sheaf at the bond should be six feet; this costs five-pence per sheaf, including the threshing of the ears. A good acre of wheat will produce three dozen fheaves, value eight fhillings and fix-pence per dozen,* and each fheaf fhould weigh fifty-fix pounds. By this method, the firmnefs of the ftalk is preferved, and rendered more valuable for the purpofes of thatching buildings,† &c.

Barley and oats are threfhed by the quarter. Price from one fhilling to one fhilling and fix-pence per quarter.

A good acre of oats will produce two waggon-loads of ftraw.

The land is now confidered in its higheft ftate of ftrength and vigour; and it is thought by moft farmers, that every fucceeding year reduces its value; nor can this be wondered at, when the fubfequent courfe of cropping is ftated.

It is no unufual thing to have three or four fucceffive crops of corn, nay, fometimes five or fix without an intervening fallow, or fallow crop; greateft part of the ftraw is fold, nor is the land fown with artificial graffes till it is no longer able to bear corn.

---

* Ear-pitching is the provincial term for this management, and the fheaves thus prepared are called reed-fheaves. They are in general ufe for the purpofe of thatching, for which, indeed, they are folely intended. The practice is not confined to Mendip, but is in common ufe through great part of the diftrict. The workmen are very dexterous in making, and the thatchers no lefs expert in ufing it; and at the fame time that it makes a covering more durable than any other of ftraw, it is of fuch fuperior neatnefs, that the thatched buildings of this neighbourhood excite the admiration of many ftrangers coming from other parts where this practice is not known.

A dozen fheaves will cover a fquare of one hundred feet. Price of laying them up (new work) three fhillings per dozen. A fecond or any fucceeding coat, two fhillings per dozen. Mending, four-pence per fheaf. R. P.

† Some people difpute this point, and fay, that the hollow tube of the wheat-ftraw admits the air, and that its decay is thereby accelerated, and affert (from experience) that threfhed ftraw is more durable than unthrefhed. J. B.

This

This mode of treatment, together with the coldnefs of the climate, has hitherto operated as an effectual bar to the fettlement of opulent and more enlightened farmers; but I am well perfuaded, than if even one of that defcription were to fettle here on a farm of a proper fize, viz. five or fix hundred acres, he would, according to the farmer's phrafe, " find himfelf at home," and his example would foon be followed by many others.

Cabbages, turnips, potatoes, carrots, parfnips, vetches, flax, oats, clover, and all artificial graffes, may be fown in the higheft abundance and perfection.

The land is never glutted with rain, nor fubject to drought, and the fogs (of which fo much is faid) are prevalent only in the winter feafon.*

It cannot be denied, but that a cold wet fummer, fuch as that of 1792, is peculiarly unfavourable to the ripening of corn on lands of fuch elevation, but in fummers like the laft, few countries could vie with it.

Though I am no advocate for farms of an *exceffive* extent, yet I think, that on foils, and in fituations fuch as Mendip hills, they fhould not be lefs than four or five hundred acres. I mean fufficient to keep a flock of fheep for the purpofes of *folding*, which fhould be unremittingly purfued through both winter and fummer months. On the fallows in the fummer, and on the grafs land or in the farmyard in the winter. A wether flock would be beft calculated for the purpofe; and it is a matter of doubt with many judicious farmers, whether fheep of that kind are not equally profitable with the breeding flock, even in fituations more

---

* The inconvenience of fogs is greatly abated by the inclofing and draining of the low moor lands in the vicinity of Mendip.

mild

mild and temperate. By fuch a fyftem of management, one hundred acres might be manured every year with the fold, which, joined with occafional liming and the application of the farm-yard dung, would keep the land in a progreffive ftate of improvement, and at the leaft poffible expence.

DOUBLE-FURROW PLOUGH.

Formerly the ploughs ufed here were the moft aukward, and ill-contrived, that could be conceived, but they have in a great meafure given place to the *double-furrowed* plough, which was introduced to this neighbourhood by a fpeculative man who turned farmer on thefe lands, difregarded and defpifed by all practical hufbandmen.

Though common farmers are for the moft part backward in adopting new plans, yet I never knew any *valuable* difcovery that they did not fooner or later fall into. So it happened with the double ploughs. For ten years, did the perfon above alluded to ufe this inftrument, and was conftant in feafon, and out of feafon, in recommending it to others; (for they who have a true tafte for agriculture, enjoy themfelves in the communication of every ufeful difcovery) but all in vain, the more warm he was in enforcing its utility, the more reluctant were the common renters in adopting the ufe of it; and in all probability it would have remained to the prefent day, undiftinguifhed for its fuperiority, had not the fame been manifefted at the different trials of ploughs exhibited under the direction of the Bath Agricultural Society.

. At prefent, fcarce any other plough is ufed after the firft breaking; and, I believe, I may truly affert, that in compa-

rifon

rifon with the old ploughs of the diftrict, no lefs than fifty pounds per year is faved on a farm of five hundred acres. Another mode of management has been for many years paft introduced by the perfon before alluded to, namely, ploughing by the *acre* inftead of the *day*.

The contract is thus conducted; the mafter finds oxen and food, and the ploughman labour and driver. The latter is alfo bound to attend the cattle at all times, even when debarred from work by rain, fnow, froft, or any other caufe. The price is two fhillings and two-pence per acre for the ploughing of the rough Mendip lands when firft inclofed, (this is done with a fingle plough) and one fhilling and two-pence for all other ploughings of every defcription, with the double plough.

By this fyftem of management he has annually had more ground ploughed by *one* team, than his neighbours by *two*; and it has been no unufual thing for his man and boy to earn regularly per week feventeen fhillings and fix-pence, that is, for two acres and half per day on an average. Nay, his man has repeatedly ploughed with fix oxen (in yokes) twenty acres of land, ftatute meafure, in forty-eight hours; I mean in fix fucceffive days, reckoning eight hours per day: the breadth of the plit according to agreement not exceeding nine inches, nor the depth lefs than four inches, (when the foil was deep enough to admit thereof.)

Let us paufe here, and ferioufly confider the advantages of *contract* in comparifon with *daily* labour.* The Englifh labourer

* Many fenfible and well-meaning men have objected to *contract labour*, under the idea of its being injurious to the health and longevity of the labourer;—but though I have been in the habit of letting my work by the job or tafk for twenty years paft, I never perceived any ill effect on the health or ftrength of my workmen. Where great exertion

labourer is naturally difpofed to vigorous exertion, if encouraged thereto, either by an increafe of wages, or by the
exhilarating influence of good cheer.

Do we not fee in times of harveft a degree of activity
exhibited, unknown at other times of the year? and this at
a feafon when the heat of the weather naturally induces
fatigue.

Do not the manufacturer and artifan, almoft of every
defcription, have recourfe to contract labour? And though
their workmen earn from ten to thirty fhillings per week,
do they not find their account in fo doing, from the emu-
lation which it excites, and the perfection of workmanfhip
which it produces?

Muft it not be acknowledged, that in thofe countries
where *daily labour* is the prevailing mode, a flow and indolent habit is generated, which neither promifes nor threats
can entirely overcome, to the great injury of the common-
wealth, as well as of the farmer. Suppofe we allow the
average rate of daily labour to be fixteen-pence, and admit
that by contract, men will be excited to earn twenty-pence,
what an addition of ufeful labour would be created, taking
it in an aggregate point of view!

But I muft not enter too widely into this field of difcuffion, and fhall only add, that in refpect to the operation of
ploughing, the method now fuggefted can only be fubject to
two objections.

---

exertion and excefs of wages are forerunners to drunkennefs and debauchery, fuch confequences may follow;—but no practical man will
deny, that where daily labour prevails, a confiderable portion of the
day is wafted in fauntering, holding tales, and in a fluggifh ufe of thofe
limbs which are capable of more lively motion.

At any rate, *ploughing by the acre* cannot poffibly be attended with
any injury to the health or ftrength of the ploughman.

Firft,

First, the possibility of cattle being injured by too great exertion; and secondly, imperfection in the execution.

Both these are easily obviated by stating, that the eye of the master may see, and his judgment may direct, so as to preclude the possibility of imposition, without detection.

Dispatch at particular seasons of the year may be considered as invaluable, particularly in respect to spring and summer crops. A dry and favourable season for sowing occurs in March; by contract labour, and improved instruments, you are enabled to plough and sow *double* the usual quantity. The increased produce in comparison with a sowing in April, may be fairly calculated at more than the rent of the land, exclusive of the comparative cheapness. The same argument will hold good, in respect to flax, hemp, turnips, potatoes, cabbages, summer-fallows, &c. &c.

COMPARISON BETWEEN HORSES AND OXEN.

It is the general opinion of farmers in this district, that oxen are preferable to horses, for the purpose of ploughing, but for harrowing and all other purposes, the contrary.

The expences of keeping a team of each for the purposes of farming may be thus stated, and it will appear, that the superiority of oxen is not so great as some sanguine men have stated.

HORSE TEAM, (4)

The firſt coſt, including harneſs, cannot be eſtimated at leſs than one hundred pounds.

	£.	s.	d.
To 30 weeks keeping at hay, 12 tons at 40s.	24	0	0
Corn throughout the year ———	30	0	0
To twenty-two weeks keeping at graſs, at 3s. 6d. each horſe ——— ———	15	8	0
Repairs of harneſs — —	2	12	0
Farrier and ſhoeing ·— —	4	0	0
	£.76	0	0

OX TEAM, (6)

The firſt coſt of theſe, ſuppoſing them to be the beſt North-Devon breed, and four or five years old, yokes, bows, and chains included,* 70l.

	£.	s.	d.
To twenty-ſix weeks at hay, twenty-four tons, at 40s. — ———	48	0	0
Twenty-ſix ditto at graſs, 2s. 6d. per week each ox ———	19	10	0
Repairs of yokes and bows, and chains —	0	10	0
	£.68	0	0

Some farmers think that three horſes are equal in exertion to ſix oxen; if that be admitted, the expences of the horſe team will be leſs than thoſe of the oxen.

If an accident ſhould happen whereby a horſe is lamed, the value is much more leſſened than in the caſe of an ox;

---

* Oxen are now (January 1797) fifty per cent. dearer.   J. B.

but

but in all other respects they stand on equal ground; for horses, if purchased at the age of four or five years, are improving in value for two or three years, as much or more than oxen. And every intelligent farmer must be sensible of the folly of keeping a horse after he is six or seven years old; they should then be transferred to common carriers, &c. and agriculture should only be the medium whereby a young horse becomes, by gentle labour, inured to more severe discipline.

LIMING.

Having already stated that lime is the great article of modern improvement of these hills, I shall only add, that instances might be produced of lands letting at this time for thirty shillings per acre, which forty years ago were not worth four shillings; and the beginning of all these improvements has been by lime, whereby the acidity of the soil, impregnated with mineral exhalation, has been corrected, and crops raised on them as good as those on improved fields; and it is no less wonderful than true, that thirty cart-loads of rotten dung per acre, *previous to liming*, have had no sensible effect; but after the land has been once limed, the operation of dung is as perceptible here as on other lands. Surely this circumstance will prove, that these hills come under the description of barren land, as referred to in the statute of Edward VI. and as such be exempt from the payment of tithes for seven years. §

Before we leave the subject of liming, it may be right to inform my readers, that some have dressed their old pastures

§ It is much to be lamented, that all ambiguity in that act is not done away by a new bill explanatory of its meaning.

with

with hot lime, by which the mofs has been deftroyed, and a fine herbage produced, highly grateful to the palate of all forts of flock. The lime, after the rate of one hundred and fixty bufhels per acre, is put on the land foon after it is mown, and its effects are very durable; being perceptible for fifteen or twenty years, and it quite alters the nature of the coarfe four grafs, to which old layers are very fubject.

I confefs I am ignorant of the *whole* caufe, whereby lime produces fuch happy effects; but, however unknown the caufe, all agree that it is the moft cheap and efficacious manure that the hufbandman on thefe hills can have re-courfe to.

Here ends the detail of the Mendip hufbandry.

CHAPTER

CHAPTER VII

ARABLE LAND.

AS corn is but little attended to, in the greateſt part of this diſtrict, the mode of tillage is very defective. The ſtubbles are ſcarce ever ploughed till near Chriſtmas; and as it is the common practice to have at leaſt two crops of lent corn after wheat, the ground is ſeldom in a proper ſtate to receive graſs feeds.

Few turnips* are grown; and the land intended for ſummer fallow, preparatory to wheat, is not ploughed till the ſowing of the ſpring-corn is finiſhed,—from theſe cauſes the land abounds with *couch-graſs, cabiſes,* &c. Nor can we recommend the

ROTATION OF CROPS.

On the Clay, it is

1ſt. Beans		1ſt. Beans
2d. Summer Fallow		2d. Wheat
3d. Wheat	or,	3d. Winter-fallow and oats, with artificial feeds
4th. Oats		N. B. This will do tolerably well.
5th. Oats and graſs-feeds		

Or, 1ſt. Teazles
  2d. Wheat   } This is a pretty good courſe.
  3d. Beans
  4th. Oats.

---

* An acre of good turnips will (between the months of November and March) maintain one hundred ſheep ſix weeks, and an acre of cabbages two months. An acre alſo of good turnip-rooted cabbages, or an acre of Swediſh turnip, will maintain one hundred ſheep through the trying month of March.

It is ſuppoſed that a little hay be given with the roots.

On the Red Earth,

1ft. Oats on the lay   4th. Oats
2d. Summer-fallow   5th. Oats
3d. Wheat   6th. Oats and grafs-feed

Sometimes the grafs feeds are fown in the fecond crop of oats after a winter fallow.

On the Stone-Brafh,

(That is, the land abounding with marl.)

1ft. Wheat   4th. Barley and clover
2d. Wheat   5th. Clover.
3d. Wheat

Of this foil and its management I fhall fpeak more fully hereafter.

Fallowing is generally practifed in all thofe foils; for as turnips are little known, the farmers are obliged to have occafional recourfe thereunto to clean their land, made foul by fucceffive corn crops.

CROPS COMMONLY CULTIVATED.

WHEAT generally fown after a fummer fallow, fometimes after beans; but in confequence of inattention to the hoeing and cleaning the bean crops, the wheat is fo choaked with weeds, that this rotation is on the decline. It is the general practice to manure for wheat either with lime, dung, or the fheep-fold.

The laft produces the beft corn. Many forts of wheat are fown, and each has its advocates. In the vales, and on ftrong clay-land, the *cone* or *bearded* wheat takes the lead;—next to that, the *white* and *red hoar* or *velvet wheat*—the *brazil*—the *white Holland,* and *red lammas.* On the hills, and on all expofed fituations, the *red ftraw,* which differs

from

from the red lammas, inafmuch as every bloffom is of a purple colour. Moft attentive farmers prepare their feed by fteeping it in water, mixed with a fufficient quantity of falt or brine to fwim an egg, ftirring it well and fkimming off the light and defective grains, and afterwards drying it with hot lime; this is found a never-failing preventative of the fmut. The feed is always fown broadcaft, after the rate of two and half or three Winchefter bufhels per acre, and moft commonly under furrow, on fix-feet ridges. It is weeded in the fpring, and but feldom has any top-dreffing.

The method of harrowing and threfhing has been already explained. The produce varies from twelve to thirty bufhels per acre.

BARLEY.—Excepting the ftone-brafh or marl foil, there is very little land in this diftrict favourable to the culture of barley.

OATS may be confidered as the principal fpring crop, and, though fown on a corn ftubble, is generally productive. The quantity of feed fix bufhels.

The time of fowing March and April,* and the produce from thirty to fifty bufhels per acre.

---

* Few farmers agree in opinion refpecting early or late fowing, and perhaps no fixed time can with propriety be eftablifhed. The fuccefs, or otherwife, depends fo much on fortuitous circumftances, fuch as, the wetnefs or dryorfs of the feafon, the temperature of the air, both at the time of fowing and after, that what is fucceffful one year is quite the contrary the next.

The following rules may, I think, be fafely followed: not to fow wheat before the month of September, nor later than the beginning of November.

Not to fow till the ground is perfectly moiftened, and made clofe and firm by rain.

After the middle of February, whenever the land devoted to fpring crops is dry and healthy, begin planting beans, and fowing oats; and under the fame circumftances let all your barley be in the ground before the middle of April. J. B.

Rye and Buck-Wheat scarcely known.

Beans and Pease are sometimes sown broadcast, and sometimes planted; the latter is confidered as the best method.

Vetches are not cultivated so much as they ought.

TEASELS.

In the parishes of Wrington, Blagdon, Ubly, Compton-Martin, and Harptry, teasels are much cultivated. The head of this plant, which is compofed of well-turned vegetable hooks, is ufed in drefling of cloth; and the manufacturers of this county and Wilts are, for the most part, supplied from thefe parishes. Large quantities are alfo fent (by water conveyance from Briftol) into Yorkshire.

As this is a plant not generally known, I will defcribe its culture.

The moft favourable foil is a ftrong rich clay, or what is generally denominated good wheat land.

Sometimes an old ley is broke up, and fometimes a wheat-ftubble; the feed is fown, after the rate of two pecks per acre, in the month of April. During the fummer the land is worked over three or four times with long narrow fpades to deftroy the weeds.

In the month of November, if the plants are too thick, they are drawn out to fill up vacancies, and the plants are fet at a foot diftance. If, after this thinning, too many plants remain, another field is prepared, into which they are tranfplanted; but thofe plants which are never removed produce the beft heads.

At the next fpring and enfuing fummer the land is worked over three or four times with the narrow fpades, by which it is kept thorough clean, and the plants earthed up. This is called fpeddling.

In

In the month of July the uppermost heads begin to blossom, and as soon as the blossom falls, they are ripe. The gathering is performed at three different times. A man, with a knife made for the purpose, cuts the heads which are ripe, and ties them up in handfuls. After a fortnight he goes over the ground again, and at a third cutting the business is compleated. On the day of cutting they are carried into a house, and if the air be clear, they are taken out daily and exposed to the sun till they are compleatly dry; but great care must be taken that no rain falls on them.

The crop is very hazardous. A wet season rots them, particularly when there is much rain at the time of blossoming.

In the year 1792 there were few worth harvesting. The crop this year is but indifferent. When dry they are separated into three different parts, called kings, middlings, and scrubs; and are, after that, made into packs, containing of kings nine thousand heads, and of middling twenty thousand. The scrubs are but of little value. The average price is forty shillings per pack; and sometimes the produce is fifteen or sixteen packs an acre, at other times a total blank. There is an amazing inequality in the produce of different plants; some stocks will send forth one hundred heads, others not more than three or four.

Should not great attention therefore be paid to the selection of seed, namely, by taking it from those plants which appear to be most prolifick? This, however, is not done, but the seed is taken indiscriminately from the whole crop.

As the goodness of the crop chiefly depends on the care taken to keep the land free from weeds, leaving the plants at proper distances, and earthing them up well; and as most of the common workmen will pay more attention to their own than to another person's interest, it frequently happens that

a partnership

a partnerſhip is formed between maſter and man. The former finds ground and ploughing, and the latter feed and
labour.

At harveſt the crop is divided, and each party takes a
moiety.

The expence and produce of teaſels may be thus eſtimated
per acre.

			£.	s.	d.
To two years' rent	—	—	— 3	0	0
To ploughing	—	—	—— 0	15	0
To workmen's labour	—	—	— 3	15	0
To making out in bundles, tying together, and					
teaſel-bands, 2s. per pack	—	—	0	14	0
			8	4	0
		Profit	5	16	0
			£ 14	0	0

BY AVERAGE PRODUCE.

Seven packs, at 40s.   —   —   — 14 0 0

Tithe and taxes excepted: the firſt of which is generally
compounded for at 5s. per acre.

The working with the ſpade can only be done to advantage by the men accuſtomed to it, who are become, by
habit, ſo dexterous in the uſe of this implement, that they
will even thin out a crop of carrots.

The common hoe has been tried, and though in the hand
of a compleat turnip-hoer, it was not found to anſwer.

After the crop wheat is ſown, on one ploughing, and ſeldom fails of a good produce; ſo that it may not be quite
fair to charge the teaſels with two years' rent.

Few ſoils will bear frequent repetitions of this crop; and
the farmer finds it his intereſt to devote newly broken-up
land to this culture.   WOAD.

WOAD.

This is an article of cultivation, which, being important, as it relates to the woollen manufactory, must not be omitted. It is raised principally in the neighbourhood of Keynsham, and its quality is much esteemed.

The farmers who raise it have an opinion that the parish of Keynsham is particularly favourable to the growth and perfection of it; but this is most likely a vulgar error, for experiments are attested of as good crops elsewhere. The soil must be strong and good where it flourishes; it delights most in a deep fat loam, of a dark colour, which must have so much sand as to admit of easy pulverization. As the excellence of woad consists in its size, and the succulency of its leaf, it requires careful management as well as a rich soil. It is most commonly sown on land fresh broken up, and on narrow ridges.

The first ploughing should be against winter; the second in the spring, when the ridges should be formed; a third in April; and the last in May or June, just before the sowing of the seed.* In the intervals of the ploughing, harrowing should take place, to destroy all weeds.

The seed is sometimes sown by the best farmers in drills, for which purpose the surface should be harrowed very fine and level. The plants, in a moist season, appear in a fortnight, and in two or three weeks after are fit to hoe; they should be hoed out clean, to the distance of about six inches at least; some prefer a greater distance. In this neighbourhood, hand-weeding and thinning are generally used; and at the employ, women and children earn very high wages, especially since a cotton manufactory has been introduced in the

---

* Frequently woad is sown on ley ground, and on one ploughing, the surface being well harrowed.

parish.

parifh. The fuccefs of the crops depends much on the
hoeing and weeding, fo as to keep the ground frefh and clean.
Thus managed, three or four crops or gatherings will be
produced in fucceffion; but the firft two are the beft. The
time of gathering is determined by the full growth of the
leaves, and the firft appearance of change of colour at the
extremities; and this rule of courfe governs the fucceeding
crops.

The leaves are cut by hand, and gathered into bafkets by
women and children, who carry them to a very deep large
cart at the edge of the field. After two cuttings, the crop is
fuffered to go to feed for the next year, if feed be wanted;
but if only one crop be taken, the feed will be the finer.
When the pods turn of a dark colour, the feed is deemed
ripe. The ftalks fhould then be reaped like wheat, and
fpread abroad; and if the weather be favourable, the feed
will be fit for threfhing in four or five days.

When the green crops are carted home, the plant is
thrown into a mill, conftructed with a heavy iron ribbed
roller, fomething like that which is ufed for bruifing bark
and other fubftances; by this procefs it is cut and bruifed
to a pulp. It is then laid in fmall heaps, preffed clofe and
fmooth; and as the cruft formed on the outfide cracks, it is
clofed again to preferve the ftrength of the fubftance. After
lying about a fortnight in this ftate, the heaps are broken
up, the outfide worked into the mafs, and the whole formed
by the hand, and fometimes by wooden moulds, into oval
balls, which are then dried on hurdles, under a fhed expofed
to the fun.

They turn black, or of a dark-brown, on the outfide,
when well manufactured, and are valued in proportion to
their fpecific weight and a purplifh caft in the infide. Thus
they are fold to the dyer; and it is fcarcely neceffary to add
further,

further, that the ufe of this article in dying confifts in forming the ground of the indigo blue. The crop is generally
a profitable one. The quantity per acre near a ton and half.
The nett profit of courfe muft be governed by the goodnefs and price of the article. But it feems, on an average,
to be fo lucrative a culture, that few farmers who can raife it
ever difcontinue the practice. It however exhaufts the
land exceedingly, and, more than two years crops muft not in
general be taken. To this crop fucceed wheat and beans.*

POTATOES.

The rapid extenfion of the cultivation of this root can
only be equalled by its general utility as a food both for man
and beaft. Thirty or forty years ago it was an extraordinary
thing to fee an acre of potatoes in one fpot, and in one man's
poffeffion; now there are many parifhes in this diftrict which
can produce fifty acres. Nay, the writer of this report has
grown thirty or forty acres per year, for a fucceffion of years;
and once he had upwards of one hundred acres in one year.

* About forty years ago woad was cultivated in the neigbbourhood
of Mells; and there was in the parifh a horfe-mill for grinding, and
fheds for drying it, the property of one HARVEY, who was more generally known by the appellation of the Woadman, than his own fur-
name. Since his death it has been entirely difcontinued.

From whence this man originally came is unknown, but moft probably from fome part where this plant was in ufual culture. Small
plots of teazels, hops, &c. are fometimes feen in villages far diftant from
thofe parts where they are raifed on a large fcale. Hence one is led to
obferve the attachment which moft men have to the local hufbandry of
the diftrict in which they are born and brought up, and the confequent
difficulty of introducing a new fyftem of agriculture into any place.
The perfon migrating carries his attachments and habits with him,
whilft the neighbours, where he fettles, are unconcerned, or perhaps
contemptuous fpectators of his proceedings; and though they fee him
flourish and do well, are fcarce ever induced to relinquifh their old
ways and imitate his example. R. P.

The

The foil moſt favourable is a rich ſandy loam, newly broke up, and of a looſe texture. The ſorts cultivated are, the *kidney*, *white Scotch*, *magpie*, *rough red*, *purple*, and *ſilver-ſkin*. Rotten horſe-dung is conſidered as the beſt manure; next to that, hog's dung; and after that, all ſorts of farm-yard dung.

Lime, marl, ſoaper's aſhes, or rags, make the potatoes ſcabby. The ſeaſon of planting is April or May, and the quantity planted per acre from five to eight ſacks, (240lb.) The ſeed ſhould be changed every two years, and *large* cuttings uſed from your *largeſt* and *fineſt* potatoes. Whole potatoes have been tried, and found not to anſwer. There are various methods of planting, but they may be reduced to two, viz. the drill and the promiſcuous.

If labourers are plenty, the promiſcuous method is ſuppoſed to be the beſt. In this way the land is thrown into beds, five feet wide; intervals or alleys three feet, which are dug and thrown on to the beds.

The ſets are placed one foot apart. Let the ſeaſon be ever ſo wet, the potatoes in this way lie dry. In hoeing* alſo, acceſs is had to the plants without treading on them. They are not ſo liable to be injured by rooks; and ſuch a putrid fermentation is excited by the cloſe thick ſhade of the haulm, that the land is more meliorated, and the weeds more compleatly ſuffocated and deſtroyed than in any other method. In regard to expence there is no great difference, for in this way it may be done for a guinea an acre, and in the drill method it will coſt at leaſt twelve ſhillings. The ſame reaſoning weighs ſtill ſtronger in reſpect to taking up: dexterous labourers, by thruſting their ſpades under the po-

* In hoeing, be particularly careful to cut out all plants which appear curled in the leaf.

tatoes, avoid cutting the roots. They also, in digging, separate the *small* from the *large*. They pulverize the soil more: they can dig clean, though the land be wet: and, on the whole, the expence of digging will not exceed that of ploughing out, more than *ten shillings* an acre. If the crop be a good one, the separating the small potatoes from the large will cost more than this difference. The produce varies from fifty to one hundred and twenty sacks (24lb. each) an acre; and the general price, as human food, is from four shillings to seven shillings per sack; and on particular occasions they have been sold at ten shillings.

When dug, they are secured in pits, and if common care and attention be bestowed, they are preserved in this way through the most severe winter, without injury; but they will shrink in respect to measure about one sack in twenty.

From a series of experiments made by the writer of this report, and communicated through the channel of the Bath Society's Papers, it appears that their value, when applied to the fatting of hogs, could not be made to exceed two shillings and six-pence, or three shillings, per sack, of 240lb.: and from other experiments since made, it is probable, that no greater value can be affixed to them if applied to the sustenance of any other stock. However, this should be no discouragement, for on good land, and with good management, they may be grown for one shilling and six-pence per sack, and will furnish the farmer with a certain supply of food in those months wherein he is most distressed.

Many object to the cultivation of this root *on a large scale*, considering it in the light of a great exhauster. If the produce of any crop, so productive as this is, be sold from the farm, and consumed at so great a distance that no return can be made, I will acknowledge that such must be the effect; but if potatoes are consumed on the premises, the return of

manure,

manure, from the confumption of *one* acre, will be fufficient for *two* or *three*; and as the potatoe crop ought always to be highly manured, no deficiency need be feared in the fubfequent crops of corn, graffes, &c. particularly if wheat be banifhed as a fucceeding crop, and barley or oats fubftituted in its place.*

It is now a common practice, inftead of boiling, to drefs potatoes by fteam, and by fo doing, the quality is rendered more farinaceous, and a confiderable faving is made in the article of fuel.

---

* The reafon why wheat frequently fails after potatoes, is becaufe the frequent hoeings and digging render the land fo light and porous, that it is more fubject to the ravages of the grub, earth-worm, &c.; befide, in cold and expofed fituations, the fowing is generally protracted till the month of November, which alone is fufficient to check the practice.

N. B. The writer has known thirty-two fucceffive crops of potatoes from the fame field, and the produce as good at the latter part of the term as at the beginning. This will puzzle the theorift, with his *peculiar fubftances of nutrition.*

A large cow, tied up a month after calving, ate 2cwt. and 18lb. of hay in one week, and on the enfuing week, being given four bufhels (Winchefter) of potatoes, the confumption of hay was reduced to 3qrs. and 26lb. It appears, therefore, that a fack of potatoes is equal to 1 cwt. of hay. The quantity of milk was increafed by the potatoes, but it was thinner in quality.

CHAPTER

CHAPTER VIII.

Sect. 1. *Natural Meadows and Pastures.*

IT has been already obferved, that the grafs land of this diftrict greatly preponderates; and if it be not chilled by too much moifture, it may boaft of almoft a perpetual verdure.

On the rich marfh land near the Briftol Channel, the grazing fyftem prevails. In the vicinity of Briftol and Bath, the fcythe is in conftant ufe; and at a greater diftance nothing is fcarcely feen but the milking-pail. To which ever of thefe purpofes the land is devoted, its bounties are not niggardly difpenfed. If we view them comparatively, the hay fyftem is perhaps the moft injurious to the land, and the leaft productive of profit. This article feldom exceeds three pounds per ton; and if we confider the rifk in making, the expence of carriage, the lofs of time, and above all, the declining value of the eftate fo occupied, few arguments can be wanted to prove the impolicy of the fyftem. In fhort, I never knew a hay-felling farmer get rich.

Sect. 2. *Artificial Graffes.*

On the ftone-brafh and freeftone-grit foil, *fainfoine* takes the lead; and though the feed is very expenfive, the quantity and quality of its produce, together with its durability, make an ample return of profit, particularly if fown when the land is clean.

Next to fainfoin, *rye-grafs,** *marl grafs,* and white *Dutch clover,* are in deferved repute when the land is intended to remain

---

* The Agricultural Body is much indebted to Mr. Peacey, of Northleach, Gloucefterfhire, for his careful felection and diffemination

remain some years in grass; but when it is intended to be ploughed again in the course of a year or two, *broad-clover* is preferred to all other artificial grasses.

Perhaps there are few things in husbandry more difficult to be accomplished than that of restoring worn-out arable to a good pasture. A few hints on this subject may not be unacceptable.

The first step is to extirpate from the land all noxious weeds. This may be done by a compleat winter and summer-fallow; or, in place of the summer-fallow, by a crop of potatoes, well manured, and kept perfectly clean, and followed by winter vetches, fed off in the spring.

At the latter end of May, or beginning of June, sow one bushel of buck-wheat per acre, and when that is up, and in rough leaf, harrow in (choosing, if possible, moist weather) two bushels of hay seed, collected from the best meadow hay, half a bushel of rye-grass, four pounds of marl grass, and four pounds of white Dutch clover. The buck is intended principally as a screen to the grass seeds.

If, therefore, the harrowing should pull up some of the plants, so much the better. A thick crop is not desirable. After the buck-wheat is harvested, which will be some time in September, let the field be hayned, or shut up for the winter; and let it be fed the next summer with sheep, or any kind of cattle, except horses; the latter animal will tear up the young plants with his teeth.

---

of the true perennial rye-grass, which is in every respect so much superior to the common rye-grass, sold by seedsmen, as to justify the warmest recommendation to the practical and discriminating husbandmen. Some people have objected to this grass, under an idea that it is not so palatable as the common rye-grass. Stock it whilst young, and put double the quantity of sheep that you generally do, and this objection will vanish. J. B.

Should

Should this pasture, in the course of three or four years, decline in fineness of herbage, and become coarse and rough, which is frequently the case, give it a top-dressing of lime, or lime mixed with pond or ditch earth, or the scraping of a road made with lime-stone, or marl; and if neither of these can be procured, with coal or soapers' ashes, or any kind of compost; and two years after either of the above manures are administered, serve out some good meadow hay on it in the months of January and February, and then give it a compleat covering of rotten dung.

By this method a good permanent pasture may be obtained. If the ground so laid down be intended for *pleasure* ground, omit the rye-grass, and add to the natural grass seeds.

SECT. 3. *Hay Harvest.*

In the management and curing of the natural grass, the inhabitants of this district, particularly in those parts where it is intended for sale, are very attentive.

Women or children are employed to spread the grass after the mower. About the middle of the day it is turned, and in the afternoon put into small cocks. Next day it is again spread with great care, shaking it high up in the air, and separating as much as possible every blade. In the course of the second day, it is twice turned; and early in the afternoon, whilst the *sun's rays are strong and powerful, and the hay warm,* it is again cocked in heaps, about double as large as those of the preceding evening. On the third day it undergoes a similar process in regard to the spreading and turning; and if the weather be very fine, and the crop not exceeding thirty cwt. per acre, it will be fit for stacking;—if otherwise, it should be put into large cocks, and left till the fourth morning, avoiding on all ocasions stacking late in the evening,

evening, or in a strong dew. Should the weather be difficult, and the hay-making be interrupted by frequent showers, or by some days rain, make a point of drying it thoroughly, and then *salt it* after the rate of a peck of salt to a ton of hay; this will make it palatable to the cattle. On all accounts, avoid making a chimney in the stack, for this will inevitably make the hay mouldy and unwholsome.

Should it heat too much, and be in danger of taking fire, *turn the mow* before the heat is too far advanced. The expences of hay-making varies from eight to twelve shillings per acre.

In making artificial hay, the small cocks into which it is got the second day, are frequently turned and shook up, but *not spread*; and it requires two or three days more than natural hay before it is fit for the large mow.

N. B. One cubic yard of hay, in a mow well made and not overheated, will weigh on an average of the whole mow about thirteen cwt.

SECT. 4. *Feeding.*

The upland pastures of this district have seldom a sufficient bite of grass till May-day.

Two acres, worth thirty shillings, per acre are necessary to summer a cow well, and one acre and half for her winter provender. As it is the general practice to serve their cows during the winter with hay in the fields, the land is frequently in wet seasons so pounded, as to be unproductive great part of the summer.

In summer feeding, attentive farmers have the dung which falls from the animal scraped up and wheeled into heaps, and the thistles and rough spots frequently mown.

They also make a point of excluding horses and sheep from their cow pastures. And when their mown ground is

fit

fit to be flocked, they hayn their fummer leaze, fo as to
have a good fupply of rough grafs or rowen in the winter.
They alfo mow and feed alternately, by which means the
beft forts of graffes are preferved and encouraged.

A RECEIPT for making HAY-TEA.

BOIL about a handful of hay in three gallons of water,
(and fo in proportion for a greater or fmaller quantity) or
if the water be poured boiling hot on the hay, it will anfwer
nearly as well,

Give it to the cattle and horfes to drink when cold; or if
the cattle and horfes are any ways ill, and under cover, give
it them blood warm. This drink is fo extremely nutritive,
that it nourifhes the cattle aftonifhingly, replenifhes the
udders of the cow with a prodigious quantity of milk,
makes the horfes ftale plentifully, and keeps them healthy and
ftrong; and by this method one trufs or hundred of hay
will go as far as eight or ten otherwife would do.

The cattle and horfes do not feem to like it at firft; but if
they are kept till they are very thirfty, they will drink freely
of it ever afterwards.

The hay, after being ufed as before-mentioned and dried,
may be ufed as litter for horfes and cattle, make very good
manure, and fave ftraw, which will be a confiderable advantage, efpecially where there is a fcarcity of ftraw.

N. B. By a handful of hay, is meant as much as a perfon can grafp in his hand from a parcel of loofe hay.

And it is prefumed and wifhed, as the above method is
fo very eafy and fafe, that no perfon who has cattle, cows,
horfes, or fheep, will neglect to try it.

CHAPTER IX.

GARDENS AND ORCHARDS.

THE horticulture of this diſtrict is ſufficiently under-ſtood and practiſed, to ſupply the cities of Briſtol and Bath with a great variety and abundance of culinary pro-ductions; but there are no remarkable inſtances of ſkill in the exhibition of early field crops.

In reſpect to nurſeries, the Rev. J. BROOKES, of Cold-Hinton, takes the lead; he has eight or ten acres under a very regular ſyſtem of management. The annual expence of labour in a nurſery amounts to about twenty-five pounds per acre.

The whole diſtrict is full of orchards, which let from three pounds to ſix pounds per acre; and the fruit produced at the northern baſe of Mendip hills, viz. at Langford, Burrington, Rickford, Blagdon, Ubly, Compton-Martin, and Harptry, affords a cyder ſtrong, palatable, and highly eſteemed as a wholeſome *table* liquor. Many of theſe orchards have a northern aſpect, and are ſheltered from the violence of the weſterly winds; and it is noticed, that orchards, ſo ſituated, are the moſt regular and uniform bearers.

The favourite apple, both as a table and cyder fruit, is the *Court of Wick Pippin*; taking its name from the ſpot where it was firſt produced. It originated from the pip or ſeed of the golden pippin, and may be conſidered as a beautiful va-riety of that fruit. In ſhape, colour, and flavour, it has not its ſuperior: the tree is large, handſome, and ſpreading, and

a very

a very luxuriant bearer.* On the whole, it cannot be too strongly recommended.

Mr. Good, who occupies a large farm in Hutton, has a method of making cyder, which it may not be amiss to describe. The apples are ground by a horse-mill. The pummice is then wrung in hair bags; after which it is put into a tub and chopped. It is then ground over again, and made into a cheese, which stands in the press all night.

In the morning the press is strained as tight as it will bear by a lever or cap-staff; by these means, the cheese is made so dry, that it is cut into narrow strips, tied up in faggots, and burnt. He can make one hogshead upon eight more than by the common method. Two men make and tun five hogsheads in a day, and the horse will grind the apples in three hours.

Query. Is not the quality of the cyder injured by such close expression?

The grinding apples by a horse-mill saves much manual labour, and expedites the business of cyder-making. But whether Mr. Good's method may be the best, or most lucrative, is a matter of question, for what is gained in quantity is lost in quality; the liquor procured by the second forcible expression being certainly weaker than the first, and being mixed with it, must reduce the whole to a lower staple. No water-cyder can be made after so strong a pressure of the pummice; and as, in the common way, two hogsheads of good water-cyder can be made after seven of the best, the loss seems more than the gain.

* Grafts from this tree may be had by application to the reporter; and a sample of the fruit has been sent to Sir John Sinclair for the observation of the curious in this article.

Notwithstanding

Notwithſtanding the apparent utility of extenſive and productive orchards, many conſiderate and ſenſible men have heſitated in giving their unqualified aſſent to this ſentiment; alledging, that a plenty of cyder is the forerunner of idleneſs, drunkenneſs, and debauchery, not only among the lower claſs, but alſo among the yeomanry themſelves, who at theſe times ſpend ſucceſſive days and nights in toping and guzzling at each others' houſes. We ought not, however, to confound the abuſe of a thing with its intrinſick value.

CHAPTER

CHAPTER X.

WOODS AND PLANTATIONS.

THE country is but partially wooded, and, on account of the demand from the collieries, the wood is but very irregularly cut. Syftematic plantation is but little ftudied.

Kingfwood covers about two hundred and thirty acres. The timber is chiefly oak, but does not get to any large fize; the woods being, for the moft part, fituate at the declivity of the hills, where there is but little depth of earth. The underwood is cut for wreaths or faggots. The valleys are in general richly laden with elm, which grows fpontaneoufly in the hedge-rows, and gets to a good fize. The method practifed here of lopping off the fide branches, to what is called a befom-head, cannot be too much execrated. It is deftructive to the growth of timber, and by leffening the agitation produced by winds, deprives it of what may be deemed its falutary exercife. The effect of cutting off the lower branches is a premature delay, which firft takes place in the top of the tree, a general check is given to the circulation of the fap, and it reduces the tree nearly to the ftate of a pollard.*

On the northern declivity of Mendip hills are fome very good coppice woods; the principal are, Blagdon, Hafel, and Ubly, containing in the whole about 150 acres.

---

* This is not the worft confequence of the befom-head. Philofophers are now agreed, that trees in full verdure receive a great portion of their nourifhment from the atmofphere, by the abforbent veffels of their leaves; hence appears the impolicy of depriving a tree of that head which nature intended fhould affift in bringing the body to perfection. A. C.

These

These woods are very romantick and picturesque, and being secured from the south-west breezes, the growth is very rapid, and the profit greater than any will believe who have not had experience thereof; beside, these profits may be made annual, and are in themselves more certain than any other produce. You have only to divide a coppice of forty-eight acres into twelve parts, that is, four acres per year, twelve years growth. The more ash in these coppices the more valuable, as the poles are very saleable at the coal-pits; and I have known many instances of an acre producing in value sixteen pounds net after the expences of cutting, carriage, &c. have been deducted. This is nearly twenty-eight shillings per acre per annum, for the whole forty-eight acres, besides the accumulating value of timber-trees. It is more profitable to cut coppice-wood every twelve years, than to let it remain longer. On the southern declivity of Mendip hills, there are also some coppice woods, *Stoke wood* the principal; but these being exposed to the western breezes, are not so productive.

In the eastern part of this district there are also some large and productive woods, such as Mells, Leigh, Edford, Harwich, Compton, Camely, &c. these being near the coal-works are very valuable; interspersed also are many beautiful plantations, which are not only an ornament to the respective seats to which they belong, but are in themselves a fertile source of annual profit.

On land properly situated, no speculation can be more profitable or more pleasing than planting; the only objection is, the length of time required to bring it to perfection; but surely this ought not to have much weight, as the benefit must accrue either to the planter or his heirs; and certainly there is no way so easy of raising fortunes for younger children as by planting.

.The

The ancient foreſt of Selwood (on the verge of which the town of Frome ſtands) appears to have compriſed a woody vale of about twenty thouſand acres, about eighteen thouſand of which are now cleanſed and converted into paſture and arable land, with a ſmall portion of meadow; the remainder continuing in a ſtate of coppice-wood. The chief ſorts of timber in theſe coppices are oak and aſh, which, though not of large growth, are very good of their kinds, and find profitable markets in the neighbourhood; the oak ſelling from fifty ſhillings to three pounds ſixteen ſhillings per ton, and aſh from forty-five ſhillings to three pounds. The underwood is chiefly hazel, aſh, alder, withy, and birch; ſome of which, at eighteen or twenty years growth, ſell as high as ſixteen pounds per acre. To ſtate the profit of theſe coppices in a clearer light, I would remark, that the annual value per acre, in timber and underwood, (I ſpeak of thoſe coppices which lie towards the northern end of Selwood) is from fifteen to thirty ſhillings. Much of the open land within the limits of this ancient foreſt does not net more than ten or twelve ſhillings per acre.*

---

* Digging holes one foot and half ſquare and four inches deep, for planting young trees, may be done for two-pence per ſcore, if the land be not very ſtony; but the beſt method of planting trees is on the ſod, covering the roots with other ſods inverted, that is, graſs to graſs.   J. B.

CHAPTER

CHAPTER XI.

WASTE LANDS.

IN this diſtrict there are many commons uninclofed; the principal of which are, Broadfield-Down near Wrington, and Lanſdown near Bath. The former contains two thoufand five hundred acres, and is for the moft part a good foil, deep in earth, and eafily ploughed.

Surely the inclofing and cultivating a tract like this, fituate only eight miles diftant from the city of Briftol, could not fail of being a great advantage to the proprietors; particularly as it abounds with excellent lime-ftone, and the coalpits are only a few miles diftant.

Lanſdown comprehends nearly one thoufand acres; but as the foil is thin, and the furface perfectly fmooth, and remarkable for its excellence in feeding fheep, to which it imparts a delicate flavour, it might not be prudent to break it up, efpecially as it affords a luxurious and beautiful ride to the fojourners in Bath.

Inclofing has been of long ftanding in moft of thefe parts; many have exemplified an advance of rent more than two-thirds. The produce in many inftances has been, of wheat thirty bufhels, barley forty, oats fifty, and beans from thirty to forty per acre.

Increafe of population in proportion.

Befides the above, there are feveral thoufand acres of moor-land in what is called the North-Marfh; the prefent condition of which is difgraceful to the owners. Moft of thefe moors confift of a rich fertile pafture, overcharged with ftagnant water many months in the year, which inconvenience might eafily be removed by the methods before fuggefted.

CHAPTER

CHAPTER XII.

IMPROVEMENTS.

SECT. I. *Draining.*

NOT fo much attention has been paid to the draining of land as the object undoubtedly requires; but in fome cafes, where inclofures have been accompanied with a weeping furface, great improvements have been made by flone-draining. The acclivities from the vales are for the moft part of this quality and complexion; and if the fprings, which iffue from the fides of the hills, were taken off at their head by judicious drains, and diverted into a proper channel, the value of the land would be advanced at leaft one-third.

Main drains two feet and half deep and two feet wide, in a heavy ftrong clay foil, may be dug for one fhilling and fix-pence per rope, (twenty feet) viz. nine-pence per rope digging the drain and placing the ftones, three-pence per cart-load quarring the ftones, and three-pence per load halling. Each rope will require one cart-load and half of ftones.

Small drains, leading to the main drain, may be executed for ten-pence per rope (twenty feet.)

SECT. 2. *Paring and Burning.*

Burn-baiting, that is, cutting off the turf, drying it, and piling it in heaps, and afterwards burning it to afhes, has been tried, but no fenfible good effect, either immediate or diftant, having been experienced, the practice is relinquifhed;

K 2 and

and I rather think this procefs is beft calculated for cold, rufhy, and heathy grounds, of little or no value.

The effect of bum-baiting, even on lands beft adapted to this procefs, does not laft more than three or four years; and if followed up with fucceffive corn crops, the ftrength of the land is fo exhaufted by the forced fertility, that a reft of eight or ten years is neceffary to prepare for its repetition. If burn-baiting be practifed, it fhould be for turnips, after which only one crop of barley or oats fhould be taken, and artificial graffes fown therewith. If this rotation of crops be adopted, I fee no reafon why lands to which the manure is congenial, fhould be wholly denied the advantages of the practice.

A great deal in thefe inftances depends upon the fkill and judgment of the farmer. If he be wantonly debarred from the ufe of a valuable manure, he is injured; and if, on the other hand, he ufes it without difcretion, his landlord fuffers, and the moft indefatigable induftry will not fave himfelf ultimately from lofs, and perhaps ruin.

SECT. 3. *Manuring.*

MARL.

The parifhes of Midfummer-Norton, Stratton-on-the-Fofs, Kilmerfdon, Radftock, Timfbury, High-Littleton, Farmborough, Paulton, Ston-Eafton, Binegar, and Chilcompton, comprehend a diftrict of land, part of which is rendered remarkably fertile by the application of marl.[*]

The foil confifts of an earth more or lefs loamy, of a mixed colour, between brown and red, with a prevalence of

---

[*] Marl alfo may be found at Queen-Charlton, Chewton-Keynfham, and Burnett.

one

one or the other; very ſtony, reſembling that kind of ſoil uſually denominated corn-grit, and naturally ſo barren, that when in common field, at the beginning of the preſent century, the lands were not ſet at more than three ſhillings and ſix-pence per ſtatute acre.

By a moderate computation, this ſoil may be ſaid to occupy, in the pariſhes before enumerated, an average proportion of at leaſt one-third. At a variable depth from the ſurface an inexhauſtible ſtore of black marl is conſtantly found, which, from properties equally ſingular as to fertility and duration, has advanced the lands from three ſhillings and ſix-pence to one pound eleven ſhillings and ſix-pence, and ſome to two pounds per ſtatute acre; and this too with a very liberal allowance of profit to the occupier.

This valuable manure is raiſed in the ſummer at the average depth of about ſeven or eight fathom, by ſinking a pit or ſhaft of four feet diameter, the ſides whereof are ſecured by timber props, interſperſed with wreathings of bruſhwood, and it is drawn to the ſurface by means of a windlaſs and buckets.

The firſt bed of marl perforated is blue, two feet thick, of a ſtiff conſiſtence, and on repeated trials found in a comparative degree uſeleſs. Below this lies a ſtratum of ſtone, nine inches thick, and of a blue colour; next to which is found a bed of marl, from three to four feet in thickneſs, nearly horizontal, of a colour approaching to black, and, towards the lower part, of a ſhelly ſubſtance; the greater predominance whereof is found proportionably to improve its fertilizing property.

The expence of raiſing it, including that of ſinking the ſhaft, is from eight-pence to one ſhilling per cart-load of twenty-four buſhels. That, and carting out, ſpreading and bruſhing in, eighteen ſhillings per ſtatute acre.

Forty

Forty load is an ample dreffing for a ftatute acre, which,
at one fhilling per load, amounts to   £.2 0 0
Carting, fpreading, &c.   0 18 0
                                          _____
                          The whole   2 18 0
                                          _____

For which a manure is obtained that fecures a luxuriant
undiminifhed vegetation, not requiring any further affiftance for fifteen or twenty years. The generation of mofs
manifefts the declining effects of this manure. It is confidered as an indication for breaking up the old fward, which
is generally done. This developes a very curious and fingular phænomenon; namely, the marl fpread on the furface
forty or fifty years before, has only obtained the depth of
between five and fix inches, where it forms a regular, uniform, confolidated bed. Even at this depth its effects, although not exhaufted, are neverthelefs fo much impaired as
to demand its renewal. Will not this fact tend, in fome
degree, to elucidate its modus operandi?

While it remains within two or three inches of the furface, which is the cafe in fome inftances perhaps for twenty
years or more, it may be fuppofed to form a kind of pan
or refervoir for the nutritious and fructifying influences depofited by the atmofphere; which being there retained, and
in contact with the roots of the graffes, form fuch combi-
nations in the laboratory of nature as are beft adapted to
give vigour and permanence to the elementary principles of
vegetation. Thefe are evidently weakened when the marl,
by its defcent, gets below the roots of the graffes, and
thereby deprives them of the matrix, which feems to preferve the means of their nutrition and fupport. This may
account for the production and increafe of mofs on the fur
face, and the neceffity of marling afrefh, not only to impede
its propagation but to deftroy it.

                                                    It

It is obfervable that when marl is laid on this moffy fur-face, which accompanies an old fward, to avoid a courfe of tillage, the improvement is not equal to that of laying it on clover, or marl-grafs, the fecond year from the time of fowing.

An inconfiderable portion of thefe lands is employed in tillage under the following courfe of cropping:

1ft year.—Old fward ploughed up in Auguft.

. Wheat—harrowed in October and the beginning of November on one earth.

Produce—from twenty-five to thirty bufhels (eight gal-lons) per acre.

2d year. Wheat—fingle ploughing harrowed in as before.

Produce from thirty to thirty-five bufhels.

3d year. Wheat again.

Produce, from twenty-five to thirty bufhels.

Sometimes barley with or without fallow.

Produce fifty-fix bufhels.

4th year. Peafe with two or three ploughings.

Produce, from twenty to twenty-five bufhels.

Then winter-fallow as a preparation for next year.

5th year. Barley and clover or marl-grafs.

Produce, forty-eight bufhels.

6th year. Clover or marl-grafs.

When mowed, produce from thirty to forty cwt. per acre.

7th year. Clover or marl-grafs fed.

Defective and ruinous to the land as the firft three years' rotation of crops may appear, it is neverthelefs with little variation uniformly purfued; and, with little abatement of produce, is renewed for another feven years fucceffion.— Even a third is carried through by many farmers, accom-panied

panied with fallowing for some of the wheat crops, and affifting the land with a fprinkling of farm-yard manure. Even a fourth fucceffion, with lefs wheat and more barley, is carried on by a few confiderable farmers in the diftrict; but from the lightnefs of the foil, and the difficulty of keeping weeds under, the crops fail, notwithftanding a more liberal ufe of manure.

A fyftem of cropping, fo very perverfe and erroneous, carried to fuch a length on land rented at thirty or forty fhillings per acre, muft in the end involve the farmer in a yearly lofs, and cannot but aftonifh every one; more efpecially if it be recollected, that this very land is fufceptible of reftoration to its former vigour and fertility at the moderate expence of two pounds eighteen fhillings per acre.†

Marl grafs* is the fpontaneous production of the marl land. It was firft noticed and collected fifty or fixty years ago by a Mr. JAMES, who lived on a farm belonging to the Marquis of BATH, in the parifh of Chilcompton. By his affiduity in preferving and propagating the feed, in the courfe of a few years it became common, and has been confidered ever fince as a valuable fubftitute for red or broad clover,

---

† As every acre of land improved by marl gives a permanent addition to the national ftock, premiums for the difcovery of it, where it has not yet been found, and for the application of it, where it is known to exift, but has not been ufed, might very probably be attended with more real and durable benefit to the community, than a multitude of others which are annually propofed by the different Agricultural Societies eftablifhed in various parts of the kingdom. Covenants might alfo be inferted in leafes, obliging the leffor and leffee, on proper confiderations, the former to be at the expence of raifing, the latter of carting and fpreading the marl on any given number of acres that may be agreed on. R.P.

* Trifolium Alpeftre.

to which it bears rather a ftriking analogy; with, however, this difference, that it will continue much longer in the land.

When the marl lands are laid down to graffes, trefoil or white Dutch clover is fown in the proportion of feven pounds to twenty pounds of marl-grafs or broad-clover, which enriches, diverfifies, and by its early vegetation and blofloming, produces a carpet the moft beautiful and picturefque that can well be imagined.

Marl has been repeatedly tried on the loofer red earth lands, and on freeftone grit foil, in different parts of the diftrict, without producing any good effect. It has alfo been carried fome miles out of the diftrict, and applied to the light red earth of the lime-ftone lands, with no better fuccefs.

The contiguity of the parifhes to Bath and Briftol not exceeding a mean diftance of nine miles, acceffible by good roads, and which afford markets of almoft unlimited confumption; the luxuriance of the pafturage, the early vegetation in the fpring, all concur to render dairies a very eligible, as it is a general mode of occupation; yet notwithftanding on the larger farms, if a greater proportion were devoted to tillage, 'fince they produce wheat and barley of excellent quality, and require, under a judicious routine of crops, little manure but the firft marling for fifteen or twenty years, both landlord and tenant would derive confiderable advantage therefrom.

The landlord might levy an additional rent of ten fhillings per acre on the lands fo converted to arable, under a leafe of twenty-one years, compelling the tenants to drefs with marl four years previous to the expiration of the term, by which means they would be left in a very good ftate of proof.

The

The tenant would be amply repaid his advance of rent, not only by the general certainty and superabundance of his crops, but by the application of the farm-yard manure, arising therefrom, to his red earth lands; which he may well do without injury to the former, and thereby find an equivalent, in their improved state, for the advanced rent.

Rational and well-founded as this change of management must appear to every intelligent and unprejudiced man, it has nevertheless many formidable obstacles to encounter. The landlord's groundless apprehensions of injury to his lands, under even a well-regulated course of tillage; his prepossession in favour of dairies and grazing, neither of which tend in any great degree to impoverish or exhaust the soil; the rich and beautiful complection of the surface so gratifying to the eye during the greatest part of the year; his reluctance to build or enlarge barns, stalls, &c.; the frequency of modules for tithe of cows; the easy rate of agistment, and other vicarial tithes; with his rooted aversion to the payment of corn tithes, however moderately levied; the smallness of many of the farms; and lastly, his dread of innovation on the accustomed practice of his neighbourhood, all concur to diminish the quantity of arable land. It must be admitted, that farms under one hundred pounds per ann. might not bear the expence of suitable buildings, to accommodate the plan here suggested; but since this, on every scale, would be proportioned to the size of the farm, the advance of the rent, exclusive of interest on money expended thereon, would secure to the landlord an augmentation of income deserving his notice.'

With respect to tithes, the tenant would readily submit to the increased amount, and would find more than an adequate compensation in the abundance of his crops, and the moderate expences of tillage. Yet so revolting is tithe,

though

though unaccompanied with severity in its application, as to induce the land-owner and tenant to forego a positive advantage rather than comply with its demands.

In the parish of Kilmersdon there is a species of soil usually called a freestone-grit, of a light brown colour, stiff, clayey, and abounding in stone. Underneath, at various depths, is to be found a blue marl, which, on repeated trials, has not hitherto been known to communicate any improvement. This marl is not readily soluble when exposed to the air; but retains its clay-like quality, which renders it unfit either to pervade, or incorporate with the soil. These lands are sometimes devoted to tillage; but are soon exhausted, and left to poverty and rest for seven or eight years, when a similar course of management is resumed. Present value from five to six shillings per acre.

COURSE OF CROPS.

1st year. Lay broke up in the spring. Summer fallow.

2d year. Wheat sown early in October.

Produce, twelve bushels per acre.

3d year. Oats.

Produce, sixteen or twenty bushels per acre.

No clover; the soil will not support it. If sown, it gradually declines through want of sustenance.

Here ends the cropping without manure. Mr. WALWYN, of Kilmersdon parish, fourteen or fifteen years ago tried sainfoin in this soil. The produce, from mowing four or five years successively, averaged twenty cwt. per acre. It so far exists now in some of these lands, as to keep up their value to twelve or fourteen shillings per acre. Where totally extinct, on breaking up afresh, the soil is found in better proof than in its pristine state. Notwithstanding this experiment,

accompanied

accompanied with effects so obviously beneficial, yet the example has been but very little, if at all, followed in the neighbourhood, although surrounded by several hundred acres of a similar quality. However, a gentleman of large fortune, and proprietor of the greatest part of this barren district in the same parish, has for two or three years past attempted its melioration, by summer fallowing and turnips, to some parts of which he gives four or five ploughings and harrowings. Its texture is already considerably loosened.— Barns, stalling, and farm-yards, are provided on a large scale, in a situation to command the whole. Within a reasonable distance he can procure a supply of sand and coal-ashes; a resource too valuable to be overlooked. With a relish for agricultural improvement, a practical attention to its progress, and the conveniencies before mentioned, there is little doubt, but that in the course of time he will be enabled, in no trifling degree, by a judicious system of cropping, to fertilize this very intractable soil.

LIME.

The liming system of improvement has been fully detailed in the account given of Mendip hills. Green crops are seldom ploughed in as a manure, nor are the drainings of the farm-yard collected into reservoirs as they ought to be.

Bones, rags, night-soil, horn shavings, soot, &c. which in some countries are highly esteemed, are here little regarded. In short, too much confidence is placed in the natural richness and fertility of the soil.

SECT. 4. *Weeding.*

Some attention is paid to the weeding of the wheat crop, but little to the weeding of lent corn. This branch of rural economy is too much neglected.

SECT.

SECT. 5. *Watering.*

The watering of pastures is not much known, though the advantage resulting from that practice in neighbouring counties is not questioned.

The intermixture of lands embarrasses the operation of individuals in that respect, and this seems likely to prevent a practice from becoming more general, which numerous springs and rivulets would otherwise favour.

The water issuing from Mendip hills is unfit for this purpose, carrying with it noxious mineral particles, destructive to vegetation.

More will be said of watering when we come to the southwest district of the county.

CHAPTER XIII.

LIVE STOCK.

Sect. 1. *Cows.*

AS the cows are all devoted to the dairy, preference is given to that fort which gives the moſt milk and of the beſt quality; or, in the farmer's language, to that ſtock which makes the moſt goods, whether it be butter, or cheeſe, or both; hence it follows, that in point of carcaſe they are very deficient. They are moſtly of the ſhort-horned breed; and though the fine long-horned cows of North-Wiltſhire have been tried, and ſtrongly recommended by ſome, yet the general run of dairymen are ſtrongly attached to their own breed.

As this is a ſubject of ſome magnitude, let us beſtow on it a few moments attention.

In the choice of ſtock, the buyer ſhould principally attend to the purpoſes for which that ſtock is deſigned, and to the nature and quality of his land.

If his principal object be rearing, either with a view to fat himſelf or to ſell to others, the form or ſhape of the parent ſtock ſhould firſt be regarded.

That frame of body, which is accompanied with the greateſt portion of valuable fleſh, and the leaſt offal, is to be preferred.

An aptitude to fat in youth is alſo an object of great importance. By an attention to theſe points, the farmers of Leiceſterſhire and other counties have ſo attracted the notice of emulous breeders, as to ſell their ſtock at a price

scarcely

fcarcely credible to a plain old-fafhioned farmer. But, however we may admire their care and ingenuity, does it follow that we are to be led aftray by the extravagant ideas which fome people entertain of their fuperiority? A heifer of three or four years old, which difcovers a difpofition to fat, feldom proves a good milker, and is by our farmers turned out of the dairy. Befide, I have been informed that the great breeders are frequently obliged to have the affiftance of Welch nurfes for their calves, through a deficiency of milk in the parent animal. Is this a recommendation of them to the dairyman?

As a confirmation of the idea that handfome flock are feldom good milkers, I fhall advert to the North-Devon breed, and I believe in all other refpects there is not a more valuable in the kingdom.

In that part of the kingdom, little attention is paid to cheefe or butter; but if a cow produce handfome flock, it is all that is required of her; and it frequently happens that a farmer, with ten or twelve cows, has but little more of thofe articles than is fufficient to fupply his family.

The Somerfetfhire dairymen generally keep their good cows till they are ten or twelve years old, at which time their value is reduced to four or five pounds each. A long-horned cow, at that age, might be worth eight or ten pounds; (I mean of the middling breed) here is then an apparent deficiency of four or five pounds; but when we reflect that the keeping of one is worth ten fhillings a year more than the other, the lofs is not fo apparent; and if we admit, that the fhort-horned will make half a hundred of cheefe more per year than the long-horned, the balance of profit is then in favour of the former.

I do not mean by what I have faid to detract from the merit of Mr. BAKEWELL, or other great breeders of the North.

North. I only wish to recommend a discriminating principle, and to deter the credulous farmer from *too hasty* a dereliction of principles and practices founded in experience, and to which he has been long accustomed.

I may be here told, that the foregoing premises, from which conclusions are drawn unfavourable to the long-horned cow, are delusive; that a North-country breeder would laugh at the idea of keeping a cow till she is ten years old; that at six years, or at the farthest at seven, she ought to be in the possession of the butcher.

But, coolly and calmly, ask a practical cow-keeper at what period of life a cow makes the most goods, and he will tell you between the age of six and twelve years old. I have known cows continue good milkers till they have passed their twentieth year.*

When cheese only is made, the annual produce per cow is from three to four cwt.

Many dairy farmers, in the vicinity of Bath and Bristol, make butter and half-skimmed cheese; in either way, the annual produce per cow is from eight to twelve pounds, including the calf, and profit of pigs.

From three to four acres of land will keep a cow throughout the year.

---

* The discriminating principle recommended, is a very necessary one, and deserves particular attention. It may here be observed in general, that in many parts there is a sort of cattle, as it were provincial, hardy, thriving, and well adapted to the soil on which it is bred. Let the cautious farmer furnish himself with the best of this sort which he can select, and if he must improve, as it is called, let him not lose sight of the discriminating principle, but do it with wariness and discernment. And as very little of the dairyman's profit is expected from sale of the carcase, if his cows are well kept, and yield him a good quantity of rich productive milk, it will be immaterial whether they have long horns, short horns, or any horns at all. R. P.

If

If kept on hay alone, a middle-sized cow will eat one hundred and three-quarters per week during the winter month, and on an average thirty hundred in the whole winter; this calculation is formed on a supposition that she calves between Christmas and Candlemas. If turnips or cabbages be given, she will eat, of the former two hundred, and of the latter one hundred and half in twenty-four hours, and the quantity of hay will be lessened about one half.— Heifers are put to the bull when one year and half old; and very few calves are reared for bulls or oxen, and no more of the female kind than just sufficient to keep up the stock.

Next to the selection of a proper sort, good keeping when young is of the first importance; and it has been observed, that calves, after being turned out to grass, should have but little water given them. The first winter each calf will eat about sixteen hundred of hay.

Sect. 2. *Sheep.*

In the North-East part of this district, that is, in the vicinity of Bath, a very large and good race of sheep are bred; the wethers of which are commonly folded till they are between two or three years old, and then grazed. Some of these sheep, when well fatted, run to thirty or forty pounds per quarter. Mr. MOGER, of Woolverton; Mr. DAY, of Foxcote; Mr. YOUNG, of Camerton; Mr. HOLBROOK, of Corston; and Mr. SMITH, of Twerton, are the principal breeders; and this sort of sheep, having a large quantity of tallow, is highly approved by the butchers. There is also the native Mendip breed, a sort that will thrive on the poorest soil, and fatten on such land as will scarcely keep other forts alive. Pasturage ever so dry and exposed will feed this kind. They are very hardy, and their wool fine. The

L

mutton

mutton is also excellent for the table, being full of gravy and of a rich flavour.

The large heavy loaded sheep of Leicestershire and Lincolnshire have been tried; but the great doubt lies whether this sort of sheep would bear folding; if not, they are inadmissible, as folding is the *fine qua non* of good husbandry, on the sheep and corn farms* of this district.

Under the auspices of the Bath Society, unto which his Majesty was graciously pleased to present a Spanish ram, a

---

* Some time ago the Leicestershire sheep-breeders were modest enough to express only their *doubts* of the utility of *folding* sheep, but now they do not hesitate positively to condemn the practice, and to represent it as altogether ridiculous and absurd. " It is only (say they) robbing the *pasture* land to support the *arable*. It cannot increase the quantity of manure, nor can the benefit attending it be a sufficient compensation for the injury done to the flock."

In a rich fertile country, where the quantity of arable land is small, and in mere subserviency to the breeding or grazing system, where dung is plenty, and can be put in the corn land at a small expence, and where each ewe is valued at four or six pounds, it is not to be wondered, that the folding system should be held in contempt and derision; but I will be bold enough to repeat, that in a poor exposed and extensive corn farm, the soil of which is light and stony, it is the *fine qua non* of good husbandry.

Let me ask these gentlemen, whether the downs of Wilts and Dorset would wave with luxuriant corn if folding were abolished? No. The farmer would plough and sow to little purpose, were his fallows to remain untrod with the feet, and unmanured by the dung and perspiration of these useful animals. Beside, in the hot summer months, nothing is so grateful to the flock itself, as fresh ploughed ground; and sheep will, of their own accord, retire to it when their hunger is satisfied. The following may be some of the reasons why these gentlemen set their faces against this useful practice:

1st. Their sheep are too valuable to be kept in sufficient numbers for folding.

2dly. Their inability to walk to any great distance.

3dly. Their liability to disorders from too great heat of body.

J. B.

new

new breed of sheep has been lately introduced, which bids
fair to exceed all others of equal size, in quantity and quality of wool, accompanied with a carcase by no means despicable; but as these crosses of breed are found sometimes
to degenerate, I shall not be too warm in recommendation
till a farther trial has been made, and experience has confirmed their superiority.

More sheep would be kept in this district, were it not for
the disposition of the land to bring the foot-rot.

The marl land in particular generates this disorder; and
though the following receipt will make a temporary cure,
yet it is a very difficult undertaking thoroughly to keep the
feet sound. The scab is also a troublesome and infectious
disorder. The goggles or rickets is a disorder not much
known: it attacks sheep between one and two years old,
and no method of cure has yet been discovered.

RECEIPT FOR THE SCAB ON SHEEP.

One pound of quick-silver
Half ditto of Venice turpentine
Half a pint of oil turpentine
Four pounds of hogs-lard.

Let them be rubbed in a mortar till the quick-silver be thoroughly incorporated with the other ingredients.

RECEIPT FOR THE FOOT-ROT.

Roman Vitriol
Verdigrease
Gunpowder, and
Linseed-oil, made into an ointment.

ANOTHER.

One spoonful of turpentine
wo ditto of crab-verjuice.

SECT. 3. *Horfes.*

There are but few horfes bred in this diftrict—the farmers are principally fupplied by dealers who attend the
North-country fairs. Farriery is in the hands of men
equally conceited and illiterate; and thefe ufeful animals frequently die of a difeafe called the *dotter.* Few people are
aware of the expences which attend the keeping of a team
for *road* work.

The following being taken (as an average of feven years
paft) from an account kept by a perfon whofe accuracy may
be depended on, needs no apology:

TWO TEAMS, NINE HORSES.

	£.	s.	d.
Two waggoners 61l. turnpike 50l. expences 27l. 6s.	137	6	0
Corn of all forts	110	10	0
Brewers' grains four-pence per bufhel	38	19	0
Hay, at three pounds per ton	74	0	0
Harnefs-maker	9	12	0
Tilts, lines, &c.	11	0	0
Blackfmith	27	10	0
Farrier	3	1	0
Wear and tear of waggons	20	0	0
Ditto of horfes	30	0	0
Straw	16	0	0
	*£.477	18	0

Or nearly 240l. per team.

---

* This calculation affords a very fubftantial reafon why *trawnters*,
as they are called, (that is, men who keep horfes and waggons for
hire) feldom get rich.

Cutting

Cutting ſtraw into chaff is much practiſed, but I doubt its utility in reſpect to horſes. The food, in this method, paſſes into the animal's ſtomach without proper maſtication, and in my opinion affords but little nutrition. For oxen, cows, and all ruminating animals, the practice may be advantageous.

SECT. 4. *Hogs.*

The vaſt number of hogs fatted in this diſtrict are for the moſt part bought at Briſtol market of Welchmen, or of itinerant drovers, who travel through the county. They are fed chiefly with whey, ſometimes a little corn is given to finiſh; and their fleſh is of a fine colour and delicate flavour; their weight when fatted from ten to twenty ſcore. Thoſe few that are bred, are of various ſorts:—1ſt. The native white, with large ears and long body. 2d. The Berkſhire, black and white in colour, and of a compact round form. 3d. The Chineſe. 4th. A mixed breed.

In breeding hogs, nothing ſhould be more attended to than *warmth* and *cleanlineſs*; without theſe, the moſt liberal allowance of food will not avail; and as there is a great difference in the quantity of food neceſſary to ſupport hogs of different ſorts, though of the ſame age and ſize, experiments are wanting to aſcertain their different degrees of perfection. In the writer's opinion, the beſt ſort of hogs he ever ſaw, was ſent to a friend of his from Mr. ASTLEY, a great breeder of ſheep in Leiceſterſhire.

The writer of this report has been in the habit of folding hogs on his paſture land, feeding them with raw potatoes.

The improvement of the land has been aſtoniſhing; and when hogs are kept on a large ſcale, the practice cannot be too warmly recommended.

SECT.

SECT. 5. *Rabbits.*

Some years fince there were many warrens in this diftrict, but the only ones now left are, Charter-Houfe, Temple-Down, and Ubly, containing about fixteen hundred acres. Both the flefh and fkin of the rabbits, bred on thefe warrens, are much efteemed; and they fell, when in feafon, (that is, from November to January) for two fhillings and fix-pence a couple, fkins included. Could coneys be preferved from the depredation of *two-legged* and *four-legged vermin*, the occupation would be very profitable; but one fnowy winter drives them off the warrens never to return, and wipes out the profit of many favourable years.

SECT. 6. *Poultry.*

The great demand in Briftol and Bath naturally induces an attention to the rearing and fattening of all kinds of fowls. Of late it has been found that potatoes, boiled and mixed with the fkimmings of the pot, or with any other fat or greafy fubftance, is the cheapeft food that can be given to all kinds of poultry, and fattens them in a few days, making the flefh of a moft delicate colour and flavour.

SECT. 7. *Pigeons.*

Thefe are confidered fo ravenous and mifchievous, that few are kept.

SECT. 8. *Bees.*

It is to be regretted that thefe ufeful infects are fo little attended to.

Suppofe in each parifh of the county there were kept only ten hives, and the average produce of each hive was twenty pounds of honey, this would amount at the prefent price to near five thoufand a year, befides the value of the wax.

Though

Though many directions have been given in books for the prefervation of the lives of bees, and at the fame time taking away their ftores, it does not appear that any of them has been practifed in this county with fuccefs.

After they have fwarmed, driving them out of the full hive, and putting an empty one in its ftead, has fometimes anfwered the purpofe.

This fhould be done early in the feafon, fo that the bees may have time to collect a ftore of food before winter.

CHAPTER XIV.

RURAL ŒCONOMY.

SECT. 1. *Labour.*

THE rate of wages, in hay and corn-harvest, is about nine shillings per week, with dinner and beer; at other parts of the year about seven shillings, with small-beer or cyder.

Time of labour in the summer from six to six; in the winter from daylight till it is dark.

SECT. 2. *Provisions.*

In the year 1793 wheat was six shillings per bushel, (Winchester) barley four shillings and six-pence, oats three shillings and three-pence, beef four-pence halfpenny per pound, mutton four-pence halfpenny, pork five-pence, butter nine-pence,* and cheese, six months old, forty shillings per cwt. Now, viz. January 1797, wheat is at seven shillings, barley three shillings, oats two shillings and three-pence, per Winchester bushel; beef at six-pence, mutton five-pence halfpenny, pork seven-pence, butter one shilling per pound, and cheese fifty-six shillings per cwt. The prices of all grain are declining rapidly; and it is probable, that before the conclusion of the year 1797, they will be very low indeed.

---

* In the years 1795-6 wheat was at fourteen shillings per bushel, barley five shillings, oats three shillings and nine-pence, beef five-pence, butter ten-pence, and cheese fifty shillings per cwt.

In

In the alarming scarcity of bread-corn, and the dearness of all other grain, which was felt in the years 1795-6, the attention of mankind was naturally directed to an investigation of those causes from which that distressing evil might have originated. Various were the opinions of mankind on this subject; and the chief causes stated, were, the *consolidation of farms*, the *combination of farmers, jobbers, and millers*; the *consumption made by the distillers*, the *oppression of tithes*, the *sale of corn by sample*, and lastly, the *increased luxury of the times*.

Though all these causes have undoubtedly contributed in part to produce the effect, which we have had so much reason to deplore, yet I think the great operating causes have been, *scanty crops of corn, the prevailing disposition of converting arable to pasture*, and the *unavoidable waste which must inevitably accompany war*.

From the year 1791 to 1796 we had not a first-rate crop of corn. The summer and autumn of 1792 were a continued series of wet weather; both corn and hay were greatly injured in harvesting, and consequently the little corn that was well secured, advanced in price; but under all these unfavourable circumstances, the old stock in hand was so considerable, that the price in 1793 did not exceed (in the county of Somerset, at least) seven shillings and six-pence per bushel, Winchester. The produce of 1793 being a middling crop, wheat did not experience much advance, till a probable deficiency in the crop of 1794, accompanied with nearly a total failure in the crop of pulse, was discoverable. Its advance then was very rapid, and great part of the old stock being exhausted, apprehensions were entertained of an absolute famine. We may, therefore, from the foregoing statement, draw this fair inference, that three out of the five years before referred to were *deficient in produce*; and that the crops of 1791 and

1793,

1793, though tolerable, were not fufficient to make good the deficiency of the three unproductive years.

For argument fake, let us fuppofe the average produce of a good crop to be twenty bufhels per acre, and the average confumption of the kingdom eighteen bufhels?

Let us alfo fuppofe the average produce of 1792 and 1794 not to exceed fourteen bufhels, and that of 1795 not to exceed twelve bufhels per acre, the amount will then ftand thus, admitting that 1791 and 1793 were good years of produce:

1791,	- - 20	bufhels per acre.
1792,	- - 14	ditto.
1793,	- - 20	ditto.
1794,	- - 14	ditto.
1795,	- - 12	ditto.

       80 Produce of five years.
       90 Confumption in ditto.

       10 Deficient, or two bufhels per acre per annum.

Admitting that three million of acres are annually fown with wheat, a deficiency of two bufhels per acre, of produce, compared with the confumption, would require an annual importation, for the above ftated five years, of 750,000 quarters.

Now, according to a certain writer, the importation from foreign countries, for eighteen years, ending January 5th, 1789, amounted to only 42,657 quarters of wheat, and 283,175 quarters of oats per annum.

From the ftatement made in the firft report of the Select Committee appointed to take into confideration the means of promoting the cultivation and improvement of wafte land,

it

it appears that the total increase, in the consumption of cattle and sheep, for the last sixty-two years, amounts to the enormous number of 32,854 head of cattle, and 203,290 sheep, or nearly one-third *for the metropolis alone*; and as the size and weight, both of cattle and sheep, have probably increased at least one-fourth since 1732, such augmented proportion ought to be added to the calculation of consumption. This denotes such an increase, both of inhabitants and of luxury, as must have been attended with a proportionate consumption of butter, cheese, hay, &c.; and if extended to the whole kingdom, clearly accounts for the increased price of the before-mentioned articles, and is a sufficient apology for that predilection for *pasture* land, which, for many years past, seems to have been universally manifested.

In the course of the last thirty years, the price of labour, butter and cheese, beef and hay, have advanced in price nearly fifty pounds per cent. Barley and oats have also advanced thirty or forty per cent. Not so *bread corn*. If we except the last two years, that article has advanced but little; and perhaps the average price of the last thirty years, namely, from 1764 to 1794, is not much higher than that from 1734 to 1764.

Let us now advert to the consolidation of farms, to which the multitude have attributed the late scarcity; and here I cannot help remarking, that without farms, at least moderately large, I much question the possibility of extending an improved agriculture; and were the prevailing wish gratified, and the plan of small farms adopted, such a measure must be attended with a total extinction of that energy and spirit which are the life and soul of adventure.

What would be the operation of such a system in trade, were the clothier, the cotton manufacturer, the artisan, to be restricted to a limited capital? Why, a total dereliction of all

all that animation and exertion which have gained to them
a trade with the whole world, and which have rendered
their late and prefent improvements the object of general
admiration and aftonifhment.

An equal divifion of farms never has exifted, nor could
it continue, if it had. The unequal ability of tenants, the
affiduity and œconomy of fome contrafted with the indolence and diffipation of others, the diverfity of foils, the
mode of manuring, courfe of cropping, proximinity or diftance
from large and populous cities and towns, and variety of
flocking, are all fo unfettled in their nature and qualities,
that what might be *right* in one inflance, would be *wrong*
in another.

Let me afk the advocates for fmall farms what occafioned
that confolidation of them, which they fo much reprobate,
and to which they attribute, in a great degree, that dearnefs
which the nation now experiences. Was it not becaufe the
large holder could afford to give more rent than the fmall?
And how was this to be done, but by an increafed produce?
And if an increafed produce was the confequence, how could
fuch a meafure operate in the way ftated?

But fome will fay, does not the confolidation of farms
act as a check to population? I fay, no.

The ideas of large farmers are more expanded than thofe
of fmall. The extent of their capital; their more liberal
education, and more general intercourfe with the farmers of
other diftricls; the diffemination amongft thofe of knowledge, by means of books and agricultural focieties, whereby
difcoveries reach them long before they can poffibly be
known to the finall farmer; all thefe comparative advantages concur to introduce a fyftem of *cropping*, *cleaning*, *manuring*, and *flocking* the land, by which the neceffary manual
labour on a farm is greatly increafed. And what difference
is

is it to the publick whether this manual labour be performed by the little *farmer himself*, or by the *hired labourer* of the large farmer?

True it is, that where cottages are levelled, and the married labourer is obliged to give way to the domeſtick or *ſingle* ſervant, then its operation may be in ſome degree fatal to population; but for this a remedy might be deviſed.*

On the whole, I am of opinion, that any ſyſtem adopted by the Britiſh Legiſlature to limit the extent of farms would be unwiſe and injurious in its operation.

Let it not be inferred, from the preceding remark, that I am an advocate for farms of an *unlimited* extent. No. A farm ſhould never be ſo large as to preclude the poſſibility of good management. Where this limitation (as to corn or grazing farms) may be fixed, it is difficult to ſay, for the reaſons before ſtated; perhaps in no caſe ſhould they exceed ſix hundred pounds per annum. This is large enough to produce, with good management, a ſufficient profit to render its occupier independent and comfortable.

As to dairy-farms, they cannot well be too ſmall.

One even ſo low as ſixty or ſeventy pounds per annum will afford a comfortable proviſion for a family, be wholly conducted (ſerving cattle excepted) by the females of the houſhold; and the male part thereof might increaſe their income by occaſional work done for their more opulent neighbours, the corn farmers of the diſtrict.

But the moſt formidable objection to large corn farms ſtill remains to be anſwered, this is, the capacity which large capital gives the holders of withdrawing the produce from

---

* Let a tax be put on all unmarried male-ſervants beyond a certain number living and lodging in a farmer's houſe, and let the produce go to the induſtrious married cottager.

market,

market, and thereby producing an artificial fcarcity; to which may be alfo added, the practicability of combination to enhance the price much beyond a due proportion.

In years of plenty, when the foil produces more than is neceffary for the confumption of its inhabitants, the man who holds back from market a *part* of this fuperfluity, fo far from being an object of condemnation, ought rather to be an object of applaufe, in as much as fuch conduct tends to preferve a greater equality of price than could otherwife exift.

In the latter end of the year 1791, and the beginning of the year 1792, the price of wheat did not exceed fix fhillings per bufhel.

The wet fummer of 1792 occafioned an advance of price, but even then it did not exceed feven fhillings and fix-pence per bufhel, nor did it much advance till 1794, when the drought of the fpring having occafioned a total failure of pulfe, and a poor crop of wheat, the price advanced rapidly, and at laft reached the enormous value of fourteen fhillings per bufhel.

Other caufes befide this deficiency of the crop may have contributed to this alarming and melancholy event; but if the foregoing obfervations are founded on fact, we may fafely infer that the late dearnefs of wheat is eafily accounted for, without having recourfe to the combination of farmers, the monopoly of jobbers, or to any other of the caufes before enumerated.

It arofe from *three years out of five of deficient produce. The almoft total failure of pulfe in the year 1794, and the deftructive ravages of war,* which has not only leffened importation, but has inevitably produced in our fleets and armies a wafteful expenditure of this neceffary article of human food.

CHAPTER

CHAPTER XV.

POLITICAL ŒCONOMY, *as connected with or affecting* AGRICULTURE.

———

SECT. 1. *Roads.*

PUBLICK roads pretty good, confidering the traffick upon them. Parochial ones ill managed, and bad; notwithftanding good materials for keeping them in repair are near and abundant. But fome examples are beginning to be fet of more judicious management, by throwing the fides to the middle, thereby widening the fpace of paffage, and making drains at both fides. This obvious piece of œconomy cannot be too much imitated.

SECT. 2. *Canals.*

The *Somerfetfhire Coal Canal,* which has two branches, the one commencing at Paulton, the other at Radftock, and both communicating with the Kennet and Avon canal; the *Dorfet and Somerfet Canal,* commencing near Nettlebridge, and extending through Frome to the county of Dorfet; and the *Ilchefter Canal;* are the only three canals for which acts have been obtained. Another was attempted which was intended to commence at Pill near Briftol, and to communicate with the Grand Weftern canal at Taunton. This Briftol and Weftern canal, as it was called, might have been carried near fifty miles without a lock, and for the moft part through a ftrong clay foil. It would, in conjunction with the Grand Weftern canal, (an act for which has been obtained) have delivered coal to the inhabitants of

the

the county of Devon at nearly half the prefent price; and yet all thefe benefits were loft, and a fcheme, fraught with publick good, as well as private convenience, was fruftrated by a certain nobleman, merely becaufe he conceived that he had not been treated by the oftenfible promoters of it with becoming deference and refpect.

SECT. 3 and 4. *Fairs and Weekly Markets.*

Many fairs are held in this diftrict, but Bath and Frome are the only towns which have a weekly market of any confequence.

SECT. 5 and 6. *Commerce and Manufactures.*

The principal manufactures in this diftrict are thofe of woollen cloth, and knit worfted ftockings, which, in the town of Frome, as well as Shepton-Mallet, are confiderable; and from the number of hands therein employed, muft have fome effect on the agriculture of the neighbourhood.

The town and parifh of Frome are found to contain nearly feventeen hundred families, or about ten thoufand people; more than one-third of which are actually and immediately fupported by the manufactures fpoken of; befides a vaft number of the lower order of people in the adjacent villages. In this town, the annual quantity of cloth manufactured has lately been found to be more than one hundred and fifty thoufand yards. In Shepton, the inhabitants may be reckoned fix thoufand, and the cloth manufactured one hundred and twenty thoufand yards.

Juftice and impartiality compel me to remark, that the woollen manufacture, in almoft all its branches, has been for fome years paft, and is now rapidly decreafing in its heretofore moft fertile fource of national benefit; namely, in furnifhing labour adapted to the different periods and

flages

flages of life. Machinery *muft* and *will* be univerfally introduced, otherwife the diftricts, where *it is not ufed*, muft be facrificed to thofe where *it is*. Would the legiflature interfere to fufpend its operations, or limit its progrefs? This would be incompatible with its wifdom and juftice. To allow only its *partial eftablifhment*, would be oppreffive; to admit of *none*, would be ruinous; becaufe fuch machinery, with its appendant branches of manufacture, and a *few individuals* allotted to each, is not only fufceptible of, but it is prefumed will fhortly be, in a ftate of migration. In Yorkfhire, where it has received a degree of perfection, and an extent of eftablifhment, beyond that of any other part of the kingdom, I have been informed, from indifputable authority, that before the prefent war, the great demand for the produce of the manufactures left but few, in comparifon, to refort to agriculture for fupport. What the prefent fituation may be, in this momentous relation to national profperity, I am not able circumftantially to defcribe, but general rumour ftates it as a melancholy reverfe.

Whether the introduction of machinery for the expediting carding, fpinning, &c. will enable the manufacturers to make more cloth, or whether a number of the poor muft be driven to feek fubfiftence by other labour, may, perhaps, be beft afcertained by experiment. If the revival of the export of kerfeymeres and fine cloth fhould take place, and fufficient ftock of wool can be obtained, the decifion will be in favour of the former part of the queftion, and all will be well; but fhould the prefent check on the export long continue, or fhould it be found that by the hands now in employ, and the machinery already in ufe, the whole ftock of wool (which is moft certainly a limited article) fhall be wrought into cloth in nine or ten months of the year; the full-grown and aged labourers in this manufacture will be

M   ferioufly

feriously diftreffed. Landed property in the neighbourhood will be heavily burthened; and the children muft migrate and feek fubfiftence by other employ where it can be found. Should this be the cafe, many other profeffions and employments, which are either mediately or immediately connected with this manufacture, or otherwife dependant on the populoufnefs of the neighbourhood, will be ultimately affected. Further, the agriculture of the Weftern part of Wiltfhire, and the North-Weftern part of Dorfetfhire, muft partake of the confequence of fuch a migration; for the lands about Frome or Shepton not being well adapted to tillage, the inhabitants are chiefly fupplied with corn and grain from thofe counties. The affiftance of machinery was had recourfe to by the manufacturers of Frome and Shepton from abfolute neceffity; for had they continued in the old method, their trade muft have been loft; and indeed *now* the North-country manufacturers are beforehand with them, particularly in the application of water, the beft *primum mobile* of all machinery. *

It is much to be feared, that the improvements already made, and thofe now going on, will ultimately be the means of diffeminating manufactures in other countries, to the prejudice of the export trade of Britain.

There are alfo feveral mills on the Avon for preparing iron and copper, and fundry others for the fpinning of worfted, and fpinning and weaving of cotton. The effect on agriculture has been confiderable; the pay of men, in the

* The prudence of the North-country manufacturers was highly confpicuous, in their introducing the cotton manufacture fully-into their neighbourhood, before they much extended machinery in their woollen;-thereby firft fecuring full employment for the poor, and then enjoying all the advantages which machinery could beftow. A.C.

time of harveft, has been greatly advanced, and that of women and children doubled.

It may be faid, that this diftrict cannot boaft of any practices in agriculture which are peculiar to itfelf; the cultivation of teazles and woad excepted.

Its advances in receiving the improvement of more enlightened agriculturifts are very flow, notwithftanding it has
the advantage of a very refpectable Agriculture Society, which
has been eftablifhed in Bath near twenty years. From the
tardinefs before mentioned, it feems difficult to devife any
means to engage a ftronger defire of improvement. *Draining their wet lands, folding fheep on their uplands, feeding
their cows during winter in the farm-yard, and more frequent
marling,* naturally prefent themfelves as the chief objects of
notice; and it is efpecially defirable, that thefe practices
might be ftrongly urged, if any means could be happily
found to do it effectually.

MIDDLE DISTRICT.

CHAPTER I.

GEOGRAPHICAL STATE AND CIRCUMSTANCES.

SITUATION AND EXTENT.

THE middle divifion of the county is the largeft, being that part comprehended between the Mendip hills on the North-Eaft; Quantock-hill and the foreft of Neroche on the South-Weft; parts of Devonfhire and Wilts on the South-Eaft; and the Briftol Channel on the North-Weft. It includes the city and borough of Wells, the boroughs of Bridgwater, Ilchefter, and Milbome-Port, and the market-towns of Axbridge, Shepton-Mallet, Glaftonbury, Brewton, Caftle-Cary, Wincanton, Somerton, Langport, Yeovil, South-Petherton, Ilminfter, Crewkerne, and Chard, toge-ther with their adjacent parifhes and villages, amounting in the whole to between four and five hundred thoufand acres.

CLIMATE AND SOIL.

The climate of this diftrict may, for the moft part, be pronounced mild and temperate; but on fo varied a furface an uniformity of foil cannot be expected.

On the borders of Wilts and Dorfet the lands are high, and partake of the foil and management of thofe counties;

fheep-sheep-walks and corn conftituting the principal parts of hufbandry. The farms are here large, and _olding_ is unremittingly purfued. Wheat is feldom fown without _two_ foldings; and fallowing every four or five years is the general practice. The corn produced is of a good quality, and finds a ready fale at Wincanton, Bruton, and other markets.

The next divifion of this diftrict, namely, the country around Shepton, Bruton, Caftle-Cary, Ilchefter, Somerton, Langport, Petherton, and Ilminfter, is exceedingly fertile, both in corn and pafture; abounds with good orchards and fine luxuriant meadows, and is altogether as well cultivated and as productive as moft parts of the kingdom. In fome parts, flax and hemp are produced in great abundance, which, together with wool, furnifh the raw materials for extenfive manufactures. Weftward of this, Polden and Hamhills rife boldly to the view, and conftitute fome of the inferior lands of the county. The foil on thefe hills being very thin, and the eftates difpofed in fmall portions of common field, no confiderable improvement can be effected without a fundamental change in the fyftem of management.

Hence we defcend into the marfh or fen-lands, which are divided into two diftricts, namely, _Brent-Marfh_, and the _Bridgwater_ or _South-Marfh_. Brent-Marfh is that portion of land comprehended between Mendip-hills and Poldenhill on the North and South, Bridgwater-bay on the Weft, and extending to Wells and Glaftonbury on the Eaft.

This marfh may alfo be divided into two parts, feparated by a tract of elevated land, on which ftand the parifhes of Allerton, Mark, Blackford, Wedmore, &c. Through the Northern level runs the river _Axe_, emptying itfelf into the Briftol Channel at Uphill; and through the Southern the river _Brue_, emptying itfelf into Bridgwater-bay near Burnham.

This

This country has been heretofore much neglected, being deſtitute of gentlemen's houſes, probably on account of the ſtagnant waters, and unwholſome air; but of late many efforts have been made to improve the ſoil, by draining and incloſing, under a variety of acts of parliament. The beneſit reſulting therefrom has been aſtoniſhing. The rhynes and ditches neceſſarily cut to divide the property, together with the deepening of the general outlets, diſcharge ſo much of the ſuperfluous water, that many thouſand acres, which heretofore were overflown for months together, and of courſe of little or no value, are become fine grazing and dairy lands; to the great emolument of the individual poſſeſſors, as well as the beneſit of the community. The quantities thus incloſed in Brent-Marſh, within twenty years paſt, under authority of parliament, are as follows:

ACRES.

Wedmore and Mear	4,400	} together with 1,100 acres of turf-bog as yet unimproved.
Compton-Biſhop	300	
Glaſtonbury —	1,500	Ditto 300 ditto
Weſthay, &c. —	1,700	Ditto 1,000 ditto
Mark ———	2,000	
Huntſpill —⁀	1,200	
Shapwick ———	100	
Blackford —	900	
Wookey ———	900	
Weſtbury —	450	
Bleadon ———	400	
Weſt-Pennard —	250	
Eddington ———	1,000	Ditto 400 ditto
Stoke and Draycot	800	
Nylands ———	350	
Wells —	1,150	
	17,400	2,800 of turf-bog.

Of thefe feventeen thoufand four hundred acres, fix parts out of feven are cleared of ftagnant water, and rendered highly productive: on the turf-bog but little improvement has hitherto taken place.* There remain about three thou-fand acres to be inclofed, which (the turf-bogs excepted) will compleat the divifion of all the moors within the Brent-Marfh diftrict. It is not to be underftood, that the local drains, under fuch a variety of acts, and at fuch different times, can have the moft perfect influence on the country; particularly when it is confidered, that the river Axe has no barrier to the tide, which flows feveral miles, and choaks the lower part of it with *flime*, to fuch a degree, that many thoufand acres adjoining the upper parts of the river are, in confequence thereof, very much injured. Were a barrier, with proper fluices, erected near the Briftol Channel, fome of the moft confiderable windings of the river fhortened, and the fhallow parts deepened, not only the moors, but the *old inclofures*, would be benefited thereby, to the amount of at leaft five thoufand pounds per annum.

The river Brue drains a much more confiderable part of Brent-Marfh than the Axe, and has a barrier to the tide (which rifes there no lefs than twenty feet in height) with fluices therein, at Highbridge; but its foundation, and the apron and cills of the fluices, are at fuch a height above low water mark, that the drain is very imperfect, and the loweft lands, which lie fome miles up the river, are frequently in-commoded by the land floods.

On the confines of the Brue are two heath or turf bogs: one on the north fide containing about three thoufand, and the other on the fouth containing about fix thoufand acres.

* Ten thoufand fheep have been noticed in one year in the parifh of Mark, before the inclofing and draining took place.

On

On these bogs scarce any pasturage at present grows.—
They are a composition of porous substances, floating on
water, and imbibing it like a spunge. They are observed to
rise with much wet, and sink in dry weather. The principal
use to which they are appropriated is that of fuel to the surrounding parishes. As it is an object of the first importance to the country to have these bogs perfectly drained
and consolidated, I shall endeavour to suggest a plan whereby
this desirable effect may, in my opinion, be attained.

The cause of the inundation and drowning of this level
arises from the outfalls being choaked up either by the collection of sea-mud in the river, or by the elevated land lying
between it and the Bristol Channel. Of course, nothing
more is necessary than a removal of those obstructions to the
outfalls, which will open a free passage and quick current to
the land water; this being effected, the turf-bogs, which are
now five or six feet higher than the adjacent land, would
subside, and the porous earth become consolidated, and fit
for all the purposes of vegetation.

The annexed plan, drawn by Mr. WHITE, the surveyor,
will sufficiently explain the object in view, and excite the
attention of all parties interested.

By the levels thus delineated, (the accuracy of which, I
think, may be depended on) it appears, that the spring-tides
are nearly on a level with the surface of the turf-bogs, and
that by the proposed outlet an additional fall of ten feet
will be acquired. Such a drain, reduced to an inclined plane
of a foot in a mile, would, in all probability, discharge all its
stagnant waters.

A farther explanation is unnecessary, as the plan will convey a more distinct idea of the general design than words.

The present outlet at Highbridge is not only of insufficient
depth, but is situate so far *inland*, that the slime and mud

choak

choak up the river, and the current is not rapid enough to diflodge the fame.

I am aware that many of the proprietors of land in Hunt-fpill, Mark, &c. will object, under an idea that their lands will be made *too dry*, and that in the fummer feafon their ftock will be deftitute of water. But this objection, and indeed every other drawn from the apprehenfion of a too liberal difcharge of water, may be obviated, by *placing katches at the different bridges*, which will be neceffary both for pub-lick and private accommodation.

An improvement of fuch magnitude cannot be effected without the authority of parliament; and all perfons re-ceiving benefit muft be burthened with a rate proportionate to the advantages derived. This affeffment may be made by commiffioners duly appointed, but fubject to an appeal to the court of quarter-feffions; and the drains, when finifh-ed, fhould be put under the view of the court of fewers.

I will now endeavour to give a hafty fketch of the pro-bable coft, and fubfequent improvement: but in this I do not pretend to accuracy; fuffice it to fay, that the apparent benefit fo far exceeds the utmoft latitude of expence, that no folid objection can lie on that head.

Brent-

Brent-Marsh and the River Axe Drainage.

DR.   £.

	£
To act of parliament, gaining consents, &c.	400
To sluice at letter *a* near the river Perrott	600
To twelve miles of new drain, average depth fifteen feet	12,000
To lowering river Brue three miles	1,500
To purchase of land	2,000
To bridges, hatches, &c.	2,000
To sluice on the Axe near Hobb's boat	500
To one mile and half of new drain	1,500
To lowering the river Axe six miles	1,000
To purchase of land	1,000
To commissioners, surveyor, &c.	2,500
	25,000
To balance of profit	331,250

CR.   £. 356,250

	£
By 9000 acres turf bog improved, at the most moderate computation, 15s. per acre, making 6750l. per annum, twenty-five years purchase	168,750
By 15,000 acres of flooded land improved 10s. per acre, or 7500l. per annum, twenty-five years purchase	187,500
	£. 356,250

On the side of the river Axe, the expence of a compleat drainage would not exceed five thousand pounds; and there can be no doubt that the low lands near Axbridge, Cheddar, Nyland, Draycot, Rodney-Stoke, Westbury, &c. would be improved at least four thousand per annum. As a farther stimulus it might be urged, that the air would be rendered

dered more healthful, and the exhalations which now rise
from so large a body of stagnant water, and are wafted by
the winds to the high corn-lands of the Mendip-Hills, to
their great detriment, would be unknown.

Were the turf-bogs reclaimed and made productive, I
think this district might be considered as one of the most
fertile in the kingdom. The yales are formed principally
by mud, carried down by the rivers which flow through it,
and deposited there by the tides opposing the current thereof.
Many ages must have been required to effect this, but it is
evident that the whole of this district is raised to a confiderable height above its original level; and that the turf-
bogs were in former days dry and firm land, not subject to
inundation from the sea, or to the stagnation of the river
waters; else, how can we account for timber trees of great
dimensions, both oak, fir, and willow, being found at the
depth of fifteen or twenty feet, standing in the same erect
posture in which they grew; and reeds and other paluftrine
plants, at the same depth and in the same posture. Human
bones, furze-bushes, and nut-trees with nuts, have been
found at the same depth. Now it is manifest, that neither
furze nor nut-trees will grow under water.

It appears therefore probable, that the whole of this level
was at a former period dry, firm land; and that by some
violent convulsion of nature it became of a sudden inundated.* This is in some degree confirmed by the extraordinary depth of the clay or found ground, on the verge of

---

* Some objections may be brought against this idea of sudden inundation, from the upright position of the sedge, as discovered in digging the Sedgmoor drains. Had this Moor been drowned by a sudden
flood, it is reasonable to suppose the sedge would have been proftrated.
                                                                J. B.

the

the *Highlands*; and it is well known, that in many parts of this kingdom the sea has gained on the land, and in other parts the land has gained on the sea.

The improvement of such a tract of unproductive land would impart the most pleasing sensations to the mind; and I verily think, that *two* grand drains, accompanied with proper lateral ditches, such as I have now suggested, would increase the rent of this district eight or ten thousand pounds per year.

The profit which has attended the improvement already practised during the last twenty years is, I should think, a sufficient incentive. Scarcely a farmer can now be found who does not possess a considerable landed property; and many whose fathers lived in idleness and sloth, on the precarious support of a few half-starved cows, or a few limping geese, are now in affluence, and blessed with every needful species of enjoyment. Disorders of the body, to which the stagnant waters heretofore subjected them, are now scarcely known: and the inhabitants for the most part arrive to a good old age.

SOIL.

The soil of these moors may be comprehended under four divisions:

1*st*. Strong, dry, and fertile clay, of a considerable depth.

2*dly*. Red earth, of various depths, from one foot to six feet, covering the black moory earth of the heath.

3*dly*. Black moory earth on the surface, with a substratum of clay at various depths.

4*thly*, and *lastly*. The turf-bog.

The first of these descriptions of land may be considered as of the best quality, being highly productive, and particularly so in a wet summer. If shut up early in the spring, it

will

will produce from two to three tons of hay per acre. Its value may be eſtimated from two to three pounds per acre, and it is for the moſt part devoted to grazing.

It is no leſs remarkable than true, that this land will fat ſheep nearly as well in the winter as the ſummer, if not ſtocked more than one to an acre.

The vaſt advantage reſulting from the incloſure of the waſte lands in the pariſhes before enumerated, is ſo maniſeſt, that whoever runs may read.

A moiety of the manor of Wedmoor might have been purchaſed, about twenty years ago, for twenty thouſand pounds. It is now worth ſeven thouſand pounds per annum. The improvements in Huntſpill, Mark, Mere, Glaſtonbury, Eddington, &c. &c. are nearly ſimilar. In the latter hamlet, ſingle rights of common, when incloſed, have been ſold for more than eight hundred pounds; and all this without any concomitant inconvenience. At firſt the ſcheme was highly unpopular, and its firſt promoters were on the eve of falling a ſacrifice to popular fury and reſentment, but by coolneſs and perſeverance they weathered the ſtorm: all parties are now ſatisfied, and acknowledge the wiſdom of the meaſure. Nor has the advance of the poor's rate been in any degree equal to what has been experienced in neighbouring pariſhes, where no incloſure has taken place, as will be ſhewn by the following ſtatement:

WEDMOOR.

| Amount of poor-rate ſeven years previous to the incloſure £2132 | Amount of poor-rate 7 years ſubſequent to the incloſure £2342 |

HUNTSPILL.

| Ditto - - - - - 1561 | Ditto - - - - 2204 |

MARK.

MARK.

Ditto - - - - - 1985 | Ditto - - - - 2163

MERE.

Ditto - - - - - 2016 || Ditto - - - - 2170

An increased population necessarily accompanying such an occupation of productive land, must inevitably be attended with a proportionate advance in the poor's levy; besides, men cannot, in an instant, by any, even the strongest incentives, be roused from a state of sloth to a life of labour and activity. To this may be added, that a great part of the extra levy arises *from the high demand for county stock*; and it is found that for several years past the rates are declining, notwithstanding the poor are treated with much more liberality than heretofore.

The division of property, on these lands, is effected by ditches eight feet wide at the top, three feet and half wide at the bottom, and five feet deep, which may be cut in the strongest clay for twenty-pence per rope; and on the black ground and red earth at sixteen-pence per rope, which is about one penny per cubic yard.

At these prices a good workman will, in the summer, earn three shillings per day, and in winter two shillings.*

These rhynes discharge their waters into the rivers; and sluices are occasionally made to keep back water, in times of drought, for the use of the stock.

The graziers, on these strong clays, are fond of large inclosures, and object to the planting any trees, or hedges; alledging as a reason, that they harbour flies, which teaze the cattle, and check their progress in fatting: trees also prevent a free circulation of air. Experience confirms the wis-

---

* Can any excavating machine execute this work at a cheaper rate!

dom

dom of this theory. Many also are of opinion, that one piece of forty acres will sooner fat a given quantity of oxen, or sheep, than two pieces of twenty acres each. All, however, do not agree in this sentiment; and the opponents urge, that animals eat with greater relish, when frequently changed from one field to another, than when they are confined to one.

As no satisfactory experiments have ever (to my knowledge) been recorded on this subject, let us reason a few moments thereon.

It is difficult to decide in this case from *experiment.* Two pieces of land, perfectly alike in quality, or two sets of flock, exactly similar, cannot easily be found; we must, therefore, form our opinion from some other data. The argument made use of by the advocates for change is, " that of giving " the food to the cattle *fresh* and *fresh*;" but this seems not to be conclusive. Independent of the division-fence (which occasions a lofs of pasturage unfavourable to the small allotments) there must be an equal number of blades of grafs in either cafe, and the cattle may vary their feeding as much in one instance as in the other; for in the large inclosures they will not be seen in the evening where they were feeding in the morning. The grand enquiry is, *do the cattle,* or *do they not, consume more grafs in one way than the other ?* I think they do, and shall not hesitate (though with great diffidence) to give my opinion in favour of a change of food; and this for the following reasons:

When an animal is turned into a piece of grafs, he takes a furvey of the whole field, for the purpofe, I presume, of selecting that kind of herbage which best pleases his palate.

This perambulation does not much injure the grafs, for if it be not very rank indeed (and graziers should be careful that it be not fo) it will soon rise after the animal's tread.

He

He then becomes contented, and, during the time of his abode, feeds in the same manner as he would were the piece ever so large. After one or two months' residence in a large piece, the animal becomes disgusted with his situation, and tired with his food; the grafs is tainted by his breath and by the effluvia of his dung; he bellows for change, and traverses the field, consuming, or rather destroying, more grafs with his feet than with his mouth.

In ever so large an inclosure (properly flocked) every part of the field is tainted with the breath of the animal some time or other in the courfe of twenty-four hours, and it is aftonishing how soon they become disgusted; in changing from field to field it is not fo. Every fortnight or three weeks bring a fupply of untainted food, which gratifies their palate, and a change of scene amufes them, and increases their comfort and enjoyment.

The only manure ever put on these lands, is the contents of the drains and ditches; and this, with judicious manage-ment in the method of grazing, is fufficient to keep them in unabating fertility.

Some of this clay land, when tilled, has been known to produce ten or twelve fucceffive crops of wheat, without an intervening fallow or fallow crop. I was fhewn a field in the parifh of Mark, which had growing in it the *nineteenth* crop of wheat; and I verily think the produce was not lefs than fifty Winchefter bufhels per acre. No manure had been put on it during the whole time, fave the contents arifing from the cleanfing of the ditches. The flubble was mown every year, and carried off; two ploughings only were given it, after which the wheat was fown in the months of No-vember or December, under furrow, in eight-furrow ridges, after the rate of two bufhels and half per acre, chopping the clods, and fmoothing the furface of the ridge with a fpade.

N   The

The average produce per year, for the whole eighteen years, was eftimated to exceed thirty-five bufhels per acre.

This aftonifhing fertility of foil can only be afcribed to the invigorating principle of the faline particles with which the land is impregnated. They enable it to produce a fuc-ceffion of crops, which in common land would reduce the foil to a mere *caput mortuum.*

Notwithftanding this encouragement to tillage, the plough lies idle, and nineteen parts out of twenty remain in grafs, though it is apparent that the value of the land, in fee, might be gained in a few years.

The fecond defcription of foil found in this diftrict, namely, a ftrong red earth over a pure clay, poffeffes alfo many good qualities; it is neither fubject to injury from an excefs of wet weather, nor does it burn in a drought.

This foil, formed by a depofit wafhed from the hills, may be confidered as a fine vegetable mould, and, if tilled, is ca-pable of bearing a variety of crops in the higheft perfection. Its value is about forty-five fhillings per acre, and its pro-duce of hay about two tons.

Black moory earth is the third fort of foil found in this level, and on it extraordinary improvements have been effected, by covering the furface with a thick coat either of clay or red earth.

In its natural ftate it is in a great meafure unproductive, yielding fcarcely any herbage, fave carnation grafs, rufhes, and other aquatic productions. The deficiency of this foil arifes from the want of tenacity. The beft means of im-provement is *compleat draining*, and after that a liberal co-vering with clay or red earth; thefe will freely incorporate with the foil, and make it fufficiently firm. After fuch im-provement, no kind of land is more productive, particularly in a dry fummer.

I have

I have this year feen land of this defcription, fpring-fed till the 12th of May, yield by the 24th of June two tons of hay per acre; and Mr. LAX, on his farm at Godney, has, for five years paft, kept twenty cows and a bull throughout the year on thirty-five acres of land. His plan is to winter *bayne** fifteen acres. This, on an average of feafons, is fit to be ftocked the beginning of April, and is fed till the 12th of May. By this time the remaining twenty acres are in fufficient ftrength to take the cows, and will keep them till the after-grafs of his mown ground is fit to receive them; then the unfed grafs in the fummer-leaze is *fkimmed*, which yields from five to ten cwt. of hay per acre; this is given to the cows when they are dry, namely, in the months of December and January. After they have calved, which is from the beginning of February to Lady-Day, they are fupplied with the beft hay; here are more than thirty tons of hay produced, fo that twenty cows cannot poffibly want winter provender.

Not many years fince this farm was part of an extenfive moor, inclofed by Act of Parliament, and was purchafed by Mr. LAX, of the Commiffioners, at fifteen pounds per acre, to which add five pounds per acre for draining and claying, making in the whole twenty pounds per acre, at five per cent. the rent will be twenty fhillings per acre.

---

* It is *old* Englifh, and found in all books and laws relating to forefts.

DEBTOR.

DEBTOR.	£.	s.	d.
To rent of thirty-five acres, at 20s. per acre	35	0	0
To taxes, highways, &c. — — —	1	5	0
To dairy women, and all other incidental expences, twenty-five shillings per cow — —	25	0	0
To expences making fifteen acres of hay, at twelve shillings per acre — — — —	9	0	0
Ditto skimming and making summer-leaze hay	3	0	0
To fences — — — — —	1	15	0
To interest of capital — — — —	7	10	0
	82	10	0
Profit	117	10	0
£200	0	0

CREDITOR.	£.	s.	d.
By sixty cwt. cheese, at fifty shillings per cwt.	150	0	0
By twenty calves — — — —	15	0	0
By butter — — — —	15	0	0
By hogs — — — —	20	0	0
£200	0	0

Though the produce of cheese, in comparison with the general produce of the county, was small, it must not be supposed that the deficiency arose from any want of food, but principally from the cows being young, and of a small breed.

The last species of soil is *the Turf Bog*.

The surface of this soil is of a light, spungy, tough texture, full of the fibrous roots of plants, and withal so matted together, that a spade or knife must be made very keen to

penetrate

penetrate it. Immediately under the turf, or fward, is found the vein of black moory earth, fo unlike in its nature to the peat which lies underneath, that when cut with it, and dried, it will fall off and feparate from it.

This mould is of good quality, and will bear both natural and artificial grafs in great abundance. It is alfo an excellent manure for clay or any other heavy land. This black moory ftratum is from one to two feet in thicknefs, and underneath is found the peat, which is from three to fifteen feet in depth.

Under the peat is a bed either of clay or fand; the peat is full of flaggy leaves and hollow ftalks of rufhes. Thefe vegetable matters are accompanied with a fubftance like pitch, of a bituminous nature, which lies between the ftalks of the rufhes and the leafy remains, and conftitutes the inflammable part thereof. It is ufed as the common fuel of the country, and makes a clean and pleafant fire, particularly well adapted to the purpofes of the dairy. An acre of land will furnifh an immenfe quantity, infomuch, that in the parifh of Catcott it has been fold, for a term of twenty-one years, as high as thirty pounds.

There is no great difficulty in the mode of curing peat. In the months of May and June it is cut out with a keen inftrument into the fhape of bricks, left fingle on the ground for a few days to dry, by which time they lofe part of their moifture, and become firm enough for piling in pyramidal heaps of about a waggon load each; in this ftate they are compleatly dried, and then fell for ten fhillings per waggon load on the land where they are dug; and the price of digging and carrying is five fhillings per load. Though the outer covering or fward of this boggy land will burn, yet it is not much efteemed as fuel, being foon confumed.

Before

Before I fuggeft a method of improving thefe bogs, let
let me advert to the probable caufe of their prefent fterility.
I conceive then, that ftagnant water is the grand operative
principle which has for ages kept the fuperftratum buoyant,
and fwimming as it were on its furface; this lifts up and
fwells the foil, making it fhake and give way on treading.
In confirmation of this idea, it is found, that at the depth of
four or five feet the black earth becomes a mere pulp, in
which an iron rod will defcend with a trifling exertion to
the furface of the clay; and it invariably happens, that the
worfe the bog the deeper the clay.

In the third defcription of land, ftated at the beginning of
this difquifition, the clay is found at the depth of three, four,
or five feet, and gradually finks thence to the loweft part of
the peat bog, where it is found at the depth of eighteen or
twenty feet. If, therefore, the furface of the two forts of
land were equal, one foot of ftagnant water on the clay of
the former would be accompanied with fourteen or fifteen
feet on the clay of the latter. Such a body of water con-
tinually remaining at all feafons of the year, (for in the dryeft
fummer I conceive its diminution does not exceed three or
four feet) cannot fail of rendering the furface cold and unproductive.

Agreeably to this theory, the furface muft rife in the winter, and fubfide in the fummer months; and this is verified
by fact, for certain fixed bodies are feen over the moor at
certain feafons, which cannot be defcried at others. *

* Some may fay that another caufe, befide that which is here given,
might contribute to this phenomenon, viz. a copious fog at certain
times hovering over the moor, by which fome extraordinary refrac-
tions are known to take place, and exhibit the appearance of objects
apparently *above* the horizon, which in reality are *below* it. A. C.

If

If thefe premifes be admitted, it follows, that the only radical cure muft be *compleat draining*, and after that, *burning
the matted furface*; the *former*, I think, may be effected in
the manner before ftated, and the *latter* in the following way,
without any great difficulty or expence.

In the months of March or April, when the land is dry,
let it be ploughed as deep as fix ftrong horfes can plough it;
this will coft about twenty fhillings per acre. In this ftate
let it remain till the fod is dry enough to burn, then fet fire
to the plit as it lies, or clfe provide yourfelf with fome keen
cutting knives of about a foot in breadth, the cutting part
of which fhould be of a femicircular form; with thefe, let
the plit be cut into parts of about two feet and a half in
length, and let your burners reduce them to afhes as faft as
poffible, which being fpread equally on the furface and
ploughed in, fow the ground about the middle of May with
one bufhel and a half of buck-wheat per acre, two bufhels
of ray-grafs, and five pounds of white Dutch clover. The
coft of all this will be nearly as follows per acre.

	£.	s.	d.
Firft ploughing	1	0	0
Cutting the plit and burning	0	12	0
Spreading the afhes	0	3	0
Second ploughing	0	5	0
Harrowing	0	1	0
One bufhel and half of buck-wheat	0	6	0
Two bufhels of ray-grafs	0	5	0
Five pounds of Dutch clover	0	4	0
Tithe	0	3	0
	£2	19	0

N. B. If the furface be very tough, it might be right to
have two crops of buck-wheat.

Should

Should the fubfequent fummer be moift, it is probable that the produce of buck-wheat might be equal in value to the expenditure; but fhould it even entirely fail, the artificial grafs will amply repay the expence and exertion of the hufbandman.

After the buck-wheat is harvefted, let lateral trenches be cut at the diftance of thirty-five feet, emptying themfelves into the great drains; thefe trenches fhould be twelve inches wide, and fixteen inches deep, and will coft about one penny per rope (twenty feet) or about five fhillings per acre.

The contents of thefe trenches being for the moft part black mould, will be excellent manure for the artificial grafs, and fhould be fpread thereon without delay. It might be advifeable for the firft year or two, either to mow or feed with fheep, avoiding the tread of heavy cattle till the land has fully fubfided; and if clay or red earth could be procured within a moderate diftance, give it an occafional fprinkling therewith, after the rate of thirty or forty cart-loads per acre.

I have not the leaft doubt but with this management, or with fomething fimilar thereunto, the turf-bogs might be all reclaimed, and made worth twenty-five or thirty fhillings per acre. And as a proof thereof, I need only inftance the vaft improvements already made, and ftill carrying on with unremitting affiduity, by Mr. Moxham, of Glaftonbury, whofe exertions in this way highly merit the warmeft encomiums.

Without the affiftance of the plough, he has, by draining and earthing, advanced land of the foregoing defcription from one fhilling per acre to thirty fhillings. His expences, it muft be allowed, are great, for he puts one hundred cartloads, nay, in fome inftances, one hundred and fifty cartloads of red earth per acre, which being halled one mile and a half or two miles, the coft muft be more than ten pounds

per

per acre; yet notwithstanding this bountiful and expensive manuring, the advance in the value of the land amply compensates; for the original price of these bogs was two pounds per acre *in fee*, and many hundred acres may now be bought at that rate.

Mr. MOXHAM contends, that a covering of red earth, such as he bestows, is absolutely necessary to kill the old sward; and it must be admitted, that the end proposed is effectually obtained; but then the land is for some time unproductive, and the expence is also so enormous, that few farmers would have courage to go through so costly an experiment.

How far the plan of proceeding, which I have before suggested, is or is not more eligible, I shall leave to Mr. MOXHAM and to my readers to determine.

Mr. MOXHAM has planted firs and alder hedges on these bogs with great success, and has made various striking improvements, to the great astonishment of his neighbours, who could not conceive such things possible.

In short, he is justly entitled to the thanks not only of the labouring poor, but also of the community, for his persevering industry and activity.*

No

---

* This turbary-land, as it is called by the proprietors, is a portion of heath-moor appropriated for digging turf for fuel. It is dug out by the people of Glastonbury in pits of five or six feet deep, which are hollowed out on the sides as far as they can do it with safety, leaving a crust on top of the part hollowed, which makes it very dangerous to walk over it. The people of Mark (the adjoining parish) dig their turf in ditches, which I think a better method. I have levelled about 70 acres of this turbary-land, by taking the sward and sufficient of the uppermost earth to fill up those pits. This peat or turf earth, in its natural state, is very soft; and those pits, if not filled up, swell up from the bottom, and in twenty or thirty years will be sufficiently solid to be cut for turf again. When they are levelled, they sink down again into

No country can afford greater encouragement either to the grazing, dairy, or corn farmer, than this; the falubrity and mildnefs of the climate, and the fertility and ftrength of the foil, enable the occupier to devote his land to either purpofe with an almoft certainty of fuccefs; and the annual profit, over and above his rent, cannot fail, as a fource of wealth and independence. The dairy farms are fmall, feldom exceeding two hundred pounds per year; the grazing farms are large, and very detached.

It is obvious, that the profits of the dairy exceed thofe of the grazier nearly in the proportion of two to one; and as one hundred pounds per year will afford a comfortable fubfiflence to a family, fmall farms are beft calculated to increafe population, and to rear up an induftrious race of independent yeomanry. Excepting the Bifhop of Bath and Wells, there are few proprietors who ftand feized of more than fix or eight hundred pounds per annum, and for the moft part from one hundred to two hundred pounds per annum; and more than nine-tenths of the land are employed in pafture,

---

into hollows, fo that I have been obliged to level fome of them again four, five, and fometimes fix times, before I could venture to lay on good earth. I have then covered the land with from one to two hundred put-loads of rich fandy mould on an acre, fuch as is dug out of the rivers, or left by thick floods on the fides of the rivers, of a grey colour. This makes great improvement, produces a very good herbage, and by letting in on it from the river three, four, or five thick floods in the fpring, on about fifty acres of it, (which I do by means of a double funnel or trunk of two feet fquare each, without injuring my neighbours, having made flood-banks to keep it in) I have been able to make very good heifer-beef without their feeding on any other ground. Some part of this turbary-land I cannot flood; on this, when it is properly fettled, I propofe to put fome heavy earth. This heath-moor turbary-land has been fold in its original ftate from about forty fhillings to eight pounds an acre; the Wefthay turbary-land, in the adjoining parifh of Meer, fells for about forty fhillings an acre.

WILLIAM MOXHAM.

The old arable was found not to pay for ploughing, and has therefore been laid down.

Some few farmers, however, have enriched themselves by giving four pounds per acre for some rich dry and newly inclosed land, on which they have grown fifty bushels of wheat per acre for ten years succeffively, without fallow or manure of any kind.

Where there is so much to approve, I am sorry there should be any thing to condemn, but truth compels me to state, that a shameful inattention prevails as to their breed of cattle; and scarcely can an inftance be produced of a farmer's giving more than ten pounds for a bull, or three pounds for a ram; yet, notwithstanding this general neglect, many are accustomed to sell their home-bred team of four oxen, when fat, for one hundred pounds; and sheep in great abundance, that weigh from twenty to thirty pounds per quarter. The elevated corn-lands were formerly in open common fields, but every effort has been made to divide and inclose them; the tenure, however, (great part being under the fee of Wells, and other churches, under charity endowments, and under queen ANNE's bounty) has operated as a check to the neceffary exchanges. None of thefe common field lands will let for more than fifteen shillings per acre, whereas, if inclosed, they would let for twenty-five shillings.

Though there are many things in the practices of this diftrict deferving both commendation and imitation, I cannot help obferving, that the procefs of *making hay* is not among the number.

In this respect, they are the moft egregious flovens I ever beheld. It is no unufual thing to fee cocks of about a load each remain in the fields two months after they are made; and before the rivers were lowered, and the country drained, thefe these cocks were frequently carried away by a sudden flood. When conveyed to a large mow, no care is taken either in making or securing it; it is seldom thatched; some indeed make their mows in a conical form, by which means they suffer but little injury, but for the most part they are left flat on the top, and the winter rains soak from the top to the bottom, without shame or regret on the part of the owner. In their summer pastures they are equally slothful; docks, thistles, nettles, and other weeds, cover nearly a quarter of the land, and, wafted by winds, the seed is disseminated on the lands of their more careful neighbours. Ofttimes have I observed, that where nature is most bountiful, her gifts are least prized. This is the case with the farmers here; so quick is vegetation, even in the winter season, that the cattle (unless it be unusually severe) scarce ever want a bite of grass; and a deficiency of winter provender is scarcely known.

I presume it is on the same principle that the Scotch gardeners excel the English; having more difficulties to encounter, their exertion and care are proportionate thereto.

THE SOUTH MARSH

Is bounded on the North-East by Polden-hills, on the South-West by the river Parrett, on the North-West by Bridgwater-bay, and on the South-East by Ham-hill, &c.

That part thereof which lies nearest the sea is higher than the interior part, owing to the great deposit of sea-mud left at the high spring-tides for ages past; and it is also better drained, in consequence of being near the outlet, where the greatest fall of draining exists. (This observation also extends to the lands of Brent-Marsh.)

The river Parret is the principal drain of this marsh. It has no *barrier*, and the tide flows up as far as Langport,

filling

filling its banks, and frequently penning the land-floods over the moor, and meadows adjoining; fo that near thirty thoufand acres of fine land are frequently overflown for a confiderable time together, rendering the herbage unwholfome for the cattle, and the air unhealthy to the inhabitants. An act of parliament was lately obtained for draining a confiderable part of this fenny plain called *King's-Sedgmoor*, which, together with the adjoining inclofed meadows now flooded, amount to about twenty thoufand acres. This defirable end is nearly accomplifhed, by having the outlet or fluice many miles lower, in the river Parret, than formerly. Nothing could be more unpopular, at its outfet, than this undertaking; and every obftacle, which prejudice and ignorance could fuggeft, the promoters thereof had to encounter.

About the year 1680, King JAMES laid claim to the foil of this moor, and formed the defign of improving it by a compleat drainage; but fo perverfe were the owners of the adjacent lordfhips commoning with their cattle on it, that they oppofed the fcheme with all their might; and difcerning that they could make no juftifiable claim to the foil, offered to affign to the king four thoufand acres, in lieu of his right thereto, and to lay out the refidue, being nine thoufand five hundred and twenty-two acres, among their lordfhips; which being accepted of by the king, there were allotments then made to each manor according to the following proportions:

Names of Manors.		Acres.
Dunwear	To the heirs of Sir Robert Chichester, &c. ——	346
Stawell	To Sir John Stawell —	274
Sutton-Mallett	To John Mallett, efq; ——	234
Bawdrippe	To Walter Long, efq; —	218
Brogney	To Thomas Muttlebury, efq;	70
Middlezoy	To R. Warr, efq; Sir R. Strode, &c.	567
Moorlynch	To the heirs of Mr. Floyer —	354
Highham	To Henry Lord Gray ——	708
Netherham	To the heirs of Sir Ed. Hext —	264
Beere	To Sir William Courtney, &c.	229
Aishcotte	To Sir Thomas Cheeke —	526
Horfey	To Sir George Horfey ——	370
Chedzoy	To Earl Pembroke —	412
Weflon	To Sir Peter Van Lore, &c. —	582
Othery	To Sir Edward Trent, &c. —	428
Somerton	To Tho. Hill, efq; James Rife, efq; and Burgeffes, &c. —	1505
Graynton	To the heirs of Mr. Watts —	291
Pitteney	To Earl Northampton, and Sir J. Hanham ——	569
Compton-Dunden	To Sir J. Strangway, and Baronet Portman ——	548
Walton	To Sir Thomas Thynne —	540
Street	To Andrew Whittington, &c.*	488
	Total acres ——	9522
	Befides for the king —	4000

Memorandum. That thefe allotments are rated proportionably, after the rate of two hundred and eighty-two acres

---

* Dugdale.

of the moor (by the perch of fifteen feet) to every hundred acres of the severals.

In the reign of *King William*, a similar attempt was made. An act was obtained for draining it, but by some means or other its operation was entirely frustrated. This projected and useful improvement lay dormant till the year 1775, when it was revived by *Mr. Allen*, then member of parliament for Bridgwater. Sanguine of success, and highly impressed with the idea of its importance, he purchased a large number of rights, and having obtained a signature of consents, went to parliament; but not having interest enough in the house to stem the torrent of opposition, all his delusive prospects of profit vanished, and he found himself left in a small but respectable minority. Though Mr. Allen met with so warm an opposition, yet there were not wanting many lords of manors interested, who expressed their decided approbation of the measure, in a *general point of view*, but objected to the mode by which it was conducted, and to the men who were the ostensible movers in the business. After this defeat, nothing was done till the year 1788, when a meeting was held at Wells to take into consideration the propriety of draining the said moor, and dividing it into *parochial allotments*. At this meeting Sir Philip Hales presided; and after much abuse and opposition from the lower order of commoners, who openly threatened destruction to those who supported such a measure, the meeting was dissolved without coming to any final determination.

The leading idea was, however, afterwards pursued, with great assiduity, by Sir Philip, and his agent Mr. Symes of Stowey; and by their persevering industry, and good management, matters were brought into such a train, that application was made to parliament in the session of 1790, for leave to bring in a bill for draining and dividing the

said

faid moor into parochial allotments, among thirty parifhes and hamlets therein ftated; and alfo among fuch other parifhes as may prove a right to feeding the fame. In the fpring of 1791, this bill paffed into a law; and the commiffioners, acting under the powers thereof, held their firft meeting at Bridgwater in June 1791.

I have been thus particular in ftating the progrefs of this bufinefs, merely to fhew the impropriety of calling publick meetings, with a view of gaining fignatures of confent, or taking the fenfe of the proprietors in that way. At all publick meetings of this nature, which I ever attended, noife and clamour have filenced found fenfe and argument. A party generally attends with a profeffed defign to oppofe, and truth and propriety have a hoft of foes to combat.

Whoever, therefore, has an object of this kind in view, let him acquire confent by *private application*; for I have frequently feen the good effects thereof manifefted, by the irrefiftible influence of truth, when coolly and quietly adminiftered; and it has frequently happened, that men, hoftile to your fcheme, have, by difpaffionate argument, not only changed their fentiment, but become warm partizans in that caufe which at firft they meant to oppofe.

This never could have been done at a publick meeting; for after men have once joined the oppofition, their pride will not permit them to retreat.

How far the commiffioners appointed under this act have difcharged their truft, time will fhew; but the general opinion of their conduct feems to be flattering; and thofe who at firft fuppofed that the act carried with it the feeds of its own diffolution, are brought to confefs, that the prefent appearances are highly promifing.

It cannot but be fuppofed, that in the inveftigation of four thoufand and fixty-three claims, (of which only one thou .

fand

fand feven hundred and ninety-eight are allowed) and in making compenfation for a large portion of land, neceffarily cut through in making the great drain, many caufes of offence muft be given; but, I truft, neither partiality, negligence, nor corruption, can be imputed to them; and if they have erred, it has been an error of the head, and not of the heart.

Previous to the prefent drainage, this moor emptied itfelf into the river Parrett, fome miles above Bridgwater, and the fall from the moor was very trifling. Hence it followed, that the leaft flood covered it with water, and in that ftate it frequently remained many months. It was at firft fuggefted, by many people whofe abilities the county held in high eftimation, that nothing more was neceffary for the purpofe of draining the moor, than the opening and widening thefe old outlets; but it occurred to the commiffioners, that fuch a partial and ineffectual mode of procedure could not produce a radical cure. They therefore fet themfelves about to difcover a convenient place of difcharge lower down in the river, by which a greater and more rapid defcent might be gained.

An old fluice, called Dunbald-Clize, prefented itfelf as the defired fpot; and on levels being taken by Mr. WHITE, an eminent furveyor, it appeared that an extraordinary fall of nearly ten feet could be acquired; and that the defcent from the upper part of the moor to this outlet, (a diftance of about twelve miles) was nineteen feet, or about one foot and a half in a mile. The only objection which could be brought to the meafure, arofe from a confideration of the great expences which muft be incurred by cutting through two miles and a half of elevated land.

No alternative, however, prefented itfelf. It appeared that this plan muft be adopted, or the work would be incomplete.

o   Juftified

Juflified therefore by the concurrent opinion of Mr. WHITE, and of Mr. JESSOP, (whofe advice was taken) they proceeded boldly; and having erected at a great expence, and under numerous difficulties, (arifing from the morafly nature of the ground on which it was built) a ftrong fubftantial *fluice,* they proceeded to make a channel or cut fifteen feet deep, ten feet wide at the bottom, and fifty-five feet wide at the top.

It is impoffible to defcribe the ridicule which this undertaking excited. Some thought the commiffioners mad; others, and by far the majority, afcribed the boldnefs of the plan to the liberality of the proprietors, in allowing the commiffioners three guineas per day for attendance and management; and drew this fage conclufion, that the work would never be finifhed, but would be protracted till the expences *would equal* the value of the moor.

Uninfluenced by letters, or by menaces, the commiffioners perfevered; and they have the fatisfaction of feeing the principal difficulties overcome; and of hearing thofe very men, who were moft violent againft the meafure, acknowledge their error, and candidly confefs that the work is well executed, and promifes to be effectual.

It may be neceffary, by way of inftruction to others engaged in fchemes of the like nature, to ftate, that had the drain been made lefs wide at the top (and the opponents infifted that it fhould have been only twenty-fix feet wide) it would have collapfed, or fallen together; as it was, there were numerous and alarming flides, the repairing of which coft a confiderable fum, and there can be no doubt, but fomething of this kind will happen for years to come; for the fubftratum, at the depth of fixteen feet, is fo foft and morafly, that it gives way to the fuperincumbent clay, and rifes up in the middle of the drain.

This

This cut from the Dunbald fluice to the moor (a diftance of about two miles and a half) coft four-pence per cubic yard, or in the whole about three thoufand two hundred pounds; and the parochial drains, which were twelve feet wide at the top, four feet wide at the bottom, and fix feet deep, coft on an average two fhillings and feven-pence per rope (twenty progreffive feet.) Expenfive as this undertaking inevitably muft be, yet the benefit refulting from it will moft amply repay; for without faying any thing of the injury done to the health of the inhabitants in the circum-adjacent country, and which this drain, by rendering the air more falubrious, will totally remove; we may fairly ftate, that the probable improved value cannot be eftimated at lefs than four hundred and fifty thoufand pounds.*

The total amount of the expenditure is now afcertained; and it may give fome fatisfaction, if I inform my readers the fum total thereof. The following ftatement of the account *Dr.* and *Cr.* will approach pretty near the truth; but let it be underftood, that this calculation is made under the idea of *parochial fubdivifions*, without which little benefit will refult either to the publick or individuals. The principles which I have, in my report on the North-Eaft diftrict, fixed as *data, incontrovertible, viz.* That all commons, however rich and fertile the foil, are unproductive of profit, in confequence of *overftocking*, muft be here adhered to; and this argument is equally applicable to old inclofures. Let a farmer put *ten* head of cattle into a given piece of ground where only *five* fhould be depaftured, and the cattle will be

---

* If we add to this the capital neceffary to ftock this moor, the publick utility and importance of the undertaking will be more ftrongly manifefted. J. B.

of

of lefs worth after the grafs is confumed, than they were before: Of what value then is the land?

KING'S-SEDGMOOR.

Dr.	£.	s.	d.
To act of parliament, and all other incidental expences ———	1,628	15	0
Intereft of money borrowed ———	3,239	4	11
Commiffioners ———	4,314	7	8
Clerk ——— ———	1,215	19	0
Surveyor ——— —	908	12	6
Printers ——— ———	362	6	3
Petty expences — —	575	11	1
Land purchafed ——— ———	2,801	4	11
Drains, fluices, bridges, and roads —	15,418	2	8
Awards and incidentals ———	1,160	0	8
	31,624	4	8
To which add for fubdividing in each parifh —— ———	28,000	0	0
To original value of the moor, fay 10s. per acre, at twenty-five years purchafe —	150,000	0	0
	209,624	4	8
Profit ———	365,375	15	4
	£. 575,000	0	0
Cr.			
By 12,000 acres, at 35s. per acre, and 25 years purchafe — ———	525,000	0	0
By Improvement of 4000 acres of adjacent land, at 10s. per acre —	50,000	0	0
	£. 575,000	0	0

The

The above is the real expenditure taken from the commiffioners books, and about feven hundred acres have been fold to difcharge the fame.

N. B. Had the commiffioners been empowered to fell land at the commencement of the bufinefs, the expenditure would have been reduced five thoufand pounds by the difference in the intereft accompt.

This is not the only improvement, for by the addition of fuch a quantity of rich and productive grafs land, the upland inclofures, and common fields, may be greatly advanced in value. In fhort, it is difficult to point out all the benefits likely to accrue from this grand but arduous undertaking; befide, though the original value of the moor per acre is ftated to be ten fhillings, this is done merely with a view to give the arguments againft the inclofure the greateft weight; and perhaps it would have been more juft to have ftated its value at five fhillings per acre, or even lefs than that, for a right of ftocking could be rented for half a guinea per year.

Nor is the improved value at all exaggerated. On the contrary, I am confident it will exceed thirty-five fhillings per acre; for even in dry fummers three tons of hay per acre have been cut on inclofed lands adjoining or near the moor, the foil of which lands is in no refpect better than that of the moor.

Befides King's-Sedgmoor, there are other fimilar tracts of land on the adjacent rivers Tone and Yeo, on which no improvement has yet been attempted, namely, Normoor, near North-Petherton; Stanmoor, Currymoor, Weft-Sedgmoor, &c. near North-Curry; Weft-Moor, near Kingfbury; Wet-Moor, near Muchelny;* amounting in the

---

* Moft of thefe moors are now (1797) inclofed or inclofing.

whole

whole to about ten thoufand acres, independent of many
thoufand acres of low flooded inclofed lands, which might
be greatly improved by judicious draining.

Many of thefe moors are fuperior in their quality to
King's-Sedgmoor; and the example now fet before them
will, I truft, remove the mift from the proprietors' eyes, and
make them fee, in a true light, their own and the publick
intereſt.

Thefe lands would be fairly worth forty fhillings per acre
the moment they were drained and divided; and if taken
from the tenants, the original eftates would not be reduced
in their annual value one farthing.

But on this fubject, I have before enlarged very fully, and
fhall, therefore, only remark, to thofe who are influenced by
a humane regard to the right and comfort of the cottager,
that very few habitations of that defcription are to be found
near thefe moors; and a great part of thofe which do exift,
poffefs rights, which, when divided, may be worth two or
three hundred pounds; and if fold, will enable a man to
rent an eftate of one hundred pounds per annum, and to
keep twenty or thirty cows, in the management whereof his
whole family would become ufeful; and habits of induftry,
care, and œconomy, would by degrees be eftablifhed.

Adjoining this extenfive plain on the South fide, lies a
tra 2 of elevated land, compofed principally of fea fand and
fhells, well adapted to the purpofes of tillage, and in its nature fo fertile, that potatoes, turnips, carrots, hops, madder,
liquorice, and indeed almoft every root or plant ufeful in
hufbandry, might be grown on it in high perfection.

The arable is for the moft part in common fields, and
though exhaufted by conftant cropping, lets for near thirty
fhillings per acre. The wheat produced is of prime quality;
and as to barley, it is fuppofed that Chedzoy, Wefton-Zoyland,

land, Middlezoy, and Othery, produce the beft in the county. Were the common field lands of thefe parifhes divided into feparate property,* a portion of the new allotments in Sedgmoor annexed, and the whole comprized in farms of four or five hundred pounds per year, and let to fome enlightened fheep and turnip farmers, thefe parifhes might vie with any in the kingdom, both as to the *quantity* and *quality* of produce; but this cannot be effected whilft the lands are held by the prefent tenure. They are now occupied by fmall farmers holding under lives, fome one life, fome two, and a few three, and in fome inftances without any power or profpect of renewing.

The declivities of the hills, North and Eaft of Sedgmoor, are as barren as thofe before ftated are productive. The finer particles of the foil have for ages been wafhed into the moor by heavy rains; and the remaining mould is fhallow and fterile. When the moor is drained and made productive, this loft fertility may be in fome degree reftored, by carrying the produce of the moor to the uplands, either by the fheep-fold, or by confuming the hay thereon.

A great part of thefe high lands are in tillage, but the expence of ploughing is fo great, and the produce fo fmall, that it is matter of aftonifhment to me how the farmer can gain a livelihood. Somerton and Compton-Dundon, two confiderable parifhes to the Eaftward of Sedgmoor, are for the

---

* An attempt was lately made by the inhabitants of Wefton-Zoyland to divide and inclofe their common arable fields by act of parliament, but the fame was violently oppofed by the bifhop of Bath and Wells, under the idea that the tithes would be reduced by the application of the land to grafs inftead of corn. To fubvert this doctrine, which I conceive to be illiberal and oppreffive, I will be bold to affert, that *one half* the quantity would, under a fyftem of improvement, produce more than the *whole* does now.

moft

moſt part the property of the Earl of Ilcheſter; and I know
no pariſhes in the county ſo ſuſceptible of improvement.
The arable lands in common field lie ſo detached and divided, and the eſtates, farm-houſes, &c. are on the whole ſo
badly diſpoſed, that vaſt improvements might be made by
judicious exchanges, and by a proper arrangement of the
property. The ſoil is naturally good, and around the town
of Somerton is a multitude of gardens, which ſupply the
adjacent markets, even ſo far as Wells and Shepton-Mallett,
with early peaſe, beans, potatoes, &c. and in the month of
Auguſt with cucumbers by cart-loads; theſe they raiſe on
hillocks, under which is placed about two buſhels of *horſe-
dung*, collected in King's-Sedgmoor by children, and brought
to their gardens on the backs of, or drawn in carts by, aſſes.

There is a large market held every three weeks at Somerton during the ſummer months, and to it is brought an
immenſe number of ſheep, principally of the Dorſet breed,
together with oxen and other cattle; theſe are purchaſed by
graziers occupying the rich graſs land of the county.

On the ſummit of Polden-hill the corn land is for the
moſt part in common fields, and under the following courſe
of huſbandry: wheat, beans, fallow. The general produce
of wheat twelve buſhels per acre, and of beans the ſame;
very little barley or oats; but in the incloſed fields clover
and vetches thrive exceedingly; and if the farmers were to
have more of theſe articles, and plough leſs, they would
find their account in ſo doing; for nothing will bring a
farmer to poverty ſo ſoon as *poor corn land.*

From the nature of the ſtone on the ſurface, as well as
from ſome trials lately made with the borer, I have reaſon
to think, that on the Northern declivity of Polden-Hill may
be found a vein of marl which paſſes through the pariſhes
of Coſſington, Chilton, Eddington, Catcott, Shapwick, and
Aſhcott,

Afhcott, and from thence extends to Butleigh and Kingf-welton.* Should it prove of good quality, the difcovery will be highly important, and be the means of advancing the lands to treble their prefent value. This marl has been tried at Butleigh and Kingfwelton, and I believe with fuccefs.

It is not improbable that the fame vein extends to Yar-lington near Caftle-Cary, where it has been dug and ufed with great advantage by J. ROGERS, efq; whofe improve-ments both in agriculture and planting are very meritorious.

I cannot pafs over this neighbourhood without noticing the pleafant and fertile parifh of Caftle-Cary, which, both in refpect to foil and climate, cannot well be excelled. I could wifh fome fpirited agriculturift would here try, whe-ther the exclufive power of growing hops is confined to Hants, Kent, Worcefter, and a few other counties. The luxuriancy of the wild hop, the richnefs and depth of the foil, the mildnefs of the climature, and the fecurity from violent winds, all confpire to render fuch a fpeculation pro-mifing. The confumption of the county in this article is immenfe, and I have no doubt but I could felect in diffe-rent parts of it many hundred acres, as well adapted to this culture as any lands at Farnham, and at one-fourth the price which is there given; befides a much eafier accefs to manure of all kinds, and a greater and cheaper fupply of poles.

In Caftle-Cary potatoes are grown on a very large fcale, and it is no unufual thing to get one hundred and fixty facks (two hundred and forty pounds each) per acre, the average price about five fhillings per fack.

---

* There is likewife marl (but never much worked) about Doulting and Cranmore, and perhaps in various other parts of this diftrict.

MINERALS, &c.

Many attempts have been made in different parts of this diftrict to find *coal*, and pits to a confiderable depth have been funk at Glaftonbury, Chard, and other places, but no regular vein can be found; and it is the univerfal opinion of intelligent colliers, that there is no coal South of Mendip-Hills. Indeed fome will fay, that the ftrata run in a regular direction from South to North, through the whole kingdom of Britain.

WATER.

Irregation is but little practifed in this diftrict; there is, indeed, near the town of Ilminfter, fome land watered with the wafh of the town, the good effects of which are manifeft.

Some of the marfh-farmers alfo, on the river Brue, cut openings in the banks of the river in the winter months, and overflow their land with the thick water defcending from the hills.

This practice is certainly right.

CHAPTER III.

BUILDINGS.

THE old farm-houses are ill constructed and improperly
situated, but *new* ones are much improved in point of
uniformity, regularity, and convenience. Too much attention cannot be paid to this branch of rural management.
Instead of being placed in vales, and at some extreme part
of the estate, the farm buildings should be situated on some
high and central spot, so that the produce of the manure
arising therefrom, may be conveyed to and fro at the least
possible expence and trouble. So situated, the running of
the yard, stables, &c. might be collected in a reservoir, and
discharged from thence over the pastures with great ease
and advantage. Lime also might be occasionally thrown
into the reservoir, stirring it well previously to its being discharged on the land. The benefit to be derived from such
a practice is inconceivable.

Convenience in the disposing and connecting of the
buildings is also of material consequence. The straw-yards
should be placed at the front and backside of the barn, and
the stack-yards at each end. The barn should be filled
through an aperture or sheaf-hole, and not in the usual
way by waggons drawn on the floor to the great injury of
the same. Granary (if any be necessary, which I much
doubt, as all corn should go to market as soon as threshed)
should be over the waggon-house. The hog-sties and poul-
try-yard as near as possible to the dairy. The stable detached from the other buildings for fear of fire. In short,
every thing about the farm should be so contrived and disposed that the business may be done with the greatest possible ease and dispatch.

CHAPTER

CHAPTER IV.

MODE OF OCCUPATION.

THE greatest part of that rich tract of land, called Brent-Marsh, was, a few centuries ago, either the property of the Crown, or of the Abbey of Glastonbury. Many of these manors have been since dismembered, and I believe we may now say, that half this country is occupied by the owners.

The following tables of Mr. RICHARD LOCKE, of Burnham, will shew the great advance in the value of the land in the course of forty years.

No. I. Valuation in 1755.				No. II. Valuation in 1796.			
Quality of the Land.	*Price per Acre.*			*Quality of the Land.*	*Price per Acre.*		
	£.	s.	d.		£.	s.	d.
No. 1	1	5	0	No. 1	3	10	0
2	1	2	6	2	3	5	0
3	1	0	0	3	3	0	0
4	0	17	6	4	2	15	0
5	0	15	0	5	2	10	0
6	0	12	6	6	2	5	0
7	0	10	0	7	2	0	0
8	0	5	0	8	1	15	0
9	0	2	6	9	0	10	0

The same Mr. LOCKE adds, that every marsh farmer, occupying two hundred acres of land, does, or at least ought to grow, twenty acres of wheat, milk twenty cows, and feed twenty oxen and heifers, besides sheep and other cattle. And to shew the vast influx of wealth to this country, he engages to name fifty farmers, within the distance of a few miles, worth ten thousand pounds each, on an average, of their own or their father's getting, within the space of fifty years past.

In the middle part of this district there are many large proprietors, and rent is universally paid in money, without any personal service: great confidence exists in the Eastern part of this district, viz. about Wincanton, Horsington, &c. between the landlords and tenants. Estates are there principally held on mere *verbal* engagements, and scarce an instance can be produced of a breach of faith on part of the landlord, or suspicion on the part of the tenant.

Between Yeovil and Taunton, including the parishes of Martock, Puckington, Barrington, Kingsbury-Episcopi, Lambrook, South-Petherton, Ilminster, Hinton St. George, and the adjacent places, lies a tract of strong loamy land, from sixteen to thirty inches deep, on a substance of clay: a more pleasant country can rarely be found. The proprietaries are large, and the estates are mostly held by lives, under the lords of the fee: there are, however, many freeholders who possess from one hundred to seven hundred pounds per annum.

The farms are from forty to six hundred pounds per annum, and are composed partly of rich grazing and dairy land, worth from thirty to forty shillings per acre; partly orchard, from two pounds to three pounds ten shillings per acre. Sheep-walks, from fifteen shillings to twenty-five per acre; and the arable, from twenty shillings to twenty-five shillings per acre.

The rich pasture land is partly grazed with heifers, and partly devoted to the dairy. Few farmers milk their own cows, but let them out to a class of people, scarcely known in other counties, called *dairy-men*. A herd, of a good

breed,

breed, will now let for feven or eight pounds per cow; a certain portion of land is devoted to their fummer keeping, and a fufficient quantity of hay is provided by the farmer for their winter fuftenance.

This practice of letting dairies muft have originated either from *pride* or *indolence* on the part of the farmer's houfhold, and ought, in my opinion, to be checked by the landlord.

When the female part of a farmer's family is unemployed, (and, without a dairy, that muft be the cafe throughout great part of the year) diffipation, folly, and extravagance, take the lead, and domeftick care and induftry are entirely forgotten. Gentlemen of fortune fhould therefore fet their faces againft the practice, and refolve never to let an eftate to a farmer whofe family was too proud, or too indolent, to undertake the management of the different departments thereof.

LEASES.

The rack-rent leafes are generally for feven years, and the covenants confine the quantity of land in actual tillage, the number of crops, the mode of feeding, to fpend the produce on the premifes, to fell no hay, not to plough the meadow or pafture land, not to relet without confent, and for want of affets to re-enter.

There are few things that operate as a more powerful check to an improved agriculture than *fhort leafes*; and it were to be wifhed, that all lords of manors, poffeffing eftates leafed out on lives, would continue to grant renewals; and by fo doing, I verily think, they would promote their own intereft; for though it muft be acknowledged, that the leafing out a property upon three lives, at the ufual price of fourteen or fifteen years purchafe, is unfavourable to the intereft of the *grantor*, yet I think, that when an eftate has been fo leafed out, it is more his intereft to renew, than to run

againft

againſt the lives; for if compound intereſt of money be ſet againſt the reverſionary income, the latter is ſoon ſwallowed up. Great advantages would alſo reſult to ſociety from the general adoption of ſuch a meaſure; for it is well known, that eſtates falling into hand, are greatly reduced in value, let the reſtrictions in the leaſe be ever ſo judicious. In confirmation of this idea, do we not ſee that lands held under the church, under corporations, and under charity endowments, &c. *where renewal is certain*, are nearly in as good a ſtate as freehold property, and eaſily to be diſtinguiſhed from lands held under private lords, where ſuch renewal is frequently withheld. Various are the opinions reſpecting the comparative advantage attending the purchaſe of freehold and leaſehold property. In favour of the former, the natural, and indeed laudable pride of man ſteps in, and decidedly determines. Moſt men wiſh to poſſeſs property independent of all controul; and the ſuits and ſervices exacted under many leaſes, are a relict of feudal tyranny, highly diſguſting to men fond of freedom and independence; but let us have recourſe to figures, and we ſhall find that two men ſtarting together *with one thouſand four hundred pounds each*, and purchaſing, the one a freehold eſtate, of fifty-ſix pounds per annum, at twenty-five years purchaſe, and the other a leaſehold for three lives, of one hundred pounds per annum, at fourteen years purchaſe, would be in very different ſituations at the end of twenty-one years. Calculating the intereſt of each at five per cent. and allowing *three* renewals, at two years purchaſe, (clear income) the leaſeholders eſtate, of one hundred pounds per annum, (nett) would, at the expiration of twenty-one years, coſt him 1205l. 18s. and the freeholders eſtate, of fifty-ſix pounds per annum, (nett) would, at the expiration of the ſame term, coſt him 1900l. 1s. as the following calculation will confirm.

FREE-

FREEHOLD, 56l. per annum, (net) and 25 years purchase.

£.					£.		
	1400	0		Brought up	1513	19	
Add Interest	70	5 per cent.		Add Interest	75	14	
	1470	0			1589	13	
Deduct rent	56	0		Deduct rent	56	0	
	1414	0	1st yr.		1533	13	8th yr.
Add Int.	70	14		Add Int.	76	14	
	1484	14			1610	7	
Deduct rent	56	0		Deduct rent	56	0	
	1428	14	2d yr.		1554	7	9th yr.
Add Int.	71	9		Add Int.	77	14	
	1500	3			1632	1	
Deduct rent	56	0		Deduct rent	56	0	
	1444	3	3d yr.		1576	1	10th yr.
Add Int.	72	4		Add Int.	78	16	
	1516	7			1654	17	
Deduct rent	56	0		Deduct rent	56	0	
	1460	7	4th yr.		1598	17	11th yr.
Add Int.	73	0		Add Int.	79	19	
	1533	7			1678	16	
Deduct rent	56	0		Deduct rent	56	0	
	1477	7	5th yr.		1622	16	12th yr.
Add Int.	73	17		Add Int.	81	3	
	1551	4			1703	19	
Deduct rent	56	0		Deduct rent	56	0	
	1495	4	6th yr.		1647	19	13th yr.
Add Int.	74	15		Add Int.	82	8	
	1569	19			1730	7	
Deduct rent	56	0		Deduct rent	56	0	
	1513	19	7th yr.		1674	7	14th yr.
							Brought

	£.	s.			£.	s.	
Brought up	1674	.7	14th yr.	*Brought up*	1849	16	
Add Int.	83	14		Deduct rent	56	0	
	1758	1			1793	16	18th yr.
Deduct rent	56	0		Add Int.	89	14	
	1702	1	15th yr.		1883	10	
Add Int.	85	2		Deduct rent	56	0	
	1787	3			1827	10	19th yr.
Deduct rent	56	0		Add Int.	91	7	
	1731	3	16th yr.		1918	17	
Add Int.	86	11		Deduct rent	56	0	
	1817	14			1862	17	20th yr.
Deduct rent	56	0		Add Int.	93	4	
	1761	14	17th yr.		1956	1	
Add Int.	88	2		Deduct rent	56	0	
	1849	16			1900	1	21st yr.

Freeholder's purchase of fifty-six pounds per annum, nett, allowing five per cent. compound interest, stands him at the end of twenty-one years in £1900 1 0

First purchase - - - 1400 0 0

Lofs 500 1 0

LEASEHOLD,

LEASEHOLD, 100*l.* per annum, nett, and 14 years purchase.

£.	s.
1400	0
Add Interest 70	0
1470	0
Deduct rent 100	0
1370	0 1st yr.
Add Int. 68	10
1438	10
Deduct rent 100	0
1338	10 2d yr.
Add Int. 66	19
1405	9
Deduct rent 100	0
1305	9 3d yr.
Add Int. 65	5
1370	14
Deduct rent 100	0
1270	14 4th yr.
Add Int. 63	11
1334	5
Deduct rent 100	0
1234	5 5th yr.
Add. Int. 61	14
1295	19
Deduct rent 100	0
1195	19 6th yr.
Add Int. 59	16
1255	15
Deduct rent 100	0
1155	15 7th yr.

£.	s.
Brought up 1155	15 7th yr.
Add renewal 2 yrs. purch. nett rent } 200	0
1355	15
Add Int. 67	16
1423	11
Deduct rent 100	0
1323	11 8th yr.
Add Int. 66	4
1389	15
Deduct rent 100	0
1289	15 9th yr.
Add Int. 64	10
1354	5
Deduct rent 100	0
1254	5 10th yr.
Add Int. 62	14
1316	19
Deduct rent 100	0
1216	19 11th yr.
Add Int. 60	17
1277	16
Deduct rent 100	0
1177	16 12th yr.
Add Int. 58	18
1236	14
Deduct rent 100	0
1136	14 13th yr.
	Brought

£.	s.		£.	s.
Brought up 1136	14	13th yr.	*Brought up* 1241	6
Add Int. 56	17		Deduct rent 100	0
1193	11		1141	6 18th yr.
Deduct rent 100	0		Add Int. 57	1
1093	11 14th yr.		1198	7
Add renewal 200	0		Deduct rent 100	0
1293	11		1098	7 19th yr.
Add Int. 64	14		Add Int. 54	18
1358	5		1153	5
Deduct rent 100	0		Deduct rent 100	0
1258	5 15th yr.		1053	5 20th yr.
Add Int. 62	18		Add Int. 52	13
1321	3		1105	18
Deduct rent 100	0		Deduct rent 100	0
1221	3 16th yr.		1005	18 21st yr.
Add Int. 61	1		Add another renewal 200	0
1282	4		1205	18
Deduct rent 100	0			
1182	4 17th yr.			
Add Int. 59	2			
1241	6			

Leafeholder's purchafe of one hundred pounds per annum, (nett) allowing five per cent. compound intereft, ftands him at the end of twenty-one years (admitting three renewals at two years purchafe nett income) in the fum of £1205 18

Profit — — 194 2

Firft purchafe — 1400 0

Free-

	£.	s.	d.
Freeholder's lofs at five per cent.	500	1	0
Leafcholder's profit at ditto	194	2	0
Difference	£.694	3	0

N. B.   A deduction fhould be made from Leafcholder's profit, for lord's rent and heriots, and fomething from free-holder's lofs, for increafing value of timber; but thefe will not be fufficient to invalidate the general conclufions.

The great caufe why leafcholds are held in low eftimation by the commonality, arifes from the improvidence of the general holders, who for the moft part expend the whole income of their eftates, without laying by a fund for the purpofe of renewal; hence it follows, that their eftates fall into hand, and the owners are reduced from a ftate of comparative affluence to beggary; at which event, the general exclamation is, *Who would have leafehold property?*

CHAPTER VII.

ARABLE LAND.

Flax and Hemp.

FLAX.

IN the rich fertile country, extending from Wincanton, through Yeovil, to Crewkerne, flax and hemp are culti vated in great abundance, the value of which is in proportion to the skill and spirit with which it is cultivated.

A crop of flax greatly depends both on the management of the land previous to sowing, and on the goodness of the seed.

To raise it to advantage, it should be sown on new broke-up ground, ploughed once, and the surface hacked. It should be harrowed once before sowing, and twice after. Seed imported from Riga, and sold at about fourteen shillings the bushel, is to be preferred; and the produce for two or three years may, without change, be sown again; April and the beginning of May are the months for sowing, and the quantity two bushels and a half per acre.

The great damage done to flax in its growth is by weeds; and if those people you employ to weed it be not careful, they may do more harm with their feet, than their hands can do good. At any rate, the weeds must not be suffered to get head of the flax, for if they do, it will become stunted in its growth, and get to no height.

When the plant is arrived at its growth, and is in full blossom, which in common seasons will be about the beginning of July, it is fit to be pulled, if the grower has a greater regard to the produce of the stalk, than to the seed.

However,

However, it is a common practice to injure the whole crop for the sake of the seed; and to let it remain till the seed begins to ripen, so as to have both flax and seed. In this case, the land suffers greatly; for flax seeded is a great impoverisher, but if pulled whilst in blossom, is an excellent preparative for turnips, which should always follow a flax crop instead of wheat. The great reason why the Irish, and indeed most foreign flax is finer than the English, is, because they pull it early, and sow particular spots purposely for seed; and, perhaps, it would be politick in government to grant a bounty on all foreign flax seed sown in this kingdom, so as to reduce the price of foreign seed nearly to a level with our own; by this, the growth of flax (and with it the linen trade) would be encouraged, which has of late suffered considerable diminution by the restrictions to its cultivation imposed by land-owners, under the idea of great injury done to the land by the culture of this plant.

After the flax is pulled, there are two methods of working it; the first is called *rating of it*, that is, steeping it in water in order to loosen the rind, and separate it from the stalk; and the other is called *dew-ripening*, which is the spreading it on grass land, and by rain and dew producing the same effect. The early flax is mostly watered, which is done by laying the bundles in a pond or reservoir of soft water, and keeping them down by stones, or any other heavy bodies. In the course of seven or eight days the rind will be sufficiently loosened, and they must be taken out of the water, spread abroad, and dried. In this part of the operation, great skill and attention are necessary; for if it be left in the water too long, the threads become rotten and useless to the manufacturer; it is, therefore, more adviseable to take it out *too soon*, than to leave it *too long* in the pits. Those who raise flax for the seed and stalk both, go through an operation

tion

tion called ripling; this is, separating the feed from the stalk, by passing the flax through a kind of comb before it is watered. These combs are made of iron, and the teeth are so close that the heads cannot pass through, and are consequently pulled off.

It is observable, that the land on which rated flax is spread to prepare it for housing, is greatly improved thereby; and if it be spread on a coarse sour pasture, the herbage will be totally changed, and the best sorts of grasses will make their appearance. Having myself cultivated flax on a large scale, and observing the almost instantaneous effect produced by the water in which the flax was immersed, I was induced some years ago to apply it to some pasture land, by means of watering carts, similar to those used near London in watering the roads. The effect was astonishing, and advanced the land in value ten shillings per acre. This liquid is much superior to animal urine. The practice I therefore strongly recommend to the cultivators of flax; possibly it may not be a new idea, but I believe it is seldom so applied.

The second method, namely, dew ripening, may be carried on immediately after the flax is pulled, or it may be dried and mowed; and in the months of February or March the seed may be stamped from the stalk, and the latter spread on the grass land to ripen.

The principal manures made use of by the growers of flax are, the sheepfold, woollen rags, horn shavings, and lime; and it is no unusual thing for the farmer to find ground, manure, ploughing, and all team work; and the labourer to find seed, and all manual labour, dividing at the conclusion the produce, in a way similar to that before stated in the *travel* account. The expence and produce of an acre of watered flax may be thus estimated:

Dr.

Dr.	£. s. d	Cr.
To rent of land, &c.	2 0 0	
To manure —	2 10 0	
To ploughing ——	0 8 0	
To hacking —	0 5 0	
To harrowing and		
rolling ——	1 4 0	
To feed and fowing		
(Riga) —	1 15 0	
To weeding ——	0 10 0	
To pulling —	0 6 0	
To halling to pits and		By 40 dozen of
watering. [N. B.		flax, at 7s. 14 0 0
The price of this		By bounty 4d.
depends on the dif-		per flone - 0 10 4
tance! —	0 10 0	(allowing 1s.
To taking out of pits,		for expences)
halling, fpreading,		
drying, and houfing	0 14 0	
To braking, fwing-		
ling, and dreffing		
40 dozen, at 1s. 4d.	2 13 4	
To tithe —	0 5 0	
	12 0 4	
Profit ——	2 10 0	
	£. 14 10 4	£. 14 10 4

To this profit may be added the fucceeding turnip crop,
and the improvement of the land by the manure; without
thefe, it cannot be confidered as very lucrative, for it is precarious; and if a dry feafon follow the fowing, it frequently
happens

happens that the flax does not get to any height, and is
scarcely worth pulling. Some people may think the expences over rated; but if they consider that the calculation
is made under the idea of an acre *statute measure*, and also
that it includes beer, tools, and many other trifling articles
of expence, they will be disposed to acknowledge it to be
correct—at least, I can say, that it is drawn from my own
experience of its truth.

HEMP.

THE culture of Hemp and Flax agrees in many respects;
but in their nature and form they are widely different. In
flax, the male and female embrio are lodged in the same
flower; but in hemp the male is found on some plants, and
the female on others; they are, therefore, called *male* and
female hemp; that which has only flowers is the *male*, and
that which has seeds is the *female* hemp. The male is ripe
five or six weeks before the female, and they both arise from
the same seed.

Hemp likes a deep, rich, dry, sandy loam, and abhors a
cold wet clay; a piece of woodland, grubbed up, generally
answers well. It requires fresh land, good tillage, but seldom
dung: even land exhausted with other crops, *if well tilled*,
will produce good hemp, and if properly managed, will leave
the land as clean as a garden.

The quantity of seed per acre about three bushels, and
time of sowing April or May; great care must be taken to
keep off the birds, for they are very fond of the seed, and
their time of feeding is principally before sun-rise, and
within half an hour of sun-set. Compleat weeding is as
necessary for hemp as for flax.

About the beginning of August the male hemp will be
ripe, and great care should be taken that the pullers do not

trample

trample and injure the female hemp left standing. It must be gathered into small bundles, and nothing more is necessary than to dry it in a proper manner, so as to make it fit for working.

In managing the female hemp, particular regard is to be had to the seed; care, therefore, must be taken in drying it. After it is tied up in bundles about the size of a yard round, it should be set up in the sun for three or four days; but if the weather be difficult, it may be stacked in small mows of about a waggon-load each, where it may remain till it is thoroughly dry, and fit to be housed; a little wet does not injure the *stalk*, but it greatly damages the seed. An acre of land will produce from twenty to thirty bushels of seed; and the stalk of the female hemp is more valuable than the stalk of the male. The watering, braking, and dressing of hemp, is so nearly like those operations on flax, that I shall not detain my reader any longer on this article, and shall only add, that in many cases the crop is more profitable than that of flax.

TURNIPS.

In this part of the county turnips are also grown on a large scale. They are univerfally sown broadcast, once hoed, and for the most part fed on the land as a preparation for barley.＊

Wheat, barley, oats, beans, and peafe, are in general culture; but there is nothing in the mode of management worthy of notice.

Clover is the grafs generally sown; and their courfe of hufbandry,—1ft. Wheat;—2d. Turnips;—3d. Barley;—4th. Clover, Vetches, Flax, Hemp, Peafe, or Beans;—and 5th. Wheat again.

＊ When working oxen are fed with turnips they fhould not have water. J. B.

The crops of the *large* farmers are greater than thofe of the *fmall*, owing to their fowing more turnips and vetches, and confequently keeping a larger folding flock. Some of the arable land, being in common field, is in the following courfe, 1ft. Wheat;—2d. Barley;—3d. Clover, Vetches, Potatoes, &c. and then Wheat again. Thefe crops are comparatively fmall; wheat is found to fucceed better after flax or hemp, *(provided they be not feeded)* than after potatoes or beans.

Fallowing is not practifed; the prevailing opinion is, that corn crops, equally good, may be obtained after turnips, clover, potatoes, peafe, vetches, beans, hemp, flax, &c. (if well manured and kept clean) with thofe after a compleat *fummer fallow*. " Thefe are enlightened farmers!"

Let any man vifit this country, view their crops, and the condition of the land, and many arguments will not be neceffary to make him an *antifallowift*, at leaft, on foils like thefe.

The large farmers carry all their dung on their *pafture* land, (excellent!) and fupport their arable by folding, lime, horn-fhavings, rags, &c.; but the fmall farmers act directly the reverfe. The large farmers all plough with oxen; the fmall farmers with horfes. A renter of fixty pounds per year muft keep *three* horfes, for he cannot plough with lefs; and one of five hundred pounds per year will not keep more than *eight*; here is a comparative faving of twenty horfes, and juftifies my former predilection for large *corn* farms.

CHAPTER VIII.

GRASS.

THE Natural Meadows and Pastures of this division are kept in high condition; and their Artificial Grasses may vie with any in the kingdom.

CHAPTER IX.

GARDENS AND ORCHARDS.

BEFORE I take my leave of this rich district, it may not be amiss to say something of their orchards, to the production of which, the land is peculiarly adapted. Permit me, therefore, to state, by way of encouragement to planting, that there is scarcely an orchard that will not let for four or five pounds per acre; and if the trees are planted at proper distances, viz. sixty feet every way, the pasture suffers but little injury; the strength of the soil enables the trees to throw forth a multitude of roots sideways, near the surface; it is, therefore, of the utmost importance that they should be placed at proper distances. In confirmation of this idea, a tree thus placed in an orchard belonging to Mr. BATH, of Mark, has frequently produced four hogsheads of cyder; and the tenant told me, that he would give for it one guinea per year for a term of twenty-one years. The tree is not more than forty years old. Most orchards are planted *too close*. The desire of having a great deal of fruit upon a little ground, is the cause of so doing; but the method defeats the purpose. When an orchard is first planted, sixty

feet

feet appear an immenfe diftance; and I have known many, who, acknowledging the advantage of diftance, feel loth to admit fo great a vacancy, and have planted at thirty feet, with a full refolution of rooting up every other tree at fifteen or twenty years old; but alas! this is fcarcely practicable; after a tree is brought to full bearing, an infurmountable reluctance to eradicate it occurs, which arguments, however powerful, cannot overcome; and after all, many rational farmers are of opinion, that orchards planted at great diftances feldom bear well.

The forts of apple in beft eftimation are, Royal Wilding, White-Styre, Court of Week Pippin, Pounfet or Cadbury, Flood-Hatch, Black Pit Crab, Buckland, Mediate or South-ham, Royal-Jerfey, Woodcock, Red-Hedge Pip, Old-Jerfey, and Redftreak.* They are grafted on crab ftocks in the nurfery, with any grofs growing fruit.

As foon as the ground for the orchard is ready, plant your trees, and be particularly careful not to plant them deep in the ground. After about four years, lop their heads and graft them with the fruit you moft efteem, taking care to adapt your grafts to the ftock. In other words, let your grafts, and the trees on whofe heads you graft, be as fimilar in refpect to luxuriancy as you can; on this a great deal depends.

It is found, that a luxuriant grofs-growing graft will never fucceed on a flow-growing ftock, and fo *vice verfa*. It may alfo be obferved, that fome excellent forts of fruit are na-turally fo flow of growth, that a man, inftead of planting for himfelf, plants for his grandchildren; and if you endea-vour to force them (which is often injudicioufly done) with

---

* A four yellow apple, ftreaked with red on the fun-fide, be its name what it may, is undoubtedly a good cyder fruit. A. C.

luxuriant

luxuriant flocks, you occasion disease. The tree never becomes large or lasting, and the fruit will be tasteless and insipid.

Great care should be taken to secure the trees whilst young from the nabbing and rubbing of cattle, and more especially sheep; but in this respect the planters in this county are not very attentive, nor is there any thing worth notice in their management of the fruit.——The average price of the article is about thirty shillings per hogshead.

CYDER-MAKING PROCESS.

The fruit being properly matured, every necessary utensil ought to be set in order for cyder-making; the mill, press, tubs, casks, and pails, clean washed, and suffered to dry before they are used.

Several methods are practised for converting apples to pommage; but the two most chiefly in use are, the bruising stone with a circular trough, and the apple-mill. The best internal construction of a mill seems to be that which has two pair of rollers, the upper pair being stuck with coggs and dags; and the under pair being of very hard wood, turned smooth, and worked with coggs only. The upper rollers grinding the apples to a coarse pommage, and the under ones squeezing it to a very fine pulp.

The apples being, by either of the foregoing methods, properly bruised, the pommage is carried to the press, and a square cheese made thereof, by placing very clean sweet straw or reed between the various layers of pommage, or else by putting the same into hair-cloths and placing them one on another.* To this cheese, after standing a while, a

---

* It is of importance, that the straw or reed be sweet and perfectly free from any sustness, lest the cyder be impregnated therewith.—Particular care ought also to be taken to keep hair-cloths sweet, by frequent washing and drying, else the ill effects of their acidity will be communicated to the cyder.

flight preffure is at firft given, which is gradually increafed, until all the juice or *muft* be expreffed; after which, this *muft* is ftrained through a fieve and put into veffels.

Thus far cyder-making is a mere manual operation, performed with very little fkill in the operator; but here the great art of making *good cyder* commences. Nature foon begins to work a wonderful change in this turbid liquor; and by fermentation converts it into a wholfome, vinous, heart-cheering beverage, nearly equal to the juice of the grape itfelf.

It is well known, that there are various ftages of fermentation in thefe juices, each of which changes the very quality and nature of this fluid; but the principal, which are to be particularly attended to in the inftance now under confideration, are three; namely, the *vinous*, the *acetous*, and the *putrefactive*. The firft converts the *muft* from its turbid fulfome ftate, to a tranfparent fpiritous liquor.

If the juice be expreffed from *four* apples, this fermentation is perfected in two or three days; but if from *fweet* apples, not under a week or ten days.

The next ftage of fermentation gives an acidity to the vinous liquor before fpoken of, convérting it to vinegar.

This fermentation begins foon (frequently in few hours) after the vinous is ended; and, if the fermentation be improperly haftened by heat, *before* the vinous is perfected. The third (and all fucceeding fermentations) difengages an alkali from the liquor, and gives it a tendency to putrefaction.

To regulate the firft, and to check the others, is then the great bufinefs of that cyder-maker who would attach to himfelf the fatisfaction and fame every one is emulous of.

Let us, therefore, confider how thefe ends are beft attained.

It

It is well known, that fermentation should not by too much heat be carried on rapidly, nor by extreme cold too slowly; as in each cafe the fermenting body will be injured. Hence it appears, that a certain degree of warmth, or rather imperceptible heat, conduces best to regulate this operation. This degree of warmth may be understood to rest between thirty-eight and forty-six degrees of Farenheit's thermometer. If then the warmth of the cellar in which new-made cyder is placed be between these points, we may expect (no adventitious cause interrupting) that the vinous fermentation will commence and go on with due regularity.

It has been observed above, that fermentation is an intestine motion of the parts of a fermentable body; this motion, in the present cafe, is always accompanied with a small hissing noise and evident ebullition; the bubbles rising to the surface, and there forming a scum or soft spongy crust over the whole liquor. This crust is frequently raised and broken by the air as it disengages itself from the liquor, and forces its way through it. These effects continue while the fermentation is brisk, and at last gradually cease. The liquor now appears clear to the eye, and has a pungent vinous sharpness upon the tongue.

Now is the critical moment which the cyder-maker ought not to lose sight of; for if he would have a strong and generous liquor, all further sensible fermentation must be stopt. This is best done by racking off the pure part into open vessels, and placing them in a more cool situation for a day or two: after which, it may again be barrelled and placed in some cool place for the winter.

It is possible, however, that a variety of avocations at the season of cyder-making may take off too much of the farmer's attention from this branch of œconomics, and give opportunity to the acetous fermentation to come on, ere he

is

is aware of it. What remedy (it may be afked) has he to prevent the ill effects thereof running to full extent?—Several have been tried; fometimes with a degree of fuccefs, at other times wholly unavailable.

The moft popular ones are the following:—a bottle of French brandy, half a gallon of fpirit extracted from the lees of cyder, or a pailful of old cyder poured into the cafk, foon after the acetous fermentation is begun; but no wonder if all thefe fhould fail if the cyder be ftill continued in a clofe warm cellar. To give effect to either, it is neceffary that the liquor be as much expofed to a colder atmofphere as conveniently may be, and that for a confiderable length of time. By fuch means, it is poffible to reprefs the fecond fermentation in a great meafure; and if a cafk of *good* cyder cannot from thence be obtained, a *tolerable* one may.— Thefe remedies are innocent; but if the farmer or cyder-merchant attempt to cover the accident occafioned by negligence or inattention, by applying *any preparation of lead*, let him reflect that *he is about to commit an abfolute and unqualified murder on thofe whofe hap it may be to drink his poifonous draught.**

* Should, however, any one be wicked enough thus to fophifticate a cafk of cyder, his villainy may be detected in the following manner: Make a decoction of orpiment in lime water, drop a fmall quantity hereof into a glafs of fufpected cyder, and if it has been impregnated with any preparation of lead, its colour will foon change to a brown, dirty red, or black; but if it be genuine, its colour will remain nearly the fame. Some liquid liver of fulphur will have a fimilar effect. Bifhop WATSON directs us to boil together, in a pint of water, an ounce of quick lime and half an ounce of flowers of brimftone, a few drops of this liquor being let fall into a glafs of cyder containing lead, will change the whole into a colour more or lefs brown. Effays, vol. iii. p. 371.

In the 4th and 5th vol. of the Bath Society's Papers, there are feveral valuable papers on the pernicious effects of lead veffels in dairies, which deferve publick notice and attention.

Q   Stumming

Stumming of cyder is a provincial phrase, signifying the fuming a cask with burning sulphur; and is thus performed: take a strip of canvas cloth about twelve inches long and two broad, let it be dipped in melted brimstone. When this match is dry, let it be lighted and suspended from the bung of a cask (in which there are a few gallons of cyder) until it is burnt out: the cask must remain stopped for an hour or more, and then be rolled to and fro, to incorporate the fumes of the match with the cyder, after which it may be filled. If the stumming be designed only to suppress some slight improper fermentation, the brimstone match is sufficient; but if it be required to give any additional flavour to the cyder, some powdered ginger, cloves, or cinnamon, &c. may be strewed on the match when it is made:—the burning these ingredients with the sulphur will convey somewhat of their fragrance to the whole cask of cyder; but to do it to the best advantage, it must be performed before the vinous fermentation be fully perfected.

To perfect a vessel of cyder, after the foregoing steps have been taken, it will be found necessary now and then to supply the waste occasioned by evaporation and insensible fermentation with fresh cyder; and about the beginning of April following to give it a final racking. At this time a commixture of cyder made from the Jersey or any other luscious and sweet apple, with that of the four apples, may be recommended, to give it a general regular colouring.— Should, however, a higher colour be required than what results from such commixture, a small quantity of burnt or melted sugar, prepared in the following manner, will produce the desired effect: Take a pound of sugar, and put it into a stew-pan with a little water, and place it over a clear fire, stirring it frequently till it turns black; take it off the fire, and as cools apply some cyder thereto, by little and

little;

little, and continue ftirring it till it be thoroughly mixed. This colouring tinges to perfection, is very cheap, gives no luscious sweetness, but rather an agreeable bitternefs, and thus recommends itself to the nicer palates.

Soon after this, in the fame month, the cyder may be bottled; and by the month of June the owner may expect to find himfelf poffeffed of a rich, pleafant, and wholesome liquor.

" If there be a general characterillick of good cyder fruit, " it feems to be this: that the apple be of a yellow or light " red ground, tinged with red ftreaks on the fun fide, of a " fmart acid flavour, with firm but juicy parenchyma;—if " it poffefs thefe criteria, be it called by what name foever " it may, it will, doubtlefsly, make good cyder."

CHAPTER

CHAPTER X.

WOODS and PLANTATIONS.

THE low lands are badly wooded, and planting in general shamefully neglected, particularly a very profitable part of it, viz. the elm and the willow, both of which thrive in this soil, and the latter is much wanted for the purposes both of the thatcher and fisherman.

There is, in the eastern part, an extensive chain of wood from the parish of East-Cranmore through Downhead, Cloford, Whatley, Elm, &c. several miles in length, besides other woods of considerable importance. On the borders of Wiltshire is a large forest, which extends from Pen-Selwood to within three miles of Frome.

This forest was disafforested about the seventh of Charles I. and divided into three portions, one whereof was allotted to the lords of manors, another to the commoners, and a third to the crown. The latter was sold off to the adjoining landholders. Sir Richard Hoare, bart. Thomas Southcote, esq; the Duke of Somerset, William Beckford, esq; the Earl of Corke, and the Marquis of Bath, are the owners of the greater part of the woods now remaining. No great quantity of woodland, in this tract of country, has been grubbed within the last forty years, but much new ground has been planted during that period, particularly on the hills belonging to the Marquis of Bath, Mr. Beckford, and Sir Richard Hoare, very much to the profit of the owners, as well as to the ornament and convenience of the country.

These woodlands are, in general, in a state of coppice wood, with an intermixture of timber, chiefly oak; but the soil, foil, particularly in the vallies, being in general of a ftrong yellow clay, is of fo cold and retentive a nature, that vegetation is exceedingly flow; and the oak trees, though fpringing up fpontaneoufly, in great abundance, are fo apt to get moffy and dead topped, that few of them come to a large fize; and yet, on account of its vicinity to good inland markets, which are never overflocked with underwood or timber, the profit from woodland, under any tolerable degree of management, may be fairly taken at nearly double the value of the adjoining land in an arable or pafture flate; and the profit arifing from the new-planted hills, particularly the fandy parts of them, has been, in many inflances, near ten per cent. on the original expence of planting and fencing.

Surely no greater inducement can be held out to the owners to preferve the old woods, or to plant new ones, in foils and fituations fo favourable to their growth, and in a country that would fuffer very materially for want of wood, if deprived of this refource.

But as the profit arifing from thefe woods depends very much on the mode of management, it will not be thought improper to give a few general rules, taken from the appearance of fuch of thofe woods as are *well managed*, to the owners of thofe woods that have a very different appearance, and that appearance not occafioned by any apparent difadvantages of foil or fituation.

The natural defect of thefe woods, particularly that part of them which abounds with oak timber, has already been ftated to be the flownefs of their growth. This proceeds from three caufes:

1ft. The native coldnefs of the foil.

2dly. The expofure of a great part of the woods to the fouth-weft wind.——And,

3dly. The injury the woods receive from cattle.

In

In proportion as thefe defects have been obviated by art, the woods may be faid to be well or ill managed. Draining the cold wet parts of them is the obvious remedy of the firft-mentioned defect. Screening them from winds, by fkirting with Scotch fir and other hardy plants, and keeping them moderately thick of timber, are the beft remedies for the fecond. But both thefe remedies will be ufelefs, unlefs a ftrict attention be paid to the fences, fo as to keep the woods from being cropped by cattle. This is particularly hurtful to flow growing timber, and by it thefe woods (though in very few inftances fubject to common rights) are very materially injured.

Wherever, as is the cafe in the greateft part of the woods, oak timber is the natural produce of the foil, it fhould, by all means, be encouraged; and as its growth to a certain period is ufually very rapid, and afterwards altogether as flow, it fhould be cut when that period of ftagnation commences, and a frefh fet let up to fupply the deficiency.

There are many inftances in thefe woods, where, although the underwood cannot by the beft management be made worth more than eight pounds per acre at fixteen years growth, yet at leaft twelve fmall oaks, worth twenty fhillings a-piece, may be cut regularly at every round of the wood, from every acre, and that without injury to the underwood.

No fyftem will pay equal to this; the underwood, inftead of fuffering from the multiplicity of trees, will abfolutely be better than without any. The fhelter afforded by thefe trees making amends for the damage done by the dropping from them; efpecially as afh underwood, on which the value of coppice wood greatly depends in this country, (and which does not grow well under the dropping of timber) does not in general thrive well in thefe cold foils.

The

The underwood that thrives beſt in them is oak, willow, alder, and above all *birch*. Theſe kinds of wood will, if proper attention be paid to them, be fit to cut at ſixteen years growth; if cut oftener, the wood will ſcarcely be large enough for the purpoſes of the country; and if ſuffered to ſtand much longer, the timber is apt to receive a check from the cold winds, when deprived of the ſhelter of the underwood. The coal-pits near Mendip furniſh a never-failing market for the poles of this underwood, and the demand for the domeſtick uſes of the country is fully ſufficient for the reſidue; and as not only this end of the county of Somerſet, but alſo the adjoining part of Wiltſhire, depend on theſe woods for oak timber, the demand is, and always will be, equal to the ſupply.

From the produce of theſe woods charcoal is ſometimes burnt for the uſe of the manufacturers. The wood is then cleaved and heaped into what is called a cord of wood, the dimenſions of which are,

$$. \ 8 \text{ feet } 4 \text{ inches long,}$$
$$4 \text{ do. } 4 \text{ do. high,}$$
$$2 \text{ do. } 2 \text{ do. broad.}$$

The price of cleaving and heaping from 1s. 10d. to 2s. 3d. per cord. The expences of burning one hundred cord of wood, the value of which for fuel is ſix ſhillings per cord, may be thus eſtimated:

	£.	s.	d.
Cabin for the man — — — — —	0	5	0
Burning 263 ſacks of charcoal, at 6d. per ſack	6	11	6
Halling ditto, at 6d. per ſack — —	6	11	6
Unloading — — — — —	0	12	0
Wear and tear of ſacks — — —	3	10	0
	17	10	0
One hundred cord of wood, as fuel, at 6s.	30	0	0
	47	10	0

PRODUCE.

Two hundred and fixty-three facks, of nine bufhels
    each, at 4s. 10½d. per fack   —   —   64   2   1½
From which deduct   —   —   —   47 10   0

Balance in favour of charcoal in comparifon with
    fire-wood   —   —   —   — £.16 12 1½

As to the new-planted woods, particularly thofe on the
high parts of Rodenbury-hill, Witham-park, and Kingfettle-
hill, although all kinds of wood grow well upon them, (and
efpecially upon the fandy parts of them) provided they are
planted in maffes fufficiently large to fhelter themfelves from
the winds, yet nothing appears to grow fo well as fir, and
particularly *Scots fir*. An occafional mixture of filver fir,
fpruce fir, and larch, on fome of the beft and moft fheltered
fpots, and a general thin mixture of beech and other foreft
trees, add certainly very much to. the *variety* and *beauty* of
the plantations in which they have been introduced; but in
point of *profit* the Scots fir ftands unequalled, for rapidity
of growth, for fuperiority in value when grown, and above
all, for its ability to bear the cold expofure of the country.

There are inftances on thefe hills, on land not worth, in
a ftate of pafturage, three fhillings per acre, that plantations
of Scots firs, of thirty years old, are now worth eighty
pounds per acre,[*] and the demand for this kind of wood in-
creafes as faft as its ufes, becaufe more and more known.
A great encouragement furely to cover the refidue of the
land, of this defcription, with plantations; efpecially when

---

[*] This is proved by ftating, that at eight feet and a half diftance,
fix hundred and forty trees ftand on an acre; and that they are worth,
at a low computation, two fhillings and fix-pence each.

it is confidered that this kind of application of the land not only contributes fo wonderfully to the improvement of the eftate on which it is made, and to the employment of the poor of the neighbourhood, but that it alfo adds fo much to the beauty, the comfort, and the convenience of the country for many miles round.

The coldnefs and fournefs of the foil of this part of the country, and particularly of thofe parts that were once in wood-land, tend much to depreciate its value in cultivation, either as arable or pafture land.

In an arable ftate it produces few forts of grain kindly. It will not at all do for barley; it is in general too poor and ftubborn for beans, and only a very favourable feafon can infure a good crop of oats; wheat is its favourite crop, and this is fometimes late in ripening, and is frequently purchafed at the lofs of two or three years rent, and of more dung than the pafture part of the country can afford to lofe. And the peculiar inaptitude of this foil to return to grafs, after it has been once ploughed, (and more efpecially, as is too often the cafe where it has been burn-beaked) is an infuperable objection to its being ufed in any kind of convertible hufbandry. In a ftate of grafs land, the latenefs of the fpring, and confequent length of the winter, reduce its value very much, even in the only mode of application to which it is at all adapted, viz. " the dairy."

The great improvement of which the cold part of this country is capable, may be expreffed in a few words, " Shorten the winter." This is to be done principally by draining off the fuperfluous water; as the fprings of fo many principal rivers, viz. the *Frome*, the *Cale*, and the *Brew*, rife in this neighbourhood, the land muft every where be full of it; and fecondly, by treading the wet land as little as poffible in the winter; but, on the contrary, winter hayning,
wherever

wherever it is practicable, and of course mowing early in the summer, and endeavouring as much as possible to mow and feed every piece of land alternately.

Nothing has contributed more to the improvement of the cold wet parts of this country, than the plan which seems daily to gain ground, of building sheds for housing cattle in the winter. This not only prevents the land from being poached out in wet seasons, whereby the sward is frequently trod out of sight, but also produces dung, of which the land is so much in want, and of which it has hitherto had so little; it being a well-known fact, that many pieces of land have been constantly mown *every year* within the memory of man, and that frequently not earlier than August, without the least return of dung, or any other manure whatever, save only the assistance supposed to have been given them by the foddering of cattle thereon in the winter, and which, in wet seasons, has certainly done more harm than good. *

Those

* The remark, p. 77; that nature has wisely provided a manure within itself, which in most soils may be found near at hand, and congenial thereto, is applicable to these cold unprofitable lands. It is presumed that these also may from themselves be supplied with a plentiful and permanent manure, so as to make them convertible to tillage or pasture. The means of effecting this is, by burning the clay of the same lands in such manner as to reduce it to a state of pulverization fit for spreading on the land, which, as an indispensible preliminary, must first be properly drained. This was practised many years ago by Mr. PARSONS, of West-Camel, on a pretty large scale, and with remarkable improvement of a wet clayey soil. His method was, to carry all the earth and clay from his drains, (which were open ones) ditches, &c. to one place, where letting it remain some time to dry, he made a fire with wood on the ground, gradually adding thereto his materials till the whole was sufficiently burnt; and he was so great an adept, that (as he said) he knew by the smoke when the fire was of a proper degree of heat for pulverising the clay without burning it to brick. At the time of his saying this, he had a very good specimen of his skill, a

very

Thofe parts of this diſtrict which have a coɔering of red loam, particularly in Witham-park, and thofe which lie on the deep fand vein which runs through Kilmington and Yarnfield, have been much improved by chalk, from Brad-ley, Long Knowl, &c. and by this affiftance may be very profitably kept in tillage; but the want of a permanent ma-nure for the cold clays, which comprife the greateſt part of this diſtrict, is a very great objection to the ploughing them at all, and a ſtrong recommendation to the keeping them in a ſtate of paſturage.

Wherever there is, in this cold country, an appendage of arable land to a dairy farm, and which is certainly not only uſeful, but abfolutely neceffary, on account of ſtraw for making dung; care ſhould be taken to prevent the tenant from ufing any part of the ſtall-dung on the arable land, fo as to oblige him to buy lime, rags, aſhes, and ſuch like, for

---

very large heap as finely pulverifed as the burnbake from earth and weeds in a garden. With this he mixed any other fort of manure which he could get, and carried out all together, either on his paſture or arable land, to the very great improvement of both. As there is, in different parts of the kingdom, an immenfe quantity of this fort of land, the fubject merits a ferious confideration; and if by a kiln, or any other contrivance, clay could be burnt at an eafy expence, with certainty and difpatch, the improvement of thefe lands would, or might, be fuch as nearly to double their prefent value, to the great increafe of private property and national riches. Materials for this can never be wanting, as the drains, whether open, or ſtoned, parings of the ditches, &c. will afford a confiderable fupply; and if more be defired, a fmall portion of the field may well be fpared, with a view to the melioration of the remainder.

The prefent is faid to be an enlightened age. It certainly is an age of experiments, which, in fome inftances, are profecuted with the greateſt ardour, though, at the fame time, to the queſtion, *cui bono?* no fatisfactory anfwer can be given. In this cafe the *bonum* is obvious and extenfive, and the beſt way of accomplifhing it is an object highly deferving the attention of the Board. R. P.

the

the latter, and to referve the whole of the ftall dung for the grafs land.

Every encouragement fhould alfo be given to induce the tenant to underdrain the land, or, if the landlord has already made the drains, to preferve them. He fhould alfo be obliged to mow and feed the land alternately, and induced, by proper cattle-fheds, to take his cattle off the wet lands fome time in November, whereby he would not only fave treading out his land, but alfo be enabled to get early grafs ; he would by that means alfo be enabled to mow early in the fummer, and of courfe to get a good crop of after-grafs, which he might preferve till a late period in autumn, and by thus fhortening the winter *at both ends*, he may be enabled by *art* to reduce it nearly to the length it generally is, in more favoured fituations, and thereby, in a great meafure, cure the *great natural defeƐt of the country.*

CHAPTER

CHAPTER XI.

WASTES.

THE largeft uninclofed (*upland*) common in this diftrict, is the foreft of *Neroche*, containing about eight or nine hundred acres.

The right of flocking on this common belongs to the parifhes of Ilminfter, White-Lackington, Donyat, Broadway, and others; and in regard to quantity is unlimited. For want of proper draining, this common rots the fheep, and is of very little value. If inclofed, drained, and cultivated, it might be made worth from twelve to twenty-five fhillings per acre. Next in fize is White-down, near Chard. There are a few other fmall uninclofed commons in different parifhes; but their total amount does not exceed four or five hundred acres.

Of the moor, or low marfhy lands, there cannot be lefs than eight thoufand acres.

The land in open field, is, for the moft part, in fmall pieces of one, two, and three acres each. Were proper exchanges made, and the fame divided into pieces of ten or twelve acres, it would be advanced in value eight or ten fhillings per acre.

CHAPTER XII.

IMPROVEMENTS.

GREAT attention is paid to draining by all the sheep farmers. The common drains are sixteen inches wide, from twenty to thirty deep, and are for the most part *turf drains*; and when the turf is strong they are found very durable.

Paring and burning but little practised.

CHAPTER XIII.

LIVE STOCK.

OXEN.

GRAZING MANAGEMENT.

THERE are two methods of fatting oxen, the one called summer, the other winter fatting; the first is thought the most profitable, and accompanied with the least risque.

In the first method, they are purchased in February, and are for the most part of the Devon sort, bred either in the Northern part of that county, or in the lower part of Somersetshire. They are bought in good condition, and cost from eight pounds to fifteen pounds each; during the interval between February and grass time, they consume each about ten hundred or twelve hundred of *inferior* hay, viz. the skimming of their summer leaze. When at grass, they

are

are allowed from one acre to one acre and a half each ox, and some add one sheep to each ox. Horses, if any, are kept very sparingly, not at any rate to exceed one to twenty acres of grazing ground. These oxen will be fat, some before and some soon after Michaelmas, paying for their keep from three shillings and six-pence to four shillings per week.

Frequent bleeding, in small quantities, is found to accelerate their fatting.

The next flock are bought in June, July, and August, and are not of so good a sort, being either home-bred or Welsh, and cost from six to eight pounds. These follow the flock purchased in February, and are sometimes stall-fed in the winter, and sometimes fatted in the field; in either case they have the best hay, and good attendance.

They are fat in April and May, and sell from twelve pounds to fourteen pounds each.

A grazier occupying two hundred acres of land may fat yearly one hundred head of oxen, to which add two hundred and seventy sheep and ten colts, constituting altogether a profit comfortable, but by no means *exorbitant*.

The account may be thus stated :

GRAZING.

GRAZING.

Dr.	£.	s.	d.
To rent of 200 acres, average value 40s. an acre	400	0	0
To tithe and taxes, fay	50	0	0
Feb. To fifty oxen, at 11l.	550	0	0
July. To fifty oxen, at 7l.	350	0	0
To mowing and making fifty acres of hay, at 10s.	25	0	0
To fkimming and making fifty acres of fummer-leaze, at 3s.	7	10	0
To wages throughout the year, befides the farmer's labour	50	0	0
To accidents	20	0	0
	1452	10	0
To profit (intereft of capital and accidents included)	277	10	0
	*£1730	0	0

Cr.			
Oct. By fifty oxen, at 18l.	900	0	0
May. By fifty oxen at 13l.	650	0	0
By profit on feventy fheep, fummer kept	40	0	0
By profit on ten colts	40	0	0
By profit on two hundred fheep winter fatted, and fold in April unfhorn	100	0	0
	£.1730	0	0

* Nothing can be more pleafing and fatisfactory, to a farmer engaged in the department of grazing, than a power of afcertaining the feparate pay of each particular ox, fheep, pig, &c.; this may eafily be accomplifhed by means of a weighing engine. For the weight of the ox, &c. when bought, being thereby exactly determined, the animal fhould be then numbered in the horn, a book correfpondent to fuch number being opened, in which the weight fhould be then inferted, and a column opened for the purpofe of inferting remarks made during the progrefs of the animal's fatting.

The oxen, when fat, are driven to the London, the Salisbury, and the Bristol markets, at the following expences,
(salesman's commission included:)

London, 12s. per head
Sarum, 5s. ditto
Bristol, 3s. ditto.

They are nine days travelling to London, a distance of
one hundred and thirty miles. It is difficult to say which
may be considered as the best market; but the general opinion seems to be, that the London market is calculated
for those only who attend it regularly every week, the price
of beef per stone greatly varying according to the plenty or
scarcity in the market.

Some farmers graze heifers in preference to oxen, buying
them in about the months of March and April, and selling
them in October and November. The profit amounts to
forty shillings or fifty shillings each for their summer food;
and the land is stocked after the rate of one heifer to each
acre, together with a considerable number of sheep both in
summer and winter; and it is thought by many, that this
method of occupation is more profitable than the former.

Others fat two-years old wedders of the Dorsetshire and
Somersetshire breed. The Dorset sort are purchased about
Michaelmas, at Sherborne and Stolford fairs, price from
twenty shillings to thirty shillings. No hay is given in the
winter, unless the weather be uncommonly severe, or the
ground covered with snow. They are sold fat between
February and May, and weigh from twenty to thirty pounds
per quarter. A few oxen accompany the sheep, which are
bought in the spring, and fatted the ensuing winter. It is
the universal opinion, that sheep are not so profitable stock
as oxen.

R   It

It is no unufual thing for fome of the graziers to give their prime oxen a *fecond* fummer's grafs. In this cafe they are brought to a high flate of perfection, and in all probability they pay more the *fecond* year than the *firft*; for it is well known, that an animal nearly fat will confume much lefs food than a poor one.

Ewes and lambs are alfo the flock of fome farmers; they are purchafed partly in the autumn in lamb, and partly in the fpring with the lamb by their fides, and are moftly of the Dorfetfhire or Mendip breed.

All the graziers of this county are partial to the red oxen of Somerfet and Devon; and you feldom fee a North-country ox in their poffeffion. They will not allow that the Northern oxen poffefs any comparative merit, either for labour or flaughter; perhaps fome allowance fhould be made for long-eftablifhed prejudices; but it muft be admitted, that in the London market, to which fat oxen are brought from all parts of the kingdom, the Somerfetfhire (next to the Galloway Scot fatted in Norfolk and Suffolk) appear to bear the belle, both in refpect to finenefs of grain and internal fatnefs; and there cannot be a ftronger proof of their merit than the increafing demand for them with the moft eminent graziers of Leiceflerfhire, Oxfordfhire, Warwickfhire, &c. many of whom regularly attend the fairs both of Devon and Somerfet, as purchafers of them lean; and I have been credibly informed they find a good account in fo doing. As to myfelf, it is with reluctance that I hazard an opinion on this fubject; refpecting which, men of long-eftablifhed experience are fo much divided, and on which fuch various opinions exift. But I cannot help remarking, that if the fuperiority of the Northern fort were fo confpicuous as the great breeders of the North affirm, how is it that fome of their beft friends and moft ftrenuous fupporters

in the *fheep line* defert them here, and give an unqualified preference to the Weftern breed? It is not likely that
a wary and confiderate farmer would travel one hundred
and fifty or two hundred miles to purchafe flock, with all
the manifold inconveniencies and rifque which muft attend
the driving fo far, if he could purchafe equally cheap and
good at home.

Nothing is more cenfurable than an injudicious partiality;
and this principle ofttimes leads men haftily to run away
with ideas unfupported by fact; but when long experience
and frequent trial have produced conviction, a farmer would
be equally inexcufable, were he to refift the influence naturally produced in his mind thereby.

The red breeds of Devon and Somerfet have been pro-
greffively increafing, and they are now partially difperfed
over great part of the kingdom; and in refpect to their qualities as a *labouring* animal, I never heard but one opinion,
and that opinion I can myfelf confirm from large and long
experience, namely, that they are *the beft in the kingdom.* In
refpect to their qualities as a *fatting* animal, I will not fpeak
fo decidedly, for I verily believe they have many rivals; the
French, the Galloway Scot, the Leicefter and Oxfordfhire,
the Herefordfhire, the Glamorganfhire, the Suffolk polled,
are all good grazing cattle; and in almoft every county may
be found in the hands of the moft fpirited and attentive
farmers, a valuable fort highly fuperior to the general run
of the county; and I muft again repeat, that the fafeft plan
which a farmer can adopt is that of improving his breed by
a judicious felection of his beft females, and by procuring
fuch males as are eminently diftinguifhed for perfection in
thofe points wherein his females may be found deficient.
A total change of flock is frequently accompanied with lofs
and difappointment; and if the attempt fucceed, you are for

R 2 a confiderable

a confiderable time driven to the neceffity of fatting all you breed; for the rooted prejudice of the graziers in favour of the prevailing fort of the county, whatever they may be, cannot eafily be overcome; and you may in vain expect at market a price adequate to your care and exertion.

Notwithftanding what has been faid, there are certain well-founded axioms in the grazing fyftem relating to the fhape of the animal, which cannot juftly be difputed. Delicacy in the horn, head, and neck; deepnefs and roundnefs of the carcafe, widenefs of the loins, elafticity in the flefh, fmall bones, accompanied with a thin fkin: thefe, with many other points which might be enumerated, are confidered as effentials, and are feldom unaccompanied with an aptitude to fat.

The fame partiality which I have here ftated to exift among the Marfh farmers in favour of the red oxen, was, a few years fince, as ftrongly manifefted in favour of the Dorfetfhire fheep; but of late the *polled* breed of the lower part of the county gain ground, and are in high efteem.

These fheep are bred in the neighbourhood of Dulverton, Bampton, Wivelifcombe, &c. they are well made, yield a large fhear of wool, and fat quickly; but they might, in my opinion, be greatly improved by a crofs with the Leicefter, to which they have in fize and fhape fome degree of affinity. The objection made by the breeders in that diftrict to a crofs with Leicefter is, that what they might gain *externally*, they fhould lofe *internally*; and that the deficiency in the fat of the infide would fo difgrace their fheep in the eye of the butcher, that they would lofe their old cuftomers.— Surely this reafoning is fallacious; for, on a fuppofition that the infide fat of a fheep were by this intermixture to be reduced fix pounds per fheep, (and I think this as much as it poffibly could be) the deficiency, at four-pence per pound,

would

would amount to only two shillings; five pounds extra weight of the carcase would pay this; and if the buyer were to allow the butcher for this defect, all reasonable objection on his part is done away; and, on the other hand, the grazier need not be alarmed, for he may rest assured, that the increase of the carcase will amply repay the want of inside fat.*

A list of FAIRS *to which the* SOMERSET GRAZIERS *resort to buy* LEAN STOCK.

SOMERSET.

Binegar, Whit Wednesday and Thursday
Bishop's-Lidiard, April 5
Bridgwater, June 24, Oct. 2, and Dec. 28
Broomfield, Nov. 13
Bagborow, May 23
Bristol, March 1, and Sept. 1
Castle-Cary, Tuesday before Palm Sunday, May 1, and Whit-Tuesday
Chard, first Wednesday in May, and in November
Comb St. Nicholas, Wednesday sen'night before Christmas-day
Dulverton, July
Frome, Feb. 24, and Nov. 24
Lansdown, August 10
Milverton, October
North-Petherton, May 1
Pensford, May 6, and Nov. 8
Priddy, August 21
Somerton, Monday before the 30th of January, Oct. 30, Nov. 8, and the first great market the Tuesday before Easter, and four other markets every three weeks after
Taunton, June 17, and July 7

---

* The foregoing account of grazing was written in the year 1794, since which a great advance has taken place, both in the price per acre, and the value of the land. J. B.

Ubley.

Ubley, September 4
Wellington, Thurfday before Eafter
Wells, May 14, July 5, Oct. 25, Nov. 30
Wefton-Zoyland, Sept. 9
Wivelifcombe, May 11 and 12
Yeovil, June 28, and Nov. 17
Shipham, Nov. 17.

DEVON.

Afhbrittle, February 25
Axminfter, Wednefday after Pack-Monday
Barnftable, September
Chudleigh, Eafter Tuefday
Churchinford, January 25, 26
Crediton, April , May 11, Auguft 21
Exeter, Afh-Wednefday, Whit-Monday, Lammas-day, and Dec. 6
Hatherly, May 21
Honiton, July
Oakhampton, Tuefday before Lady-day
Ottery St. Mary, Tuefday before Palm-Sunday, and the Wed-
    nefday fe'nnight after Whitfunday
Sandford-Peverel, April
South-Molton, April 12
Tiverton, Trinity-Tuefday, and Oct.
Great-Torrington, third Saturday in March, May 4, and Mid-
    fummer
Witheridge, April

Fairs at which Fat Cattle are fold.

Axbridge, February 3, and March 25
Backwell, September 21
Banwell, January 18
Bridgwater, fecond Thurfday in Lent, Oct. 2, and Dec. 28
Briftol, March 1, Sept. 1
Burnham, Trinity-Monday
Eaft-Brent, Auguft 26
Huntfpill, June 29
Priddy, Auguft 21
Wedmore, Auguft 2

Wells,

Wells, October 25, November 30

Somerton, Tuesday before Easter, and every Tuesday three weeks till Midsummer

Weston-Zoyland, September 9

Mark, Tuesday before Whitsuntide, and September 15

Wollavington, October 18

Langport, second Monday in Lent.

COWS.

The cows of this district being intended chiefly for the purposes of cheese-making, the profit arising is in proportion to the quantity and quality of the milk; size, therefore, is not attended to, but principal regard is paid to the breed whence she sprung. The dairy-men think it more profitable to have a small breed *well fed*, than the best breed in the world *scantily kept*; and the cow that gives milk the longest is most esteemed.* The time of calving is from the

---

* The cheese of this district is much admired, particularly that made in the parishes of Mear and Cheddar.

It is for the most part purchased by jobbers, and sent through the medium of Weyhill, Giles's-hill, Reading, and other fairs, to the London market, where it is sold under the name of *double Glocester.*

The method of making has been so often described, that I shall not trouble my readers with a minute detail thereof. The annexed short account of the process I shall only premise, with observing, that cleanliness, sweet rennet, and attention to breaking the curd, are the principal requisites in cheese-making.

PROCESS OF CHEESE-MAKING.

When the milk is brought home, it is strained into a tub, and about three table-spoonfuls of good rennet put therein, (supposing the quantity of milk sufficient to make a cheese of twenty-eight pounds) which remains undisturbed about two hours, then it becomes curd, and is properly broken; when done, three parts of the whey is taken therefrom and warmed, and then put into the tub again, where it remains about twenty minutes; the whey is again put over the fire, made nearly scald hot, and put into the tub to scald the curd about half an

hour;

the beginning of February to Lady-day, and they take great care to keep their cows well three weeks or a month before they calve; the milk will rise in proportion to the goodness of their keeping; very little attention is paid to the nature or sort of the bull. The calves (those few excepted which are reared to keep up the stock) seldom live a month ere the butcher's knife cuts the thread of their existence; and cheese-making begins in March, from which time it continues till December.‡

The calves which are reared are fed principally with cheese-whey, and in May they are turned to grass and left to shift for themselves;† some careful dairy-women have

tried

hour, and then part of the whey is taken away, and the remainder remains with the curd till it is nearly cold; the whey is then poured off, the curd broken very small, put into the vat and pressed, where it remains nearly an hour; and then is taken out, turned, and put in again and pressed till the evening, when it is taken out again, turned, and pressed till the next morning: it is then taken out of the vat, salted, put into it again with a clean dry cloth round it, and remains in the press till the next evening, when it is taken out again, salted, put into the vat without a cloth, and pressed till the next morning; and then it finally leaves the press, and is salted once a day for twelve days.

‡ The number of calves fatted in this district is immense—four hundred fat calves have been sold in Shepton-Mallet market in one day. To this market, butchers from the neighbourhood of Bath and Bristol resort, and convey the carcases (whole) to those cities in one-horse carts. The veal is delicately white—small in size, viz. from sixteen to twenty-four pounds per quarter. The best is brought from a small village called Batcomb; and its excellency may, perhaps, be ascribed to their giving the calves small doses of metheglin in the milk, and keeping them in a dark place.

† In the South-Eastern part of this district, where the dairy land is chiefly applied to the making of butter, and skimmed milk cheese, the calves are taken from their dams at a fortnight or three weeks old, and suckled with skimmed-milk until the middle of May, when they

are

tried to increase their growth, by giving them whey after they are put to grass; but this plan is reprobated as doing more harm than good. When they become yearlings, they are subject to a disorder provincially called the *quarter-ail*, which is a mortification beginning at the hock, and proceeding with astonishing rapidity to the vital parts, occasioning death in a very few hours. The first symptom is lameness, and no cure has yet been found; the quarter affected becomes intirely putrid, whilst the other quarters are in a sound state. This disorder is, I think, the same with that known in Norfolk under the name of *gargut*; nor is it confined to these counties, but is, I believe, generally known; and an investigation of the cause of the disorder, which might lead to the discovery of a cure, is well worthy the attention of all agricultural bodies.

Cows are subject to a disorder called *the yellows*, something similar to the jaundice in the human species. This disorder frequently affects the udder, and brings on a false quarter, that is, a deprivation of milk in one teat, accompanied with a swelling and inflammation. For this, however, I can suggest a remedy which seldom fails, viz. flour of mustard mixed with any liquid, two ounces a dose, and repeating the same two or three times in the course of twenty-four hours.

The heifers are put to the bull in July, when they are about one year and half old; and the prevailing opinion seems to be, that those which are kept from the bull a year longer do not turn out *good milkers*. The average produce

are turned out to grass at home, or sold at some distant market for the same purpose. A few dairy-farmers, in this part of the district, have adopted the practice of making flax-seed and hay-tea, and mix it in the milk, with which the calves are suckled. This practice appears to answer very well, for the last month or six weeks of suckling. A. C.

of a dairy per day, may be calculated at about three gallons
per cow, from Lady-day to Michaelmas, and from Michaelmas to Chriftmas one gallon per cow per day.

Cows are kept till they are fourteen or fifteen years old,
and when fatted they feldom get to a higher price than
feven or eight pounds.

A dairy-maid can manage twenty cows fo far as relates
to the in-door work. The grofs produce of a dairy frequently averages twelve pounds per cow, and in fome particular inflances fourteen pounds; but this can only be done
when cheefe is at the prefent enormous price of near fix-
pence per pound twelve months old; and fat hogs at fix-
pence per pound.

The following eflimate of the expences and produce of
a dairy, fuppofing the land and the cows to be of the *firft
quality*, may, I truft, be confidered as tolerably accurate.

DAIRY TWENTY COWS.

Dr.	£.	s.	d.
To two milkers forty weeks, at 3s. per week	6	0	0
To a man's labour, winter serving cattle, changing their pasture, felling cheese, &c. —	4	0	0
To dairy-woman, 4s. 6d. per week ——	11	14	0
To dairy utensils, candles, salt, brushes, mops, and all other articles ——	4	6	0
To arnotto ——	1	0	0
To rent, thirty acres of summer pasture, 40s.	60	0	0
To skimming the same, and making six tons of hay ——	3	0	0
To rent of fifteen acres mown ground, 40s. —	30	0	0
To making the hay, say thirty tons, at 12s. per acre ——	9	0	0
To tithe, taxes, &c. say ——	10	0	0
	139	0	0
To profit, interest of money, and the decreasing value of cows included ——	113	10	0
	£252	10	0

N. B. A large dairy might be kept for 25s. per cow.

Cr.			
By ninety hundred of cheese, at 45s.* ——	202	10	0
By calves ——	15	0	0
By butter — ——	10	0	0
By hogs ——	25	0	0
	£252	10	0

* At this time (January 1797) cheese of last year's making is worth three pounds per hundred.

On

On a comparison of this with the grazing account, it is apparent that the dairy occupation is more profitable than grazing, for this amounts to fifty shillings per acre, whereas the other is only twenty-eight shillings per acre. On account of population, the dairy system ought also to be preferred, as one grazing farm of two hundred acres would afford a comfortable livelihood to four dairy families.

I am aware, that should these observations induce an increase of dairies, and consequently a more liberal supply of cheese, such a declension in the price of that article might take place, as would bring all things again on a level, and advance the grazier's profit to an equality with that of the dairy-man.

Be this as it may, I think dairies should be encouraged; for the arduous domestick labour and incessant employment which they bring on the female part of a farmer's family, will always prevent an undue increase thereof, unless their profits on a comparison are very great indeed. But whilst I thus recommend encouragement to the pail, I must do it with this proviso, that a different mode of management be adopted from that now practised.

The cows of this district are almost universally depastured in the fields both summer and winter; in consequence of which, the dung produced even by a large dairy is trifling indeed; hence arises a manifest declension in the fertility of the land, and you may distinguish a grazing from a dairy farm at a great distance. In this exhausted state the dairy land must remain, unless a different system of management be successfully inculcated. Were I to suggest a plan of improvement, it would be the following: Let all dairy farms be accompanied with a due proportion of arable, perhaps a *fourth part*; let proper stalls and bartons be erected as a residence for the cows during the winter months; let cabbages,

turnips,

turnips, and potatoes, be grown for their winter fubfiftence; but above all, let them be well littered, and kept perfectly clean. By thefe means, a large fupply of dung may be procured at a little expence; and if the farmer wifh to increafe the quantity, he need only dig up the wafte earth on the borders of the highways, and make a layer therewith in his farm-yard. This will abforb the urine, and when mixed and incorporated with the dung, will conftitute a manure highly fertilifing. It cannot be fufficiently regretted that this practice fhould be fo feldom adopted; for repeated experiments have taught, that one hundred acres of land thus managed, will keep more cows than one hundred and fifty acres under the prefent fyftem. *Artificial* graffes will enable the dairy-man to turn his cows out a month or five weeks earlier than he was accuftomed to do on *natural* grafs, and turnips, &c. will fupply them with winter provender; fo that the confumption of hay will be greatly reduced, and more land may be devoted to fummer pafture. It may be here objected, that the quality of the cheefe and butter may be injured: of this I have my doubts. Artificial-grafs, in the months of March and April, will make as good butter or cheefe as natural grafs; after this, the cows fhould be put to the natural pafture, and the former fhut up for mowing.

As to the effect of turnips and cabbages, I will obviate every difficulty by ftating a fimple recipe, whereby all difagreeable flavour may be entirely prevented in the making of butter; and as to cheefe, there is but little made at that feafon; and if there were, the palate muft be nice indeed, which could diftinguifh a difference of flavour.

RECIPE.

When the milk is fet abroad in the leads, put one gallon of boiling water to fix gallons of milk. It may alfo be prevented

AGRICULTURAL SURVEY

vented by diffolving nitre in fpring water, and putting about
a quarter of a pint to ten or twelve gallons of milk when
warm from the cow.

SHEEP.

In the South-Eaft part of this diftrict, the fheep are an
improved fort of the Dorfet, and many confiderable ewe
flocks are kept to the amount of four to fix hundred each ;
they begin lambing about Chriftmas, and the lambs are
weaned in May.[*] After the lambs are fhorn, which is at
Midfummer, they are worth about fifteen fhillings each.—
The produce of an ewe, fold at three years and three quarters
old, may be thus ftated:

	£.	s.	d.
Two lambs, at fifteen fhillings[†]	— 1	10	0
Wool both of ewe and lambs	— 0	12	6
Folding	— 0	15	0
Ewe	— 1	8	0
	£.4	5	6

The ewes, forward with lamb in October, are fold to the
graziers who fupply London and Bath markets with houfe-
lamb, and fometimes they bring thirty-five fhillings per
head, though folded to the time of fale.

Some farmers buy wedder lambs about Midfummer
(fhorn) at fifteen fhillings, and keep them about twenty-two
months, conftantly folding them: they are then fold (un-
fhorn) to the graziers occupying the marfh lands, at the
price of twenty-feven to thirty-eight fhillings each.

---

[*] Would it not be more advifeable to protract the lambing to
March or April?

[†] Lambs have been fold in the autumn of 1796 for nearly double
this price.

		£.	s.	d.
Folding	—	—	1	0	0
Wool	—	—	0	4	0
Average price fold at	—	—	1	12	6
			2	16	6
Deduct first cost of lamb	—	—	0	15	0
		£.	2	1	6

The latter flock requires lefs care than the former, and
at the fame time enables the farmer to manure more land;
for they may be folded through the whole winter on the
pafture land.

The number of fheep kept in this diftrict is immenfe,
and folding unremittingly purfued.*

Lately fome of the *Leicefter fheep* have been brought into
this diftrict by Mr. POSTER near Yeovil, and by Mr.
LOWMAN near Crewkerne. The carcafes of fome have
been fold in Crewkerne market, and were remarkably fat,
and highly efteemed for their delicious flavour; but with all
thefe good qualities, if they cannot walk a mile to the fold,
they never will gain much ground in this country.

*The Sheep-breeding fyftem of White-Lackington and its
neighbourhood.*

In a regular flock of three hundred ewes, it is neceffary
to rear all the chilver or female lambs; for if the twins are

---

* Mr. JEANES, of Alhampton near Caftle-Cary, has exhibited before the Bath Agricultural Society repeated proofs of his fkill in the
cure of rotten fheep; and has, in his poffeffion, a variety of corrobo-
rating teftimonies, under the fignature of refpectable fheep-farmers,
who have availed themfelves of this ufeful difcovery.,

fufficient,

fufficient, after all accidents, to keep up a regular fucceffion, it is as much as can be expected.   The flock then will confift of

> 150 Chilver lambs
> 150 Ewes from one to two years old
> 150 ditto from two to three years old
> 150 ditto three years old.
>
> 600 in the whole.

From this ftock are fold one hundred and fifty pur (male) lambs, and one hundred and fifty old ewes, yearly.   The lambs are fold about Midfummer, and the old ewes are bought by fucklers, for the London market, in September or October, about which time they begin to drop their lambs.   The ftock ewes are folded for eight months, viz. from the beginning of April to the end of November; and the fale ewes are folded about three months.   Four hundred and fifty fheep will amply manure one-third of an acre each night; and this is confidered as far fuperior in its effect to dung, or to fifteen quarters of lime, which is the fubfti-tute with people who do not keep a flock.   By the follow-ing comparifon, the value of the fold may be fairly efti-mated:—

	£.	s.	d.
Fifteen quarters of lime, at 1s. 6d.	1	2	6
Carriage feven miles	0	15	0
Mixing, fpreading, &c.	0	5	0
	£.2	2	6

The before-mentioned flock will annually fold upwards of fixty acres; and the value of fuch manuring will amount to one hundred and twenty-feven pounds ten fhillings; but as it muft be admitted that the benefit of the fold is not fo

durable

durable as either dung or lime, we will deduct one-third, and call it eighty-five pounds.

If the pur-lambs are not fold, but kept on, they are conftantly folded till they are two years and a half old, at which age, by good keeping on vetches, clover, and turnips, they are brought to the value of two guineas to two pounds fifteen fhillings, and are then fold to the grazier to finifh.

By this fyftem of folding, the fheep are kept free from the *foot-rot*; and as the grafs is not tainted by their refting on it, more fheep can be kept per acre.

Produce of a Flock of three hundred Ewes.

	£.	s.	d.
One hundred and fifty male lambs, fold at Midfummer, after being fhorn, at 1l. 1s.	157	10	0
Wool of three hundred lambs, at 2s.	30	0	0
Ditto of one hundred and fifty young ewes at 4s.	30	0	0
Ditto of three hundred full-grown and aged ditto, at 3s. 6d.	52	10	0
One hundred and forty old ewes, fold in September, at 40s. each	280	0	0
(N. B. Ten allowed for accidents)			
Folding fixty acres	85	0	0
	£.635	0	0

One fhepherd at eight fhillings per week will take care of the flock, change the fold, and have time for other work; and the hurdles will be attended with an annual expence of about three guineas.

Corn, after the fold, is much greater in quantity, and better in quality, than after any other manure.

s   Paffing

Paffing from Crewkerne to the Southward, you enter one of thofe excavations, or large vales, for which this county is remarkable; comprifing the villages and hamlets of Clapton, Seaborough, Wayford, Woolmingfton, Partington, Cricket-Thomas, Winfham, &c.

Within this vale commences a diftrict of twenty miles fquare, (one half in Somerfet and the other in Dorfet) which ought to be noted for fupplying the fummer markets at Exeter with *weanling calves*. Thefe calves drop in February and March, are fuckled by their dams for three weeks, when they are houfed, and fuckled by hand with warm fkimmed milk until the month of May, at which time they are fold to the drovers for the market before-mentioned. At Exeter, they are bought by the Devonfhire farmers, and depaftured for three or four years, when they are difpofed of to the Somerfet graziers, who fatten them for the London market: thus we fee, that part of what is called the Devonfhire breed of cattle is the produce of a finall diftrict of the counties of Somerfet and Dorfet; a breed which will probably, ere long, be generally acknowledged to be equal to any other in the kingdom.

The dairy at Ayfhcombe farm, within the parifh of Wayford, is a good fpecimen of the Devonfhire breed.*

---

* Mr. WHITE PARSONS alfo, of Ilchefter, has exhibited before the Agricultural Society at Bath, for the premium offered by that Society, a young bull of his own breeding, together with the fire and dam of the *Devonfhire* race; and all breeders of horned cattle were challenged by him to produce, at the faid exhibition, any three of equal value for flock; but no competitor appeared, and the premium was defervedly adjudged to him.

CHAPTER

CHAPTER XIV.

RURAL ŒCONOMY.

THIS county is very populous, and the wages low, notwithstanding there are very confiderable manufactures.

Men's daily labour in winter is 1s. per day, with cider.*

Ditto in fummer 1s. 4d. ditto

Women's daily labour in winter is 6d. per day, with cider.

Ditto in fummer 8d. ditto

Mowing grafs 1s. 4d. per acre, and one gallon of cider.

barley 1s. od. ditto ditto

Reaping wheat 4s. od. ditto, two gallons and half of cider.

And all other labour proportionably cheap.

Price of provifions fomething lefs than in the North-Eaft Diftrict of the county.

---

* Wages are now (1797) advanced one-third at leaft.

CHAPTER

CHAPTER XV.

POLITICAL OECONOMY, *as connected with or affecting* AGRICULTURE.

ROADS.

FEW countries can boast better turnpike-roads than may be found in this diftrict.

From Wells to Bridgwater, and from Crofs to the fame town, they are, comparatively fpeaking, as fmooth as a gravel-walk. This may, in a great meafure, be attributed to the great attention paid to the breaking of the ftones, which is done by men with fmall fledges in a fitting pofture; and the ftones are reduced to the fize of a pigeon's egg, at an expence of fix-pence per ton weight.

CANALS.

An act was obtained, laft feffions of parliament, for cutting a navigable canal through the Eaftern part of this diftrict, and the fame is now in execution. It commences at the collieries near Mendip, and, paffing through the town of Frome, divides itfelf into two branches, one joining the Kennet and Avon Canal near Bradford, and the other extending itfelf through Wincanton to the borders of Dorfetfhire.

MANUFACTURES.

A confiderable clothing manufacture has been lately eftablifhed, by fome gentlemen of Wiltfhire, at Chard; and

round

round Ilminster, Chard, Crewkerne, Martock, Yeovil, &c. there are confiderable manufactures of narrow cloth, from four to feven fhillings per yard; the quality of which, both for appearance and duration, is not furpaffed in the kingdom. In thefe, great numbers of men, women, and children, are employed; but the country being very populous, there is no want of hands in agriculture.

There are alfo many manufactures of coarfe linen, fuch as dowlas, tick, &c. alfo of gloves, girt-web, &c. all of which give animation, wealth, and comfort, to the inhabitants of this rich and delightful region.

SOUTH-WEST DISTRICT.

CHAPTER I.

GEOGRAPHICAL STATE AND CIRCUMSTANCES.

THIS divifion of the county has nearly an equal portion of rough mountainous hills, and rich fertile flopes and plains.

The climate, particularly of that part which is called the *Vale of Taunton-Dean*, is peculiarly mild and ferene; and the foil highly fertile and productive. The eye is agreeably relieved by a judicious mixture of arable and pafture; and if it be contrafted with fome parts of the Northern Diftrict, it may emphatically be called the Land o *Canaan*.

There are, however, certain parts North-Weft of the faid vale which are mountainous, and fubject to that mutability of weather, and moifture of air, generally found on elevated fituations.

Quantock, Brandon, and Dunkry-Hills, may be noted for their wild and rugged fcenery; and the part which is called *Dunkry-Beacon*, is the higheft land in the whole county.

This diftrict may be fubdivided into two leffer diftricts, including, 1ft. the parifhes of Taunton, Wilton, Trull, Pitminfter, Bifhop's-Hull, Bradford, Buckland, Ninehead, Wellington,

lington, Sampford, Hill-Farrence, Oake, Norton, Cheddon, Staplegrove, Thurloxton, North-Petherton, Monkton, Kingston, Cothelston, Bishop's-Lidiard, Heathfield, Halse, Ashpriors, Fitzhead, Milverton, Langford-Budville, Thorne, Bathialton, and Runnington.

These parishes comprehend what is generally called the *Vale of Taunton-Dean.*

SOIL.

The foil is a rich loam, interfperfed in fome places with clay, as part of Bradfield, Buckland, North fide of Wellington, part of Sampford, Hill-Farrence, Ninehead, Oake, and Heathfield ; and in other parts with fand, or a lighter mould ; as Kingston, Bishop's-Lidiard, Halfe, Fitzhead, Milverton, Langford, Thorne, and Runnington.

Thefe hundreds, together with that of North-Curry, are principally held under the churches of Winchefter and Wells, and the lands are chiefly poffeffed by fmall proprietors.

The fecond divifion of this diftrict includes the parishes of Combflory, Bagborough, Stowey, Stoke-Courcy, Crowcombe, Stogumber, Williton, Watchet, Dunfter, Minehead, Porlock, Timberfcombe, Cutcomb, Withypool, Winsford, Dulverton, Wivelifcomb, &c. &c. together with the foreft of Exmoor.

The foil of fome part of this diftrict is but little inferior to that of the former; but the hills and forefts are for the moft part left in a flate of nature. The corn land is in general good; and the watered meadows in the parishes of Crowcombe, Stogumber, Monkfilver, Nettlecomb, Dinniford, Dunfter, Dulverton, &c. are as good as any in the county. If we appreciate land by its capacity to keep ftock throughout the year, *watered meadows* are invaluable; and it is to be hoped, that the different reports, which will no doubt

doubt be fent to the Board of their importance, will induce a general application of water, wherever it be of good quality, and there is a poffibility of conveying it. A great part of thefe watered lands lie on fleep declivities; and as the water paffes quickly over them, and never lies ftagnant, not a rufh can be feen; this is not always the cafe in *low* water meadows, which for want of proper draining are much incommoded by them. Meadows which lie in a low fituation and nearly on a level, fhould be thrown up into convex beds about thirty or forty feet wide, along the ridges of which the water fhould be conveyed, flowing regularly at the different outlets, and having a free paffage in the trenches lying between the beds.

The expence of doing this feldom exceeds fix or feven pounds per acre, and the benefit is frequently twenty or thirty fhillings per acre per annum.

Excepting thofe inflances where water paffes through a town, or after fudden floods carries with it rich particles of vegetative matter, the lands receiving it near the fpring-head, are fuppofed to be the moft benefited; and the quicker it is made to pafs over the land, and the greater the *impetus* given by a large quantity thrown at once, the quicker and more powerful are the effects.

The firft watering commences in November, and is continued with regular intermiffion from that time till February. Thefe meadows are frequently, in this temperate climate, fit to receive ewes and lambs, as early as Candlemas; and a conftant and regular fucceffion of food from that time to the beginning of May, enables the farmer to view his flock with the utmoft complacency, and to look with pity on his neighbours, deftitute of fuch a refource in thefe trying months.

At the beginning of May, the land is unflocked and again watered; after fix or feven weeks they mow from thirty cwt. to forty cwt. per acre.   *Eftimate*

Estimate of the value of such Land.

	£.	s.	d.
Spring-feed from Candlemas to May-day —	1	5	0
Thirty-five cwt. of hay per acre, at 30s. per ton	2	12	6
After-grafs to November ——	1	1	0
	4	18	6

Confidering it as connected with a sheep and corn farm, all estimates must be below its real value; for it is well known, that, according to the probable plenty or scarcity of food in the months of February, March, and April, does a farmer apportion his stock for the whole year. Should turnips fail, his only refource is the hay-mow; his ewes suffer, his lambs become stunted and of little value. His meadow-ground devoted to the scythe is *spring fed*, whereby he suffers a diminution of ten hundred of hay per acre. Thefe are but a few of the many evils attendant on a deficiency of food in the months before-mentioned, and must raife the importance of water-meadow in the eyes of all difcerning hufbandmen; befides, thefe lands require no dreffing, but will preferve an undiminifhed vegetation from year to year, and will enable the farmer, by means of the fheepfold, to enrich his other lands without injury to thefe.*

---

* On the demefne of J. F. LUTTRELL, efq; of Dunfter-Caftle, a large tract of land, in a convertible courfe of tillage, is manured with water. The ufual rotation of crops is, 1ft. Wheat on the ley; 2d. Turnips; 3d. Barley and artificial graffes.

It is then fuffered to remain in pafture two years, and during that time it is, at ftated intervals, regularly flooded by a ftream defcending from the adjacent hills.

The courfe is then renewed, and this has been the conftant practice for many years.

The produce has been in general very confiderable, viz. of wheat forty or fifty bufhels, and of barley fifty and fixty bufhels per acre.

A 5

As the different modes of irrigation have been long before the public in a treatise published by Mr. Boswell, of Piddletown in Dorfetshire, and by other writers in different parts of the kingdom, I shall not further enlarge upon this subject, than merely to caution the farmer, unexperienced in this branch of improvement, not to feed with *sheep* in the *autumn*; for, though it may be done with the utmost safety in the spring, it is frequently fatal in the *autumnal* months.

CHAPTER

CHAPTER II.

STATE OF PROPERTY.

THE major part of the five hundreds of Taunton-Dean, confifts of cuftomary lands of inheritance, held under the Lord Bifhop of Winchefter, paying an annual rent. Thefe cuftomary lands pafs by furrender, paying to the lord fines and heriots on alienations. There are alfo many fingular cuftoms within the manor, difficult to be underftood even by the tenants themfelves. The defcent is called that of *Borough-Englifh*, with fome variations. The wife is heir to her hufband; and it is no uncommon thing for a widow, on the death of her hufband, having children by him, to marry again, and carry her eftate into her fecond family, to the difinheritance of her firft.

If the fines, heriots, and other incidental incomes within the manor, were commuted with the lord, for an increafe of the annual high rents; the lands enfranchifed by act of parliament, and to pafs in defcent as other lands of inheritance by common law; the income to the bifhoprick would be more certain, and the prefent inconveniencies avoided. In courfe of time, the proprietors would enlarge their poffeffions, and the manor would be brought into farms of fufficient extent for the employment of a team, which is not the cafe at prefent.

CHAPTER III.

MODE OF OCCUPATION.

THE farms in this divifion are rather lefs than in the laft, but the hufbandry is much the fame, only there is more land in tillage. The mountainous lands are uncultivated, and are depaftured with fheep and young bullocks.

In the vicinity of thefe uncultivated hills, viz. at Bicknoller, Elworthy, Brompton-Rolph, and Old-Cleeve, oats are the principal corn crop; barley and wheat are grown but on a fmall fcale.

The rotation of crops varies from that of Taunton-Dean. Here wheat is generally fown on the ley, and none but very ftiff land is fallowed. Turnips are much cultivated, but they are very lavifh in the confumption, giving too large a fpace of ground to the fheep at a time, making thereby great wafte.

The dry uplands are devoted to tillage, and the rich lowlands to grazing or dairy. On the former, wheat, beans, peafe, and vetches, are the principal crops; and thofe lands which are capable of improvement by watering, (of which there is a confiderable proportion) are fo managed as to produce excellent fpring-feed for ewes and lambs, together with abundant crops both of hay and after-grafs; but the water being frequently fcarce, the water-courfes are frequently a fource of litigation.

There are very few eftates entirely in pafture. Every little farmer is fond of the plough; but in moft of thefe fmall farms, where there is not fufficient employment for a team, the occupier's fituation is not better than that of a day-labourer.

Much

Much of the arable land will fpontaneoufly produce a variety of excellent forts of grafs, and fhortly become good pafture, if laid down in an hufbandlike manner. The artificial graffes here fown are, broad and white clover, trefoil, and ray-grafs, called here *evergrafs*. Many farmers think the latter impoverifhes the foil; but they fubftitute no other perennial in its ftead.

LEASES.

By the cuftom of the manor of Taunton-Dean, the tenant is not, without a licence from the lord, to let his cuftomary lands for more than a year and a day; but to encourage good hufbandry, it has been ufual of late years to grant rack-rent leafes for feven, fourteen, or twenty-one years.

The tenant covenants with the landlord, not to fow rape, hemp, or flax; thefe crops being confidered as great exhauflers, making no return in manure. It has alfo been common to allow the tenant church and poor-rates; but it is to be doubted whether the poor are in this cafe better provided for, although the rates for their maintenance increafe; for the occupiers, when no ways interefted, are apt to be remifs in looking into the poor's concerns.

Of late years, this burthen has been thrown on the tenant, by way of raifing his rent.

At the commencement of the term, it is ufual for the landlord to put the premifes in compleat repair; after that, the tenant finds reed, fpars, and carriage of materials, during the term; and the landlord, timber, ftones, and lime. The handicraftfmen are paid between them.

In this way, the landlord and tenant being mutually interefted, the expence of repairs is leffened, and the buildings are kept in better order.

The

The tenant alfo covenants to take care of ſtapling and timber trees, and to carry one hundred and twenty horſe-ſeams (about twelve cart-loads) of dung, or fifteen hogſ-heads of lime, or a proportion of both mixed with earth, on every acre of land converted to arable, and to take but three crops of corn before the ſame quantity be renewed. He alfo covenants never to ſow two crops of wheat in ſuc-ceſſion, nor to convert to tillage any maiden or old paſture without leave, under the penalty of five pounds an acre per annum for the remainder of the term.

CHAPTER IV.

IMPLEMENTS.

THE ploughs, drags, harrows, rollers, waggons, and carts now uſed, are much the ſame as they have been for ſixty years paſt. Of late, indeed, the double-furrow plough has been introduced, and ſeems to gain ground; all who have tried it acknowledge its fuperiority for light foils, and for ploughing the barley or turnip land.

CHAPTER V.

INCLOSING, &c.

FENCES.

THE beech hedges, around Dulverton, Dunster, &c. are not only beautiful to the eye, and an excellent fence and shelter, but are a source of annual profit to the proprietors.

The banks on which they are planted are six or seven feet high, and between four and five feet wide at the top; the mouldering of the sides is frequently prevented by a dry stone wall, four feet high. There is no ditch; and the hedge consists of three rows of beech, planted on the top of the bank, at about one foot distance. Their growth is very rapid, and they seem to defy the destructive qualities of the sea-breeze, so fatal to the white-thorn and most other plants; when at maturity, the middle row is cut to the ground, and the outside rows plashed. The quantity of fuel supplied by these hedges is very considerable; and the only objection that can be made to them is, that the earth used in the construction of the banks is so considerable a quantity, that a large portion of the field is robbed of its vegetable matter, and rendered for some years unproductive.

CHAPTER VI.

ARABLE LAND.

THE common fields in this diſtrict are ſo few, and the unincloſed waſtes (a portion of Blackdown and Pick-eridge-hill excepted) ſo inſignificant, that little improvement can be made in that way. There are a few low common meadows, where frequently the hay crop (provincially, *the tonſure*) belongs to one man, and the after-graſs to another, by which means ſuch lands are totally neglected, being nei-ther drained nor manured.

The waſte lands, on that part of Blackdown which lies within this county, are ſuppoſed to exceed a thouſand acres; they are ſo ſituated on the declivity of the hill, that floats might eaſily be made to convey the water, iſſuing from the ſprings, over the land.

And if the water ſhould not be found to fertilize, it would not be difficult or expenſive to convert theſe floats into drains, and thereby render the ground more dry and healthy.

The occupiers of eſtates contiguous to theſe hills ſtock them with young cattle in the ſummer months, but the diſtant tenants reap little or no benefit.

On ſome of their land they have fallows, and wheat al-ternately, manuring with lime.

A mixture of the earth of the headlands with lime and rotten dung, is the general manure for the ploughed lands, and ſoapers' aſhes and rotten dung *alone* for the paſture.

The method commonly adopted for mixing the earth, lime, and dung together, is, to carry the dung and ſpread it on the headlands, or on heaps of earth collected on different

T parts

parts of the field, and then put the unflaked lime on the dung, covering it up with earth till it is flaked, and fit for mixing; but as the lime is by this method diffolved upon the dung, the richeft part of the manure is confumed by the lime, or carried off in vapour.

Drilling has been tried in this part of the county, particularly by two farmers of Halfe, and by Mr. ANDERDON of Henlade. On light poor foils, it has been found to anfwer, but in rich ftrong loams, the corn has proved too rank.

Mr. ANDERDON has drilled all his corn for twenty years paft. At firft he formed an experimental field of four acres, divided into feveral equal parts, where he tried drilling various crops, in comparifon with fowing them broadcaft, and finding his drilled and horfehoed crops of beans, wheat, peafe, turnips, &c. fufficiently encouraging to proceed to acres, he has continued the practice ever fince; by which means he has certainly improved his land, and eradicated weeds.

He at firft ufed WILLEY's drill plough for fowing double rows, which is to be feen in the repofitory of the Society of Arts in London.

With this, he drilled two rows, about a foot afunder, on five-feet ridges, leaving intervals of four feet for horfe-hoeing. Since, he has drilled fingle rows on ridges of three feet, by which means he keeps his ground cleaner, and has a produce equally good with the double rows. Of wheat, he generally reaps from fifteen to twenty-four bufhels per acre, which is about the average of the wheat crops of his parifh fown in the broadcaft way.

In the year 1791 he reaped from one field twenty-nine bufhels per acre. The field was drilled in fingle rows, three feet afunder; this may be called the Tullean method of drilling, and was practifed many years ago by that enlightened

ened agriculturift JETHRO TULL. The prevailing method of the prefent day is, to drill at intervals of fix, nine, or twelve inches. Though the practice of drilling corn has been highly extolled by fome, and aftonifhing inftances of produce recorded, yet the writer of this report cannot find that it gains ground in the county of Somerfet. If the advantages refulting from the practice were fo great as they are reprefented, furely the common farmers would adopt it. The faving of feed would alone be a fufficient inducement, and in a national point of view would be worthy the attention and encouragement of the legiflature. *Experience*, that beft guide in all agricultural purfuits, has fhewn that there are fubftantial objections to the practice, and they may be comprifed under the following heads:

1ft. The difficulty in getting compleat drilling and hoeing machines, and labourers fkilful enough to conduct the procefs.

2d. The danger of having too *thin* a crop, whereby it is rendered more fubject to ruft, blight, mildew, and the effect of wind, than *thick* broadcaft crops.

3d. Ranknefs in the ftraw, fubjecting it to drop before the grain is perfected.

4th. Latenefs, and irregularity in ripening.

Let us now ftate the advantages :

1ft. Saving of feed.

2d. Strength and vigour communicated to the land by well-timed hoeings.'

3d. Deftruction of weeds.

How far thefe advantages counterbalance the difadvantages, I fhall not take upon me to determine. I can only fay, that my trials (and they have been repeatedly made on a large fcale) have been uniformly unfortunate. In dry feafons, the drilled corn, particularly barley, has been not only

late,

late, but *uneven* ripe, and this is an infurmountable obftacle to the fale of it for the purpofes of malting; and in wet feafons the growth of the ftraw has been fo encouraged by the hoeing, that it has dropped before harveft, and the grain has been but of little value. Laft year I divided a ten-acre piece, and drilled part with white Poland oats, in equidiftant rows of one foot, after the rate of one bufhel and a half, and fome part after the rate of two bufhels and a half per acre.

This was done the beginning of April; three weeks after I fowed *broadcaft* the remainder of the field, with the fame fort of feed, after the rate of fix bufhels per acre. Though fown laft, the *broadcaft* was ripe a fortnight before the *drilled*. The grain was of better quality, regularly ripe, and the produce ten bufhels per acre more. The drilled crop, *fown thick*, was better than the other. Were I to renew my practice of drilling, I would (particularly in fpring crops) depofit nearly double the quantity of feed recommended by the advocates for drilling, and at leaft a month before the ufual time of fowing broadcaft.

For beans, peafe, vetches, turnips, potatoes, carrots, and all grofs-growing plants and roots, *drilling* cannot have a more warm advocate than myfelf; and with refpect to wheat crops on light fandy foils that are fubject to weeds, the operation of hoeing, which neceffarily follows that of drilling, may frequently be of effential fervice not only to the wheat crop, but to the fucceeding ones; but with refpect to corn in general, and particularly *barley* and *oats*, I muft for the prefent demur, at leaft, till I have feen better proofs in favour of the drill fyftem. Perhaps, indeed, the ill fuccefs which I have experienced, and particularly the late ripening already mentioned, might have been owing, in fome mea-

fure,

fure, to the fyftem of faving feed being carried to too great
an excefs.*

I cannot

---

* After giving every tribute of merit to the author of this Survey,
which Mr. ANDERDON thinks he richly deferves, Mr. A. feels himfelf, in fome meafure, called upon to fay fomething to the objections
flated againft the practice of drilling, which carry with them very
great plaufibility. And, indeed, the firft objection muft be totally
admitted, in all its force.

To the fecond, he anfwers, His wheat crops, though not always
free from fuch complaints, (when general) have been lefs fubject to
ruft, blight, and mildew, than broadcaft crops; and never more fubject than thefe to the ill effects of wind. But frequently, when the
wind has blown the ftanding corn, fo as to bend it on one fide, and the
weight of the ears has kept it in that pofition, no injury has enfued,
the corn has flood very well, and fo as to be eafily reaped.

To the third objection, he admits, that the ftraw is ranker, but
ftands ftiff, and is not more fubject to fall than the broadcaft; generally, not fo fubject.

Thefe advantages attending his drilled and horfe-hoed crops, Mr.
A. imputes to the effects of his making ftone-lime a principal ingre-
dient in his compoft-heaps.

To the fourth objection. He puts in his wheat crops in good feafon, and has never failed of reaping them by the middle of Auguft.
But, in very expofed fituations, he thinks this objection may be fatal,
though he has never found it fo in the vale of Taunton. As a proof
of his harvefting his drilled wheat in good order, as well as in good
feafon, his bailiff affures him, he has not reaped a bufhel of grown-
wheat in the courfe of thirteen years paft.

As a demonftration of the fair chances of drilled crops, he has
threfhed one field of drilled and horfe-hoed wheat of laft harveft (not
the beft) which grew on hilly ground. It is a field of three acres, and
produced fixty-three bufhels and one peck. It was reaped July the
30th, (1794) and there cannot be a finer fample of wheat for feed, or
for the miller. This crop was fecond wheat.

Mr. ANDERDON drilled a field of oats, without horfe-hoeing, in
equidiftant rows, except one part fown broadcaft, by its fide, for an
experimental trial. It was a light bad fort of oat, the Tartarian, but
both very good crops. No one, by the eye, could diftinguifh which
was beft. On cutting and threfhing a perch of each fort, adjoining

I cannot difmifs this fubject without paying a juft tribute of approbation to that ingenious mechanic and enlightened agriculturift, the Rev. J. COOKE, whofe drill-machine, and horfe-hoe are well adapted to the purpofes for which they are defigned. Though we cannot accord on the fubject of the drill-hufbandry, I muft give my unqualified affent to his general principles refpecting the preparation of land for arable crops; and I verily think, that his inftruments called the *fcuffler*, and *fcarifier*, are the beft contrivances I ever beheld, for the pulverization of the foil, and the deftruction of weeds.

The ufual feed-time for wheat is November, but it is frequently fown after turnips, fo late as January or February, notwithftanding which, the crop is ripe and harvefted, in a favourable feafon, by the middle of Auguft. Coloured peafe are planted about Candlemas, white peafe are planted at Lady-day, horfe-beans from Candlemas to Lady-day; oats are fown in March, barley in April and the beginning of May; peafe are harvefted rather before wheat, barley at the end of Auguft, oats and beans in September.

Of wheat they generally fow two bufhels, peafe four bufhels, beans five bufhels, planted by women with dibbles or fetting-fticks promifcuoufly all over the land, and the crop is feldom weeded; oats five bufhels, barley three bufhels and a half per acre.

Of late a few farmers have drilled their beans in rows twenty inches afunder, horfe-hoeing them; others thirteen or fourteen inches afunder, hand-hoeing the alley, at the

---

to each other, in the beft part of the field, the broadcaft produced at the rate of fixty bufhels an acre, the drilled at the rate of feventy-two bufhels, yielding a fuperiority of twelve bufhels per acre in favour of that drilled. R. P. A.

expence of four shillings per acre; in both these ways, they have deposited nearly the same quantity of seed as in the promiscuous planting, especially in the closer rows.

The produce has been uniformly superior to those planted in the old method, and the land kept cleaner for ensuing crops.

Rotation of crops on the clayey loam.

1st. Fallow manured with ten cart-loads of dung, and sixty or eighty bushels of lime per acre, mixed with the earth of the head-lands.

2d. Wheat	5th. Clover
3d. Beans	6th. Clover
4th. Barley	7th. Wheat.

The grub has of late years so attacked the wheat sown on the clover lays, that this practice is in some measure discontinued.

In the foregoing rotation, the crops are good; seldom less than twenty-five or thirty bushels of wheat, and the same quantity of beans. The beans are planted promiscuously, after the rate of five bushels of seed to an acre; and after beans they sometimes sow the winter vetch; feed it twice in the spring, and prepare the land for wheat.

In no county are the farmers more attentive to the mode of sowing wheat, or laying up their lands in such form as to secure them from injury by winter rains; and the quality of the grain is such, as to induce the farmers of Sussex, Hants, and Berks, to purchase it for *seed* at Weyhill fair at a great price; seldom less than ten shillings and six-pence per bushel.

An implement called a mattock is much used here, and is peculiar, I believe, to the West of England; it is of great service in sowing wheat and pease on clay lands; the ridges consist of six furrows, with a furrow left unploughed between each ridge, which is called a *comb*. The labourers

with

with a mattock chop the furrows abroad, and bring part of
the earth againſt the comb; the ſeed is then ſown and harrowed with two horſes abreaſt, each horſe going on the
comb; they then (with a plough called a combing plough)
divide it; the plough being conſtructed to throw one half
of it as a furrow to the right, and the other to the left;
the labourers then go over the ridges a ſecond time with
their mattocks, and ſtrike thoſe furrows towards the middle
of the ridges, which effectually covers what grain the harrows may have left uncovered, and leaves the ridges in the
ſhape of a neat aſparagus bed.

This method is very well calculated for clayey and wet
lands, where it would be dangerous for the cattle to trample
on the ground.

An acre a day is the uſual quantity ploughed.

On light loam, the following rotation is practiſed.

1ſt. Wheat. 2d. Peaſe. 3d. Barley. 4th. Winter-
Vetches, which produce a good feed by the latter end of
March or beginning of April, and are fed a ſecond time at
the latter end of May; the land is then ploughed once, and
ſown with turnips, which are hoed and conſumed before
Chriſtmas; and 5th. Wheat again.

A better ſyſtem is adopted by ſome, viz. ſubſtituting barley as the fifth crop, on which clover is ſown. The clover
is well manured the enſuing winter, ſpring-fed, and cut in
the autumn for *feed*; after which wheat is ſown on one
ploughing as the ſeventh crop.

In the pariſh of Biſhop's-Lidiard they frequently plough
their wheat-ſtubble ſoon after harveſt, give it a good dreſſing
of rotten-dung, and let it lie in ridges during the winter.
In the months of February and March they ſow carrots,
which are fit to be dug up the latter end of July; they then

ſo

sow turnips or plant cabbages, and after thefe sow barley
and grass seeds. On rich sandy loam this husbandry cannot be too much extolled.

It is not the general practice within thefe hundreds to
give the arable land a compleat fallow. They more frequently introduce what they call *a pin fallow*, which is
ploughing after vetches, clover, or beans, two or three times,
to prepare for a fucceeding crop of wheat. In this way
they put on a good dreffing of rotten dung before the laft
ploughing. *

RHUBARB.

At Williton near Watchet, the Turkey rhubarb has been
cultivated, and brought to great perfection by Mr. BALL,
furgon, of that place. His management of this root having
been particularly defcribed in the annual publication of the
Society of Arts, &c. I fhall not notice it here, and fhall only
add, that equal attention and fuccefs have attended the exertions of JAMES BERNARD, efq; of Crowcombe, in the
fame article, though in a different climate and foil.

Mr. BERNARD has alfo lately introduced to this country
fome fanners from Norfolk, whofe example, it is to be
hoped, will excite in the neighbouring renters a difpofition
to clean and meliorate their land, by turnips and other improving crops.

---

* The general mode of carrying the harveft crops in this part of
the country is a ftriking object to a farmer from a different part of
the kingdom—it is on horfes' backs. The face of the country is indeed fo generally fteep as to render this cuftom not furprifing to a
fpectator—even manure is conveyed to the land by fingle horfes, in a
dung-pot fixed on each fide of a pack-faddle. In carrying corn, a
large wooden crook on each fide of the faddle is laden with the fheaves,
and when difcharged in the barn, or at the mow, the horfe is ridden
away to be reladen, and in this way greater expedition is made than
by waggons, or any other mode of conveyance. U. C.

CHAPTER VII.

ORCHARDS.

BEFORE I quit this rich and delightful vale, I muſt not
paſs by unnoticed, their orchards, from which cider is
made in the higheſt perfection. There are many gentlemen
in the neighbourhood of Taunton who ſell their beſt cider
for five or ſix pounds per hogſhead; and it is ſuppoſed that
they poſſeſs an art, peculiar to themſelves, of conducting the
fermentation, and thereby preſerving a rich and delicious
flavour.* The beſt fruit delights in a ſtrong clayey ſoil, and
it

---

* In part of this county, the art of making ſweet rich *cider*, which
ſells from three to five or ſix guineas per hogſhead, is reduced to a
ſyſtem; and there are ſome perſons who, on being furniſhed with a
ſufficient quantity of apples, undertake to make and carry it through
the whole proceſs at the price of fifteen ſhillings a hogſhead. But the
method of doing this they endeavour to keep a profound ſecret. The
writer of this note, who is in poſſeſſion of this method, and has practiſed it ſucceſsfully for his private uſe, deſirous that all makers of cider,
who think it worth their attention, may profit by it, takes this opportunity of making it more generally known:

PROCESS.

The apples being ripe, but not rotten, and all of the ſame ſort, that
the fermentation may be more uniform, grind and preſs them moderately, but by no means cloſely. Pour the liquor into a tub to kive,
and when the brown head (which will riſe on it ſooner or later as the
weather is more warm or cold) begins to crack, and the white froth
appears in the cracks level with the ſurface of the head, it muſt be
drawn off in order for tunning into your veſſel. At this time a great
deal of feculence is thrown to the top, as well as depoſited at the
bottom, and if the liquor is continued longer in the tub, the head will
ſink, the bottom riſe, and a ſtrong fermentation take place, which it
will be difficult to ſubdue, and which carries away the ſweets. Proceeding

it is common to mix a certain quantity of bitter apples, which add much to its quality for keeping; but unless great attention be obferved in making, the labour is in vain; for cider requires much greater nicety of management than malt liquors. The apples are fuffered to fall off the trees, or when thoroughly ripe, are picked with great care.* They are then put in heaps to ferment, and remain in that ftate for three or four weeks; after they are ground, and the liquor is expreffed, it is fuffered to remain in tubs, from thirty to forty hours, when a fcum, or froth, will rife on the top; this they narrowly watch, and when it breaks, they rack for the firft time into veffels; after which, unremitting attention

---

ceeding in your operation, tun into a hogfhead veffel three pail-fulls or about fifteen gallons of this cider. This done, burn in the veffel a ftrong match made with nearly a quarter of a pound of ftone brimftone, ftopping the bung as clofe as poffible, that none of the fume may efcape. When the match is quite burnt out, open the bung, and immediately pour in four ounces of fweet fpirit of nitre. Put in the bung tight again, and roll the veffel ftrongly for near half an hour, by which time the fmoke of the match will be deftroyed and taken up by the liquor. Then fet the veffel in its place, fill it to within a finger's breadth of the top, but no higher, and let it ftand till the month of February. In this month it will be coming fine, and muft be watched attentively, and examined frequently by a peg in the barrel. When perfectly fine, it muft be immediately drawn off and turned into the fame veffel, after wafhing out the lee, burning alfo at this racking a fmaller brimftone match. It is directed to be drawn off *immediately* when quite fine, becaufe a very few hours produce an amazing alteration. It becomes turbid and foul, the fecond fermentation is commenced, the fweets fly off, and all the preceding trouble is rendered of no effect. R. P.

* I would here particularly caution all farmers poffeffing orchards, not to fall in with the ufual cuftom of beating down the apples with fticks. Early in the autumn the buds for the fucceeding year are formed, and being tender, are foon deftroyed. To this violent attack on the branches may, in a great degree, be attributed the fuppofed incapacity of trees to bear fruit two fucceffive years.

is

is neceffary to prevent *exceffive fermentation*, by early and frequent rackings.

Where the natural foil is not good of itfelf, fuch manure fhould be mixed with it as beſt fuits its temper.

If the foil be a cold heavy clay, horſe-dung, coal, and ſoaper's aſhes, will bring it to a due temperament.

If it be light and hollow, marl, or mud from ponds and rivers, highway dirt mixed with lime, cow dung, &c. will mellow and inrich it; and if the ſpade be occaſionally employed to dig around, without wounding the roots, a fruit tree may be made to bear more abundantly, and to produce richer fruit.

Improvement of the heads is alſo of as much confequence as of the roots; and this fhould be particularly attended to in the early growth of apple trees. This is reckoned a very material part of tree huſbanding, for according as the head of the tree is firſt trained, ſo it will grow in a form more or leſs regular. Even in old orchards, judicious pruning has frequently made unfruitful trees bear in great abundance.

CHAPTER

CHAPTER VIII.

WOODS, &c.

THIS divifion does not abound with *oak*, but *elm* grows in hedges, and if their heads are not unfairly lopt, get to a fize fufficiently large for the keels of fhips of war. For the moft part they grow from the inchors or fuckers of the neighbouring trees; probably fome from feed. Few are planted from nurferies, nor is there often any occafion for it, elm being the fpontaneous production of the country.

Their heads or fide-branches are feldom mutilated, it being underflood that the ftem fwells in proportion to the fap that is drawn from the root to the head.

There are many coppices (chiefly of oak underwood) on the declivity of Quantock and other hills, but they are under no fyftem of management. Their value, at prefent, of twenty years growth, is from four to ten pounds per acre.

CHAPTER IX.

WASTES.

IN an Agricultural Survey of the county of Somerfet, it
will naturally be expected that particular notice fhould
be taken of the foreft of Exmoor; its vaft extent, and ca-
pability of improvement, render it an object well worthy of
attention.

This foreft extends from North to South about eight
miles, and from Eaft to Weft ten or twelve; containing,
according to an accurate furvey lately made, about nineteen
thoufand nine hundred acres. Nearly at the centre of this
large tract of land is an eftate called *Simonfbath*, inclofed,
and confifting of about two hundred acres, with a dwelling-
houfe, licenfed and frequented as an inn; and all offices belonging to it convenient for the management of the farm,
and tranfacting the concerns of the foreft. Here the
forefter has an annual fale for the fmall horfes that are bred
on the furrounding hills; and here alfo, during the month
of May, he meets the farmers from all the country round,
who enter in his books the number of fheep which are depaftured with him, at the rate of five-pence per head. The
fmall horfes (in the whole upwards of four hundred) are
not taken into better keeping, nor to more fheltered grounds,
during the fevereft winter. When the fnow covers the
foreft to the depth of many feet, thefe hardy animals are
feen in droves, traverfing the little vallies and fheltered parts,
gathering their fcanty fare from the banks of rivulets and
warm fprings; but the fheep are almoft all driven off for the
winter, in the months of November, December, and January, according as the feafon is more or lefs fevere.

The

The river Barl runs adjoining to this estate, but resigns its name on being joined by a small stream, about two miles to the East, called the Ex. This stream takes its rise in a low swampy spot of ground, about two miles North-East of Simonsbath, and runs to the other end of the forest; becomes, when joined by the Barl, a very considerable river, and in its passage to Exmouth, passes by Bampton, Tiverton, and Exeter, to which, and Exmouth, it seems to give name, as well as to this extensive forest.

Into these rivers, Barl and Ex, a number of small rivulets from every direction are constantly pouring their streams; and, should ever a general inclosure be attempted, offer an opportunity of watering some hundreds of acres. The water in these rivulets seems of the purest kind; it is not impregnated with any noxious mineral, and the soil, beyond any doubt, is favourable to vegetation.

On the summits of the hills, and especially on the West and North, are *swamps* of many acres extent. They are cut up as turf, at the rate of eight-pence or twelve-pence per thousand, paid to the tenant of the forest, and would be an inexhaustible stock of fuel to any inhabitants settling on the better part, as well as of black peat for burning lime, working iron, smelting ore, or any manufacture where fire is used.

The roads are in general, as might be expected in so large a tract of land without inhabitants, very bad, and in some places scarcely passable. But the whole abounds with materials to make them firm and comfortable, at an easy rate, and few bridges would be necessary.

Excepting a few willows and thorns by the sides of the rivulets, not a tree or a bush, out of Simonsbath estate, is to be seen on the whole forest; but plantations of most kinds need no more shelter, nor better soil, than is to be met with here.

here. Oak, firs, beech, and elm, would thrive in all the
parts capable of tillage. And a very large proportion of the
whole needs but the spirit, and the fortune, of some one or
more of our wealthy gentlemen in England, whose attention, if turned this way, sanctioned by the royal proprietor,
would render the forest of Exmoor, in a few years, as fair
a prospect as the surrounding country; and not an useless
and void space, as it now is, in the map of the county of
Somerset. The term *useless*, however, may be said by some
to be misapplied, when the quantity of sheep is mentioned
that is depastured on it. From the best information to be
had, twenty-two thousand are summered here, besides the
four hundred horses beforementioned; but the race is so
small, and their value so trifling, that little profit accrues to
the owner. Veins both of copper and iron have been discovered, that might be worked to advantage, considering
how convenient the situation is for shipping off the produce ;
Porlock, Lymouth, and Combmarten, all sea-ports, not
being more than nine miles distant from the centre of the
forest.

From each of those places, and also from Ilfracombe and
Barnstable, vessels are every week passing to Wales (where
founderies have been long established) in *ballast*. A large
vein of lime-stone is known to pass from East to West near
the centre of the forest, and proper stone is found for building on almost every part. And to compleat the whole, *slate*
of a good quality has been dug up in large quantities not far
from Simonsbath; and there is every reason to think it may
be found in other places. Water is in plenty in every part,
as beforementioned: and several market-towns are within
a few miles of the forest. Large tracts of land are well
adapted for the tillage of flax, which is known to thrive
best on old or unvegetated ground, with a strong deep soil.

The

The grain which thrives in the adjoining parishes would, no doubt, flourish here; and a ready sale would be found in the neighbouring markets, or by being exported from the ports on the Bristol channel.

The ashes, arising from the weeds and other extraneous matter on the surface being burnt, mixed with lime, would be a first dressing, preparatory to a crop of turnips or corn.

From the produce of the crops would arise manure for future tillage; and what is now a barren waste, might be made worth from five to twenty shillings per acre.

The plan for inclosures and buildings on the forest, I would recommend, is this: Let there be a small town or village erected near the middle, suppose by Simonsbath-house, which should form proper residences for artificers and husbandmen, to be employed in building farm-houses, and inclosing many a comfortable estate round them. From this centre town, or village, it would be easy to get a supply of provisions and all other necessaries, as a butcher, baker, shopkeeper, &c. might be there settled. And, till other houses or villages should be built, labourers, artificers, and workmen, might find lodgings, provisions, &c. in the bordering parishes, many of which, at this time, have more labourers than they can well employ. The method of fencing, cultivating, manuring, &c. would vary but little from the plan adopted on Mendip hills; and if prosecuted with vigour, would tend to lessen the poor's rates, and would train up a rising generation to care and industry, instead of theft and idleness.

Besides Exmoor, there are several hundred acres of uncultivated land around Dunkry, and on Quantock and Brandon hills.

CHAPTER X.

IMPROVEMENTS.

EXCEPTING fome peat turf on Blackdown, there is fcarcely any fenny land to be met with. On foils any ways inclined to a weeping furface, great attention is paid to draining, which is done by digging the drains deep, filling part of them with clean picked ftones, and covering with earth to the depth of fix or eight inches. Where ftones are fcarce, fhoulder trenching is practifed, but thefe are liable to be filled up with the workings of the mole,† unlefs water conftantly runs in them.* On the whole, perhaps *open* drains are preferable to *covered* on grafs land.

All tenants are reftricted in their leafes from paring and burning, and the practice is fcarcely known.

---

† The workings of the mole are a very flender objection to the ufe of fhoulder trenching; for if the pipe be funk two feet deep in the clay, as it always ought to be, it is very rarely ftopped; but if it fhould fo happen, the remedy is eafy without much coft or labour. In point of expence, it is three-fourths cheaper than ftone draining, the average price of the former being three-pence per rope of twenty feet, of the latter one fhilling. If the drain be cut eleven inches wide, the fhoulder left four inches on each fide of the pipe or channel, the inverted turf will have a firm bearing of eight parts in eleven; and it muft be very rotten indeed, if the remainder three inches ever fall in. Of near a hundred acres adjoining each other, thus drained in the laft three years, not one pipe has yet been ftopped by the working of the mole or otherwife, though the lands are fkirted by a large wood; and woods are very frequently a fecure retreat and nurfery for that animal. R.P.

* The great fkill of draining land confifts in cutting off the water at its fource. One deep drain, judicioufly placed, will frequently preclude the neceffity of any other; in moft inftances, fuch a drain fhould be near that part of the declivity from which the fprings iffue. This depends on the pofition of the clayey fubftratum, and on the height

of

CHAPTER XI.

LIVE STOCK.

THE stock of Taunton-Dean is principally neat cattle and sheep; the former of the *North Devon*, the latter of the *Dorset* breed, both excellent of their kind. Many graziers prefer the oxen bred in this district to those of Barnstaple, South Molton, Torrington, &c. and the sheep are considered as equally profitable with the Leicestershire breed, which have been introduced, but do not gain ground.

The dairy farmers are accustomed to take in sheep to keep during the winter, viz. from the beginning of October and November, to the 5th of April; the usual prices are, for hog sheep five shillings, and for ewes seven or eight shillings per head. The Dorsetshire flocks are greatly improved by this custom, and the price of keeping is on the advance.

Oxen are principally used, and are for the most part worked in yokes; some, however, are advocates for working singly in harness, and there can be no doubt but oxen may be used more to advantage this way than the other. The shape of an ox's breast is peculiarly ill calculated to bear the pressure of the bow; and when worked hard in pairs, they

---

of the reservoir from whence the springs are fed. A judicious survey of the adjacent land, and a liberal use of the borer, are necessary preliminaries to a cheap and effectual remedy for wet land, and there are few men in the kingdom possessed of equal skill in this department of agriculture with Mr. ELKINGTON, of Lancashire, whose fame is not confined to the county in which he lives, but is known and acknowledged in many parts of the kingdom.

are

are apt to get into a habit of leaning againſt each other, by which their progreſſive motion is much impeded. But o f all methods, that which is praᏟiſed in Portugal, Flanders, ſome part of Ireland, and other countries, namely, working them by the *head* and *horn*, is, in my opinion, the beſt.

I once faw on the farm of Lord SHANNON, near Cork in Ireland, three ploughs at work on a ſtrong ſoil, drawn each by a pair of oxen abreaſt, in a manner ſimilar to the application of horſes in Norfolk. The harneſs conſiſted of a long rein of untanned leather, which was fixed to the yoke, and then interſeᏟed the horns two or three times; after which it paſſed from the back of the horn over the forehead; to prevent the bruiſing of which, a *matting* was placed of ſufficient thickneſs to ſecure it from injury. In this way the animals *puſhed*, rather than *drew*, and with ap-parent eaſe ploughed an acre a day each without a driver, turning at land-end with as much docility as horſes. His lordſhip informed me, that two moderate-ſized oxen had, ſome time before, drawn home from the corn-field, (a diſ-tance of two miles) in a French ſkeleton cart, as many ſheaves of wheat as weighed upwards of three ton, and with no apparent extraordinary exertion.

SHEEP.

There are two ſorts of ſheep in this country, the one a native breed, without horns, well made, and covered with a thick fleece of wool, weighing in general ſeven or eight pounds; the other a ſmall horned ſheep, called Exmoor ſheep, bought, when hoggits, at South-Molton market, (April 12) at about ten ſhillings to fourteen ſhillings each, and fattened on turnips. The firſt is a valuable ſort, not much unlike the Leiceſter breed; and their fleeces may be conſidered as a moſt profitable article to the breeder, as
they

they fometimes reach even the weight of twelve pounds, and fell at about ten-pence per pound. The fale ewes are put to the ram about the latter end of July, and the flock ewes about a month after. Young rams are preferred, as it is fuppofed that old ones degenerate the quality and weight of their wool. The wethers of this breed, when two years old, and fatted on turnips, attain the weight of about twenty-five pounds per quarter; and being driven to Briftol market (a diftance of near fixty miles) are fold, without their fleece, in the months of May and June. *No folding practifed.*

The fecond fort are kept on the foreft of Exmoor, or the adjoining hills, for two or three years, merely for the annual profit of their fleeces; the weight of which feldom exceeds four pounds. They are fattened on turnips, and fold without their wool. Weight of carcafe from fourteen pounds to eighteen pounds per quarter.

Though thefe fheep in appearance are vaftly inferior to thofe before defcribed, being in their youth fubject to a precarious fubfiftence on the forefts and hills, it is the opinion of many fenfible farmers that they are altogether as profitable flock.

OXEN.

The oxen of this country are large, well made, and beautiful animals. They are almoft all red. They are yoked at three years old, and worked till they are five or fix, when they are fold to the graziers, at prices from ten pounds to twenty-two pounds each ox.

---

* Is it not very extraordinary, that, in fo hilly a country, this method of manuring land fhould be almoft unknown? Perhaps the weight of their fleeces may indifpofe the fheep for lying too clofe together, without creating the fcab or fome other diforders.

CHAPTER XII.

RURAL ŒCONOMY.

THE price of labour, throughout the whole diftrict, is nearly the fame, viz. Men, through the year, one fhilling per day and beer; women, for weeding and common work, fix-pence per day; and for mattocking the wheat and hay-making, eight-pence per day. But contract labour is gaining ground daily; and in this way men will earn fourpence or fix-pence per day more than at day-work.

PROVISIONS.

The price of provifions is comparatively moderate. In Taunton the beft beef, mutton, veal, and lamb, may be had by agreement with the butchers, at four-pence per pound the winter, and three-pence halfpenny the fummer half year; turkey, three fhillings and fix-pence; goofe, three fhillings; ducks, two fhillings and fix-pence a couple; and fowls, two fhillings; fifh, at certain times, very cheap.

N. B. This was in 1794.

FUEL.

Coal is brought from Wales. The quality bad, and the price high. Wood gets fcarcer and dearer every year.

CHAPTER XIII.

POLITICAL ŒCONOMY.

MANY attempts have been made by the principal wool-growers in this diftrict to eftablifh an annual fair in or about the centre thereof, for the fale of their wool; but hitherto the wool-buyers have rather fet their faces againft the meafure:—this is the more extraordinary, as it muft be apparent, to men converfant with this bufinefs, that the prefent mode of buying at the *farmers' houfes*, and giving indifcriminately the fame price for wool of very different qualities, is not only unjuft, but manifeftly injurious in its confequences.

Were the fleece to fetch a price in proportion to its clean-nefs and finenefs, (which is the cafe at eftablifhed fairs) the grower would be excited to care and attention in thefe refpects.

MANUFACTURES.

About a century ago the woollen manufactures in the town of Taunton were in a very flourifhing condition, and of courfe fome of their benefits devolved to the agriculturift; but of late years the warmth of party at the elections of their reprefentatives in parliament has run fo high, that it has not fubfided from one election to another; by which means manufactures declined, and have been removed to Wellington and other places. So that it may fairly be inferred, that if the right of election to members in parliament has been injurious to any borough in the kingdom, it has been fo to this.

There

There are, however, fome hopes that trade may revive here, as the carding and fpinning machinery has been lately introduced with confiderable fpirit and perfeverance. Some gentlemen in this town have lately formed a connection with the patentees poffeffing the fecret of making cloth without either fpinning or weaving; and the famples they have exhibited gave flattering hopes of fuccefs.*

Though the trade of Taunton has declined, yet confiderable manufactories are carried on at Wellington, Wivelifcombe, and other places; and many thoufand hands are employed therein.

It cannot be totally foreign to our purpofe to mention the falmon and *herring fifhery* of Porlock, Minehead, and Watchet, which for fome years paft has been carried on to fome confiderable extent.

The lower claffes of people have, in confequence, obtained a cheap and wholfome food, particularly fince the legiflature has taken off the duty on falt ufed in curing the latter of thefe fifh for *home confumption.*

It were to be wifhed that this fifhery could be further promoted and encouraged, as it would be a means of furnifhing employ, during the winter, for thofe failors who are engaged in the lime-ftone, and culm trade, during the fummer months.

Their frequent journies acrofs the Channel make them excellent pilots; and a hardy and fkilful race of failors would occafionally recruit that grand bulwark of the nation—the *Royal Navy.*

---

* This plan of making cloth is now (1797) intirely abandoned—at leaft, in this and the neighbouring county of Dorfet.

A RECA-

A RECAPITULATION

OF THE

HINTS FOR IMPROVEMENT,

ALREADY SUGGESTED in the PRECEDING PAGES,

WITH SOME

ADDITIONAL REMARKS.

———

1ſt. *Incloſe and cultivate all Waſte Lands ſuſceptible of Improvement, and divide and·incloſe the Common Fields.*

VERY few gentlemen of landed property in this county have ſhewn that attention to the advancement of rural œconomy, or to the improvement of agriculture, which a ſcience of ſuch importance merits: this is the more extraordinary, as their own intereſt is ſo deeply involved, and ſo great examples have been ſhewn them by the nobility and gentry of other counties, and even by Majeſty itſelf.

It is no uncommon thing for untitled gentlemen to apprentice the younger branches of their family to trade, for five or ſeven years: And why not to agriculture? It cannot be becauſe the former is a more reſpectable occupation than the latter. I rather think, it is becauſe the acquirement of knowledge in the one is conſidered as more difficult than in the other. The general opinion ſeems to be, that any one may become a farmer: How egregiouſly are they miſtaken who think thus! I have known both,

and

and can truly say, that more experience, care, assiduity, patience, and attention, are requisite in a farmer, than in a tradesman of any description whatever.

The various causes which have operated to retard the progress of improvement, have been so fully stated before, that I shall only add, by way of encouragement, that the lands of Mendip hills, inclosed and cultivated in the course of the last thirty or forty years, are now worth nearly ten thousand pounds per annum, which in their original state did not exceed fifteen hundred pounds; and the advantages attending the inclosing and draining the low lands have been still greater.

It was naturally expected that so great an accession of arable land would introduce such a plenty of corn (particularly of oats) in the adjacent markets, as would be accompanied with a proportionable diminution in price; but no such consequences have followed. The average price of oats for the last twenty years has not been less than eighteen shillings per quarter, *Winchester measure.* From this circumstance, some have been foolish enough to question the presumed advantage, exultingly crying, " Is not corn dearer " than it was before? Are not the poor's rates equally high? " Where then are the happy consequences derived from the " measure? Corn could not have been dearer, had no inclo- " sure taken place." Hold! the price of every article varies according to the plenty or scarcity in market; and if the *home* supply be not sufficient for the consumption, other markets at a distance must be resorted to. This would have been the case in the neighbourhood of Mendip hills, had no inclosure taken place. The counties of Wilts and Dorset must have supplied the deficiency; and the *carriage* alone would have amounted to ten per cent.

2dly.

2dly. Where Lands are situate on bleak and exposed eminences, improve the climate by judicious and extensive plantations.

Though I am no advocate for standard trees *in fences*, yet I think large and many plantations, in elevated situations, are not only ornamental, but profitable.

In this part of the kingdom, they should be placed on the *South-west* side of a farm, as the wind from this quarter is most injurious. The *Scotch fir* will endure almost any severity of climate, and the *beech* will resist the destructive influence of the sea-breeze; next to these, in point of hardiness, are the *larch*, the *sycamore*, the *ash*, and the *birch*.

Such plantations may be placed at the angles of the large fields, or on spots too rocky and uneven to admit the plough. They should be planted when young, and great care should be taken to secure them from cattle; this is best done by a stone wall, for hedges are liable to be broken down by sportsmen, and the work of many years may be destroyed in one night. A spirited planter would rather see cattle in a field of ripe corn, than in a new-made plantation. The damage in one instance is only partial, in the other it is nearly irreparable.

3dly. Wherever marl, lime, or chalk, can be procured within a reasonable distance, neglect not a liberal use thereof; and if destitute of such resources, be careful to make as much dung as possible by folding sheep, housing all sorts of cattle, preserving urine, collecting woollen rags, malt-combs, ashes, horn shavings, bones, &c. &c.

In the Northern part of the county of Somerset, both marl and lime are in great abundance. The former is dug for about eight-pence per ton; and as it is the produce of

the

the land to which it is applied, the carriage is very trifling. There can be, therefore, no excuse for those people who possess such a treasure, and yet forbear the use of it. Wonderful, however, as it may appear, I can assure my readers, that there are large tracts possessing this valuable manure unwrought; and in those parts where it is applied, a repetition of it seldom takes place in less than twenty-five or thirty years; so that a liberal manuring does not exceed one shilling and six-pence per acre per annum, and for this, there are many instances of an almost immediate advance of rent of twenty shillings per acre.

Lime is still more plentiful than *marl*, and, within a distance of six miles from the coal-pits, may be burnt for sixteen or eighteen-pence per quarter. Its beneficial effects are universally known and acknowledged, and yet, strange to relate, a second application thereof seldom takes place in less than fifteen or twenty years: this reluctance may be attributed to the baneful effects, not of lime, but of an injudicious and exhausting course of cropping.

Allowing that arable land may be injured by a too liberal use of this manure, it must be allowed, that with pasture no such consequences could ensue. Lime, like marl, kills all the coarse sour grasses, brings sweet and beautiful herbage, grateful to the palate of all cattle; it forms a kind of pan under the surface, by which the nutritious particles of dung are kept longer within the reach of the roots of plants, and is the means of making *ten* loads go as far as *twenty* when applied without a previous liming. Its activity is not abated in the course of three or four years; for if the land be broken up at that distance of time, its effects are as visible in the subsequent crops of corn as if it were immediately applied. Happy then are those farmers who possess such advantages, and have the sense and spirit to use them.

How

How would a Devonfhire farmer rejoice, were he to find limeftone and fuel on the fame eftate. In that part of the kingdom, to the honour of the county be it fpoken, they frequently fend twenty miles for lime, and give four-pence and fix-pence per bufhel at the kiln; and our wife-acres of Somerfet will fcarcely beftow carriage, were the landlord to give them the lime.

Where neither marl, lime, chalk, nor any other fimilar fubftance dug from the bowels of the earth, can be procured, it behoves the farmer to be earneflly folicitous to fupply their places with either animal or vegetable manure. For this purpofe, let him mow all his ftubbles for litter, houfe his cattle during the winter months, fold his fheep, grow a large portion of turnips, cabbages, vetches, rye, &c. keep a numerous flock, and be moderate in the extent of his corn land.* Great attention alfo ought to be paid to the management of dung when made, for by neglect great part of its ftrength may be loft. When properly foaked with urine, it fhould be conveyed in its ftrongeft ftate to the turnip land, or any other deftined to receive it, in a *low waggon* inftead of a cart. Thefe waggons fhould be made to open at the fides, and the contents fhould be depofited in large heaps of ten or fifteen loads each, with confiderable elevation; and it fhould be fhook abroad with as much care as a gardener takes in making a cucumber-bed. By thefe means, a ftrong fermentation is excited, and turning is unneceffary, and perhaps injurious.

---

* Particular care fhould alfo be taken to root out docks, thiftles, and other pernicious plants, which, if allowed to bring their feeds to perfection will be difperfed by the wind, to the infinite prejudice of all the furrounding lands; and the richer thefe lands are, the fooner will thefe noxious weeds be propagated.

From

From thefe heaps, p'aced at fuc'i diflances as to manure *one* acre, it may be wheeled and fpread for two-pence half-penny per load.　In this method of hauling out dung, three waggons, four horfes, and five men are employed; namely, one waggon and two men loading in the yard, another wag-gon and two men unloading in the field, and the third waggon and driver going backward and forward.*

Wherever wafte earth, mud from ponds, highway dirt, afhes, &c. &c. can be procured, compoft heaps fhould not be neglected; thefe are beft calculated for pafture land.

Such a conduct will entitle the farmer to a great produce, and keep his land in good order; but all this will not do without

4thly. *A regular and well-conceived rotation of Crops.*

This I confider as the moft promifing feature in good farming; and if it were generally adopted, would increafe the produce of the land *threefold.*

A cuftom prevails in this county, and indeed in moft others, of fubjecting a portion of land to continual tillage, and of interdicting the plough on all the other; this origi-nated from improper conduct on the part of the tenant.—

---

* In the application of dung, the farmers of Somerfet begin at the wrong end. It is almoft the general practice to manure for the *wheat* crop, whereby the wheat land is made foul, and though there is a great burthen of ftraw, there is but little corn.

How much more beneficial would it be, to apply all the dung to potatoes, turnips, &c. and to the artificial graffes, making wheat the laft crop in the courfe? It is alfo ufual to manure the turnip land im-mediately before fowing; but I have experienced great advantage, and more decided certainty of a crop, by manuring in autumn on the ftub-bles, ploughing the fame in, on a fleet furrow, and letting it remain in that ftate during the winter months.

No fooner is the plough put into his hand, than he ufes it without mercy, harraffing the land with conftant crops, till its fertility is intirely exhaufted.

The landlord, alarmed at thefe baneful effects, endeavours to counteract the progrefs by reftraining claufes, and thefe are indifcriminately applied both to *good* and *bad* farmers; and are confidered by the one as *highly neceffary*, and by the other as *exceedingly grievous*.

Were we to advert to the general practice of the tenants, we fhould be led to juftify the caution of the landlord; but were we to calculate the lofs yearly incurred by fuch reftrictions, we fhould have caufe to regret that the covetoufnefs of the occupier fhould have rendered neceffary a conduct fo inimical to the general weal of the kingdom.

In refpect to low meadow land, or very rich pafture, there can be but one opinion, viz. *that it fhould fo remain*; but it muft be allowed, that there are in this kingdom large tracts of old grafs land, *moffy, hide-bound,* and, comparatively fpeaking, *unproductive.* Land of this defcription might be greatly improved by *ploughing*; and if the following courfe of crops, and mode of manuring, were adopted, would be left, at the end of three years, of double the value it was in the fward.

ON LIGHT LAND.

1ft. Peafe or oats on the ley.

2d. Vetches fed off, and the land manured with lime or the fheepfold, preparatory to turnips.

3d. Barley and artificial grafs feeds.

In which, let it remain till the graffes fail, and the land again becomes moffy; then renew the courfe.

ON HEAVY LAND.

1ſt. Beans on the ley.

2d. Spring fallow, well manured, and cabbages.*

3d. Oats and artificial graſſes.

Then remain as before.

The foregoing courſes of cropping cannot poſſibly injure the land, and by them fallowing is excluded, which (unleſs in particular inſtances, ſuch as great foulneſs, or dearth of manure) I do not think neceſſary.

5thly. *Enlarge the upland corn farms; erect proper buildings and conveniencies for the ſhelter of the cattle in the winter months, thereby inviting ſubſtantial and well-informed farmers, of more enlightened countries, to ſettle upon them.*

I have before ſtated the advantages of large corn farms, buildings, &c. and ſhall, therefore, only add, that nothing ſo much contributes to the progreſs of good huſbandry as example. One good farmer in a pariſh (particularly if he take no pains to make proſelytes) will in a few years convert all the reſt; the ſuperiority of his crops, the advancing fertility of his land, the thriving ſtate of his cattle, the abundance of manure, all plead daily in favour of his ſyſtem, and will, in the end, produce conviction even in the moſt bigoted mind.

---

* The cultivation of cabbages on *heavy* land cannot be too ſtrongly recommended. It puts the clay land farmer on a level with his neighbours occupying light land, and as a farther encouragement, I can aſſert, from experiments repeatedly made, that *two* tons of cabbages are equal to *three* of turnips, that they are leſs ſubject to injury from froſt, and that the expences of cultivation, compared with turnips, do not exceed five ſhillings per acre.

I know

I know no method by which general improvement can be more promoted, than by difperfing the farmers of thofe counties, whofe practices are held in the higheft eftimation, among thofe parts of the kingdom on which the light of good hufbandry has never fhone. . This would introduce into general practice the Turnip Hufbandry of the Eaftern diftricts, with all its concomitant advantages.

The foil and climate of the county of Somerfet is peculiarly well adapted to the cultivation of this root; and were the pafture lands lefs rich and productive, neceffity would oblige the farmer to have recourfe to this root for winter fubfiftence. At prefent, the quantity of land devoted to this purpofe is trifling indeed, and in moft inftances the hoe is never ufed, nor are turnips confumed with any degree of œconomy.

Though the rent of the land in the elevated parts of this county may be confidered high, there are advantages which more than compenfate; thefe are, its rich and productive quality in all feafons, the facility with which it may be ploughed, the eafy accefs to marl, limeftone, and coal, goodnefs of roads, vicinity to markets; and laftly, the high price of produce. The laft-mentioned advantage is alone fufficient to induce a refidence; for it frequently happens that corn fells twenty per cent. dearer here than it does in the Eaftern counties.

6thly. *Improve the Stock by a judicious selection of Males and Females for breeding; and be particularly careful to choose a Male handsome in those points wherein the Female may be deficient.*

In this department of hufbandry, the farmers of Somerfe are very inattentive, though they all acknowledge that the proper ftocking of a farm is of the higheft importance.

x In

In confirmation of this, I need only inform my readers, that few inftances can be produced of a bull being fold for more than fifteen pounds, or a ram for more than five pounds. As to ftallions, there are but few bred; the mares are ferved by horfes brought every fpring from the Northern counties, and without this crofs the breed would be contemptible indeed.*

It is not within the compafs of my undertaking to enter upon this article at large; fuffice it to fay, that it is a thing of great confequence to the hufbandman; and the only caution to be obferved, when he introduces an alien flock by way of improvement, is, not *to change from rich land to poor,* or *from a warm to a cold climate.*

7thly. *Leffen the number of Horfes, and encourage the ufe of Oxen.*

It is univerfally acknowledged that too great a portion of land is employed in raifing food for horfes; and it is alfo as certain, that a draught horfe, if well fed and kept in houfe thirty weeks of the year, will confume twelve quarters of corn, and thirty cwt. of hay, befide grafs; this may be confidered as the produce of four or five acres of land, which, under common cultivation, would maintain nearly three men. If, therefore, the riches of a country confift in the extent of its population, and that population can only be advanced by increafing the means of fubfiftence, it follows, that every man who keeps an unneceffary horfe is an enemy to his country, by retarding the increafe of his own fpecies

---

* A tax on ftallions and bulls would encourage the attentive breeder, by increafing his cuftom, and enlarging his price, and would leffen the number of ill-bred and ill-fhaped males of each fpecies.

Navigable canals would alfo greatly tend to reduce the number of horfes, and, wherever the fituation is fuch as to admit of them, fhould be encouraged.

To a fpirit of fpeculation and gambling the country is indebted for the canals now cutting; but though the rage has fubfided, yet, I truft, the probable advantages will infpire the prefent adventurers with fufficient fpirit and vigour to profecute their undertaking to its full completion.

The county is rich, populous, and abounds with all thofe heavy articles of traffick, which will render water conveyance profitable to the fubfcribers, and beneficial to the public; and if the cuts be made of fmall dimenfions, the coft will be trifling; the confumption of land, and the invafion of private property, infignificant: fuch a canal could only be confidered as a large ditch, and might be fo multiplied as to anfwer the purpofe of turnpike-roads.

8thly. *Amend the Publick Roads.* *

Nothing fo much contributes to the improvement of a county as good roads; before the eftablifhment of turnpikes, many parts of this county were fcarcely acceffible.

Seven or eight horfes were neceffary to draw a waggon loaded with *two* tons weight, and fcarcely ever exceeded the diftance of twenty miles a day; now, the fame number of horfes will draw *five* tons, and travel thirty or forty miles. This is an immenfe faving of labour, and yet the eftablifh-

---

* In fome parts of the kingdom road clubs are eftablifhed. Thefe are very good Inftitutions, and ought to be adopted in every county. Rules and orders of fuch clubs may be feen in the appendix to the Worcefterfhire report. The reluctance which individuals fhew to the preferring indictments, renders fuch an affociation peculiarly neceffary.

ment

ment of fuch roads was as unpopular, and the probable
benefit as little credited, as thofe of canals are now. The
money collected at the gates was confidered as a burthen,
and the publick were for fome time loaded with an extra
charge for carriage. This, however, did not laft long, for
in the courfe of a few years, a diminution in the price of
carriage univerfally took place, and it has gradually fallen
from that time to this.

Before the turnpike-roads were eftablifhed, coal was carried on horfes' backs to the diftance of fifteen or twenty
miles from the collieries; each horfe carried about two hundred and a half weight. Now one horfe, with a light cart,
will draw ten hundred weight, or four times more than the
horfe could carry: Can an infignificant toll be put in competition with this faving?

In refpect to private roads, I would recommend a repeal
of the law compelling flature labour, and changing the fame
to a compofition in money.

Whenever a farmer is called forth to perform flatute-
labour, he goes to it with reluctance, and confiders it as a
legal burthen from which he derives no benefit. His fervant and his horfes feem to partake of the torpor of the
mafter. The utmoft exertion of the furveyor cannot roufe
them, and the labour performed is fcarcely half what it
ought to be.

This would not be the cafe, were the furveyor to receive
in money the highway tax; he could then employ fuch
workmen as would do him juftice, or, if they were indolent
or infolent, he could difmifs them.

9thly. *Encourage the use of such ploughs, and other instruments, as are best calculated to expedite work and do it well.*

Admitting that there are only one hundred and fifty thousand acres of tillage in the whole county, and that the same are ploughed on an average twice; allowing also that one-third of this is of so hilly a nature that a wheel-plough cannot be used to advantage, there will remain one hundred thousand acres capable of being turned with the *double furrow* plough.

For the sake of argument, let it be also admitted that three horses, a man, and a boy, with the common plough of the country, will turn an acre a day, and that the double plough with four horses, and the same number of attendants, will turn two acres. The number of acres will of consequence be ploughed in half the time, and the difference in expence cannot exceed two shillings per day. Here then might be a saving of twenty thousand pounds per annum in this article alone, besides the inestimable advantage of expediting work at certain seasons.

Some may doubt the possibility of making the double plough so generally useful; but I can truly say, I have never yet found an instance where it could not be worked to advantage; and it is well known, that, in the various trials made under the auspices of the Bath Society, on lands of the most *difficult nature*, the double plough has always gained the prize.

In the counties of Wilts and Dorset, where three large and powerful horses are put to a single plough, the saving by such an instrument would be immense; and this I can confirm, by the testimony of some eminent farmers of the first-

named

named county, who, in confequence of my recommendation, have introduced them on their refpective farms, with great profit and fuccefs.

10thly. *Sow early in expofed and cold fituations, and be particularly careful not to plough or harrow in wet weather.*

The neceffity of this caution is fo well known to all practical farmers, that I need not, I truft, enforce it.

11th. *Deftroy Rats and Mice.*

The depredations of thefe vermin are too important to be overlooked. A fenfible farmer of my acquaintance thinks, that by them and birds a twentieth part of the corn of the kingdom is devoured. Corn in barns they have free accefs to, and it is very difficult to keep the mows on ftadles free from them. If they are not brought in from the corn field, a ftick, a rake, a pike, or any other body carelefsly placed againft the mow, will introduce them.

Deftructive, therefore, as they muft be, it behoves all farmers to make their flaughter a general concern, and it might be done by a parifh rate.

12th. *Introduce Threshing Machines.*

Thefe are common in the Northern parts of this kingdom, and in Scotland; and from the accounts I have received, anfwer the purpofe, threshing the corn both well and expeditioufly. There appears to be but one objection,‡ which

---

* A fimple engine for weighing cattle *alive* is alfo a defirable thing.
‡ Query. Is the ftraw equally palatable to the cattle?

is, the leſſening of *in-door* labour in the winter months. As a ſubſtitute for which, let the farmer houſe all his cattle, drain his wet lands, collect manure, &c. and employ the barn-men in theſe occupations.

13th. *Let all Unmalted Corn be ſold by weight.*

The different meaſures of this kingdom, and the confuſion incident thereto, were ſo notorious, that great pains have been taken by the houſes of parliament to introduce one general ſtandard meaſure, and the acts of the legiſlature have been followed up by the moſt active exertions of the magiſtrate.

By theſe means, the Wincheſter meaſure is pretty general, and in reſpect to this county I may add, to the *great benefit of the ſeller*, and the *great loſs of the purchaſer*. The calculation in reſpect to the comparative price between the old and new meaſure, was formed on the difference between eight and nine gallons, but this is erroneous; the old meaſure of the county was not leſs than nine gallons and a half, and in ſome inſtances ten gallons, ſo that the buyer gives ſeven or eight per cent. more than he ought to give; and I humbly think that *weight* would be a better ſtandard, as the drier and plumper the corn is, the heavier it weighs.

14th. *Grant Long Leaſes.*

All farmers who have ſpirit enough to improve their eſtates, ſhould have ſome ſecurity for being reimburſed the expence. Where a man's tenure is precarious, and ſubject to the whim and caprice of a landlord, little improvement can be expected. Upon unimproved farms, ſuch as waſtes, commons, &c. newly incloſed, a conſiderable expenditure is

necessary

neceſſary to bring them Into order. Here the tenant ſhould have a leaſe of twenty-one years, and the rent to advance at fixed periods; for inſtance, ſuppoſe the land in its original ſtate to be worth, when incloſed and accompanied with neceſſary buildings, five ſhillings per acre; this rent, if the tenant is to pay all expences of cultivation, ſhould continue ſeven years; at the expiration of which time, he ſhould be advanced to ten ſhillings, and at the end of fourteen years, to fifteen ſhillings per acre.

Or the following method might be adopted; let the landlord pay all expences of cultivation, manuring, &c. and charge five per cent. on the expenditure, allowing the periodical advance to be proportionably leſs. At all events, the intereſt of the tenant ſhould be better preſerved than at preſent; but this is ſo copious a ſubject, that I muſt forbear entering into it, not doubting but it will be ably treated by ſome of your numerous correſpondents.

15th. *Sow more Sainfoin on the ſtone-braſh lands, and on all other ſoils congenial thereto.*

16th. *Roll all Graſs Land once a year at leaſt, with a heavy roller, and abſtain from ploughing your Arable Land in wet weather.*

17th. *Set all Peaſe and Beans in lines from North to South, and hoe them twice at leaſt.*

18th. *Devote at leaſt one quarter part of your Turnip Land to the Ruta-Baga or Swediſh Turnip.*

This root will bear the utmoſt ſeverity of weather, and will remain ſound when the other turnips are all rotten. The ſeed ſhould be ſown the beginning of May, and treated in other reſpects like the common turnip. The root does not attain the ſize, but is much weightier, and conſequently more nutritious.

19th. As in every point of view this county appears from its soil and situation to be better adapted to *grafs* than arable, it deserves enquiry, whether stock could not profitably be kept on *grafs land alone*, without the aid of winter roots. The argument for ploughing arises from a wish of having straw to make manure, and turnips to support stock in the winter season. But whenever the plough is put into the hand of the generality of farmers, the land is from that time in a state of degradation, and its value reduced at least 10s. per acre, in comparison with contiguous grass land.

Grafs, therefore, should be considered as the ultimate improvement of land in the Western part of the county of Somerset.

CONCLUSION.

THIS county does not raise grain sufficient for its consumption, nor are the climate and soil of many parts thereof favourable to corn farming; yet, were all the improvements before suggested to take place, there cannot be a doubt but that the produce of the soil might be increased at least onethird.

The advanced rent which might be produced by draining the marshes, and by inclosing and cultivating the common fields and waste lands, may, according to the most moderate calculation, be thus estimated:—

No. of Acres.	Description.	Increased Rent.			Total Increase.
		£.	s.	d.	£.
30,000	Marsh lands	0	15	0	22,500
20,000	Common field	0	5	0	5,000
65,000	Uncultivated waste	0	5	0	16,250 per ann.
					43,750

To

To which may be added, a capacity of improvement in the arable and pasture lands *inclosed*, of at least five shillings per acre, amounting to more than 213,000l. per annum, which increased rent, at thirty years purchase, would exceed six millions.

These blessed effects would be the natural consequence of that spirit of industry which publick encouragement would excite, would add greatly to the capital of the nation, and be much more valuable than any foreign conquest of treble the amount. Would to God that nations would learn wisdom, and instead of coveting distant territory, improve to the utmost *that* which they possess!

IT now only remains for me to apologize to the honourable Board, for the desultory and procrastinated way in which this Report has been executed.

The various publick as well as private business, in which I was engaged prior to my undertaking this survey, could not be dispensed with; I have, therefore, only had it in my power to snatch an occasional hour from other numerous avocations. Had not my general knowledge of the county, and particularly of the Northern and Middle districts, enabled me to write on its practices without a personal survey, I must have declined the undertaking. As it is, I have felt, and still feel, a considerable portion of regret that I did not resign the appointment, as the Board might have then selected some person possessed not only of more leisure but of superior ability.

With

With a fincere wifh that the eftablifhment of an Agricultural Board may be attended with all thofe happy confequences, which its moft fanguine fupporters can defire,

I remain,

Their moft humble fervant,

J. BILLINGSLEY.

Afhwick-Grove, Oct. 4th, 1794.

ERRATA.

Page 16, line 6, for *Wirton* read *Weston.*

—— 60, l. 5, f. *qualifying* r. *qualitying.*

—— 110, l. 18, f. *thirteen cwt.* r. *one hundred cwt. three quarters.*

—— 101, l. 3 from the bottom, f. *irregation* r. *irrigation.*

—— 116, l. 6, f. *1l. 4s.* r. *4s.*

—— 130, l. 3 from the bottom, f. *because* r. *become.*

—— 162, l. 8 from the bottom, f. *diftinguish* r. *diftinguifh.*

—— 163, l. 9, f. *o* r. *of.*

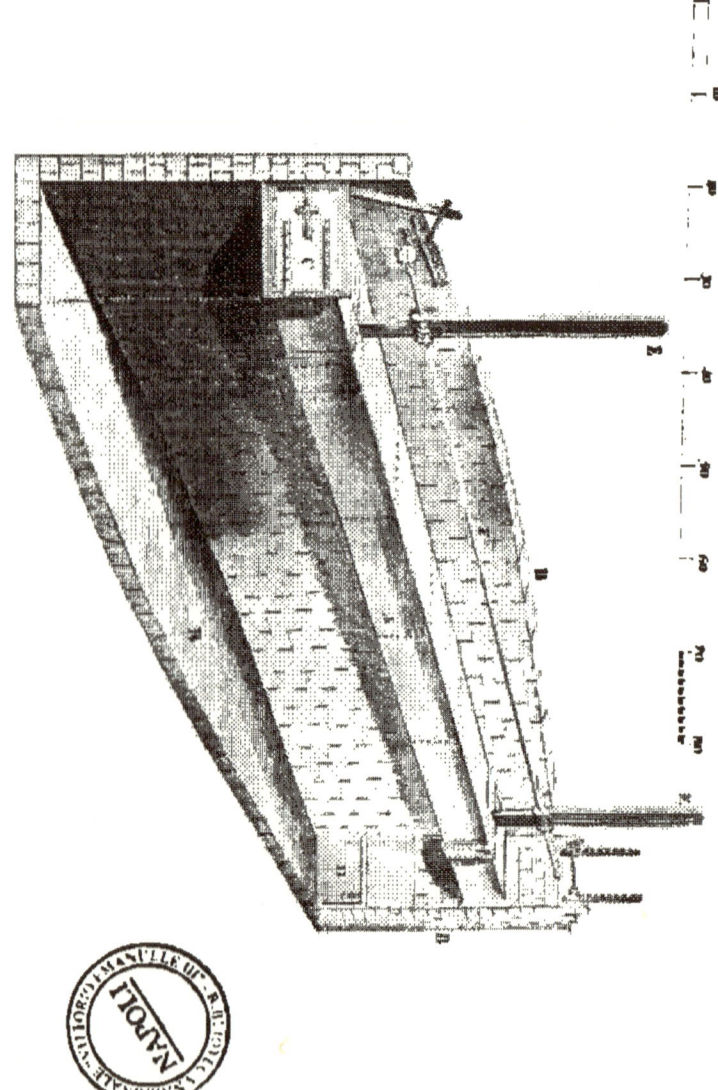

A DESCRIPTION OF

ROBERT WELDON's

HYDROSTATICK or CAISSON-LOCK,

Which is now building and nearly completed

On the Somerset Coal-Canal near Coomb-Hay,

ABOUT THREE MILES FROM BATH.

———————

AS many impediments arife in the progrefs of Canals;
First, From a want of water to fupply locks in dry
feafons and elevated fituations.

2*dly.* In croffing valleys by expènfive aqueduéts;

3*dly.* Tunneling through hills and high grounds;

And 4*thly,* The great delay occafioned by paffing many
locks where the unevennefs of the country renders it unfavourable for canals;

R. WELDON, after having devoted many years ftudy and
indefatigable labour to avoid thefe difficulties, and to accomplifh this great objeét, now offers to the publick a defcription
of his Hydroflatick or Caiffon Lock.

The drawing annexed prefents a perfpeélive view of the
machine or contrivance by which the conveyance is to be
effeéled, and of the infide of a lock, or pound, in which it
is immerfed.

A. confifts of a trunk or caiffon made of wood, and of
dimenfions equal to the reception of a commercial veffel of
twenty

twenty-five or thirty tons burthen, at each end thereof is a door-way, which the boat, &c. is to be floated through into or out of the caisson, and being received therein, and the door then shut, with a given quantity of water to float the boat, and counterpoise the caisson, so as to make it the same specifick gravity with the water in which it is immersed; it may then be easily raised or lowered at pleasure, either by destroying the equilibrium, by admitting a small quantity of water into the caisson through a valve constructed for that purpose, or by discharging a similar quantity through another valve, or by chains and rollers, as in the drawing annexed, from one level to another, and the boat be floated from the caisson into the canal; the water in the caisson and that in the canal having both the same level whilst the conveyance is effected.

B. is one side the bottom, and one end of the lock or cistern in which the caisson is immersed, which is built of free-stone, and of the following dimensions, viz. from the foundation to the top of the wall sixty-six feet, length from out to out eighty-eight feet, width in the middle twenty feet, ditto at each end eleven feet and half, and the perpendicular height from the surface of the lower canal to that of the upper canal forty-six feet.

C. The door at each end of the caisson, which shuts into a rabbet, the frame projecting about three inches beyond the door when shut.

D. An aperture at each end of the cistern or lock, communicating with the upper and lower canal, with a sliding door or gate, which are counterpoised like a common sash, and wound up by wheel and pinion, to receive the end of the caisson, to which it is closely fitted at the time the boat is received or delivered.

R. WELDON,

R. WELDON, having devoted the whole of his time to the superintendance of this great work since the commencement of it, he hopes will be a sufficient excuse for not having the whole history of it ready for the press, but flatters himself to have it complete to lay before the publick (with engravings and references to every part distinct, and carefully copied from the original drawings after which the present machine is constructed) in a few months.

Extract from an Account of a Provision made upon an Inclosure, for supplying the Poor with Fuel.

(Communicated by EDWARD PARRY, esq.)

UPON the inclosure of the parish of Little-Dunham, in Norfolk, in the year 1794, being Lord of the Manor, I got a clause inserted, directing the Commissioners to set out a parcel of land to be called *the Poor's Estate*, to be vested in the lord of the manor, rector, churchwardens, and overseers of the poor for the time being, and to be let by them for twenty-one years on lease; the rents and profits to be laid out by them in fuel, to be delivered at the cottages of the poor, in such proportions as the trustees should think proper.

Although the prejudices of the poor, against the inclosure, were very great before it took place; the moment they saw the land inclosed, and let as *the poor's estate* for twenty-one years by auction, at the rate of 5cL a year, (although only estimated by the Commissioners at 2cl. a year) they were highly gratified; and have indeed great reason to rejoice, as they will now be most amply supplied with that great comfort

fort of life. This was fo evident, that fome neighbouring inclofures have followed the example, and it appears to me to be advifeable that fuch a plan fhould be generally made known.

The firft idea was to fell the land, and place the money in the publick funds, in order to produce a larger income; but I found that was not underftood by the poor: they faid they might at any time be deprived of the money, and they had no intereft in the land inclofed; whereas, in the mode purfued, they confidered themfelves as having a permanent and improveable eftate, which their children would inherit. Thefe prejudices are valuable; as in their confequences they produce, if attended to, induftry and content.

I have had occafion to obferve, as to fuel, which is certainly an important article to the poor, that where there are commons, the ideal advantage of cutting flags, peat, or whins, often caufes a poor man to fpend more time after fuch fuel, than, if he reckoned his labour, would purchafe for him double the quantity of good firing.